RYNE DOUGLAS PEARSON
CAPITOL PUNISHMENT

"DEATH, DESTRUCTION AND THRILLS . . .
A TOUGH, HARD-POUNDING STORY
THAT IS DIFFICULT TO PUT DOWN . . .
Capitol Punishment races along at breathtaking speed . . .
Not likely to be forgotten in a hurry."

Orlando Sentinel

"RIVETING ACTION . . .
AN ENGAGING PLOT . . .
A HIGH-TECH THRILLER."

Kirkus Reviews

"CHILLINGLY PRESCIENT . . .
Intensity and a troubling verisimilitude . . .
Besides establishing a frightening criminal conspiracy,
Pearson effectively juggles a cast of
FBI agents, politicians and civilians."

Publishers Weekly

"A WELL-WRITTEN AND WELL-PACED WORK."

Library Journal

"GRIPPING . . . PLAUSIBLE . . .
AS FASCINATING AS IT IS FRIGHTENING . . .
There's effective suspense and solid entertainment
to be found in *Capitol Punishment*."

The Observer

RYNE DOUGLAS PEARSON

CAPITOL PUNISHMENT

AVON BOOKS ⬖ NEW YORK

AVON BOOKS
A division of
The Hearst Corporation
1350 Avenue of the Americas
New York, New York 10019

Published in hardcover by William Morrow and Company, Inc.; for information address Permissions Department, William Morrow and Company, Inc., 1350 Avenue of the Americas, New York, New York 10019.

First Avon Books Printing: August 1996

AVON TRADEMARK REG. U.S. PAT. OFF. AND IN OTHER COUNTRIES, MARCA
REGISTRADA, HECHO EN U.S.A.

Printed in the U.S.A.

RA 10 9 8 7 6 5 4 3 2 1

For Lou,

the bestest of friends . . .

ACKNOWLEDGMENTS

To Irene, for understanding.

To R.H., S.H., and M.G. . . . words combined are ideas.

To Clyde Taylor, for the support.

To Tom Colgan, for liking good stories.

*To Bob Shuman, for being an instant supporter when
things were crazy.*

The Surly Bonds of Earth

"Nine-one-one, what is your emergency?"

"I'm not sure," the woman answered, her small baby cooing softly in her arms. "The house across the street from me, well, this guy kind of stumbled out the front door and fell down. He's just lying there on the walkway."

"So a man collapsed. Did you hear or see anything else?" The 911 operator had already alerted the county's fire-rescue dispatch, as well as the sheriff's department.

"No. I was just doing dishes when I noticed it. Should I go check and see if he's all right?"

"No, ma'am. Just stay where you are. Now, do you know who the man is?"

"I don't know his name, but I've seen him at that house before. There's only two of us on this road so you don't miss folks too easily. God, I hope it's nothing bad."

"Don't worry. We have a sheriff's unit rolling and fire-rescue will be there soon. Twelve-twelve Riverside, correct?"

The woman nodded to herself. "Right near Alamo."

"Thank you. Help will be right there."

The call, a medical emergency, warranted a code three—lights and sirens—response, but in the sparsely populated area in the north of Los Angeles County there was little to get in one's way in any case. Eleven Adam Seven, a two-man unit out of the Los Angeles Sheriff's Department Antelope Valley substation, had been given the priority call just a minute earlier. In the time since, Deputies Phillip Pearl and Danny Contreras had covered a mile and a half, leaving a low rooster tail of dust rising from the two-lane asphalt road in their wake.

"Right turn coming up," Contreras warned his partner behind the wheel.

Pearl saw the sweep in the road and lifted his foot off the gas and began a steady push on the brake, the nose of the black and white cruiser diving for the road. "Hang on."

A good grip on the Chevy's door-mounted armrest kept Contreras planted firmly upright as his partner swung into the turn at thirty miles an hour. Ahead of them was a bare stretch of road with two houses coming at them fast.

"Twelve-twelve's on the left." Contreras undid his safety belt with his left hand and grabbed a flashlight from the charger as the cruiser pulled to a stop on the wrong side of the street.

"I'll put us ninety-seven and get the med kit," Pearl said.

"Gotcha. I'll check our victim." Contreras stepped from the car and walked a few paces to its front, where he stopped and checked his surroundings. His academy days were long behind him, but the training he'd received there, and the bullet he'd taken a few years after that, had ingrained in him a simple rule to live by: Don't rush in. He scanned the front lawn, just greening in a wet autumn after a relentless summer, and the street side of the tan-colored house. Just as reported, lying outside the open front door was a body. From ten yards it looked about as lifeless as lifeless got, but the only way to know for sure was to get up close and personal. He'd done hundreds of body checks in his career, but had never been able to distance himself enough from the deceased to make the act just another part of his job. Maybe, though, this check would yield some sign of life. Just maybe.

Contreras trotted around a surprisingly green hedge toward the victim. Nearer the open entry door he slowed, checking the darkened interior as best he could from his position in the bright sunlight. Nothing was obviously amiss, so he knelt down and lightly pressed two fingers against the man's neck in search of a carotid pulse. His other hand probed the body for telltale signs of trauma—blood, bruising, etc.—but found only a sticky wetness soaking the victim's shirt. He pulled his moistened hand away and sniffed at the liquid, but it had no scent. A swipe of his hand on his uniform pants cleaned it off. His fingers stayed on the neck for a few more seconds until further searching was fruitless. They no longer had a victim . . . they had a body.

He started to stand to tell his younger partner not to bother with the med kit, but never made it out of his crouch.

Pearl slammed the trunk lid after removing the orange med kit, walked toward his partner and the victim, and froze near the hedge at what he saw. Contreras, who had been giving the man a quick once-over just a few seconds before, was no longer crouched at his side. Instead, the twelve-year veteran was in a heap atop the body of their victim. His face, lying sideways on the man's chest, was a blank mask of clenched teeth and vibrating features, the eyes open, falling back into their sockets, and the mouth puffing reflexively.

The med kit hit the ground as Phil's rover came out of its belt holder. "ELEVEN ADAM SEVEN—OFFICER DOWN! TWELVE-TWELVE RIVERSIDE!"

He vaulted the low hedge, gun coming out to cover the open door—*Was there a shot? I didn't hear any-*

thing!—and was at his partner's side in an instant, his hands easing him off the body as he searched for some reason for the collapse. Air passed in and out of Danny Contreras in strange spurts, but it was unnatural, reflexive, like the death throes of a landed fish. Like no breathing action Pearl had ever seen or heard. He searched for some cause, some reason for his partner's collapse. It was as if an invisible assailant had struck his partner . . . had struck . . . had—

Then Deputy Phillip Pearl knew. He was three years out of the academy, a former military policeman and veteran of the Gulf War. With just a few seconds of life remaining, the intensive training he'd received after arriving in Saudi in the fall of '90 came back to him. But all it brought was the realization that there was nothing to be done. He heard sirens in the distance, strange, high-pitched warbles that stretched out to long wails, then became loud snaps as violent as thunder as his brain stopped processing auditory signals in any recognizable way. He thought briefly about reaching for his rover, but couldn't. His body would not respond to even the simplest command. Arms and legs seemed like separate entities functioning on their own.

CRACK!

He thought he felt motion, in his face or head, maybe, but couldn't pin it down. What little of his vision that had lasted this long then faded to blackness, leaving him trapped, somehow still sensing something, his mind wandering as he tried to focus on his family, thinking of them this last time. This very last—

"All rise."

Judge Malcolm Horner entered his ninth-floor courtroom from chambers to the sound of the marshal beckoning all in attendance to stand. The ten-year veteran of the federal judiciary walked straight to the bench without looking to the gallery, an assembled mass of litigants, press, and interested parties that filled the long, narrow courtroom in the Edward Roybal Federal Building in downtown Los Angeles to capacity. Two low steps up put him on the granite-faced riser that supported the bench, an imposing cube of wood and marble that, when viewed from the back of the courtroom, had the appearance of an altar. Had the architects had the space they might have added a vaulted ceiling to complete the image of a cathedral. God over the law, the law over man.

That impression was not lost on John Barrish, though he denied the existence of a deity, as well as the power of the state to judge a man for his beliefs. And that's exactly what this was, Barrish knew. The papers of officialdom might say *United States* v. *John Barrish*, but they really meant State versus Freedom. A nonexistent God could not pass judgment on him, and a corrupt, hegemonic government could certainly not break him and make him deny who he was, from where he came, or the right of his kind to take their place in history. They feared what he stood for. They feared those who stood with him. They feared the truth.

"Be seated," the marshal said, his voice carrying in the cavernous room.

Barrish lowered himself and sat stoically next to his court-appointed lawyer, a Jew with some constitutional zeal, and faced the judge without looking at him. An African. How appropriate, Barrish thought. The State had chosen one of those who had bastardized the America of long ago to sit in judgment of him. There were twelve others chosen as tryers of fact, of course. All his "peers." Four of those were Africans. Two Mexicans, he thought, though one might be of purer Spanish blood. He had no mixed features common to the blending of the Spanish conquerors with their Indian slaves. Four appeared to be white, but appearances were just that. A surface reading was often treacherous when looking for a person's true heritage. That required the study of their ancestry farther back than some influences that had altered their skin color. His two Asian "peers," for example. The eyes of one belied Spanish ancestry—the Spaniards were mighty people at one time, Barrish knew from study. More rounded eyes, probably from the Philippines. Narrow eyes close together. Japanese. That was the mark of the other. Twelve people. Mongrels. Some purebreds. None were his peers. The sham was so obvious it was ludicrous.

Seymour Mankowitz leaned a bit to his right and touched his client's elbow with his. "Look at his face, John."

Barrish didn't.

"Do you see that?" Mankowitz suppressed a smile. "See his expression? He didn't buy it."

Barrish heard his attorney's hopeful words, but placed little stock in them. He knew the power of the State. He knew it well. It had taken almost all that was his, all that he had worked for. His home. His business. Those were the costs of an unrelated civil action brought by a group of lazy Africans, the darlings of the State. With this, a criminal action, they were trying to take his freedom, to take him from his family. Those things they could do. But one thing they could not. One thing remained his wherever he might be, in whatever circumstances he was placed. Everything they could usurp from him and still John Barrish knew he would have his fight. It couldn't be reasoned out of him, stolen from him, or beaten from his fiber. In fact, every attempt to weaken his resolve, every trial, every character assassination hurled at him through the media, every penny robbed from him by the State's thieving IRS, every single thing they had done in pursuit of that elusive goal had had more than an opposite effect. Resolve, however strong, was no longer an issue. They had pushed so hard that the line between man and mission had faded to inconsequential. John Barrish *was* the fight now. The fight was him.

"Counselors, would you approach, please," Judge Malcolm Horner said as he looked down upon the parties to the trial.

Mankowitz left his client with a soft grip on the shoulder and followed his opposite, Deputy U.S. Attorney Leah Cobb, to the bench, his eyes casually glancing down for a peek at the lines of the high-cut panties he had come to believe she favored. They stepped onto the riser and drew close. Horner had open before him a file containing Mankowitz's motion for dismissal.

"Ms. Cobb, I wanted to give you one last chance," Horner offered. "Anything?"

Leah Cobb thought she saw sympathy in the judge's face, as though he wanted her to have some way, some brilliant legal maneuver, to make Mankowitz's motion worthless. But she didn't. She had almost nothing. Her case, her way of tying John Barrish to the murder of four little black girls in a Los Angeles church, was at rest beneath a gleaming grave marker that did not do FBI Special Agent Thom Danbrook justice. Only he could definitively tie John Barrish to the guns used to murder those four children as they practiced for a Christmas concert. Because of the many months he had spent undercover, he could have pointed his finger at the man whose hate dwarfed his diminutive physical stature and say that he had purchased the weapons from one of his brother hate groups. But the cliché was irrefutable: Dead men told no tales. Thom Danbrook was dead, as dead as Leah Cobb's case against the leader of the Aryan Victory Organization, and neither could be resurrected.

"Your Honor, unfortunately I have nothing more," Leah said.

Horner looked at the prosecutor for a long moment, hating what had to come next. "Ms. Cobb, the government has had the opportunity to present its case. In the context of the trial as a whole the jury would be your judge, but—and I never like to do this . . . in any case— at this point it is my responsibility to determine if you've done your job. I'm sure you've done your best, but you haven't sufficiently impugned Mr. Barrish to warrant continuing this trial.'' He saw the youthful attorney cast her eyes downward briefly. She was angry at herself, Horner knew, though he also was certain she could have done nothing to overcome the situation pure chance had put her in. ''And delaying that conclusion any further will do no good. You had an additional six months fol- lowing Agent Danbrook's murder to rework your case.'' Danbrook was her case, Horner knew all too well. Or, more properly, his testimony would have been. But a chance encounter with two murderers had robbed Thom Danbrook of his life, and Leah Cobb of her only way to show that Barrish was more than just an ignorant ob- server of a plan that had resulted in four black children dying a horrible death, trapped in a church as bullets cut them down. Horner felt her anguish. He also felt his own rage at having to set John Barrish free. ''Step back, please.''

Mankowitz took the lead this time. The front rows of the gallery could easily see the contrasting expressions on his and the prosecutor's faces. A hushed murmur rose from those in attendance.

''You're going home, John,'' Mankowitz whispered.

Barrish swallowed, still not ready to believe it. He had narrowly escaped prosecution for the same crime by the State of California because of a lack of evidence, a bullet dodged until the federal government had decided to take a crack at him under the guise of ''violating the civil rights'' of the dead African children. For over a year now he had been held without bail in federal custody in the towerlike Metropolitan Detention Center in down- town Los Angeles. Locked up like an animal. Subjected to the taunts and brutality of the African inmates. Slurs and hateful threats had been hurled at him. So had choice bodily excrements left to ferment for days in foam cups just for that purpose. All while his keepers laughed at the display. He had expected no less from the Africans, and no more from the agents of the State. Was it going to be over now? he wondered, still looking defiantly straight ahead.

"Would the marshal please bring the jury in." In a moment the twelve citizens were in their place on the courtroom's left wall. "Mr. Mankowitz, would you and your client please stand." Horner watched as the self-described leader of the Aryan Victory Organization rose with his attorney. Such a small man, the judge thought. Physically and otherwise. Yet this man was hate, and he inspired that in those who would do his bidding. And he was about to be let loose upon the world once more.

Horner waited for a few seconds before beginning. "It is the opinion of the court that the government has failed to present sufficient evidence against the defendant to warrant the continuation of this trial. The motion to dismiss offered by the defense is hereby granted." The background murmur became a soft gasp. "Ladies and gentlemen of the jury, thank you for your attentiveness and service. You are dismissed from this case. The marshal will see to your needs." Rather quickly, with shared looks of surprise, the twelve jurors filed out for the final time. And then it was time for the most distasteful part of what had to be done. "Mr. Barrish, the charges brought against you in this case are hereby dismissed. Accordingly you are remanded from custody and are free to go. Good day, everyone."

The gallery and litigants stood as the judge left, and a few reporters tried to move to the front of the court. Three very serious federal marshals stopped them four rows back.

Deputy U.S. Attorney Leah Cobb stood motionless, just staring at the empty bench, looking right after a few seconds. "You have no idea what you've done, Mankowitz."

Seymour Mankowitz looked the prosecutor's way, smiling. His eyes traveled halfway down her slender body. "And you have no idea just how fine an ass you have, Leah." He ended the retort with a leer that was meant more to anger than to invite. It was enough to motivate her quick departure.

"You'd better get him down to the basement," a huge marshal suggested to Mankowitz. "The crowd's already gathering out front."

"Okay." He turned to his client. The man was still looking blankly ahead, at nothing in particular. His chest was rising and falling more than Mankowitz had ever noticed. Relief. That had to be it. "John. Let's go."

The two men followed a small phalanx of marshals to a service elevator out of view of the press. It took them directly to the restricted area of the basement parking garage.

"He has transport, right?" the big marshal asked Mankowitz.

"I have everything I need," Barrish told the big African, turning away and walking toward the blue Aerostar waiting with its side door open.

"I tried to tell him it would be better to have some protection leaving here," Mankowitz told the marshal.

"No skin off my back," the marshal said, thinking to himself that a lynching by that very large and very dark crowd out front might be very appropriate, considering . . .

John Barrish climbed into the van and took the middle seat as the door was closed. His wife grabbed him around the neck in a hug that was so tight it was almost painful.

"John. John." Louise Barrish kissed her husband's neck and started to cry. "John. You're coming home."

John felt the warmth of her tears rolling onto his

cheeks. He reached up with both hands, gripped her shoulders, and broke the hold she had on him. "Get off of me!"

Louise fell away as her husband pushed her toward the large tinted window on the van's left side. Her hands came up to her face, the tears falling upon each trembling finger.

John looked to her with the eyes she remembered. They also contained the look she had wished would be gone. Somehow gone. "This isn't the time."

"Pop." Toby Barrish looked back to his father from the passenger seat, his lazy right eye askew. "You look strong."

"Always," John answered, happy more than anything to see his two sons after so long a separation. "Stanley, where are we going?"

The younger Barrish boy adjusted the rearview mirror to see his father. "We have a place."

A place, obviously provided by his one remaining benefactor. Four walls and a roof. Not a home. That had been taken by the State. Still, it would serve the purpose. A place to eat, to sleep, to think. And to prepare.

"Do we have it yet?" Barrish asked his eldest son.

Toby looked back, smiling. "Freddy picked it up today. I'm gonna get it from him tomorrow."

"Good," John said, his head nodding confidently.

Stanley glanced at his father in the mirror as he wound the van up the serpentine driveway to the street. "So we're going to do it?"

John gave his son a look that caused him to turn away from the reflection of the man who'd given him life. He flashed on the seemingly endless days spent penned in by concrete and steel. "Yes, Stanley. Now more than ever."

It was eagerness, Toby realized. And anger. His father was a master at harnessing the power of the latter, in himself as much as in others.

"There's a bunch of niggers out there," Toby warned his father.

John snapped his head toward his eldest son, which was enough of an admonition.

"Sorry, Pop," Toby said, knowing exactly what his transgression was. "Africans." Many people referred to his father as a refined racist because he didn't run around in a white hood saying "nigger" every time he opened his mouth. But Toby saw no difference in the terms. African. Nigger. Coon. It didn't matter, though he respected his father too much to challenge his views on the subject. And in due course it would not matter. Soon there would be an America populated by Americans, and what anyone called someone with an excess of skin pigment would be up to them. The Africans would be back banging their drums and taking Swahili names for themselves. The Mexicans would be back in tortilla heaven. The Japs and the towelheads would all go home. America, from the Atlantic to the Pacific, would be white, as it was meant to be. Soon. Sooner than anyone could imagine.

"You might want to duck down, Dad," Stanley suggested. "We're going out the side but there might be cameras."

"I've got nothing to hide," John declared.

"Sit tall, Pop," Toby said as light from the street above washed over the driveway ahead.

"I just thought—"

"You thought wrong, Stan," Toby said, cutting his brother's words off.

The Aerostar crested the driveway and pulled through a line of police onto the blocked-off street. Cameras were everywhere, but only a few demonstrators had figured out that the front of the Federal Building might be a *symbolically* fine place to show their anger, but the object of that anger would be nowhere near it. There were some signs, plenty of obscene gestures and shouting, and lines of hypocritical police holding back those with vengeance in their hearts. They would arrest John Barrish for his beliefs, and they would protect him because of the same. It was a duality they would come to regret in very short order.

"I'm glad you're going to be with us for this, Pop," Toby admitted. His father had conceived the entire plan some time before, nurturing all the elements until everything was in place. Even his incarceration hadn't halted the preparations. He had seen to that, seen to everything being able to go ahead without him. Still, he deserved to be part of it. "You get to enjoy it all."

John Barrish stared straight ahead at downtown traffic, not really smiling, but feeling something beyond pleasure. It was desire. A burning desire that nothing could match. "Not 'enjoy,' Toby. Savor."

It was the closest words could come, but words meant very little now. Talk was no longer cheap in John Barrish's mind—it was without value. Action was the only measure of expression worth a damn.

They have no idea . . .

ONE
First Light

You would have thought that the Super Bowl was being played just two miles from 1212 Riverside by the number of satellite trucks lining Avenue B.

"The vultures are out," Frankie observed as she eased the Bureau Chevy along the crowded roadway.

"They smell flesh," Art said, regretting his words as they became prophetic. "Damn."

"You're the one with the high-profile face," Frankie said, just before the first mike-armed reporter reached Art through the passenger-side window.

"You're Agent Art Jefferson, aren't you?" a harried female reporter asked. *Asked,* really, didn't fully convey the force of her *demand.*

Well, if they could exercise their First Amendment rights to free speech, Art could use his to push a few buttons. "What is it?" he asked, looking at his watch. "About eleven o'clock? Hey, the news starts in a few minutes. Got anything good?"

The reporter's face switched from that of a determined professional to that of a teenager in disbelief at the lame comment her parent had just made. "Come on, Jefferson. Give us a statement."

The "us" had pressed up behind and around her. Cameramen circled to the front of the car and the sides, bathing it in a dazzling glare.

"Watch your toes!" Frankie cautioned the news crews as she crept through the pack. "Feral dogs. Man."

"No statement yet," Art informed them.

"Is it true there's a spill of a chemical used in military weapons research?" a reporter asked.

"We'll have a statement later." They hated this, Art knew, being told *no!* like children. And, of course, they would react as such. But he really couldn't give them much more than they already knew. His and Frankie's quick stop at the L.A. office hadn't yielded much information, and the news they'd listened to on the drive north only mentioned a major chemical accident, possibly involving hazardous materials stolen from an Army depot in New Mexico. What really was going on was yet to be discovered.

"Why are there Army personnel here?" the closest reporter asked, pressing the attempt for information.

"Later."

"Jefferson! Come on!"

Early in his career with the Bureau, contact with the media had infuriated him. Now he knew how to play the game, and how to win. It was time for the trump card. "No comment. Let's get in there, partner."

Frankie gave the Chevy a bit more momentum and pressed through the pack, stopping at the first roadblock a hundred yards ahead. There, their identification was checked by the four sheriff's deputies manning that checkpoint. After being allowed in they drove another half-mile on Avenue B to the intersection of Riverside. Where the roads met, a sheriff's department patrol car sat blocking the streets' north and west lanes of travel. A deputy, windmilling his arm as he stood in mid-intersection, directed them right onto Riverside. Heading south now, they could plainly see the glow from the incident command post ahead. Far ahead.

"This isn't like any perimeter I've ever seen," Frankie commented. "It's got to be two miles as the crow flies."

A chemical accident, Art thought. Must be some nasty stuff if it's true.

"Slow down, partner," Art said, seeing the orange-vested deputies standing at roadside. The lights of the Chevy painted them as the agents neared, causing the wide reflective stripe on the vest's front to fluoresce and mark their positions. There were a half-dozen visible, spaced fifty or so yards apart, each holding a road worker's sign that read SLOW. To that admonition they added hand gestures, pressing downward on the air before them. The message was clear.

Frankie slowed the car to under fifteen miles per hour and continued on to the incident command post. What had been just a half dome of light on the horizon became much more as they neared. Portable light standards, their self-contained generators humming, ringed an area about a quarter the size of a football field. Two trailers were nose to rear on one side, one each from the sheriff's and fire departments. A dozen fire engines lined Riverside opposite the trailers, and, parked in the trampled sage off the road were more vehicles, including several with the familiar *G* plates assigned to government agencies. These also had the mark of the United States Army stenciled on their doors.

When you were a cop, parking was no problem. Frankie simply pulled across Riverside into the empty oncoming lane and stopped, leaving her flashers on.

"There's Lou," Frankie said.

Lou Hidalgo, the assistant special agent in charge of the L.A. office, saw their arrival and broke away from a small group he was part of to greet them.

"Lou, how are you?"

"Art." The A-SAC, his face drawn, met the two agents at the front of the Chevy. "We've got a bad one."

Agents, especially those in command, usually referred to situations as "tough" or "sticky." For the A-SAC to call this one otherwise set it apart more than just descriptively.

"How so?" Art asked.

"You heard the chemical spill story, right?"

"On the way up," Art replied.

"And the reporters asked us when we pulled up," Frankie added.

"Some road worker who dropped off a bunch of signs overheard something and then shot his mouth off," Hidalgo explained. "Fortunately he only heard part of a conversation."

"So, was Allen cooking up some more explosives?" That would explain the massive perimeter, Art theorized, and Freddy had certainly shown a fondness for things that made noise.

"I wish," Hidalgo said honestly.

Wish? "What was he doing, Lou?"

Hidalgo looked over his shoulder to a spot of light a mile off in the distance. "Somebody over there was making nerve gas."

Frankie looked to her partner just a second before he did the same. "Nerve gas?" she said. "What do . . . You mean like the military stuff?"

Lou nodded. "There's an Army guy here who knows the technical stuff, but, from what this cop brain of mine can figure, yeah. Like the military stuff."

"Jesus," Art said softly. He shivered briefly, wishing it was from the chill in the night air. "So there must have been an accident."

"That's what I gather, but only some Army guys and a couple of firefighters have been up there. The Army is keeping a tight seal on the whole area, and on the site in particular." Hidalgo paused for a second. He was shaken by all this, the agents could see. Very shaken. "Art, there are more dead in there than just Allen."

"Who?"

"Some cops. Paramedics. Someone else in the house. From what we can piece together no one knew what was going on when they showed up on-site," Hidalgo explained. "There was a nine-eleven call about someone collapsing outside the house. Two deputies were first on-scene. Then another arrived and saw his buddies down. He went in. Then a county fire rig and a paramedic unit pulled up together. One of the paramedics and a fire captain went to help them, then they went down. Thank God the other paramedic sounded a warning. He had haz-mat training and held the others back."

Art saw that Lou was emotional. "Are you okay, Lou?"

"Yeah. I'm all right." Hidalgo sniffled, then continued. "County fire got a haz-mat team out and they detected something nasty, then they asked for help from the Army. They brought in a gas detector and got a positive. Then all this happened. Three-mile perimeter. Reporters. This is big."

"But how did they ID Allen?" Frankie asked. "He wouldn't have been running around with anything that had his name on it."

"His face," Hidalgo answered. "The haz-mat team ran a cable from a camera at the scene to a truck a quarter-mile out. They did a tape of everything, all the victims, and then brought it to the ICP so they could identify the bodies."

"So they called you down to ID Allen," Frankie said. She watched a single tear roll down from Hidalgo's eye.

"No. They called me down here because one of the firefighters that went down was my son."

"Oh my God, Lou," Art said. Frankie could only bring a hand up to cover her mouth.

"I saw Luis lying there, and I recognized Allen on the ground next to him." Hidalgo stopped for a moment to regain his composure. He was a senior, Luis, his oldest boy, being his namesake. Now that was all gone. "Luis was trying to help that scum when he died. Can you believe that?"

"Lou, I'm so sorry," Frankie said, stepping closer and placing a hand on the A-SAC's back.

"Yeah. Me too." Hidalgo took a handkerchief out and wiped his nose. "Jerry said to get you guys up here since Allen was yours."

Jerry Donovan, the special agent in charge of the Los Angeles field office, had proven one thing in the time Art had worked with him: he didn't like Art. But he also didn't let that prevent him from assigning the more difficult cases to him. Maybe it was Donovan's form of quiet warfare against him, but Art had learned to live with it since William Killeen, the former SAC, had packed it in for a retirement consisting of trout-filled Montana streams.

"God, Lou, is there anything we can do?" Art asked. Actually it was a plea from a man feeling helpless. You could shoot a bad guy, but what could you do for another man's pain?

"No. It's had a while to sink in now," Hidalgo said. "I'm almost glad Marie isn't here anymore. Luis was her favorite. I'd never tell any of my others that, but I knew. You could see it when they were together." Again he paused. "I guess they are again."

Breast cancer had taken his wife two years earlier. Now this. "Lou, you should go home," Art suggested. "What about your kids?"

"My sister is with them. They don't know yet."

"We can get someone to drive you home," Frankie offered.

"I can drive myself. I just wanted to wait until you got here."

"Then go now, Lou," Art said. "Go to your kids. We can take it from here."

"All right," Hidalgo agreed. "Up in the forward

trailer is the guy you need to see. He's Army. I can't remember his name.''

"Okay. Go home. We'll call you later if there's anything you need to know.''

"Thanks, Art. Frankie.'' Hidalgo gave her hand a squeeze before walking away to his car.

"I can't believe this, Art. First his wife, and now his son.'' Frankie's mind flashed the face of her little girl briefly. How would she survive losing Cassie? How?

They could stand there, watching the taillights of Lou's car fade as he drove away, and dwell on the pain and sorrow. But there was a job to do. That there was now a very personal element attached only made it more important to get to it.

"Come on, partner.''

The agents went to the forward trailer, a solid white rectangle on wheels that was still attached to the sheriff's department pickup that had towed it there. They walked up the foldout steps into the trailer. Four people were inside, two at a communications console and two standing at a wall-mounted map. One of the latter wore an olive-drab jumpsuit with rank insignia stitched on the epaulets.

"Excuse me,'' Art said. Only the two men at the map turned. "Agents Jefferson and Aguirre from the L.A. FBI.''

"One minute,'' the military officer—a captain, Art thought—said, then turned back to the sheriff's department captain he was standing with. "If the wind gets past fifteen knots you're going to have to evacuate this area.'' A finger tapped on the map. "Remember: fifteen knots and that area gets cleared. Don't wait for my word. Just do it.'' The officer turned back to the agents. "Sorry. It's been pretty busy around here.''

"That's what we gather. I'm Art Jefferson. This is Frankie Aguirre.''

"Hi,'' Frankie said.

"I'm Captain Orwell. Don't ask the first name; my parents were cruel."

Captain George Orwell? That must have been hell for him during basic, Art thought. "We just sent our boss home."

"I'm sorry about his kid," Orwell said. "He never had a chance."

"That's what we gather," Frankie said. "*Nerve* gas?"

"The worst kind. You want to take a look?"

"You mean . . ."

Orwell looked to Art. His face might be a chocolate brown, but it was a shade lighter than the second before. "It's safe. At least as safe as it can be. We'll get you suited up. Come on."

Art and Frankie followed the captain to an Army vehicle parked a hundred feet up on Riverside. It was a modified Humvee with what could only be described as a large box affixed behind the driver's compartment. A door faced to the rear of the vehicle, and small folddown steps spanned the gap between the opening and the ground.

"After you." Orwell held the door open for the agents, climbing in after them. "Take your jackets off, and anything sharp or metal. Belts, watches, earrings."

Art slowed as he slid out of his blazer and looked down to the Smith & Wesson on his hip.

"Guns, too," Orwell said. "They'll be locked in here."

Art unclipped the holster and spare magazine and laid it on a table that folded down from the wall. He didn't like the feeling, and it showed.

"There aren't any bad guys up there, Jefferson. At least no live ones."

Frankie removed the locket from around her neck, kissing it lightly before setting it aside.

"You can stay back, partner," Art offered sincerely. He knew whose picture was in the locket, and that little girl needed a mommy. "I can check it out."

"Thanks, but no. Allen is mine, too, remember."

"Okay," Art said. It was just an offer, but he knew she wouldn't take it. In a way, though, he wished she had. The mix of him, his partners, and dangerous situations had often resulted in harm coming to the person paired with him. But that was the past. He repeated that until he almost believed it.

"All right." Orwell took three hooded camouflage jumpsuits from a cabinet and handed two to Art and Frankie. "These are MOPP suits. That stands for 'mission-oriented protective posture.' "

Frankie noticed the odd texture of the material. "What is this?"

"It's a synthetic material impregnated with activated charcoal," Orwell explained. "This is the same thing troops in the field would wear in a chemical environment. For us, though, it's secondary protection." He pulled three other garments from a separate cabinet. These were white, and had a more solid feel to them. "These are containment suits."

Art noticed the resemblance to the "moon suits" the Bureau EOD teams wore.

Orwell lifted the head of one suit to show. A clear, rigid plastic faceshield covered the front of the head portion, and inside a suspension system similar to those in hard hats helped the bulbous space maintain its shape. "This will go over the other suit, then we'll walk down to the gear area and have one of my team put the airpacks on us and seal us up."

"Getting in sounds easy," Art observed.

"You're right. It's the getting out that can kill you." Orwell smiled. "When we come away from the site we'll be covered with the nerve agent. All that will have to be cleaned off before we can even think of getting out. The joy of decontamination. It can take some time, so if either of you have to take a leak, now's the time to tell me. Otherwise it's in your pants later.''

"I'm dry," Art said. "How about you, partner?"

"As a bone."

"Then let's get suited."

Orwell started, the agents following his lead, stepping into the MOPP suit, zipping up its front closure and cinching all the flex points. They left their hoods hanging loose. Next it was into the containment suit. Large, thick boots were at its base, big enough to fit anything but the largest foot size. The trio stepped into these up to their waists and let the upper half droop over one arm in front of them. Then it was out into the night once again.

"These are warm," Frankie commented.

"You wouldn't want to do any prolonged fighting in them," Orwell said. "That's why a chemical environment is a bitch to fight in. You get hot, tired, and dehydrated awful fast with any kind of activity. Fortunately we'll have some relief from that."

"How so?" Art asked.

"Inside the containment suit, besides the air supply, we'll each have a small cooling system. It's a miniature air conditioner that will circulate cool air around the head. The downside is that it only lasts for an hour; it's a major power hog. But it is relief."

The three walked for a minute more until they were at a vehicle identical to the one they had just left. Waiting outside, with three sets of gear resting against the vehicle body, was a soldier in a MOPP suit.

"Sarge, get us set," Orwell directed.

"Okay, sir," the middle-aged NCO said. "Everyone, turn away from me. Let your suits drop and bring your arms back like I'm gonna cuff you, but farther apart."

That had a very unappealing sound to it for the agents, but the position was meant only to facilitate putting on their air supplies. The shoulder straps of the tank harness rode up their arms as the sergeant lifted the forty-pound packs onto their backs. "Cinch up your straps and I'll check 'em."

"Sarge, give them the rundown on the rebreather," Orwell requested. His familiarity with the routine put him three steps ahead of the agents.

The sergeant circled around to the front of his neophytes. He checked their harnesses with a few tugs and then took the full face-mask breathing rig from Frankie's setup in hand. "This isn't like a normal air supply that you might see a fireman or a scuba diver use. This is a rebreather. What that means is that whatever you breathe out after inhaling is directed through a chemical scrubber at the base of the air tanks on your back. About eighty percent of that gets fed back into your air supply. The other twenty percent is pumped into the waste tank. That's why you have two tanks on. One is usable air, and the other is waste. You see, if this was a conventional breather the waste you exhaled would fill the containment suit and you'd blow up like a balloon. And keep blowing up until you popped. So you'll hear the scrubber running, and you'll hear the cooling system—"

"I already filled them in on that, Sarge."

"Very well, sir. So you'll hear sounds, but if you hear a repeated beeping that means the scrubber has failed. In that case you'll have ten minutes to get to decon down the road before you start venting through tears in your suit. That doesn't mean you'll be contaminated right away, because the pressure outflow from the holes will prevent any infiltration . . . for a while."

"That sounds real comforting," Art said.

"It hasn't happened yet," Orwell said, trying to reassure the agents. But anything with a "yet" attached at its end could not fully alleviate natural fears.

"Okay." The sergeant went to the rear of his charges and activated the cooling systems, scrubbers, and air supplies on each setup. "Masks on."

Orwell slid his on easily. Art and Frankie had more difficulty, but the sergeant made sure they were properly fitted and sealed before pulling the MOPP suit hood over their heads and sealing it to the mask's synthetic frame with a heavy tape.

"Duct tape?" Art asked, hearing the familiar tearing sound.

"Too porous," the sergeant answered. "This has a zero air transference rating. Nothing in, nothing out."

"That's how we like it," Orwell said to the agents, his voice booming through the mask's built-in amplifier.

"Getting air okay?"

Art and Frankie nodded to the sergeant.

"Okay, sealing you up now." He pulled the containment suits up and over, directing them to adjust the bubble-faced top on their hooded heads.

"I feel like a damned tamale," Art said.

"A chili tamale?" Frankie ribbed him.

"I wish."

The sergeant pulled the open back of the suits closed and zipped them down. Gravity would not make these zippers come undone. Next he ran multiple strips of tape over the closure and to each side. This he spent a good deal of time on. It was not the place to make a mistake.

"Here," Orwell said, handing each agent a battery-powered lantern.

"And here," the sergeant said, taking his turn and affixing a small object to the single Velcro strip on Art's and Frankie's chests. "Remember that beeping sound I told you about? Well, if you hear a steady high-pitched screeching that means gas has gotten into your suits. If that happens, or if you feel any of these symptoms—dizzyness, sudden extreme dryness in the mouth, blurring or double vision, sudden nausea, or a headache building rapidly—take the injector I just put on the Velcro and jab it into your thigh like this." He made a downward stabbing action. "The action is automatic after that. It'll put a massive dose of adrenaline into your system which may keep you alive.''

''But I've got to be honest,'' Orwell said. ''Don't count on it.''

''Well, partner, I'm about ready for this ride,'' Art joked dryly. ''How about you?''

Frankie looked to Art through the faceshield that slightly distorted his appearance around the edges. Blurry vision? she thought. ''I prefer stuff I can see, partner. Stuff I can shoot at.''

''I hear you.''

''Sarge, let the decon crew know we're coming through,'' Orwell directed. ''Is anyone on-site right now?''

''Sergeant Fuller just pulled back through decon.''

''Then it'll just be us.'' Orwell took a belt from the ground and snugged it around the added girth of two protective suits. To this he clipped a handheld radio. ''We're off.''

Art saw the captain take a few steps toward the roadway. ''We're walking?''

''A half-mile,'' Orwell responded. ''We can't drive in. Too much of a chance of transferring the agent from the site out here. Plus the motion of a vehicle could kick up particles from the roadway that have been contaminated. You saw the orange signs coming in, didn't you?''

''Now I know what they were for.'' Art turned to Frankie. ''Time to hike.''

The trio walked onto Riverside Drive's hard surface and moved abreast at a good pace toward the lights in the distance. Two hundred yards down they moved through the decontamination area. Multiple showers were set up, their feed hoses snaking to a water truck a few yards distant. Actually the compound filling the tank was more exotic, a combination of water, detergents, and chemical neutralizers. At the bottom of each shower a separate hose ran to a series of pumps. From those a single hose went to another truck.

"You don't take any chances," Art observed, pointing to the second truck.

"That stuff will be burned on-site eventually," Orwell informed him. "On our way out we'll shower off and get swept for traces of residue. If there is any left we go through the process again. We have to leave this spot absolutely free of contamination. Then halfway back to where we suited up we dump the containment suits in that bin by the road."

"To be burned later," Art said, parroting what he'd heard from the captain.

"Correct."

"This stuff is that bad?" Frankie asked, a slight puffing coming through the amplifier. She was a sprinter in high school, not a distance runner, and the combination of additional weight on her back plus the heavy clothing was already taking a toll.

"O-ethyl S-2-disoprylaminoethylmethylphosphonothiolate. That's the chemical name," Orwell said, as if he'd simply rattled off a cookie recipe. "The common name is VX. It's the deadliest thing we have in our inventory."

"That's an awful complicated name for something that you say was cooked up out here," Art proposed, his own stamina tested after only three-fourths of their walk.

"Complicated?" The laugh mixed with feedback static from the amplifier. "Anyone can buy the necessary chemicals to manufacture any number of nerve agents. Tabun, sarin, soman. You name it, it can be made by a kid with high school chemistry, some money, and a brave streak a mile wide."

"Or a stupid streak," Frankie added.

"Like our friends up here," Orwell said. "Something went wrong. From what I could tell it was just in time."

"How so?" Art asked.

"The fellow in the house looked like he was carrying the canister that had the VX in it," Orwell said, recalling the scene from one of his three visits to the site. "About ten feet inside the door and around a corner is where we found him. The canister is right next to him on the floor. Allen is outside. I'm no cop, but it looks to me like there might have been a transfer of the VX about to go down when they had a spill. Totally unexpected, and totally irreversible."

"I thought this stuff was a gas," Frankie said. "How do you spill a gas? Wouldn't it just leak out?"

"*Gas* really isn't the proper term. Especially for VX. The correct nomenclature is 'nerve agent.' The gas misconception dates back to the mustard gas days of World War One. What you actually inhale if you are unfortunate enough to breathe in some VX are droplets. Tiny particles that are airborne because of dispersion—usually by spray canisters or warheads of some sort in wartime—or disturbance. That's our concern with motion in the area."

"So this is a liquid," Art said.

"A thick liquid," Orwell expanded. "VX has the consistency of a thin motor oil. That gives it usefulness in the battlefield because it sticks to everything." The captain pointed toward the site. "That's why we're doing that."

They were just a hundred yards away now, and from this point twin streams of water were visible arcing high into the air near 1212 Riverside. After apogee the torrents dispersed into a wide spray that fell upon the house and its surroundings like a heavy rain. Backlit by a portable bank of floodlights, the deluge was comparable to that of a mild hurricane, less the wind. Thankfully less the wind.

"That is one place I want any contamination in the ground," Orwell said. "Water helps dilute the agent and prevents it from getting airborne. If it were possible, the best thing would be to just lift the whole house up and set it in a vat of water. But a wish is just that.''

"So this washes it all into the soil,'' Art said, the first droplets of mist beginning to reach his faceshield. He prayed silently that it was only water.

"Exactly. Then all we have to deal with is the interior.'' Orwell reached up and wiped his faceshield. They were literally walking into a stationary rainstorm. "That's going to take weeks to clean up enough to dispose of.''

"The house?'' Frankie inquired.

"The whole thing. Piece by piece, sealed tight. We'll take it out in the clear somewhere and burn it. Incineration is the only real way to get rid of VX quickly. Over time it will degenerate into its base elements. But that's too long to wait.''

They were very close now, coming upon the American LeFrance fire engine abandoned by its L.A. County Fire Department crew. Ahead of that, closer to 1212 Riverside, was the empty paramedic unit from the same station as the engine. To its side was the backup sheriff's unit that had heeded a call for help. Then, stopped cautiously just shy of the house was the black-and-white that had been first on-scene, its front doors still open, the radio continuously spewing radio calls as dispatched by the sheriff's communications center.

"What about these vehicles?'' Frankie asked.

"We'll burn them eventually,'' Orwell answered, slowing the pace now. "Watch your step all around here. Try not to trip.''

"Religiously,'' Frankie assured him.

The agents rounded the front of the sheriff's car and slowed even beyond their guide's suggestion at the sight before them. It was as if they were on a movie set, observers of an eerie production that looked too real to be. The man-made rain fell steadily and danced upon the

cement walkway to the front of the house. On that walkway and on the lawn were the bodies.

"This is unreal," Frankie commented.

"It's too real," Art said, adding his own correction
to her words.

They continued carefully up the slick walkway, the
constant downpour drumbeating on the heads of their
containment suits. At the jumble of bodies they stopped.

"How long have they been out here?" Art asked,
looking down upon the lifeless forms. They appeared
waxen, the water cascading off their faces.

"Fourteen hours," Orwell answered.

Frankie squatted down next to the single body not in
a uniform. "Can I touch him?"

"Go ahead." The captain certainly didn't relish putting his hands on the departed.

Frankie reached over and unzipped Frederick Allen's
jacket. She checked his shirt pockets, then his front pants
pockets. "Just car keys. Art, you want to help me move
him." With her partner's help Frankie lifted Allen from
the right and rolled him onto his side, his body resting
upon that of Luis Hidalgo, Jr. His soaked jacket clung
to his body, the back of which was caked with mud from
the wet ground.

"Wallet," Art said.

"Got it." Frankie removed the bulge from Allen's
back pocket and looked through it. "License. He's using
the Sam Toomy alias again. A few bucks. No credit
cards." She picked through the recesses. "That's it."

Art shook his head and looked to the faces of the dead
cops at his feet. He noticed something on the lip of one.
"Look at this."

Orwell knelt with Art.

"That's a pretty nasty gash," Art observed.

"Look." The captain used a gloved finger to pry the
officer's cut lip up to reveal a shattered set of teeth.
"The result of convulsions and tremendous spasms in

the jaw muscles. See the jagged remains? That's what caused the cut. If you could look inside the mouth you'd see worse.''

"The ME is going to have a job with these,'' Frankie said.

"The medical examiner is never going to see them,'' Orwell informed her. ''These will be burned on-site.''

"What?'' Frankie stood. ''What about their families?''

"Look, the human body is a perfect host for this agent. We can't decontaminate the insides, the lungs, the digestive tract. There's no way to make these corpses safe for removal.'' Orwell eased his tone. ''I understand your feelings, but there's too much of a risk. We can't take that.''

"I still can't believe that someone could *make* this stuff,'' Art said. The sight of a man's body assaulted by an unseen killer infuriated him. Cancer was the same way. He remembered the experience of watching his grandmother succumb to that invisible killer. But that was natural. Almost expected as one progressed in years. This . . . this was created by men, and unleashed here by those who obviously had had bigger plans than what he now looked upon.

"Jefferson,'' Orwell began, sliding frustration aside. Making people understand the potential danger of these weapons was never easy. They weren't nukes, after all. Nowhere near as sexy as a mushroom cloud, but every bit as deadly. ''Do you know where the technology to make VX came from? To make most nerve agents, in fact?''

"Where?''

"Pesticides. Because that's basically what nerve agents are: pesticides for humans.'' Orwell briefly recalled a poster from a class some years earlier depicting a cartoonish bulldog in an Army uniform utilizing an old pump fogger to spray retreating mice wearing Red

Army uniforms. The caption below read *It's that simple.* "Think of what happens to a bug when you zap it with an insect killer. It becomes confused. Falls over. Twitches. Then it dies. See the similarity? All VX is, is a very potent pesticide designed to exploit the weaknesses of the human nervous system. What it does is attach itself to an enzyme our central nervous system relies on to maintain our basic life functions. It cuts off the transfer of necessary neural information. Without that control you get the spasms and the collapse of the respiratory functions."

"You're telling me this stuff is a bug killer?"

"No, but that's what British chemists were looking for when they stumbled upon VX in the fifties. And that is precisely why it is so easy to manufacture."

"But how does someone know how to do it?" Art pressed, still incredulous that anyone not connected with making these agents for military use could do so.

"Organophosphorous chemistry," Orwell said. "That's a subdiscipline of organic chemistry that deals with chemicals and their effect on life forms. Take that one step further and you know *how* to make chemicals that affect life forms. Plus the general formula has been published quite a number of times in journals over the years. If you're a good chemist you can figure out how to make VX without the formula. If not, you can just look it up."

How could anyone do that responsibly? Freedom of speech, maybe? Bullshit, Art thought. It was worse than publishing the designs for a nuclear bomb, even. You couldn't readily get plutonium or uranium, but you damn sure could buy any chemical you wanted. Even those who made narcotics illicitly bought their bulk chemicals from reputable supply houses. Idiocy!

"Hey, I agree with what you're thinking," Orwell said. The agent's reaction to the revelation was quite clear through his faceshield.

The heavy release of breath crackled through the amplifier in Art's mask. "Well, Allen may have known how to make C4 or Semtex, but I doubt he could have either dreamt this up or carried it out himself."

"No noise factor," Frankie said in agreement. But why was Allen involved in this then?

"Where's the other guy?" Art asked.

"Come on." Orwell led them into the blacked-out house.

Art followed the captain's lead and turned on his flashlight, as did Frankie. They turned right at the first hallway and immediately came upon the body.

"Do you have a name on him?" Frankie asked.

"I'm too busy worrying about the contamination," Orwell answered. "Maybe the sheriff's department does."

Art sidestepped by the captain and knelt next to their one unknown victim. Next to the fiftyish male body was a stainless-steel cylinder about a foot long and two inches across. Both ends were rounded, with a squarish valve assembly at one. "This is it, right?"

"From what I can tell it has to be," Orwell said. "There's a lab set up in one of the back bedrooms, but I haven't been able to find any other signs of the agent. No other containers. Just supply bottles and condensers with residue. I'll have those analyzed by morning to be sure that this was it, but best-guessology is yes, that's it."

"Did you see anything else of interest?" Frankie asked.

Orwell's head moved up and down behind the faceshield. "A bunch of cash in a bedroom. One of my men did a quick count—twelve thousand."

"I'm not surprised," Frankie said.

There was no need being delicate now, Art figured. He rolled the man sideways in the cramped hallway, but found nothing in his pockets. Easing him back, Art next

picked up the cylinder, testing its weight with small tossing actions. "This thing is small."

"It doesn't take much," Orwell commented.

Art thought on that for a moment, looking around the
confined hallway. "How did all this happen?"

"An accident," Orwell said. "It has to be. Probably
when this guy was handing it off to your fugitive. That
valve on top probably also activates the mixer."

"You say 'probably' a lot," Frankie said from behind
the captain.

"We prefer absolutes," Art said. "It makes the report
writing a whole bunch easier."

"What else could it be?" Orwell wondered. "This
guy here prob— makes a batch of VX for Allen, then,
when he's giving it over something goes wrong. It
makes sense."

Art nodded halfheartedly and set the cylinder down.
He could feel the sticky liquid even through the sensa-
tion-numbing gloves. "Probably."

"Can we get a forensic team in here tonight?" Frankie asked.

"Sure, but they won't be able to take anything out.
We've got a camera the haz-mat team set up that can
feed pictures back to the van. That's about the extent of
what they'll be able to take—pictures."

"We'll take that," Art said, standing and pulling
back.

"Ten minutes' lead time," the warning came over the
radio on Orwell's belt.

"Sarge is on top of the time," Orwell explained.
"Time to start heading back."

This time Frankie was in the lead as they left the
house, but Art and Captain Orwell almost ran into her
as they came through the door.

"What is it, partner?" Art asked, knowing Frankie's
I see something posture even through the added layers
of protection.

"Allen's waistband," she answered, walking toward the fugitive as the artificial rain pelted her from above.

Art came around the captain and joined his partner once again next to Allen's body, still rolled on its side. That had not changed. But something had. The thoroughly soaked jacket, which had clung to his body, had slid under the weight of the continuing downpour to the ground, revealing the back of Frederick Allen's waist.

Frankie eased the pistol from its place tucked in the small of Allen's back. It was a .380, she saw. Then she saw its other distinctive feature.

"A silencer?" Art said, cocking his head to look at Frankie. "Why the hell . . ."

"Maybe he was planning to use it," Frankie suggested. "Freddy liked noise, but maybe this needed to be used quietly."

"Against John Doe inside," Art added. "He makes the stuff, then when Freddy comes to pick it up he also plans to cut the trail off by killing him. But the guy decides to use the stuff on Freddy when he gets wise to what's going to happen."

"*That* makes more sense than an accident, considering Freddy's nature," Frankie said. Allen was a thug, pure and simple, and he preferred to solve situations with force. That fit the scenario they were envisioning, but not his involvement in the bigger picture. There was almost too much finesse in all this. Too neat for Allen.

"A gun," Orwell said, looking over their shoulders.

Art stood up again. "I think your accident theory needs reworking. But we may be glad Freddy acted true to form."

Even Frankie didn't follow Art's line on that comment. "How do you figure?"

"If he had just been an honest thug the transfer might have gone down without a hitch," Art posited. "Then this shit would be out there somewhere. And I gather from what you've said, Captain, that he could have killed a hell of a lot more people than we lost here.''

Orwell nodded. ''Many more.''

''Let's hope this was all they were able to make,'' Frankie said.

''It probably is,'' Orwell semi-assured her.

''Make *sure*,'' Art said. ''Allen may be dead but he hung with some folks who wouldn't hesitate to use any weapon they could get their hands on. I want to be damn sure none of this stuff got into the wrong hands.''

''I'll know by tomorrow afternoon,'' Orwell promised.

''Good.'' Art looked down at the grouping of bodies one more time, focusing on the youthful face of Luis Hidalgo, Jr. He saw a bright, smiling, eager expression that practically screamed at the world to *Watch out, I'm coming!* That was the day of the young man's college graduation, Art remembered. That face now was locked in a grimace, its mouth, eyes, and nose blotched with purple discoloration around their edges. But that was not how Art wanted to remember him. Unfortunately, it was probably all that Luis Hidalgo, Sr., was able to think of right now.

''Let's get out of here,'' Art said, taking the lead this time. Frankie and the captain immediately had trouble matching his pace.

Bud DiContino pulled the mouthpiece of the phone away and sipped his coffee from the mug emblazoned with the unit flash of the 358th Tactical Fighter Wing. The reunion of his old buddies from those ''interesting'' days flying suppression in Nam was four months past now, but he still felt a grin coming whenever the mug they'd presented him neared his lips. Awarded to him for being ''Most Likely to Suck Seed,'' it was ostensibly an informal commendation for being remembered as the lowest of the low when it came to flying, precisely where the Wild Weasel pilots had to drive their Thuds.

Bud thought there might be something else in the wording of the award, though. Something to do with his present position in the West Wing. Something much less flattering.

Position did have its price. Ribbing from former buddies who had been with him in his paddy-pounding days he would accept any day as atonement for the "sin" of reaching the West Wing. Brass heaven, they called it. A job, Bud knew it truly to be. National Security Adviser to the President of the United States. He chuckled softly. *Brass heaven, indeed.*

"Did I say something funny?" FBI Director Gordon Jones asked over the phone.

"Not you," Bud said, continuing the mild laugh. "It's this cup my old unit gave me last summer."

"The 'sucking seed' trinket?"

"Yeah. Damned nostalgia." Bud set the mug aside and tore the top sheet off his legal pad. "So this chem thing looks wrapped up?"

"Jerry Donovan in L.A. thinks so," Jones said. "Everything points to a botched transfer of goods."

"Greed paid off in our favor this time," Bud observed.

"Freddy Allen played the game that way. We'd been on him for a while. He killed a Treasury agent a year and a half ago."

Bud swiveled his chair to look out toward Old Executive. "Nothing on the other guy yet?"

"Later today, but, like the brief from CIA said, it does not take a rocket scientist to make this stuff."

"Then why hasn't anyone until now?" Bud asked.

"Someone did, five years ago," Jones revealed.

"I didn't hear about that."

"Good. This is the kind of thing that is better kept in the dark. Can you imagine the copycats we'd have trying to cook up nerve gas in their basements and their garages if this was all general knowledge?"

"It is in the open," Bud pointed out.

"So are the plans for H-bombs," Jones countered. "But your average Joe can't get the stuff to make it work. In this case, your average Joe *can* get the stuff but he's more likely to kill himself than anyone else. That's what happened five years ago. Some stupid college kid thought it would be neat to make some VX. He decided to do it small, just an ounce or so, and before he knew he'd done it he was flopping on the ground like a fish. Dead by the time a buddy who'd been helping him got up the nerve to call the authorities. They did the smart thing and sealed it all off until the Army could get some people there. Stupid kid."

Bud could imagine the FBI director rubbing his temples as he shook his head. "It's still scary that someone *could* produce this stuff if they wanted to."

"I know. But the genie is out of the bottle, Bud. We just have to make sure no one without any real compunction to use it ever gets near it."

"Sounds more like a hope than a plan," Bud said.

"We have to start somewhere."

The NSA tapped his pen on the blank legal tablet and turned back to his desk. "Well, the president will be glad to hear that everything is under control."

"Is he getting any more sleep?" the director inquired.

"With a baby that just started crawling?" Bud asked rhetorically. "You should see it sometimes, Gordy. The little guy is scooting around the Oval Office like there's no tomorrow, all while the man running our country is on the phone with Konovalenko or some other world leader. It makes for some interesting background noise."

"I bet."

"Anyway, thanks for the update. If anything new comes up let me know right away."

"Will do."

Bud placed the handset back in its cradle and brought both hands behind his head. He leaned back and turned again to gaze upon the gray monolith across Executive Avenue. The faded light of the late autumn morning was not flattering to the old building. Some days it looked quite nice; others, like this, it was a drab reminder of what was possible.

So similar to the way the political landscape appeared, Bud thought. His position did not normally lend itself to internal punditry, but no one in the West Wing could deny that the president was suffering from being cast in an unflattering light, much like Old Executive. The vibrancy of a new baby in the White House aside, there was trouble on the homefront. The economy was still sluggish. Jobs had not materialized fast enough for those who were planning to challenge the president in the election the following year. And increasingly the media was focusing on those efforts that were directed at dealing with issues on the international stage and asking, *Why not focus on what needs attention at home?*

As if the world would just wait until everything improved at home, Bud thought. Still, the president was in a precarious position to begin in earnest his campaign for reelection. He needed to convince the American public that he *was* making significant strides in putting the domestic economy on a track of long-term growth. The problem with that was that it would yield little in the way of tangible results to hold before the voters as proof. Image and snippets drove elections now. And too often the voter was the recipient only of a filtered, packaged view of what was really happening on the political playing field. That was the way the pendulum had swung, Bud admitted reluctantly.

''Thank God this thing didn't blow up in our faces,'' the NSA said to the empty interior of his office. All the president needed was a crisis in the states. He would have dealt with it, and the media would have crucified him for spending too much time doing so. It was a no-win situation that they would not have to live through now. Bud had no doubt the West Wing was going to be breathing a little easier because of a crisis that entered the arena stillborn. This one was dead on arrival.

Captain Orwell finished decontaminating for the second time since leading the guided tour for Art and Frankie. An hour after their departure it had been for a two-man FBI forensic team, and this last time to finish the work *he* needed to complete. He stepped out of the containment suit that was like a sauna under the noontime sun and was checked by one of his team for any residual contamination. With a clean bill of health, and still in MOPP suit and breathing gear, he trekked a quarter-mile more to the set of Humvees.

"Damn, it's hot in this," he exclaimed as the mask finally came off.

"Just think what it would be like here in summer," the sergeant said.

"Did you get a good download?" Orwell asked. He had just completed sampling residues in the containers that had once held several dozen chemicals using a remote analyzer. That information was then fed to a computer via a landline stretching more than a half-mile from the lead Humvee to 1212 Riverside.

"Perfect. She's crunching the numbers right now."

Orwell pulled his legs out of the MOPP suit and stuffed the sweat-soaked garment into a sealed drum adjacent to the Humvee. "Let's take a look at what we've got."

The two men climbed through the rear door into an electronics-crammed workspace smaller than the dressing facility of the Humvee one back. Several banks of computers and their associated equipment were mounted against one wall, with two chairs facing them. Orwell took the one with best access to the keyboard.

"She's done," the sergeant observed.

"Let's print some hard copy while we see what we

found," Orwell said. A few keystrokes sent a report to the printer, which began spitting the pages out with just a whisper. The captain, meantime, pulled the identical data up on the screen for viewing.

"Diisopropylamine," the sergeant read from the screen, noting the presence of the colorless, ammonia-smelling chemical. "There's the base ingredient for the base of the binary."

"So it was made as a binary," Orwell commented. "Interesting." He looked back to the screen. "Ethyl alcohol, dipropylene glycol monomethyl ether, and phosphine. There's the whole base."

"The guy was able to *process* it?" the sergeant wondered. "I would have bet he'd skipped the phosphine and used the extrusion method. This guy took risks."

He sure did, Orwell agreed. Using phosphine, a gas that had the potential to spontaneously ignite on contact with air, put their man a step above advanced chemist. You had to have balls to play with this stuff in a crude environment. Balls and confidence. Strange. He chose to use a more difficult method of making the VX binary base. The only reason to do that was ... *quality control?* The simpler method sometimes yielded inferior, even ineffective product because of the potential for poor manufacturing of the several reagents. Processing *with* phosphine was more dangerous, but it gave the chemist more control over the finished product. Very strange, Orwell thought.

"Did you get any quantity readings for the base?"

"Too much evaporation to tell," Orwell answered, shaking his head. He scrolled further through the data. "Here's our activator reagents."

The binary chemical weapon consisted of two parts, separated until mixed for use: the base and the activator. The base, which was a sort of generous chemical receptor, mixed with the more important activator. This activator gave the weapon its "personality." Several variations of known agents were possible depending upon how much one "tweaked" the activator, which made identification of its precise ingredients necessary in order to determine its lethality.

"Dimethyl sulfate, sulfur dioxide, ethyl—*ethyl?*"

The reading caught Orwell's eye as well.

"This says ethyl mercaptan," the sergeant said. "That should be *methyl* mercaptan."

"I know." Orwell was already reading the rest of the data on-screen, his heart rate rising.

"Sulfur dioxide," the sergeant continued. "That's right. Ethy—" He stopped, staring at the screen.

"Ethylene glycol dinitrate," Orwell said, finishing the sergeant's words.

"That's got to be wrong! It has to be!" The sergeant took the printout and read the hard copy to confirm that what he saw on the screen was not some anomaly. It wasn't. "It isn't."

"Dammit."

"Did you get a quantity on this?" the sergeant asked.

"Yes."

"How much?"

Orwell didn't answer with words. His expression said *Enough.*

"Dear God."

"Finish that sentence, Sergeant, and ask for His help," Orwell said. He stood and slid by his subordinate, heading for the door. "We're going to need it."

TWO

Before the Horse

"The Federal Bureau of Investigation has just confirmed that *the incident north of Los Angeles initially reported as only a hazardous chemical mishap was actually a potentially disastrous spill of a military-style chemical weapon known as VX,*" the CNN anchor reported, reading from news copy just handed him. "*VX is a nerve gas common to the stockpiles of the military forces of both the United States and the former Soviet Union. At a news conference just carried live on CNN, Special Agent in Charge Jerry Donovan of the Los Angeles FBI office reported that the nerve gas was manufactured illicitly by a still unidentified person and released during some sort of mishap. Donovan repeated assurances that there is no reason to believe any of the nerve gas has fallen into the wrong . . .*"

Bud DiContino muted the television as his phone buzzed.

"DiContino."

"Bud, it's Gordy."

"Hey, I just caught your man in L.A. on CNN," Bud said. "He handled it well."

The exasperation came through the phone in the form of a sigh before Director Jones spoke. "I'm not so sure. I'm faxing you something right now."

Bud heard the low hum of the whisper-quiet machine

and pulled the pages out as they came through, scanning them quickly.

"We've got trouble," Jones said, using those words that no one at this level of government wanted to hear.

Bud scanned the last page just after the director's warning. Fast reading was a necessity in government service, the need for such a skill increasing proportionally the higher one progressed. There wasn't any higher than the West Wing of the White House, and few faster than the NSA. "When did this info come in?"

"Still the speed-reading champion, I see," Jones quipped. "Less than an hour ago."

"Did . . . what's his name?"

"Donovan," Jones prompted. "No, he didn't know this. But he also didn't have any authorization to say what he did."

Bud tossed pages haphazardly onto his desk. "Dammit, Gordy! He goes on national TV and tells everybody things are under control, and then this!"

"I know, Bud."

Bud picked up the last page and read the important section of the fax once more. "This is confirmed?"

"By the Army commander on-scene. He rammed this through channels and into the Pentagon at light speed to get it here."

"Christ!" Bud exclaimed. "What's Drew have out there—a four-star?"

"A young buck captain," Jones replied. Secretary of Defense Andrew Meyerson was also sufficiently impressed with the young officer's tenacity, the FBI director knew from the call the secretary had made to pass the info along.

"That takes balls," Bud said. He thought again of the press briefing just completed. "I hope you're going to bite a big chunk out of Donovan's ass."

"I will. Don't worry. He's only been running the show out there for a while, but he knows better than to give everybody the safe signal on something like this before checking with me first. No excuse at all.''

So a SAC was going to get the riot act read to him in a major way. As necessary as that was, it still wouldn't undo the damage already done. ''So what's the plan now?''

''Silence,'' Jones said.

''This may not be the best time to close our mouths, Gordy. Think of how the press will play it. FBI flubs first by telling the public all is A-OK, then they hide their mistake when it's discovered. It doesn't look good.''

''I'm not concerned with appearances right now, Bud. That was the mistake Donovan made. He jumped the gun because he wanted this wrapped up. I've seen it before.'' And Jones had suspected the new SAC in L.A. might live up to those low standards. But the senior senator from a state that possessed forty-three electoral votes liked the smoothness of Donovan, and certain things in the political arena had to be accepted with bared teeth disguised as a smile. ''I don't want this out because it might hamper what my people are going to have to do. L.A. is going to have to figure out more than just 'who' and 'why' now. We have to add 'where' to that list. The press is going to find out at some point in any case. I just don't want it to hamper an investigation. Hey, I'll stand up to the plate afterwards and say that we fucked up royally. Until then, I don't need reporters hounding me or my agents about a bad situation gone worse.''

Jones did make his point with conviction. Bud was still uneasy about it, but he was not the number-two cop in the land. ''You know what's best, Gordy. So what is your read on this?''

''I won't know until I get something from L.A.''

''When?''

''Tonight. I'm going to talk to Donovan after we're

done. I want his assistant to oversee this. Lou Hidalgo
is his name. You know he lost a son in what happened?
A fireman.''

"Yeah, I read that in the *Post*. Is he going to be up
to it?''

"Lou is tough. But he will just be oversight. There
are a couple agents already on the investigation working
the Allen aspect of things. I'm sure Lou will use them
as lead.''

"I know from experience you have good people out
there,'' Bud said. "This Allen fellow had some pretty
nasty affiliations, didn't he?''

"Aryan Brotherhood. But they operate pretty much
behind bars, and he's been out and on the run for quite
a while. Like I said, I'll know more later.''

"Fair enough,'' Bud said, knowing some things had
to wait. But some things couldn't. "Gordy, to be safe
I'm going to have to let some people in on this.''

"I understand. Just be particular.''

"You know it,'' Bud assured the director, then hung
up. A sandwich was on his desk, calling his name, but
Bud had some calling that needed to come first. The first
number he dialed was that of the president's chief of
staff. After a brief conversation requesting a meeting he
dialed the other. It was answered by the supervising
agent of the Secret Service presidential detail.

Cat and Dog. The title of the book John Barrish held
while sitting in the overstuffed chair might have led one
to believe that the subject was rudimentary reading skills
for children. But it was not.

*There is the cat, an obvious hunter, difficult to do-
mesticate and train, cunning, yet susceptible to the dis-
traction of simple stimuli such as a string dangled before
it. Then there is the dog, a thinker, able to follow commands to a much higher degree than the cat. It learns.*

It is loyal. It obeys commands of logic presented to it. It is discerning.

The cat and the dog inhabit the planet together. They are each prolific breeders. Yet they have never mixed, never attempted to meld their distinct selves into one bastardized offspring. Why? Why?

"Because they know better," John said aloud, answering the question posed by the book's author, Dr. Felix Trent, a social and racial theorist from the early part of the century whose writings and teachings had helped a very angry and a very confused young John Barrish find the proper way to channel his energetic convictions on the subject of race.

Because they know better. The cat functions as a more primitive creature, successful in the environment it chooses. The dog functions at a higher level in its own environment. Logic tells the two not to mix. No biological reasoning need be added.

For the African and the Aryan the question is the same, as it is for all other races defined by their bloodline and simpler cultures. The African is a hunter, a gatherer, a master of an uncivilized environment whereby its natural physical strengths and lack of inhibiting moral codes allow it to thrive. The Aryan is of a higher order, an organizer, a builder, an exploiter of tools and technology. There can be no dispute to this, nor can there be a dispute that any mixing of these races, whether by habitation in proximity to one another or by, in a more serious and tragic sense, relations that produce mixed offspring, will end in disaster. The animals know better. So should we.

It was just the foreword to one of Trent's many books, but it was powerful, John thought. So simple. Separation. Was it so hard a concept to understand? It was not for him. The Africans—why people persisted in antagonizing them by calling them niggers and the like was beyond him—could have Africa. The Aryans of pure blood could have America, the country built by white people, and parts of Europe, though he believed that so much mixing had occurred there that that continent was best abandoned, surrendered to the Gypsies and their cohorts. America would be for a white man.

John closed the book with a satisfying slap that coincided with the opening of the front door. His eldest boy was back. *Finally!* he thought, hoping some questions would now be answered. "What happened?"

"I don't know, Pop," Toby Barrish said, shrugging apologetically.

"The TV said there was an accident," Barrish said, the force in his words exceeded by the menace in his posture. His feet shuffled on the living room carpet like a bull's before the charge.

"Calm down, Pop," Toby said. "I checked the stuff. It's safe."

"But what the hell happened out there?!" Barrish demanded, his small neck bulging and his teeth gritted as short breaths whistled through them.

"I don't know. Freddy was supposed to take care of things after I picked up the stuff. When I left him he was going to go back in and do it."

Barrish rubbed a hand over his head and turned away from his son. Through the doorway to the kitchen he saw his wife looking at him, her face covered with that same, weak expression of what she thought was concern. He rejected that, from her or from anyone. John Barrish did not need sympathy. He did not need pity. Both offerings were from and for the meek, and he could be characterized as nothing if not the total opposite of that.

"Pop, there's no way they can trace any of what happened to us," Toby assured him. "I was careful with Freddy. Real careful."

Barrish faced his son again. "I knew you would be. This just shouldn't have happened."

"I know."

It had to be Freddy the federal pig was talking about on TV when he mentioned a dead fugitive. Freddy was that, to be certain. But then the pig from the Internal Robbery Service had it coming, John believed. It hadn't been done cleanly, but some resistance actions were bound to be messy. Freddy simply came from a group that subscribed to the belief that the dirtier the action was, the better.

"I'm glad he's out of the picture," Barrish said. "You did good keeping him at arm's length, Toby."

"I knew he didn't fit into our group, Pop, but he served a purpose. Means to an end," Toby added as an afterthought.

"That's right," Barrish agreed. "When is the meeting?"

"Monday," Toby answered. "Stan and I are going to meet them at the zoo."

Barrish's eyes looked down in thought briefly. "Keep an eye on Stanley. He's still young."

"He just needs a little toughening, that's all," Toby said. "This'll help."

Barrish nodded acceptance of his eldest's belief. "And you watch the Africans. You hear me?" He tapped his temple with a single finger. "They may be feeble up here, but they have centuries of genes on their side in the muscle department."

"I'll be careful."

"Make sure Stanley understands that, too," Barrish admonished his son.

"I will."

The heat of the moment was subsiding now. Barrish let several breaths loose to unwind further. "I want to see it."

The words took Toby by surprise. "That's not a good

idea, Pop. You should be as far away from the stuff as possible."

"I want to see it," he repeated, his wish obviously not up for further discussion. "Tonight."

"Okay, Pop. Tonight."

THREE

Relations

Darren Griggs wondered how one man could hate so much. He had puzzled over the same question more than a year before, when the name of John Barrish sparked images of a pitiful man who was so fearful of those whose skin was of a darker hue than his that he would champion their removal from "white" America. Now, as the head of a family torn apart by the actions of that same man he had pitied, Darren Griggs knew that he could hate even more.

Yet his hate was more profound. It came from a place inside that used to be filled with a contrasting emotion. Now there was a blazing inferno there. His rage was burning, aching for vengeance, consuming its host as it searched for a target of opportunity. It had tempted him to strike out at his own family, but he resisted, burying it deeper. His wife, already destroyed by the vicious murder of her little girl, was little more than a shell of the woman she had been. His son, who had doted on his little sister like any big brother would, was now more of an adversary in their family structure than a member. He thrived on conflict, savoring it, even in the smallest amounts. Arguments with his defenseless mother. Defiance of his father. And, even though Moises was of age, this devastated his father, who had always been the closest of friends with his son. Now the rift could hardly be wider.

And what could Darren do? He himself was teetering on the brink, ready to succumb to destructive urges, which would destroy the last vestige of shaky stability in his family. And that knowledge had guided him to the logical answer to the question. There was something he could do. Something he had to do.

Darren left his car a block and a half from La Brea and began walking east, his right hand curled around the rolled-up flyer. He had memorized the address, which would be just across La Brea and south a half a block or so. He knew so from having driven by a dozen times or more in the past week, hoping each time the courage to stop and go through with it would come to him. This time it had.

As he walked he was the subject of much interest from the residents of the neighborhood. He was an outsider; that was of no doubt. Half of those whose eyes were cast upon him looked out from under the wide brims of coal-black hats, their faces framed by long, regal beards. Children with curls dangling in front of their ears stared the most at the black man walking down their street, not because he was black, but because he was not like the other black men their parents had chased out of the neighborhood. He was dressed nice, not fancy, like Mr. Katz at the shoe store. This black man was clean, and he wasn't pushing a shopping cart piled with bags and cans and blankets. He wasn't dirty, and he didn't have lots of little plastic bags in his hand. He looked almost normal, except that he was black.

Darren glanced left and right as he moved down the block. He saw some of the stares, and felt others. And he knew why he was suddenly the focus of attention. He also didn't care. There were more important things to worry about, more pressing matters at hand. He had hate to deal with; this was just fear.

The evening rush hour was almost over, and Darren had little trouble crossing La Brea. He trotted through a break in traffic and turned right, his feet moving him toward the building frontage he had memorized from numerous no-stop passes in his car. Just inside the lobby, through twin glass doors that let the bright lights spill out onto the darkening street, Darren saw the signboard. He rubbed a nervous thumb on the roll of paper in his hand and uncurled it. *Race and Hate: A Program on Understanding.* The words on the sign and the flyer in his hand were the same, and the fact that he had it at all was another product of his daughter's murder. If his son hadn't started getting into trouble with the law Darren would never have had to come down to an attorney's office two weeks before, and if that office hadn't been just a half-mile from where he now stood, and if there hadn't been a flyer stuck on his car windshield when he came out . . .

Coincidence or design, Darren didn't care. It had happened, maybe for a purpose, maybe not, but he was here, standing outside the Hanna Schonman Jewish Community Center in the heart of the Fairfax District of Los Angeles holding on to a piece of paper that told of understanding, and to a thread of hope that it could all be true.

Darren Griggs hated himself for hating others, and he wanted it to stop. For his sake, and for his family's.

With that determination he pushed the glass doors inward and followed the signs to the indicated room. The door was closed. He knew he was late, a product of his trepidation, but the cliché fit in this circumstance. Never just wasn't an option. Darren took the knob in hand and opened the door, hoping, praying desperately that his mind and heart would follow.

He stepped into the Ben Kaplan Memorial Conference Room and eased the door shut behind him. It was a large, rectangular room with three sections of seats split by two aisles, the classic theater setup. Maybe three hundred seats, he guessed, with less than a third of them filled, but all of those were packed in the front five rows of cushioned seats. At the front of the room was a stage, where the attention of the assembled group was focused. Until, of course, they turned and saw who the latecomer was. Or, more correctly, what he wasn't.

Darren saw all heads swing his way. He had expected it, in fact, just as the stares on his short walk to this place hadn't surprised him. After all, as his father had told him when he was just a little black boy in a very white L.A., *"Son, you is ten shades darker than dark. People will notice that. 'Specially white folk."* And Darren was far darker than anyone in the room—except for the lady at the front.

"Sir, come on in." Dr. Anne Preston smiled, knowing that her pearly whites would be seen from across the hall. It was her most striking feature, at least according to her boyfriend, and she hoped that it would serve as a quiet invitation to the man who had just entered to join the group. "We're just getting to the good stuff."

A few chuckles came from the crowd, and Darren forced a smile back to the speaker. Actually, he found, it wasn't that hard to muster. Somewhat less than half of the eyes in the room followed him all the way to the seat he chose, in the row directly behind the main body of people. He avoided meeting their looks, instead focusing on the lady at the podium. *Dr. Preston,* he remembered from the flyer. A psychiatrist. A woman of color, standing before a sea of white. She would be his beacon in this room. His point of reference to block out the fear he felt from the stares.

Anne waited for the new arrival to be seated before moving on, putting the obvious questions as to why this man would put himself in this place at this time with these people. She figured that those musings would be answered when all was said and done.

"I want to talk a little about perception now," Anne began. "How our perceptions, which are influenced by that old nature-nurture combination, affect everything we see, do, and most importantly, everything we *feel.*"

She pressed the projection button recessed in the lectern. The lights dimmed just a bit onstage as the slide projector hummed and painted the large white screen above and behind her with two images. One was of a black man, a close-up shot of an expressionless face and head. It was reminiscent of the famed Willie Horton mug shot, less the long hair. To the right of this was another picture, this one of a white man, dressed in blue jeans and a casual shirt, sitting peacefully on a park bench, smiling into the camera. The contrast was obvious. It also had a purpose.

"Jerome Wilkes was a thrice-convicted felon when he met Robert Foster one night two years ago, robbed him, and killed him. He shot him in the back of the head after making him get to his knees. We can only assume that Mr. Foster was begging for his life, but he had no way of knowing that the man who broke into his Atlanta home that night was on parole for another murder. Robbery, rape, murder." Anne paused for effect. The grimaced faces were her cue to continue. "Jerome Wilkes did it all, and, unfortunately for Mr. Foster, he didn't like leaving loose ends."

Darren shifted his gaze between the faces on the screen, but found himself drawn to the man of his color. *Why did he have to do that?* he wondered. His actions were what white people saw when they looked at *any* black man. Killer. Rapist. Thief. Not all black people were like that, but the hate came anyway. Inside, Darren's head was shaking with wonder.

"When you hear this story, and you see Jerome Wilkes and Mr. Foster, what do you think of?" Anne asked the audience.

"I see what I see all around us," a man answered

from his front-row seat, arms crossed tightly across a pudgy chest. Several seats to his right, the rabbi of the synagogue sponsoring the presentation leaned forward to listen. "All around our neighborhood. Look, no disrespect meant, Miss Preston . . ."

Of course not, but I stopped being "Miss" a long time ago. And earlier when you agreed with me, I recall being referred to as "Doctor Preston." It was Anne's job to read into what was said, and what wasn't, and she was damned good at it, much to her boyfriend's displeasure at times. Here, though, it would let her make a breakthrough . . . maybe.

". . . but all we see are blacks committing these crimes. You see this all the time. You hear of it every day. They walk down our block and sell their crack."

"Not anymore," another man interjected. His face was a mask of hate. "Not on my block."

"Fine, we clean up our own neighborhoods," the first man continued, "but what about the rest of the city? Or the country. Look," he said with added passion, pointing to the screen. "That's in Atlanta. The blacks there are no different than here. No different than anywhere."

"They can't fit in," a woman offered. "They don't try."

The first man's head nodded emphatically, looking at Anne.

"That's right. And so what do they do? They rob and kill white people because *we* tried to fit in, *we* worked hard, and *we* have things they want! Miss Preston, you show us these pictures and tell us this story and expect it to change our mind? It only reinforces it."

Anne wanted to smile. She always wanted to smile at this point, more than her natural tendency to do so, but didn't. "What reinforces it?"

"This!" the man half-yelled, standing and tossing his hand toward the screen. "You tell us a story about another black murderer taking a white man's life because he wanted his things! That is what we live with every day!''

Darren swallowed hard. He hadn't expected to hear the hate. Maybe feel it, but not hear it. Was this a mistake? Was coming here hoping for something to drive the hate out of his soul too much to ask? His eyes again looked to the screen. *Why? Why did you have to fulfill their prophecy?*

''You mean Jerome Wilkes?'' Anne asked.

''Yes!'' the man yelled fully now, pointing a spearlike finger at the black face over Anne's right shoulder.

Anne glanced over her right shoulder, then over her left, holding her look there as she brought a hand up and casually pointed at the smiling white face staring down upon the audience. ''This is Jerome Wilkes.''

It couldn't be called a gasp, but there was a collective sound from the audience, including Darren.

''What made you think I meant this gentleman was the murderer?'' Anne asked, pointing now at the black face above and to her right.

There was no answer. The man who had been standing looked to some of those near him, glancing briefly at the lone black face in the audience, and slowly sat back down.

''This, ladies and gentlemen, is Robert Foster. The picture you see is from his identification card. You see, Mr. Foster was an Atlanta firefighter when he was murdered by this man.'' The direction shifted back to the man who, until a minute before, had been the victim in the eyes of the people in the room. ''Jerome Wilkes is now awaiting execution for that crime.''

Silence. The hum of the slide projector's cooling fan might as well have been thunder. The only member of the audience unaware of it was Darren, whose face was now downcast, his mind assaulting itself with torturous accusations. *Racist! To your own people! The whites don't need to hate us—you're doing it for them! Black means bad! It means guilty! You're no better than the animals that killed Tanya!* He had come seeking understanding, and was now filled with confusion. The hate he had developed for those other than his own, a hate he wanted to destroy, was now targeted inward. He sat there, hearing nothing more, dreaming of ways to end this pain. To end it for good.

"This was a trick," a faceless voice from the audience said.

"You're right," Anne responded. "Your perceptions tricked you into believing what you expected, rather than the reality. You see, preconceptions—even if somewhat validated by past experience—circumvent one of our most important abilities: the ability to look critically at something. When I put those two pictures up there you immediately focused on the black face when I mentioned that a crime had been committed." She heard no dispute from the audience; not even a *Why is his head hung like that?* "Many people have come to the point where they see black as the color of danger. Yet here we have an example of something quite different."

This was a mistake. Darren wanted to just curl up in a ball and fade away. To just be gone. Gone like Tanya. His living family didn't even matter at the moment, and he had come here in the hope of resurrecting the old Darren Griggs, the real Darren Griggs, in order to save them. Now that wasn't even a possibility as he saw it. He was on a slippery slope sliding slowly toward a steep drop-off. Slowly but gaining speed.

"You all condemned the victim here," Anne said with some accusation in her tone. "Your perceptions prevented you from ascertaining the truth. Your biases prevented understanding from developing." She gestured to the smiling face of Jerome Wilkes. "You were prepared to offer sympathy to this man based upon the color of his skin." And next to Robert Foster. "And to crucify this man because of his. Color is a color, people.

A color. That's all it is. If you condemn Robert Foster because of his, then you condemn me. You condemn all people with skin darker than yours to a life of explaining why they aren't all bad. Think about it. Please. Thank you.''

Anne never expected applause at these presentations, but it did come, if slowly. First one person would politely clap—*She did do this free, after all*—before a few others—*I did think it was the black man without knowing anything else*—joined in. She stood appreciatively before them as Rabbi Samuel Levin came from his front-row seat to stand beside her.

"Dr. Preston, thank you,'' Levin said, hugging Anne. "I'm sure I speak for everyone here when I say we deeply appreciate your time, and your wise counsel.''

Some nods now, more applause. Anne guessed there were seventy-five minds in the audience that needed enlightening. Maybe she had reached five. Maybe ten. That would be a success.

But there appeared to be one mind that might need something more. Maybe something she could offer.

"There will be refreshments in the Weitzel Room, everyone,'' Levin announced. He turned back to Anne as the audience began to filter toward the door. "Will you join us, Dr. Preston?''

The man hadn't moved. He still sat there, looking downward. "I'd love to. But I may need a minute.''

Rabbi Levin saw what she was looking at. "Yes. Of course. I will see you down the hall.''

Anne walked off the stage to where Darren remained seated. "Hello.''

Darren's head jerked up, his eyes glistening.

"I'm Anne Preston.'' She stretched her hand out.

Darren looked at the hand. Somehow it seemed to be more than an appendage. Much more.

"Darren Griggs, Dr. Preston.'' He took her hand,

shook it, then let go when he really wanted to hold on for dear life.

Anne took the seat directly in front of Darren and swiveled her body to face him. "Thank you for coming."

Darren held up the rolled flyer. "I thought . . . maybe . . . I thought I might . . ." The mist in his eyes became a single tear from each that streamed over his cheeks. "I don't want to die . . ."

What? Anne might have expected a hundred reasons why this man would have come here this night, but that was not one of them. "Why do you think that's a possibility?"

"Because everything I . . . everyone I love is dying, and . . ." The tears came fully now. ". . . and I can't help them. I can't help them. I can't save my own family!"

Anne watched Darren bend forward, his head touching the seat as the sobs came in waves. She placed a hand on his shoulder, rubbing gently until the spasms ended and he sat back up.

"I'm . . ." Darren wiped his face on the sleeve of his jacket. "I'm sorry. I didn't mean to . . ."

"Do you want to tell me about it? About your family?"

Darren felt the pressure in his chest build like the forces of a mighty river checked by a dam. The floodgates were closed, but not as tightly as a minute before. Before the question was asked. *Do you want to tell me about your family?* "Yes. Yes I do."

And he did, talking almost without interruption for fifteen minutes. About Tanya's murder. About his wife's spiral into a bottomless depression. About Moises' destructive behavior. About it all.

And Anne listened, wanting to cry at times. Remembering the news stories, how terrible it had seemed then, and now a living victim of that massacre was here with her, begging for salvation.

Then, as quickly as he began laying out the state of his life, Darren stopped. He was dry. The dam had burst and had let out all that was behind it. His desire for death was no longer there, but the aching he felt for his family was.

"I'm sorry," Anne said, offering the first words one could after hearing Darren speak of his life, and of his loss.

"Thank you for listening."

"I'm not done listening," Anne said. She had to do this.

"What do you mean?" Darren asked.

"You need to talk more. Your family needs to talk. And you need someone to help you with that."

She was right, Darren knew. But it all seemed so alien now—normalcy. How could they get that back from talking? And there were other considerations. "Thank you, Dr. Preston, but I can't . . . I work hard as it is, and with the lawyer's fees and my wife's medication, I can't . . ."

"Don't worry about that," Anne said. "We need to help your family first, and think about the other things later. I'll make you a deal, though. If you want to do this, I'll forget the fee if you and your family come to my house for dinner when we have everybody on the right track again. I'd consider that payment enough. You see, I love to cook, but my girl is grown and my boyfriend is into that health-food junk." She made a face that translated plainly to Darren. It also elicited a smile. "Deal?"

Darren wanted to cry again, but for very different reasons than before. "Deal. Thank you, Dr. Preston."

Anne handed him one of her cards. "Call me tomorrow. We'll set up a first appointment."

"Okay." Darren put the card away and smiled again.

How long had it been since he smiled twice in one day? He couldn't remember. "I'll call you in the morning."

Anne watched Darren walk away, passing Rabbi Levin, who was entering.

"My God, Anne, what did you do to that man in fifteen minutes?" Levin asked. "When I left he looked like the world had fallen on him. Now he's smiling."

"The world did fall on him," Anne said. "Remember the St. Anthony shooting?"

"The church on Crenshaw? Of course. How could anyone forget that? Four children killed." Levin's head shook. His grandparents had been dragged from a synagogue in Warsaw more than fifty years before and sent to their death. Now there was death *in* a place of worship. The senselessness of it.

"His daughter was one of them," Anne said, hating the reality of it. "Tanya Griggs."

"Oh dear God. No."

Anne nodded. "After it happened he began feeling a deep hate for white people, something he'd never experienced. It scared him. He wanted it to stop, because he was starting to hate himself for hating others because of their color. Plus his family is in ruins." She really shouldn't say anymore, Anne knew. "I'm hoping I can help him, and his family."

Levin felt ill thinking of the destruction that had been wrought upon this family. Hate. It was the worst of things. Combine it with ignorance and you had a very dangerous force. That was why he had arranged for Anne to speak to members of his flock. They were good people, but they were becoming less and less sensitive to the danger of misplaced hate. The evil they saw in the world was disproportionately of a darker hue, and they were beginning to transfer their fear of real violence to fear of anyone who looked like the criminals plastered on the news. Compassion was fading from their belief systems. That frightened Levin, because it was the same thing that had happened in Nazi Germany so long ago. Induced fear became hate. Then it became institutionalized bias. Then worse. That road had been traveled. No more. Never again, especially by his people.

"Anne, you are a good person," Levin said. "Maybe I can ask Ellis to find you a spot in the Cabinet. They could use people like you."

Anne chuckled at the complimentary suggestion. Levin was a major fund-raiser for the Democrats, and had an ear in the White House in the form of Chief of Staff Ellis Gonzales. Levin's son had been a college classmate of his, and the bond stretched from family to family.

"I'm flying out for a meeting with him on Friday," Levin said wryly. "Anne Preston in the White House. Heh?"

"You have pull with both big guys, huh, Rabbi?" Anne asked, laughing.

"Occasionally."

"Well, I'll stick to doctoring, if you don't mind."

"Of course. How could we get along without you." Levin thought seriously for a moment. "Especially people like Mr. Griggs. I hope you can help fix what has happened to that family."

"Me, too, Rabbi," Anne said, knowing there was a starting point in any project. This one would be the father.

The son, however, had a very different concept of healing. Healing now held the converse of its dictionary meaning for Moises Griggs. Vengeance, strangely, carried the same definition.

There had been another presentation that night by someone purveying knowledge to an assembled group, though this one was much smaller in number than that attended by the elder Griggs. Twelve, including Moises, had come to this place to receive the offering, to receive the motivation. In church it would be called the gospel. Here, as told by Darian Brown, leader of the New Africa Liberation Front, it was a clarion call to battle.

The home of the NALF was a converted liquor store that had been looted to the rafters in the uprising of '92, and which the former Korean owners had decided to sell off so as not to have to return to a neighborhood they saw as rejecting them. And that it had, Darian Brown professed, and rightly so. Expulsion was a hallmark of the NALF doctrine, as was compensation to the sons and daughters of slaves. Compensation in the form of land, namely that of the slave states at the time of the Civil War. It was simple in Darian Brown's mind. You move out the white people, and move in the black. Instant nation building. New Africa in this case. A homeland for the blacks robbed of their ancestral roots across an ocean. Returning to a continent ravaged by white colonialism was not an option. A piece of this pie—America—was the minimum payment acceptable on a bill long overdue.

And that message held appeal for a number that, though small, was growing. Darian Brown knew it would grow to a large movement in time of its own accord, but that would allow time for the white man to chisel away at the hard edge of their determination. Softening them. Convincing many that peaceful measures would work. No. No longer. Darian Brown, a thirty-five-year-old product of the Los Angeles ghettos who had tested the bounds of the white man's law, knew that time was their enemy. "Now" was their friend. This movement needed a spark to ignite it into a blaze that nothing could stop. And it needed members, committed individuals, to make that happen.

But there were different types to serve the movement. There were workers, and there were soldiers. Darian needed soldiers now more than anything. The workers could lead boycotts, and harass businesses. The soldiers would serve a more vital role. One with risk, but one that would reap great benefits for the movement.

In any group he spoke to Darian always tried to pick who fit into which class. This night had been no different, except for the fact that he saw a potential soldier in the group. Young. Clean. Not one of the foolish gangsta types who stupidly thought the NALF was an avenue to legitimize their self-destructive behavior. And this one had an intensity to his face, as if the muscles were sculpted to a mask of stone. Rigid. Determined. A possibility. One worth approaching.

"What brings you here, brother?" Darian asked the young man as he drew a cup of coffee from the bottom spout of the tall metal pot.

Moises was surprised by the question, and more surprised by who was asking it. "Uh. I saw the poster down on—"

"I didn't ask what *directed* you here," Darian said. "I asked what *brings* you here. The 'why,' not the 'how.' "

It was so obvious as an internalized reason, but how to say it. How to explain it. *Just say it.* "I think it's time to fight."

"Go join the N-A-A-C-P," Darian suggested, his intonation of the letters dripping with mockery. "They fight for rights. Don't they?"

"Not mine," Moises answered. "Not the way I want to. Not the way that will work."

Darian nodded acceptance of the point, his lips pouting. "Well, we may have some common ground there. What's your name, brother?"

"Moises Griggs."

Darian looked behind and called over the other two who sat with him in the NALF hierarchy. "Brother Moises, this is Brother Mustafa."

"Power, Brother Moises," Mustafa Ali said, gripping Moises' hand in a shake reminiscent of the hold shared by arm wrestlers locked in battle. He wore a brimless hat inspired by the African *kinte* style, but with the NALF logo of two clenched black fists on its front.

Moises nodded, not knowing if he should respond with the same salutation given him.

"And this is Brother Roger," Darian said.

"Power, Brother Moises," Roger Sanders said, exchanging the same raised handshake. Of the three NALF men surrounding Moises, he was the tallest, fully six inches taller than Darian's five-five frame. That modest height, and some talent, had gotten him a college scholarship to UCLA, and nothing else. He was "valuable" to the white educational establishment when his physical attributes were functioning well, but when a bum knee reduced his ability it was good-bye Roger. Enjoy working at Mickey D's. Just like the slaves America had kidnapped from their homeland, Roger realized he was valued only as a thing that could perform. His ancestors had bailed cotton and tobacco. He had thrown a ball through a hoop. Until Darian Brown showed him that there was a path to respect. A real path.

Moises sipped from his coffee after the greetings. He could see others leaving the building in ones and twos. No one else had gotten the attention he was receiving, but neither had they been excluded. He looked to the faces of the three men, wondering why they had taken an interest in him. Wondering, but not concerned that they had. Darian Brown's words that night had made more sense to him than anything he'd heard in his life. More sense than the forgiveness crap that had weakened his people to the point that the whites could attack them with impunity, just like they had done to Tanya. *Tanya.*

"You know, I liked what you said . . . Brother Darian."

Darian smiled at the young man. "Good. Maybe you'd like to hear more in a few days." *After we check you out, of course.* That was a matter of prudence. The pigs had done lower things trying to infiltrate other movements.

"Yeah. I'd like that." *I'd like that a lot.*

"Then you drop on by next Wednesday, Brother Moises," Darian directed him.

"Sure." Moises read a finality in the words, as if it was time to go. As if they wanted him to go. But why ... *Of course.* They were being careful. He had just come in off the street, after all, and even an invitation to come back didn't necessarily mean they trusted him. They wanted to make sure he was for real. That was it. And if they were being that careful, then they had to be for real. They had to. They were the real thing. Real fighters.

"Wednesday, then," Darian said, reaching out for the cup in Moises' hand. The young man handed it over and left the building, the last of those who had come going with him.

Mustafa closed and locked the glass door behind Moises, then pulled down the shades on all the front windows.

"Moises Griggs, huh?" Roger wondered aloud. "I heard that name somewhere."

"I think he's legit," Mustafa said. "He's too young to be a cop."

"Check him out anyway," Darian ordered. "Now what about the meet?"

"Sunday," Mustafa answered. "Two in the afternoon."

"Where?"

"The zoo."

Darian considered the site briefly. "Good. Your choice?"

"Theirs."

"Well, at least they're smart," Darian observed. "It'd be easy to spot any cops. Okay. We do it."

Roger looked to both his comrades. "I don't like dealing with these guys."

"Because they're white, Brother Roger?" Mustafa asked.

"That, and that we don't know shit about them."

Darian had gone through this before. Roger, though bold in his thoughts, was timid in manner. Overly cautious once the worry had been put aside. "Listen, white don't mean shit. We need money to get things off the ground. Do you think this place is rent-free? Do you think the shit we'll need to really strike out comes cheap? It doesn't, Brother Roger. If someone comes along and wants us to do a job for them then we have to consider it, especially when there's as much in it for us as these guys are talking. Money from white people. Better from them than from us."

"You saw the bread they flashed us," Mustafa said. "And the guns they gave us. And there's more where that came from."

"That's what they *say*," Roger countered.

"That kind of money is worth a little risk," Darian said.

"Why us?" Roger asked. "Why'd they pick us?"

Darian looked at his comrade for a very long moment, ignoring the questioning that was now beginning to bore him. "Are you going to be asking 'why' when whitey is putting the chains back on your legs? Brother, our time is *now*."

"But we don't even know what they want us to do," Roger pointed out.

"I guess we find out Sunday," Darian said. "If we want to do it for them, we do. If not, or if we're not sure they're not pigs, hey, we walk away. But I am not going to pass up a chance for the kind of money they're talking about."

"Yeah," Roger said, nodding. "You're right. Okay."

"Good. Sunday then." Darian switched the coffeepot

off, remembering the staggering electric bill they had received the month before. Running a movement was expensive, he was learning. And things had hardly begun. "And don't forget Griggs," he reminded Mustafa. "He might be of use if everything works out."

Frederick Stimson Allen was a known commodity, but it took almost sixteen hours to piece together a biographical sketch of the mystery man who had died with him. And a bare sketch it was.

"Nick King," Frankie said, reading from the top page of her notes. She lifted her dinner, a mass of meat, onions, and condiments barely held between a kaiser roll, to her mouth and bit in.

Art's source of nourishment was somewhat less exciting: a banana and a rice cake.

"You want some?" Frankie offered, her mouth full.

"No, I know how much fat is in that. Besides, Anne is making me something later."

Frankie checked the time. Eight o'clock. "It doesn't get much later for dinner, partner."

"I know," Art said, noticing the time himself. "But Lou said to wait."

Lou Hidalgo, quite unexpectedly, had walked off the elevator just when the majority of folks were heading home for the day and told Art and Frankie to hang around until he talked to them. Then off to Jerry Donovan's office one floor up he went. That was an hour ago, and in that span of time both agents had speculated to themselves as to why Hidalgo, after the tragedy that had befallen him just a little over a day earlier, would show up at the office. No one would have blinked if the A-SAC had just disappeared for a few days to deal with the loss of his son, but there he was, that look of determination so familiar, masking any pain he was feeling.

"What do you think it is?" Frankie wondered aloud.

"We'll know soon enough, I figure," Art said.

Frankie smiled and raised an eyebrow at her partner. "Are you going to be making A-SAC decisions soon?"

Art gave his partner a disapproving look.

"What?"

"You know what." And so did he. The "what" was a job offer. More than that, really. The job was assistant special agent in charge of the Chicago field office, and the offer had come personally from the special agent in charge of that same office, Bob Lomax.

"Well . . ."

"Are you trying to get rid of me?"

Frankie looked to her cluttered desktop and scratched above her nose. "As a *friend* I just want you to consider it objectively."

"I am," Art assured her. "Now, back to now. King— what do we know?"

Frankie put the half-eaten burger back in its Styrofoam container and flipped through her notes. "Nick King. Mystery man. No driver's license with that name matches the face according to DMV."

"Did they do a visual match to rule it out?"

"For Nick King, Nicholas King, Nicky King, ad infinitum," Frankie answered. "As for out-of-state . . ." She shrugged. That would take more time, and be labor-intensive. Three days at the earliest for that information, she knew.

"Well, there wasn't any car in the garage," Art said.

"No license, no car. Maybe he flew," Frankie jokingly suggested.

"Or he was dependent on someone," Art proposed.

"Allen?"

"God, I'd hate to have to depend on him for anything." Art knew Allen better than most, having been on his case literally and figuratively for over a year. The thirty-year-old thug was a scumbag if ever there was one. Not only did he terrorize those weaker and different in skin tone from him, he had also left a trail of children from his home state of Georgia to California. Those innocent victims of his complete irresponsibility were left to be raised by young girls that Allen had charmed into the sack for a few months, weeks, or just for one night. Yes, Freddy Allen was Mr. Dependable in Art's book. "Okay, what else?"

"Twelve-twelve Riverside is a rental property owned by a bunch of old ladies in a real estate trust," Frankie continued. She was acting as the source in the familiar routine. Hashing the evidence, laying out what was known to be discussed, theorized on, challenged, and, if necessary, discarded. Her partner was playing the wall, against which the information was to be thrown to see if it would stick.

"When did King rent it?"

"Over a year ago." Frankie scanned for other information relating to the residence. "The property manager from the real estate trust said King always paid his rent on time, with a cashier's check. That was drawn from a bank in Palmdale."

"An account?"

Frankie shook her head. "King paid cash for the check. He was not an account holder."

"There or anywhere else," Art said, his brow furrowing as he thought. "No bank account that we can find. No identification. No social security number. Would you rent to someone like that?"

"Nope."

"Then why did they?"

"The property manager said she wasn't with the trust when King moved in," Frankie answered.

"That's one thing we need to find out," Art said.

"Inconsistency number nine million to check on," Frankie commented with mild humor attached. "Also, no employer that we know of."

"But he had money," Art observed.

"Someone supporting him?"

"The more appropriate word might be bankrolling," Art said.

Frankie moved further through her notes. "Okay, Nick King the person." For two hours Frankie had talked to the only neighbor of King's, probing, peeling away whatever might conceal some bit of information. "A nice man. Kept to himself."

"So he could be a serial killer," Art said, frowning.

"The neighbor only talked to him a few times. She said he spoke with a heavy accent."

Art perked up at that. He had been talking to the sheriff's commander on-scene while Frankie was interviewing the neighbor at a nearby motel, and he hadn't caught that bit of information when scanning his partner's notes earlier. "What kind of accent?"

"German, Polish, Russian," Frankie recounted dubiously. "You name the country, she thought he sounded like he was from there."

"Guttural European?"

"That narrows it down to a continent," Frankie confirmed.

"King, huh?" Art wondered. "That doesn't sound awful European."

"He could have Americanized his real name," Frankie said. "Maybe he immigrated and wanted to fit in. A lot of folks coming in have done that."

"Could be," Art half-agreed. "But everything so far points to this King fellow maintaining a fairly cryptic existence."

"You think the name is an alias?" Frankie asked.

"It would fit."

"But why?" Frankie saw Art waiting for her to propose the reasons. "What little we know points to King isolating himself. Financially, residence, identification. Protection?"

"How so?"

"Well, either King was trying to protect himself,

probably from incrimination, or he was trying to protect someone else,'' Frankie proposed.

Art followed her line of thinking and joined in. "Add Allen to it.''

"Freddy.'' Frankie thought for a moment. "If he was going to do King in, then that would point to someone wanting to be insulated from what he was doing.''

"Use King, then get rid of him,'' Art said.

"The twelve grand in cash, the remote house,'' Frankie recounted. "Bankrolling does fit into this quite well now. So someone who Freddy Allen is associated with gets King to make some nerve gas—''

"Nerve agent,'' Art corrected.

"Nerve *agent*—for whatever reason, Allen goes to get it with the intention of removing King from the picture after the pickup, but King gets wise and decides if he's going to die, then someone else is, too.''

Art nodded slowly. It felt right. There was no other way to describe the gut instinct a veteran street agent got when the pieces slid together seamlessly. He had no absolute proof yet that the scenario his partner had just laid out was anything but a theory, but he'd lay money on it being damn close to reality.

"So,'' Frankie said. "King and Allen. Who was King and how did he get involved in this, and who was Allen working with?''

"We have the center of the puzzle,'' Art said. "Now we have to find the edges.''

Frankie flipped the pages of her notepad closed and tossed it on her desk. She looked to the clock, then to the empty coffeepot on the small credenza to her side. "I'm gonna need some caffeine if this drags on too much longer.''

Art, who had his own small coffeemaker on his side of their workspace, might have agreed with her had he not sworn off caffeine. Five hours of sleep after leaving the site of the incident as the sun came up, followed by nine hours of poring through what little they knew about the entire affair at this early stage, left neither agent wanting to make this evening another long one that would stretch into the wee hours of the morning. Art knew they needed sleep, at least one good night of it, in order to start putting the final pieces of what led to the incident at 1212 Riverside together to form a coherent picture. From that picture they might then be able to identify those who had almost succeeded in obtaining what the internationally inclined politicians called a weapon of mass destruction, though Art knew that had any of Freddy Allen's kind gotten their hands on it it would be a weapon of mass murder. Whoever those folks were, they deserved the cuffs for their intentions, and the gas chamber for causing the deaths of Luis Hidalgo, Jr., and the others. Art could supply the cuffs. The other would be decided once those were on.

The sound of the elevator door sliding open and two sets of footsteps drew the agents' attention. Art stood and turned to see who . . .

"Orwell?"

Frankie joined her partner as Captain Orwell, dressed down in blue jeans and a leather jacket, approached with Lou Hidalgo.

"Art. Frankie. Have a seat." The A-SAC pulled two more chairs over for the captain and himself.

There was no mistaking the expression Hidalgo wore like a red flag. Art had noticed it as he neared. There should have been grief, and sadness, but there was something masking those emotions instead. Art suspected it to be determination. The A-SAC knew it was rage.

"What is it, Lou?" Art asked.

"As of four o'clock today, per the director, I am overseeing this investigation."

"Wait," Frankie said. "Lou, they can't dump this on you right now."

Hidalgo shook his head. "It's not like that. Cam is

out of the country, and Jerry . . . well, he has other things to deal with.''

Oh, shit. Art straightened in his seat unconsciously. The director had called the A-SAC *personally,* and Jerry Donovan was *busy?* ''Lou?''

Hidalgo faced the man who could have had the A-SAC position had his life not taken a personally tragic detour. ''Art, don't read into that. I know you. Jerry is busy, that's all. The director wants me to watch over this thing, and, that said, you two are now running the investigation per me.''

That statement perplexed Frankie. Weren't they already the de facto lead on the case because of their involvement with Allen? That silent musing lasted only until she noticed the look on Orwell's face. ''Something's wrong, isn't it?''

''This isn't going to be just a cleanup investigation,'' Hidalgo said. ''Things are a lot worse than anyone wanted.''

Dammit! Art remembered the captain's less-than-absolute assurances at the site. *Probably, huh?* ''Some of it got out, didn't it?''

The question was directed squarely at Orwell. ''Not exactly.''

''Well, exactly what does 'worse' mean?'' Art demanded.

''When I finished the analysis on the chemical residue in the containers there were some anomalies I wasn't expecting,'' the captain explained. ''I want you to understand this, so let me be precise. VX can be manufactured into two stable reagents.''

''As a binary weapon,'' Frankie recalled.

''You told us that at the site,'' Art said impatiently.

''Give him a chance, Art,'' Hidalgo said.

Orwell waited a second for the air to clear. ''The two reagents are what we refer to as a base and an activator. For VX the base is ethyl 2-[diisopropylamino] ethylmethylphosphonite. We call it QL for brevity's sake. The activator is a thicker substance called dimethylpolysulfide. When those two are mixed they yield VX. I found residue that let me estimate King could have produced enough QL for three of those cylinders."

"But there was only one," Frankie said.

"Which made sense because there was only enough residue of the ingredients for the activator for that one batch in the cylinder. I was able to estimate that because there was a clear measurement of one of the activator's components: methyl mercaptan."

"Okay, I follow you so far," Art said. "There was enough of the base for three cylinders of VX, but only enough activator for one." The captain confirmed Art's understanding with a nod. "Was the leftover base still there?"

"No. I was—"

"Wait," Art cut off the captain. "It was *not* there? You mean someone out there has half of what is needed to make twice as much VX as we had on-site?"

"No," Orwell said. "Let me finish."

Frankie gave her partner a look that told him to ease up. He was a driven one, she knew, and sometimes needed a little mothering to keep him from letting that drive push him too quickly.

"While we were doing the residue analysis we found something unexpected," Orwell went on. "Two chemicals: ethyl mercaptan and ethylene glycol dinitrate."

"Wasn't that other one *methyl* mercaptan?" Frankie asked.

"Right. These two chemicals, along with a combination of the others we identified, can be processed into an activator named triethylmonosulfide."

"An activator?" Art said. "Like the dimethyl-whatever?"

"Similar."

"What are you saying, that this other activator works

with the base that isn't accounted for?" Frankie asked.

"Yes. VX shares its base with another nerve agent that was derived from it. VZ is its name."

The two agents shared a look before Art spoke. "You mean that there is a reason to believe that someone out there has all the ingredients to make a nerve agent like the one that got loose up on Riverside?"

"Not like, Jefferson," Orwell corrected. "Worse."

"Worse?" Frankie said with surprise. "You said VX was the most deadly thing we had."

"It's the most deadly nerve agent we've produced and stocked," Orwell clarified. "VZ is more *lethal*, but it is not as useful to the military because its deliverable state reduces its persistence. Triethylmonosulfide as an activator is not a thickener, which means that, although VZ won't stick to things as readily on the battlefield, it is more readily absorbed into the human body, both through inhalation and through the skin."

"So we didn't make this stuff because, even though it would kill you better, it wouldn't hang around long enough?" Art asked incredulously.

"Basically, yes."

Art let his body fall back in the chair. It was all clear now, why Lou was running the show. Jerry had put the cart before the horse and told the world that everything was A-OK before getting any final word. *Idiot!* "So someone has this stuff."

"We have to assume that, Art," Hidalgo said.

"Enough for two of those cylinders?" Frankie inquired.

"Or containers of similar size," Orwell answered. "But that thing had to be specially made, so there's no reason to think there wouldn't be more."

Art filtered all the information that had just filled his mental data banks, trying to place what was most important in the forefront. In the lead was a question. "If this VZ stuff is more deadly, why did King make VX at all?''

Frankie seized on a possibility almost immediately. ''Maybe as insurance against exactly what we think Allen was going to do.''

That made a hell of a lot of sense, Art realized. ''Freddy goes there to do away with King, after the VZ has already been delivered. King had to sense that something was up.''

''And Freddy probably played the tough guy,'' Frankie surmised. ''Remember the surveillance tape from that liquor store he robbed last year? He didn't even pull the gun at first. You could hear him on the tape saying, 'Give me the money so I can kill you.' Then he did. Just shot the clerk in the face.''

''So he may have been equally as cocky with King,'' Art continued the line of thought. ''Telling King what he was going to do without even pulling the gun.''

''But King was prepared for that,'' Frankie said. ''There was a bathroom right off the hallway where we found King. He might have retreated that way when Allen confronted him.''

''And the cylinder of VX could have been right there,'' Art agreed. ''King just had to reach through the doorway.''

Orwell listened to the exchange with intense interest, wondering how the agents could process the possibilities so quickly, how the imprecise could be funneled into a combination of probabilities that one could almost see as reality.

''This investigation just became priority number one, Art,'' Hidalgo said.

''Clearly,'' Art said. ''Captain, you said this stuff is more potent than VX. How much?''

''The effectiveness of chemical agents is measured as LD-50. That's the amount of the substance, measured in milligrams, released per minute within a cubic meter that will kill half of those exposed without protection. VZ has twice the LD-50 of VX when inhaled, and four times when absorbed percutaneously.''

"What's the dose?" Art asked.

"For VZ you're talking point-two-five milligrams if inhaled, and four milligrams if absorbed through the skin. But VZ, unlike VX, mists extremely well into minuscule droplets, which means that anyone unprotected will almost certainly breathe in a lethal dose before they absorb it.''

Art tried to imagine so small an amount, but couldn't grasp it effectively. "And how much is in one of those cylinders?''

"My estimate is about fourteen ounces," Orwell answered.

"And how many people could that much VZ kill?''

"That would depend on a lot of factors," Orwell said. "Environment. Dispersion.''

"A ballpark figure," Art said. "Assume that there are lots of people and everything goes just right.''

The captain thought for a moment. "Figuring that half the agent would be wasted as it spread, a guess would be four to five thousand.''

The number, spoken clinically as just a combination of digits, floored the three agents.

"Five thousand people?" Frankie asked.

"In the nightmare scenario your partner gave me, yes," Orwell affirmed.

"If someone of Allen's kind has it and is planning to use it, you can bet *they* envision the nightmare scenario," Art said.

"So how do we stop them?" Hidalgo wondered for the group.

"Well, pardon my French, but Jerry's fuckup may have given us a little edge," Art observed. "Everyone knows that there was a release of VX thanks to him, and they also think that that was it. The fact that we're investigating just goes along with the incident.''

"So whoever has the VZ might be feeling more secure because they think we think there's nothing more out there,'' Hidalgo said. ''And the fact that we're still checking around to tie together loose ends might not spook them either.''

"Not if they were as careful as I bet they were,'' Art said.

"If King was insulated well,'' Frankie began, ''just imagine how tight the folks behind this are wrapped up.''

Hidalgo considered the proposition that his lead agents were laying out. ''So we press this without actually saying publicly what our real focus is?''

"I think that's our edge,'' Art said.

"But what about public safety?'' Hidalgo asked. ''If something happens . . .''

"There's no way you can protect anyone from this,'' Orwell said. ''I may not be a cop, but what Jefferson is saying is logical. The only way to protect the public is to get this stuff away from whoever might use it.''

Secrecy was not uncommon in an investigation, but Hidalgo could just imagine the media and the civil libertarians crying ''cover-up'' if something happened before the Bureau could find and secure the nerve agent. But experience told him that a wide-open investigation might simply push the bad guys deeper into hiding, or, worse, into using their trump card before it could be taken from them.

"Do it, Art,'' Hidalgo said. ''You're senior on this. Find it.'' *Find them.*

"Will do,'' Art promised, seeing the added desire in the A-SAC's eyes . . . along with the fire.

"Captain,'' Hidalgo said. ''Thanks for digging this up. You may have saved some lives.''

"I hope so.''

Hidalgo excused himself and headed back up to Jerry

Donovan's office, leaving Orwell with the two agents.

"If you need anything . . ." Orwell offered.

"I'm sure we will," Frankie said. She looked to Art. "Early morning tomorrow, partner?"

"Tomorrow, and the next day, and the next . . . We'll figure a split between us tomorrow." Art glanced at his watch. This very late dinner with Anne could end up being his last for a while. He wanted to get going, but there was one thing still nagging at him. "Captain, you said we never made VZ for our inventory, even though it was more deadly."

"But not on the battlefield," Orwell repeated from earlier. "Just because you can make something doesn't mean you have to."

"Did anyone else know how to make it?" Frankie asked, picking up on her partner's line of questioning.

"Yes."

"Did anyone actually produce it for their military?" Art pressed.

"Yes."

"Who?" Art asked.

"The Russians," Orwell answered. "Why?"

He didn't get an immediate answer from the agents, who were locked in a suspicious, almost knowing stare.

"King, huh?" Art said, repeating his doubts from earlier.

"*Da,*" Frankie agreed.

The West Executive Avenue entrance gate to the White House grounds swung open an hour shy of midnight as a light snow dusted the nation's capital. Three white Ford vans, windowless from the cab rearward, pulled in behind a government sedan, which led the small caravan around the executive mansion to a spot near the East Wing. There they stopped, met by a tall, serious-looking Secret Service agent who went to the lead car, brushing the snow off his shoulders as he walked.

"Who are the drivers?" Secret Service Agent Ted O'Neil, head of the presidential detail, asked.

Fellow agent Larry Price, stepping from the warmth of the Service Buick, pulled the collar of his overcoat up. "Tenth Mountain Division from Fort Drum. All louies."

"Good." O'Neil, the man charged with keeping the president alive for the four or eight years he was in office, walked to the back of the first van with Price at his side. The driver already had the twin doors open.

"Where are these going?" the lieutenant, wearing nothing even remotely Army, inquired.

O'Neil looked at the piles of duffels in the back of the vehicle, at least two dozen in number. "Everything's going down in my office."

"You're not going to have any room left, Ted," Price commented quite correctly.

"How often am I there?" O'Neil asked. The leader of the presidential detail, a man of great importance himself, existed on a schedule that left little time for anything other than being close to the Man. The office was really just a place O'Neil visited once a day, late in the evening, after the president had been put to bed, to complete his portion of the requisite daily reports. Then it was sleep in the small bunk stuffed among others in a small section of the East Wing reserved for the Secret Service, and then up an hour before the president's scheduled wake-up time so he could walk the Man from his private quarters to the Oval Office. Once every two weeks O'Neil went home to his family in suburban Maryland to reacquaint himself with his wife and four children. This lasted but a weekend, and already three of those had been preempted by overseas trips, and the one coming in just twenty-four hours was now just a dream fading away. O'Neil felt the pressure, dreaded the long hours, missed his family, and loved the job he did more than anything he could imagine. "Who's going to instruct us?"

Price looked down the line of vans. "The louie in the back."

"His name's Morrison," the lieutenant with the two agents clued them in.

"Tell him to bring two of the . . . what are they called?" O'Neil wondered aloud, searching his fatigued mind for the word.

"MOPP suits," the lieutenant said.

"Tell Morrison to bring two MOPP suits to the bunk room," O'Neil told Price. "You escort him and keep them in the duffels. I don't want some steward catching sight of them and letting it slip."

"Gotcha, Ted."

O'Neil backed away and let the officers and two of his detail begin the chore of lugging the seventy-plus duffels into the dark and quiet basement of the East Wing, the smaller and less important sibling of the power center on the opposite side of the executive mansion.

"JESTER is down for the night," the report came through O'Neil's earpiece. JESTER was the Service code name for the president. The first lady was TULIP. And there was a third code name the agents now had to associate with the first family.

"Is SCOOTER quiet?" O'Neil inquired, speaking into the microphone hidden under his left cuff.

"For a change," the agent reported.

O'Neil smiled to himself. The president's son was an "active" child, and one who had demonstrated that he had a pair of lungs to challenge the most bellicose inhabitant of the Hill. And the code name was quite appropriate. O'Neil had personally taken two tumbles trying to avoid the tyke as he scooted out from behind some piece of furniture in the Oval Office or in the first family's private area of the main building. He was a handful. He was also damned cute.

"Early wake-up tomorrow?" the agent asked.

"Five," O'Neil reminded the night detail leader. "He has a speech at NYU."

"All right. See you in the morning."

O'Neil pulled his wrist away and checked his watch. Morning. That would give him about four hours of sleep, which was about the norm. Not as much as he wanted, but enough. Enough for this job.

A stiff breeze blew in without warning, reminding him that he didn't have an overcoat on. But the chill was somehow welcome, just as the end of each day was welcome and satisfying. Another day behind them. The mission of the Secret Service presidential detail fulfilled. The president and his family were tucked safely into bed. As the snow tickled O'Neil's face he had a feeling that all was right with the world.

Then, as the combination of agents and Army officers came back for a second load of the gear O'Neil hoped was never needed, that feeling became more a hope than a measure of reality.

"A little wine?" Anne half-asked, half-prodded.

Art held his finger and thumb an inch apart, spreading them to an inch and a half as Anne's smile grew. He watched her walk back to the kitchen and wondered how any woman could look so good in sweats, or in nothing at all for that matter. *Ease up, Arthur. You've got all night.*

"I can feel your eyes on my behind, Art," Anne said, glancing back over her shoulder with a smile.

"Can you blame me?"

"Hmmm." She filled two glasses with Chardonnay, hers more than his, and recorked the bottle.

"You're the one trying to get me drunk, sweetheart," Art said.

Anne walked back in and sat next to her own private G-man. She handed his glass over and clinked hers lightly against it. "A girl has to get lucky somehow."

Art grunted. He was worried about being too forward all the time, then she would let loose with a line that made him feel like a prude. *You gotta love her, Arthur.* He did.

Anne leaned over, her T-shirt-covered breasts pressing against his arm, and kissed Art on the neck, tasting upward until the lobe of his ear was between her teeth. She nibbled, knowing it was having an effect by the long, slow breaths he was taking. "You like?"

"I love," Art said.

"You're going to let work keep you away from this?" To the neck again as she set her glass blindly on the coffee table, the newly free hand coming to his chest and undoing the shirt buttons from top to bottom.

"You're bad, woman."

"I'm good, too."

Art swallowed hard. "I know."

Anne pulled back, a Cheshire grin on her soft face, and rubbed his chest through the open shirt. "You know I'm just kidding about work."

"I know," Art assured her. He lifted her hand from his chest and kissed it. "I am going to be busy, though."

"Really busy?"

"A night here and there, sweetheart," he promised hopefully. "Maybe."

"It sounds important."

"It is," Art said, knowing Anne would ask no more if he didn't volunteer it, and he couldn't. "So, how was your day?"

"I did another seminar tonight," Anne told him.

"For Rabbi Levin?"

"Yeah. The sixth one." She picked her glass up and sipped slowly. "Tonight was a little interesting, though."

"Oh?"

She wondered for a second if she should say anything, but Griggs wasn't really a patient yet, and she actually wouldn't be revealing any confidential information. "Do you remember the St. Anthony's massacre?"

"Sure," Art answered. "Remember Thom Danbrook? He was the agent killed last year."

"With you and Frankie," Anne said.

"Yeah. He was involved in the investigation of the guy behind it. Thom was the one who could have closed the door on John Barrish, but he never got to testify." *Or do anything.* "Barrish walked a few days ago."

"I know," Anne said. "I had a walk-in tonight, a face that you might say would stand out in the crowd."

"Who?"

"The father of one of those four little girls."

"You're not serious," Art said. "You are."

"His name is Darren Griggs, and he's just devastated," Anne explained. "His family is in shambles. He saw the flyer and came to the seminar. He said he was starting to hate people in the same way Barrish does. Art, this man was suffocating. It was hard to talk to him because I could almost feel his pain. It has to be eating him up."

Barrish. He was free because the legal system protected him from scurrilous prosecution, but who protected those he wanted to harm? You do, Art thought. "Jesus, Anne, I don't know how you can handle what you do."

"I do it to help people like Griggs," she said, the admission worn like a badge of honor.

"Are you going to see him?"

"I made the offer. All he has to do is call."

Art saw that glint of altruism in her eye. "Pro bono?"

"Drink your wine, G-man," Anne said, skirting the issue.

Art smiled. It was her prerogative, one she seemed to

exercise often. Then again, she made enough money for four people and felt it was something she had to do. Give something back. Such a soft spot for a very strong woman.

Anne made a loose fist and tapped Art's stomach. "You may just win that race."

"Well, I'm now officially in the senior division," Art said, shaking his head. "Fifty. Can you believe that?"

Her hand opened and slid down over his belt. "You're still eighteen in certain respects."

Art put his glass down, taking Anne's and doing the same. "Come on," he said, putting his hand out. "Let's go upstairs."

She looked into his eyes, the mischief at the core of her personality seizing control. "What's wrong with right here?"

"The couch?"

Anne glanced to the soft shag carpet at their feet.

"You little devil," Art said.

"I'm a good girl," Anne protested as she slid off the couch to the floor, pulling Art with her.

"You're a bad girl," Art said, leaning closer as Anne pulled him. She eased onto her back between the couch and coffee table, which Art slid aside.

"I'm both." Anne took his head in her hands as he came close. "Tell me which one you like better."

"I will," Art said, kissing her softly and pulling away for just a second. "In the morning."

John Barrish looked upward through the windshield, gazing at the star-filled, limitless sky as Toby pulled the Aerostar into the driveway and to the storage yard's access box.

"Stan and I figured this was as safe a place as any," Toby said, taking the white plastic card from his jacket and inserting it into the slot. The arm restricting access to the facility jumped upward, allowing him to drive through.

"I missed the stars while I was locked up," John commented. "Do you remember what Trent said about the stars?"

Toby pulled in a slow breath, steadying himself for a recital of some more *wise* musings of the renowned Dr. Felix Trent, long-dead purveyor of the racial purity theories his father held dear.

"He said the stars burn bright for one reason," John began. "So that one can navigate by them. '*Chart your course by the stars you see, and ignore the rest.*' " He nodded, a wistful smile coming softly to his face. "He was a wise man, Toby."

"Yeah. We're here, Pop," Toby said, stopping and hopping out of the Aerostar.

John got out and followed his son to the door, slightly larger than one typical for a residence. Toby flipped through several keys on his ring before finding the right one for the single padlock. He opened it and hung it on the unlatched hasp, then turned the light on inside the ten-by-eight storage room he'd rented a month earlier.

"Where is it?" John asked, looking over the motley combination of boxes and old furniture piled against one wall.

Toby closed the door behind them and went to the pile. "Stan and I moved this stuff in here to make it look legit."

John watched his son paw through a box that was partially covered by a pair of old chairs. "Did Allen know about this place?"

"Nope. Just me and Stan."

"Not that it matters now," John observed. "I'm glad he's out of the picture."

"Here," Toby said, pulling both hands from the box and holding the twin cylinders out for his father to see.

"They're so small."

Toby nodded. "He asked how big we wanted them. I told him as small as they could be and still do the job."

Barrish gave an approving smile. "You did so good while I was away, Toby. Real good."

"Just carrying on, Pop."

The elder Barrish examined the cylinders visually, bending to get a close look.

"Here," Toby said. "Take one."

The stainless-steel cylinder was very cold to the touch. "Unbelievable."

"I know," Toby said with a smile. "They'll fit almost anywhere."

"When is Stanley checking out the test site?"

"Tomorrow," Toby answered. "He's got the plans of the unit already."

"How?"

"He just called and asked," Toby said, laughing. "He said he was some sort of engineer and needed space for some trouble at an overseas construction project."

"And they just sent it to him?"

More laughter preceded Toby's answer. "I mean, it's not a secret, but the guy didn't even blink, Stan said. He got the plans yesterday at the P.O. box."

Barrish smiled and shook his head. "Stanley can do good when he puts his mind to something."

"He's a sneaky little guy, Pop."

"I guess that can be useful." John turned the cylinder around in his hand, looking closely at the small black cube that capped one end. "What does this do?"

"It's the release control," Toby answered, pointing to a recessed switch and a blacked-out digital readout with two tiny buttons beneath it. "The timer is right there, flip the switch, and at the right time it all happens." Toby chuckled a bit. "We pick the time, and someone else does the dirty work."

"Who did you choose?"

"Some revolutionary outfit called the New Africa Liberation Front. They advocate some hoo-ha about giving the old slave states to the *New Africans*." Toby's eyes rolled. "Real small in number, but the guys in it have records. Freddy's AB contacts checked what kind of time they've done. All the skills we need, and the proper skin tone."

"Excellent," John commented. The foolish Africans were going to do their dirty work, and all that white America would see and hear on TV would be "Black Revolutionaries carried out a heinous attack today . . ." But that would only be the beginning. The beginning of an end. The beginning of a wake-up call, the first step in showing white America what the Africans' true self was . . . with a little help, of course. But the ends justified the means. These ends justified any means. "Absolutely excellent."

Toby saw the pleasure on his father's face. He would do anything to make that man happy and proud. But there was still a question before them. "Pop, we're getting low on cash."

"We can get more."

Toby drew in a breath, considering his father's confident statement for a moment. "We had trouble getting money from him while you were locked up."

"I'm out now, Toby," John said with a steely tone. "Monte will have to deal with me again. Besides, it's not his decision. I'll straighten him out."

Toby was glad he no longer had to deal with their reluctant benefactor, a man drawn into their fold quite by manipulation, a little willingness, and chance. A chance his father had exploited perfectly.

John handed the cylinder back and gestured at the second one. "One for the money, and two for the show."

"It's gonna be a hell of a show, Pop."

"That it will be," John agreed, thinking briefly on the

spectacle aspect of what they were about to undertake. The opening shot—the test before the show—would captivate the nation, and even the world. It would make those in power nervous. But all that would be dwarfed by what was still to come. The coup de main. To be witnessed live on television, in Moscow, in London, in Tokyo, and, most important, from Maine to Hawaii. The 270 million people who called themselves Americans would have front-row seats, and network play-by-play, as their government was dismantled in one fell swoop. How would they react? John Barrish was betting heavily on what he believed to be the answer. Betting with the confidence of a prophet. "Quite a show, son."

FOUR

Confession

He had a choice office in the Rayburn House Office Building, one that gave him a commanding view of the west front of the Capitol, and a chairmanship of one of the most powerful committees in the House of Representatives, but Congressman Richard Vorhees would have traded it all to be diving out of a perfectly airworthy C-141B Starlifter into the Uwharrie National Forest once again. Rubbing his left leg, though, as he stared out upon the glistening power center of the United States, he knew that the only battles he would fight were destined to erupt right there. The limb was hard to the touch, though softer than the one he'd had until a few months earlier. Advances in prosthesis design and manufacture made the newer, lighter limb possible, but it would never be close enough to what he had, or what could have been his. A Cuban mine had seen to that as he led his company of 82nd Airborne troops into battle in Grenada so long ago. Ten pounds of explosives and steel. That's all it took to end an Army career. And to begin one in Washington.

The new wars, Vorhees thought, as he turned his attention back to the *Los Angeles Times*. It was one of the four papers he read each day, and, like the others, a front-page story in today's edition chronicled the budget battle over funding of research for a new fighter. Of course such a benign topic would never have made it to page one if there hadn't been accusations of corruption by the anticipated lead contractor on the project, but that was a lot of bull. Everything was corrupted, the representative from Massachusetts knew. All you had to do was point a finger and you'd be right. He was corrupt. The speaker was corrupt. The president was corrupt. The system was corrupt. It was tit for tat, I'll do this if you do that. Legalized influence peddling and vote swapping, interrupted every two years by the song and dance needed to get reelected. Vorhees laughed every time he heard the complaints about when an actor came to D.C. to be president, because he knew that getting elected to Congress was the perfect training for a career in acting, something reinforced each time one of them was reelected.

Bored with the same story for the fourth time, Vorhees flipped through the pages, scanning stories on the surprising rebound of California's aerospace industry. *Wait'll they see next year's budget.* Then on to the inevitable litany of crime stories. A dead body here. A drive-by shooting there. A—*Wait.*

"Shit," Vorhees said softly, the artist's conception of the face of one dead . . . *Nick King!* . . . slapping him across the face. He read the accompanying story, including the complete account of a woman who lived near the house where the nerve gas accident happened. Nick King! It took a minute more to sink in fully. "Goddamn you, Monte!"

Vorhees slapped the paper shut and tossed it over his desk, where it fluttered to the floor in separate pieces. He leaned forward, resting both elbows on his large wooden desk, and tried to think. Think fast. *Wonderful!* He had already hurled the requisite invective at the man, the former—as of now—contributor, who had gotten him into this. *It will be good for the country, Dick.* "Yeah, damn you again, Monte."

Damage control. That was the priority now. And first? What came first?

Say something. That ran contrary to the rule about keeping one's mouth shut, but silence was no longer accepted. No longer could an elected official *not dignify such a ludicrous suggestion.* He had to say something. And fast. But what? He thought on that question for a moment before coming to a startling conclusion.

"The truth." He might have laughed if the chance for real political damage wasn't so real, but the truth was his ally in this fight. It would have to be massaged, of course, to give it the proper feel. To portray him as *terribly upset over this horrid, unforeseen twist.* And that, too, was actually true. Vorhees emerged from the anger of the previous moment, now allowing a small laugh. He was really innocent in this. But who would ever believe that? he thought. The voters, he knew, answering his own question. Convincing them took little more than thirty seconds of video and some catchy ad copy. How hard could it be?

"Mark," Vorhees said after dialing his chief aide, "get me a press conference for this afternoon . . . No, not tomorrow—today . . . I don't care how hard it is, just do it. And make sure there's press from my district there . . . Call them yourself, goddamit! Just get them here, all right . . . This is important."

Vorhees laid the phone back in its cradle, his manner surprisingly calm. He swung his chair around and looked to the Capitol again. That was where it would happen, in a suitably sedate room. Some books in the background, he thought. Maybe a flag to . . . No, no flag. This had to be him and his shame.

He lowered his head, shaking it slightly. *No.* That didn't feel right. This truth thing, and its requisite emotions, was, surprisingly, a tough act to master.

* * *

Vasquez Rocks, a popular county park north of Los Angeles, had seen much activity over the years. Formed by the geological forces of plate tectonics long before the first Mexican bandits used the giant rock formations as hiding places from which to launch raids upon arriving pioneers, the park now enjoyed favor as a place to climb and hike on the weekends. Hollywood, too, had taken notice of the somewhat alien-looking landscape, with its huge, rounded slabs of red rock jutting from the earth at near 45-degree angles, and had used the park many times in films and television shows, from the obvious westerns to the futuristic *Star Trek* series of the 1960s.

But during the week the visitors were fewer, mainly those dedicated rock climbers who simply could not wait until the weekend to travel to the more distant, and more challenging, Joshua Tree National Monument in the desert to the east of Los Angeles. There were also those who were there just to walk, to enjoy the sights. And there were those who enjoyed the solitude. And the privacy.

"Monte," John Barrish said as he approached the man from behind.

Monte Royce jumped and spun around, the somewhat disguised face of the man he had once expected never to see again just feet away. "Christ, John, you scared the daylights out of me."

John removed the sunglasses but left the large Aussie bush hat on as protection from the fine, chilly mist that was falling across the beautiful landscape. "You move fast for an old man," he said, the observation far from innocent in its meaning. "When you want to."

"What do you want, John?" Royce asked.

"I want more money, and I don't want any of the *crap* you gave my boys while I was away," he answered, his voice coming down after punching up the word he knew would carry the most impact.

Royce, his face long and lined after seventy years of

life, stared into the younger man's eyes, his breaths coming quicker. "Listen. I gave you what you said you needed before. I kept your family fed while you were locked up. I supported you." His head shook. "No more, John. I can't reconcile what you're going to do anymore with what I believe."

"Going soft, Monte?"

"No, just getting smart," Royce said. He was much larger than the odd-looking man challenging him, but there was a power to John Barrish, one that had once drawn him into his inner circle. But now, with time away from the man to be with his own thoughts, Royce was beginning to understand the place he had been, a place as alien as television had made the landscape around him appear, but infinitely more real, and frightening.

"The choice isn't yours, Monte," John said coolly.

"You don't have any—"

"Not me, Monte," John said, reminding the elderly man of an undeniable fact. "I don't think you make the decisions about the money." He chuckled a bit. "You're a middleman. A big, powerful middleman, who wouldn't want to anger his mama."

"Shut up, John, she has nothing to—"

"She has everything to do with this," John corrected his reluctant benefactor. "Now do I need to go straight to her and put a strain on that ninety-six-year-old heart of hers?"

"I can turn you in," Royce threatened. "I can tell the police everything."

John shook his head with disappointment. "You wouldn't like jail, Monte. Because, remember, if you hang me, you hang yourself . . . and your mama."

Royce didn't let his gaze break from that of the man he had once respected, but who had used him. Had used him so completely that death would be the only way out. But he was not ready for death. In fact he feared it, feared meeting a maker that would assuredly cast him into the fires of hell. No, Monte Royce was not ready for that. He never would be.

"How much?"

John Barrish looked up at the man, whose head was dripping from the hour he'd waited in the rain . . . as instructed. Humiliation. It was so easy to inflict, as it was merely a by-product of control.

"Now you're getting smart."

Director of Central Intelligence Greg Drummond leaned across his desk and handed the plain manila folder to Bud DiContino. "Take your pick. Forty-three groups, nations, or sufficiently wealthy individuals that Intelligence and S and T say could have provided the supplies *and* the technical expertise to pull this off."

Bud scanned the multiple pages before closing and handing the folder back to the DCI. "This is quick work."

"Intelligence put the press on," Drummond explained, referring to the agency directorate he had headed until just ten months earlier. Now he was at the helm of the most powerful intelligence-gathering agency on the planet. A company man heading the Company. It made many on the Hill nervous, but they would have been more apprehensive had there been another fiasco of leadership like the one that had preceded him. That was reasonably cleaned up now, just a few ripples disturbing the otherwise calm waters his ship was sailing upon. But the present situation was showing much more wave action, threatening a swell that would make navigation difficult and holding course tricky. But the youthful DCI, still older than the president he served, had seen troubled waters before, and knew the best way to sail around the offending storm, and how to sail headlong into it.

"How's Fred doing?" Bud asked. Fred Stennis had replaced Drummond as deputy director, intelligence.

"Good," Drummond answered. "Pete and Mike are bringing him along fast." Pete Miner, deputy director, central intelligence, was the number-two man at the Agency. Mike Healy was Drummond's former counterpart in the Operations Directorate and ran the spooks in the field. The combination of the two career intelligence officers had helped get the new DDI up to speed after an appointment that had created much controversy at the CIA's Langley, Virginia, headquarters. Stennis was young, too young some thought, but the thirty-four-year-old had caught Drummond's eye while working for him as chief analyst, Mideast desk, in Intelligence, making calls that some considered reckless, but that the then-DDI had recognized as bold and based on superior reasoning. One needed to do no less than that to impress Greg Drummond, and Stennis had done much more.

"Pete's off where right now?"

"Is this on or off the record?" Drummond joked.

"I've never worn a body mike," Bud countered with a smile. "Unlike some people I know."

"It worked," the DCI pointed out, a glint of satisfaction sparking in his eyes.

"That it did," Bud said. Where was the former DCI now? Some university in the Rockies somewhere, chairing the history department. *And you could have been head of some major-league think tank, Anthony.* But he had played the game like an amateur, the NSA knew, and now the once esteemed Anthony Merriweather, caught and secretly hung out to dry by his own words, was suffering a fate worse than prison. His sentence was political and professional oblivion.

"This isn't for broadcast to anyone," Drummond said. "He's in India. Should be there for a week, maybe two."

"An open-ended visit?" Bud questioned. That was almost unheard of in a town where itineraries and schedules were planned out months in advance. But then

Langley wasn't actually in D.C., in many respects.

"It could pay off," Drummond explained. "A new relationship with Indian Intelligence would go a long way in keeping tabs on the Chinese."

"Agreed," Bud said.

Drummond poured himself a cup of tea from the warming pot on the credenza. "You want one?"

"Half a cup."

The DCI poured a second and slid it easily across his desk. "So, that's what we can do for you regarding this chemical thing."

"I know it's Bureau territory, but you never know where things start."

"Gordy and I have a liaison group already set up," Drummond said, testing the steaming liquid with a quick taste. "We'll feed them whatever they need."

"Good." Bud took a generous sip of the warm brew and checked the time. "Where is Gordy? He was supposed to be here by now."

As if on cue the door to the DCI's seventh-floor office was opened by a security officer for the just-arrived FBI director.

"Sorry," Jones apologized. "I hate doing the committee spiel for a bunch of voteheads I never deal with."

"Which voteheads are those, Gordy?" Bud asked, amused by Jones's term for anyone on the Hill who had to submit to voter approval every two years. Senators, with six years between their electoral challenges, were exempt from his disdain.

"House Armed Services," Jones explained.

"Vorhees's bunch," Bud said knowingly. "Limp Dick can be a bastard when he wants to." The Honorable Richard Vorhees, a former Army captain who had lost a leg in the Grenada invasion, chaired the House Armed Services Committee, one of the most powerful groups of legislators on the Hill. And Limp Dick, a term of no endearment bestowed upon him because of the stilted gait an artificial limb caused, ran it like his own personal military command staff. That Cuban-made mine had cut more than the congressman's leg short, Bud knew all too well. It also ended what promised to be at least a trip to bird status, and maybe even a star or two in the distant future, leaving Limp Dick without the challenge, or the prestige, of command. His life was simply politics now.

"He's one of your blood brothers, Bud," the conservative Republican DCI commented with a devilishly superior wink.

"Not from the same cloth," Bud protested mildly. "I'm a Kennedy man. Vorhees is one of those Johnson Democrats. You never can keep those folks in line." An understatement, the NSA knew. Vorhees, despite his party allegiance, rarely stuck with the party line. He was as much a White House foe as a friend.

"Actually Vorhees was off at some breakfast thing," Jones said, sliding a chair over next to the NSA. "Real concerned, eh? It was the rest of the bunch playing CYA. 'Is there any evidence that the military . . .' " The director shook his head. "A waste of time, my friends."

"It's the same game we all play, Gordy," Bud reminded him.

The FBI director grunted and opened the folder he had brought with him. "Well, I know I'm supposed to share any new info I have, but I really don't have any. Zero."

"Nothing on who actually made the agent?" Drummond asked.

Jones shook his head. "Still the mystery man . . . Nick King. L.A. believes it's an alias of some sort. He's possibly a foreigner or an immigrant."

"Wait," Bud said. "I haven't heard that yet."

"Me either," Drummond added.

"Well, I guess I do have something for you. L.A. has

good information that King spoke with a pretty heavy accent."

"From?" Bud asked.

"European," Jones answered. "That's as close as they can narrow it down for now."

Drummond looked down at the list Intelligence and S&T had put together. Half of those groups and individuals listed were based or affiliated with those located on the European continent. "Some of these people share similar philosophies with Allen. Neo-Nazis. Some ultra-nationalists."

"All possibilities are being looked at, Greg," Jones assured the DCI. "But King made himself an island. Finding out who and what he was before he was that is a tough job."

"It's a damn important one, too," Bud observed.

"Everyone knows that," Jones said. He was on a mild hot seat, responsible for one of the more important investigations during his tenure as head of the Bureau.

The door to the DCI's office opened after two quick taps. Deputy Director Operations Mike Healy rushed in behind the abbreviated warning. "Turn the TV on."

"What's up?" Drummond asked, taking the remote in hand. Healy swiveled the cart-mounted set so that all could see it. "CNN, quick. Vorhees is making one whopper of a statement."

Vorhees? Bud turned his chair, as did Jones.

"About?"

Healy looked to his boss as the picture exploded from a single point of light at the screen's center, becoming an image of the Massachusetts Democrat against the requisite backdrop of filled bookshelves. "You'll see."

". . . when the situation of Nikolai Kostin was brought to my attention by Monte Royce, chairman and chief executive officer of Royce Pharmaceuticals in California. Mr. Royce, who has a facility located in my home district, had traveled to the former Soviet Union in 1993

to tour several of their pharmaceuticals plants. While there, he was contacted by Nikolai Kostin, a Russian citizen who had worked in defense-related industries during the Cold War. Unemployed after massive defense cutbacks, Mr. Kostin was desperate for a job, and wished not to follow the path that many of his comrades had chosen. Those paths led to countries unfriendly to the interests of the United States, countries such as Iran, Iraq, Libya, and others.''

"Kostin was King," Healy said.

Drummond glanced at his deputy, understanding now creeping into his consciousness. "He didn't . . ."

"Greg?" Jones asked, gesturing to the phone.

Drummond pressed an outside line and turned his phone to face the FBI director, who dialed his deputy's office at the Hoover Building.

Vorhees looked up at the cameras from his prepared statement, a gaggle of flashes going off at the same instant, then back to the two pages, which he gripped like a lifeline. *"Mr. Royce, upon returning from his trip, met with me and made the offer to give Mr. Kostin a position with his company, if I could render assistance in getting him into the country and protecting him while here. It was feared that, should Mr. Kostin's past line of work become known, he could be the target of threats from individuals opposed to his presence. The Immigration and Naturalization Service agreed to quietly help in the matter, providing not only entry but also an assumed identity for Mr. Kostin to use. Once here he became Nicholas King.''*

"INS," Jones said while on hold. "Who gave them the power to do that?"

"I wonder how Limp Dick voted on the INS budget increase," Healy wonderingly suggested.

The DCI gave a slight nod, but said nothing.

"I believed, from Mr. Royce's assurances, that this unusual undertaking would help to reduce future threats

to this nation's security by preventing a Russian weapons scientist from being lured to work in countries similar to the ones I have mentioned. At no time was I aware that Mr. Kostin was going to become involved in the activities he undertook while here. At no time.

"*Of course, I will cooperate fully in any investigation of this matter. Immediately upon learning of the situation from newspaper accounts I drafted a letter for transmittal to Director Gordon Jones of the Federal Bureau of Investigation, whom I also assured of my cooperation. Because of the ongoing investigation being conducted by the FBI, I will not make any further statements concerning this matter until it is appropriate.*"

He looked to the reporters a final time, folding and pocketing his statement as he did. "*Thank you.*"

The once brash, seemingly Teflon personality turned away from those gathered to hear his statement and disappeared through a door, the view cutting back to a white-haired anchor once the door was closed.

"What the hell was he thinking?" Bud asked the screen.

"When does he think?" Healy asked more profoundly.

DCI clicked the set off and let the remote drop on his desk with a plastic-versus-wood slap. He took the list before him and crumpled it into a ball, tossing it into the wastebasket for two points. "We have a list of one renegade Russian now."

And who else? Bud wondered, still staring at the now blank screen. The unknown. The goddamned unknown.

Frankie dropped the receiver into its cradle while still recording the information on a legal pad.

"Where are they located?" Art asked impatiently, the CNN wrap-up of the unexpected news conference running in the background. Agents Hal Lightman and Omar Espinosa stood waiting for the same information.

Frankie finished noting what Lou Hidalgo's secretary had read to her from the Chamber of Commerce directory. "Royce Pharmaceuticals has its main facility in Santa Clarita. Old Road and San Fernando."

"That's a half-hour at most from King's place," Espinosa commented.

"From Kostin's place," Art corrected. "Frankie, find out if Monte Royce is at that location or if they have a corporate headquarters somewhere."

"Gotcha," Frankie said, picking up the phone once again.

"Hal, now that we have a place of employment, you and Omar start feeding Royce Pharmaceuticals into the equation," Art directed. "All the people we interviewed, go back to them and throw Royce into the picture. See if it rings any bells."

"What about Allen?" Lightman asked.

Art mentally checked the assignments he'd given so far. He had forty agents—twenty teams—assigned to work with him fulltime, and he'd divided those into two groups: those checking on King, now Kostin, and those working on Allen. "Burlingame is running the Allen side. I think he's running down Freddy's old probation officers. Find him and fill him in."

"Okay," Lightman said with an eager nod. He and Espinosa were on their way without delay.

"Got him," Frankie said. "His secretary says he's in. I told her we want to talk to him. She said a whole slew of reporters do, too."

"Let's step on it then," Art suggested, grabbing his coat.

"I like progress," Frankie commented, following her partner to the elevator.

"So do I, partner," Art agreed, though he knew that the difference between real progress and a wild goose chase was often indistinguishable until it was too late.

* * *

John Barrish sat alone in the family room of the house he could not really call his home, staring at the television as the CNN anchor blabbered something over the live picture of Congressman Richard Vorhees trying to evade the pack of reporters as he hurried to his car. Two uniformed police officers were attempting, with some success, to keep the microphone-armed mob at a distance, allowing the limping legislator a scant fifteen feet of breathing room.

"Fucking bastard," John muttered. The idiot had to go and jump in front of the cameras and blab his head off. "You stupid son of a bitch."

"John?" Louise Barrish said, walking into the family room. "Is everything all right?"

"Everything is fine," John said tersely, the unspoken *Get the hell away from me* tagged on to the cold assurance. His wife retreated back into the kitchen without saying anything more.

Why did he have to say anything? John wondered with frustration. He had to remind himself that Vorhees didn't know anything of substance, but now the State pigs would have another target to pursue, one that did know something . . . *or too much*.

No. John wiped that thought away, focusing again on the picture of Vorhees hobbling away from the media, trying to save his own skin, all because of an error in his judgment. Because he trusted the wrong people.

That he had, John Barrish thought, but those who trusted too much were often used just as much, and Vorhees had unknowingly offered his services with no reservation. Barrish knew he could continue being angry at the half-crippled member of the State machinery, but really he wanted to laugh. He watched Vorhees try to run, doing that silly half-skipping thing that approximated a trot. The man had acted like a fool, and he looked like one, too. They could have anything from him—and they would. He was as easy to manipulate as soft clay.

John chuckled, smiling knowingly at the TV. He laughed fully now, watching the picture change as a cameraman got past the police and took a low shot of Vorhees limping up to his car, the alabaster dome of the Capitol providing a suitable backdrop. "And we're not even done with you yet, you beautiful, gullible gimp."

FIVE

Encounters

Stanley Barrish rarely looked better. The suit was new, a gray number with pinstripes subtle enough that one might think he was trying to avoid being pretentious, and the tie, chosen by his mother, had a hint of red to imply that there was a confidence despite the youthful appearance of its wearer. In one hand a soft leather briefcase said comfort mattered, as did the slightly bloused white shirt. All in all, when combined with the youngest Barrish boy's blond good looks, he appeared to be an up-and-comer in the business of his choosing.

And that he was, his choice being subterfuge, a talent Stanley had perfected as a bored student looking for intellectual adventure in the conformist schools he was forced to attend. His brother, Toby, similarly bored with an educational system that looked upon his family's racial views as abhorrent, had rebelled in a more confrontational, violent way, taking on more of a leadership role with the few friends he had. Stanley simply became one of the followers, the younger brother obediently in tow.

And that sibling hierarchy had not changed in the many years since those difficult days of Stanley's youth. Still he followed, still he obeyed, still Toby was the one to show the way. Of course that way had already been laid out by their father, but, during his incarceration,

Toby had taken over the leadership role of the family. Stanley simply faded further into the shadows, rarely expressing himself in any way that was not acquiescence to his brother's wishes. Never did he lead the way. Never did he make the big play. Never did he shine.

Until now.

"Don't be nervous," Toby told his brother as he pulled the rented car through the traffic gate and into the Metrolink parking lot at Union Station in downtown Los Angeles, choosing the first spot that presented itself.

"I'm not."

"Just take it slow," Toby instructed him.

Stanley looked at his brother, making contact with his good eye. "I can do this."

Toby nodded nervously, knowing his little brother was about to be put to the test, a test he had actually arranged for himself. A test that, if passed, would yield the final information needed to ensure success. "I know you can."

The words, sounding sincere, surprised Stanley. Approval? From Toby? Or was it just resignation, a hope that little Stan could do it and, if not, oh well. But then again, did it really matter which it was? "I gotta go."

Stanley stepped from the car, closing the door behind, and headed for the stairs to the Metro Red Line station, the feel of his brother's judging eyes on his back fading only after he began the seventy-foot descent. At the platform level he quickly oriented himself and went straight for the ticket kiosk. The environment was foreign to him, as it was to most Angelenos. The City of Los Angeles had only recently jumped upon the mass transit bandwagon, building its first true subway, the Red Line, which cut through downtown Los Angeles on its underground swath westward. Stanley, though, had familiarized himself enough with the layout and route to know which stop would be his, and he had reminded himself that, despite the absence of the turnstiles familiar in the subways of other major cities, he did have to buy a ticket from the computerized vendor. The honor system prevailed here, though only until one of the many uniformed transit cops might ask to see your stub. In a way it was farcical, Stanley thought, smiling at the kiosk-mounted screen—he was playing by the rules on his way to do something quite the opposite.

The trains at this time of the morning ran every twelve minutes, leaving just a short wait for the next one. Stanley boarded one of the surprisingly clean cars with only a small group of passengers, most dressed as he was, and took a seat facing the aisle. After the doors closed with a muffled hiss the train pulled away from the station and into a sweeping left turn that was barely noticeable in the tunnel. Less than two minutes later, just shy of a mile from Union Station, the train made its first stop, at Hill and First, disgorging those who had business at the Civic Center. That done the chain of steely silver cars continued less than a half-mile further, slowing and stopping at the Pershing Square station . . . Stanley's destination.

The ride had been less than five minutes, but it served a purpose, putting virtually untraceable distance between Stanley's final destination and the rental his brother had picked up that morning at the airport. From the platform Stanley walked up the stairs, emerging into the noise and light of downtown Los Angeles just north of Fifth Street at Hill, across from Pershing Square proper. The oasis of green amid a forest of glass and old stone was not his final stop. He stayed across from the square, walking west on Fifth with the rest of the late-morning commuters. At South Olive, waiting for traffic to clear, he looked up, seeing the towering masterpiece of engineering that dwarfed anything on the west coast of the United States. His destination. Their target.

The First Interstate World Center, located at the corner of Grand and Fifth in the heart of downtown Los

Angeles, rose like a polished cylinder of gold-tinted glass to a height of 1,017 feet. Its seventy-three stories were populated by a mix of banking, legal, and other offices that came very close to filling the 750,000 square feet of available space. At any one time during a work-day, between five and twenty thousand people were es-timated to be either working, doing business, or visiting there. This day, Stanley Barrish was among those.

"Excuse me," Stanley said to a pretty young lady at the information desk. "I'm supposed to meet Ray Har-back. He's the . . ." Stanley fished out the piece of paper he'd written the man's title on.

"He's our environmental plant manager," the girl said with a smile.

"Right," Stanley said, putting the paper back in his pocket.

"His office is on this floor, over there." She pointed west across the lobby. "Down that hallway you'll see a sign that says World Center Management. Mr. Harback's office is in Building Services."

"All right. Thank you." Stanley moved across the crowded lobby, the dingy morning light flowing through windows to his left, and down the hallway to the loca-tion he had been directed to. Inside the door to Building Services he found Harback's secretary, who showed him into her supervisor's windowless office.

"Mr. Stearns," Ray Harback said, coming around his desk to greet the visitor.

"Call me Stan," Mr. "Stearns" responded.

"Okay," Harback, jacketless and in rolled-up sleeves, agreed willingly. "And I'm Ray. 'Mister' goes with the blazer."

"I'm a loose-tie man myself," Stanley informed his host.

"Have a seat." Harback returned to his chair and closed several folders on his desk. "So, Mick at Sun-Snow pointed you my way."

"Sure did. He was a big help."

"I didn't get the whole story from him, just that you're doing a project overseas and there's trouble with the environmental systems. Is that right?"

Stanley nodded. "Trouble is an understatement. The guy who did the job I'm now jumping into was arrested for taking kickbacks from one of our installation contractors."

"Where is this?"

"Thailand," Stanley lied believably. "We have a two-and-a-half-million-square-foot warehouse facility just about finished in Bangkok, maybe six months' work to go, and the environmental system this idiot contracted for will not do the job."

Harback grimaced. "Ouch."

"The main problem isn't the actual equipment," Stanley went on, "it was my predecessor's screwed-up installation instructions. He had the support plant for the . . ." He pulled a notebook from his briefcase. ". . . let's see, for the Cansco Control Systems equipment built too far from the feed systems to be of any use."

"Yeah, I know that CCS gear," Harback said with a shake of his head. "Their pumps and their flow managers are weak. You could boost the pumps, but that wouldn't put any more product into your space. Just plain air."

Product. Stanley knew that meant the output of the environmental system, what would have been called the air conditioner and heater only ten years before. No more heat. No more cool air. Product. The research he'd done was paying off.

"So our problem is that we have an almost completed facility, a completed support unit for our environmentals, and a shipload of equipment that won't do the job."

"Ouch again."

Stanley drew in a deep breath and eased back in the soft chair. "So, my job now is to find a system we can put in place in six months, using the existing support plant, that will do the job. Mick said the system you have here . . ." Again he looked to his notes.

"The SunSnow Duo Temp Assembly 5-M," Harback said proudly, as if reciting the name of his newborn.

"Right. That's the baby Mick said might fit our needs."

"So you want to know if it does us right."

"Actually I'm sure it does," Stanley said, easing into the pitch. "Like I said, our problem is setup. Space and arrangement. Mick said you have your equipment rigged in a way that might work for us."

"Yeah, ours is a little unusual," Harback admitted. "We narrow down quite a bit above fifty, so we had to plan in some creative stacking, especially with the pumps."

Yes, the pumps. That was what Stanley had read about in a trade journal. The plans SunSnow had sent him told him all he needed to know about the pumps as pieces of machinery, but Harback would have to give him what he needed more.

"Mick said you'd be willing to show me your lay-out," Stanley said. "Kinda to give me an idea if what you've done will suit us."

"Sure," Harback said, standing. "I'd be happy to show off our baby. Come on."

Stanley stood, smiling. It was really going to be that easy.

Royce Pharmaceuticals was a sprawling complex of offices, laboratories, and other buildings dotting a neatly tended green pasture forty miles north of Los Angeles just off the Golden State Freeway. The left turn from the off-ramp pointed the Bureau Chevy directly at the facility's main gate, and at several news vehicles staked out on the facility's perimeter.

"Word travels fast," Frankie commented upon seeing

the high-tech trucks, two with their telescoping micro-
wave dishes already up as they shot for a hookup with
the relays on the nearby peaks.

"When you put on a major CYA show to the press
it's bound to," Art said, wondering briefly if Vorhees
would survive the feeding frenzy. Then he wondered if
he really should care at all.

"We're here to see Monte Royce," Frankie said as
she stopped at the guard shack, showing her FBI shield.
The armed guard examined her credentials, then peered
through the open window, hesitating. "One of our people called," she informed the guard. "Mr. Royce is supposed to be waiting." The look she gave him next was
even less than businesslike. "As in waiting for *us*."

The guard stepped back and pressed a button in the
shack, which raised the single-arm barrier. "Right at the
first lot. Park facing the main building, please."

Frankie hit the up button for the window as she muttered a less than sincere "Thank you." "A little para-
noid, don't you think?"

"Paranoia is a virtue in some circles," Art said, recalling the elaborate security measures he had been witness to during his years investigating organized crime.

Frankie pulled the car into one of several open spots,
each clearly marked VISITOR on a post-mounted placard.
Art scanned the area as he stepped from the car, noting
more security measures inside the company perimeter.
"Smile, partner."

Frankie looked up, seeing the two security cameras
mounted atop perches swivel their way. She met the unseen stare of the unseen operator, maintaining it until
entering the oversized glass doors that led into the lobby
of the main building.

"Agents Jefferson and Aguirre to see Mr. Royce,"
Art said to the receptionist, again sensing more security.
This time it was two men in immaculate suits standing
near the only door leading from the lobby to the innards

of the building. Both had their jackets unbuttoned, hands crossed hanging in the fig leaf position. It would only take a split second for either to get to the weapons they obviously carried under their coats.

"Yes," the receptionist acknowledged. She turned to one of the security guards. "Would you please escort these visitors to Mr. Royce's office?"

"Certainly." The man nodded and flashed a professional, antiseptic smile to the agents. His counterpart held the door open as the security guard led the agents through, stopping halfway down a wide hallway that was decorated in subtle earth tones. He pressed the lighted up arrow next to the elevator and followed the visitors in, hitting the 6 button.

"You'd think you guys made cruise missiles or something here," Frankie said once the door closed.

"We have competitors," the security guard said.

Competitors. Art translated that to what the man's tone said it should be: enemies. The business world really was where the next wars would be fought.

"To the right," the guard said, taking the lead again once they were off the elevator.

Wow. Frankie remembered enough of art history from college to recognize the pieces that hung along the hallway they were moving down. *Los Caprichos*, a work by Goya, and across from it *The Duchess of Alba* by the same artist. Both were from the late 1700s, she recalled, amazed that some of the knowledge had stuck with her. More works adorned the walls. Beautiful paintings by Guardi, though Frankie could not place titles with them. Another Goya. And something told her that these were not just reproductions. The artwork alone warranted the security seen so far.

The guard opened a door, letting the agents into the outer office of the chief executive officer of Royce Pharmaceuticals, then closed it and withdrew into the hallway.

"Mr. Royce is waiting," a very polite secretary said, standing from her desk and walking to the door on the back wall. "Right through here."

The agents followed the directions and were met by the reason for their visit.

"Hello," Monte Royce said as the agents entered. He stood in the center of his spacious office, halfway between the door and his desk, which was backdropped by a panoramic view of the green hillsides that would turn brown once the region's brief rainy season had ended. "I'm Monte Royce."

Art took the man's outstretched hand first, then Frankie did.

"Can I offer you anything?" Royce asked. "Some tea? Water?"

"No," Art said. "Thank you. We're fine."

Royce looked to his secretary waiting in the doorway. "Thank you, Mary."

"Mr. Royce," Frankie began as the heavy oak door closed, "I have to tell you, you have some beautiful artwork here."

Royce bowed his gray and balding head graciously. "Thank you. My mother's father began the collection over a hundred years ago. I have a few pieces here to brighten the place up."

"It does," Frankie said.

Royce motioned to two couches facing each other across a stunning Persian rug. He took a seat on one, the agents on the other. "I suspect you are not here to discuss eighteenth-century art."

"No, we're not," Art said. "We're here about Nikolai Kostin."

"Yes, Mr. King," Royce said, nodding, his almost black suit combining with his aged features to give him the appearance of a mortician expressing sympathy over a lost loved one. "I grew used to using his new name while he worked for us."

The tone of the tense Royce used in referring to Kostin tweaked an alarm in both agents, Frankie jumping on it first. "*While* he worked for you? He hasn't worked for you recently?"

Royce's eyes wandered the room for a moment, his expression and manner becoming somewhat sad as he looked back to the agents. "Unfortunately, no. His time with us was short. Just less than a year, I believe. He had, you see, a problem adjusting to our working methods. To the way we operate here. It was a matter of culture, partly, and of personality."

"He was fired, then?" Frankie sought to confirm, her notebook and pen coming out.

"Yes. Not an amicable parting," Royce revealed. "He was not happy with us for doing so."

Art had watched the man as Frankie began the questioning, measuring his reactions to each query posed. Once he jumped in, the roles would reverse, his partner becoming the observer. One to receive and record the response. The other to make a mental record of the person's manner. It was nothing discussed, being instead a process ingrained from the earliest days of their academy training. The words and the ways, it was called. Somewhere in those, sometimes far from the spoken answers, was the truth.

"And you met him in Russia?"

"Yes. In St. Petersburg. In the spring of 1993. It was a rather high-profile trip I undertook. The Russian government provided guides and a good deal of assistance in the way of transportation."

Frankie nodded, checking her notes quickly. "And you went there to . . ."

"To tour facilities with similar functions to mine," Royce explained, taking the long pause after his short response as a signal that the agent was not yet satisfied. "It was a . . . a chance to see the level of sophistication they had attained under the stifling system of state control the plant operators were subject to. In a way, I suppose, I wanted to see if there might be ways for my company to assist the industry in Russia with technical help in the form of joint ventures. Partnerships. And the like.''

"So it was business?''

"Yes. Most definitely. Though not devoid of altruism,'' Royce added with a smile. "Good can come from a profitable relationship. That is possible.''

"I guess it is,'' Frankie benignly agreed. "And Nikolai Kostin approached you as Congressman Vorhees stated?''

"I did not see Richard's statement. I was told of it.''

Richard? Art decided to take it from there. "You know the congressman well?''

"I know many people in our government well. Senator Crippen from this state is a friend, as well as Richard Vorhees. I have a facility in Massachusetts, and my mother lived in his district until a few years ago. I moved her out here then. She is quite old, you can imagine.''

In her nineties at least, Art guessed, given the visual clues to Royce's advanced age. "And—''

"But,'' Royce interjected, "to the young lady's question, yes, he approached me in St. Petersburg.''

Young lady? Art saw the smile, then the seemingly friendly head tilt his partner had mastered. *It's Agent Aguirre!* he could almost hear her screaming inside. "Back to the congressman,'' Art said. "You proposed the idea of Mr. Kostin coming to work for you to him, correct?''

"Correct.''

"And the name change. Who proposed that?''

Royce looked away again, thinking back. "I believe it was myself. You see, I understand the vociferous nature of some societal elements. People that oppose our using animals in testing, and so on. I thought that having a man on-staff who had worked in the Russian defense establishment could bring on similar actions. That, in my opinion, would not have been good for my company, or for Mr. King.''

"Kostin," Art corrected.

"Yes. Mr. Kostin."

"So he came over, it didn't work out, and he went on his way," Art said. "Is that the simple picture?"

"That is *the* picture," Royce answered.

Very straightforward, Art thought. And very clean. Too clean. "You make drugs here."

"No, we design them here," Royce corrected. "And we prefer to call them pharmaceuticals. Several other facilities actually produce them."

"Pharmaceuticals deal heavily with chemicals, correct?"

Royce nodded at Art's question.

"Are you a chemist?"

"A chemical engineer."

"I assume, then, that you know what chemicals would be required to make what Mr. King was making," Art said.

"The basic ones, yes," Royce confirmed.

"Would those chemicals be available here?" Art asked. "Would the equipment needed to manufacture nerve gas be available here?"

"Agent Jefferson, there is absolutely no way that Mr. King could have made that poison here," Royce responded, showing more animation than at any time so far in the conversation. "Absolutely no way."

"I don't think he did," Art said. "But could he have acquired either the chemicals or the equipment here?"

Royce shook his head emphatically. "Absolutely not. It is a violation of our regulations, and federal regulations, to allow that to happen."

"Mr. King was not following too many regulations," Frankie reminded him.

"Still, any pilferage would have been noticed, reported, and stopped," Royce assured the agents.

Frankie knew it was time for a new tack. "Does the name Frederick Allen mean anything to you?"

Royce's head shook as he recrossed his legs. "No. No it doesn't."

Frankie sensed something in the response, or a lack of something. A challenge was warranted. "Are you very sure?"

Royce cleared his throat. "Young lady, I am a man with many friends, several of whom share the name Frederick. But I can assure you that there is no Freddy Allen among them."

Bingo. "All right."

Art had caught it, too. It was amazing how the simplest of things could give someone away. But this was not the place nor the time to pursue it any further. In fact any additional questioning was useless for the moment. But not for long.

Frankie looked to her partner. "Is there anything else you need to ask?"

"No. Not right now." He turned to Royce. "We may have some more questions, though, if any new information comes up."

"Of course," Royce said, nodding obligingly. "I will cooperate in any way I can." He pushed off one arm of the sofa, coming to his feet. "Knowing that my former employee decided to go into so sordid a profession leaves a black mark on my judgment. I want to exorcise that, if possible. For my own peace of mind."

"Of course." Art and Frankie stood, each politely thanking the CEO of Royce Pharmaceuticals for his time, and, silently, for much more. They left his office and followed the same security guard who had escorted them in back out, exiting the headquarters of the multimillion-dollar corporation into a blustery fall breeze that had kicked up while they were inside.

"He was lying through his teeth," Art said once outside. "Hey, good snare, partner."

"Would you call someone named Frederick *Freddy* if you didn't know them?"

"He didn't call Richard *Dick*," Art answered. "Now all we have to do is find out how and why this guy was mixed up with Allen."

Whatever the executive's motivation was in becoming involved with Kostin and, she was sure, Freddy Allen, one obvious connection to the affair was very apparent to Frankie. "Money, partner."

"But why?" Art wondered. "I want to know everything we can about this guy. Especially about his finances."

"His *visit* to Russia, too," Frankie suggested.

"Good idea. Have the liaison group in D.C. run that down if they haven't already," Art directed. "Have them find out how long this trip he took was in the works, who his contacts were, where he went, et cetera."

"Will do," Frankie said, unlocking the Chevy and getting behind the wheel. Her right hand went immediately to the heater.

"This whole thing doesn't feel right," Art said as he closed the passenger door. *Scared* wasn't the word to use, at least not yet.

Harback gestured once again to the slate-gray unit after finishing his spiel. "SunSnow knows how to make things right."

"That's an understatement," Stanley commented, looking over the layout of the area and the entire system. Simple in some respects, but for his purposes there was still the nagging problem of getting to this point without sounding any alarms in those workers who were bound to see something. Whoever was going to actually place the stuff couldn't just ask Harback to . . . *or could they?*

"Ray, this is absolutely what I think my clients in Thailand are going to need. Your setup fits the bill as far as I can see. You know, what would really help is if I could get some pictures of this level and the main system. Stills and video so I could ship them over to the architects and engineers in Bangkok to convince them. Is there any way I could send a couple of my guys up next week sometime to take some shots?''

''Sure. No problem. I'd be glad to point out what they should be shooting.''

Stanley patted the bigger man appreciatively on the shoulder. ''You may have just saved my clients a hefty refit.''

''No problem at all.''

''Well, there will be a very generous consulting services fee coming your way.''

Harback chuckled, the joviality drowned out by the constant noise. ''I appreciate that.''

''Is Wednesday all right with you?''

''The day before Thanksgiving?'' Harback asked, mentally checking his schedule. Most in the building would be heading out early that day. The load on the systems would be minimal. ''Morning okay?''

''Eight would be good,'' Stanley said.

''Perfect.''

Stanley reached his hand out, shaking Harback's firmly. ''Perfect.''

Harback escorted his guest back to the ground floor and noted the appointment. Stanley thanked the man one final time, sincere in his appreciation. If only he knew, Stanley thought with a smile as he crossed the lobby, his eyes squinting at the glare from the front—

''Damn,'' Anne Preston said, her armful of books now at her feet after the collision.

''I'm . . . I'm sorry,'' Stanley apologized, squatting to help the lady pick up her books. ''I didn't see you. The glare kinda blinded me.''

"It was an accident," Anne said. "I should have seen you."

"No, I was . . ." Stanley looked up from the floor, seeing the lady's face for the first time. *She's African.* He hadn't been this close to an African in years. In fact he couldn't remember touching an African woman, even accidentally like this. "I . . . I'm sorry. I . . . I've gotta go."

Anne gathered the books as the young man handed them to her with haste. She stood from a crouch and watched him hurry from the building as if he'd just seen a ghost, then let the strange incident fade as she continued on to her twelfth-floor office.

SIX

Bulls

The forty-hour week, legislated many years before for the benefit of American workers, was but a long-forgotten dream for those gathered in the Oval Office this Saturday morning. There was coffee in a shining server, which rested on a silver tray at the center of a low table. Two platters, one of fruit slices and the other stacked with croissants, were on either side of the tray, and from the two couches and the single highback chair that framed the arrangement hands would occasionally reach in and partake of the light morning meal.

The president, sitting straight in the highback, held a saucer on his lap and sipped at the cup of Colombian blend as the man who would run his campaign for re-election, once the bid officially got under way the week after Thanksgiving, ran through a thumbnail sketch of the strategy developed over the summer months. Listening with the president were the secretary of state, the White House chief of staff, and National Security Adviser Bud DiContino, three men he saw as a troika of wisdom and honesty that could be relied upon without fail.

The outline of the route the campaign would take through the electoral minefield, presented by Earl Casey, the presidential campaign general chairman, was given as a courtesy to those men closest to the chief executive.

It was laid out for their perusal, comment, or criticism, and, as expected, it focused heavily on domestic issues. The voters, burned by promises of such in the past, as well as a still sluggish economy that refused to rebound to prerecession levels, were as skeptical as they had ever been, Casey told the group. As a political operator Casey was the best, saying what needed to be said, seeing what warranted attention, and spinning what required finessing. This was his first presidential campaign, but seven sitting governors owed their positions to the man, and the Democratic strategists had convinced the president that Casey and the team he could assemble were the ones who could keep the party in the White House for four more years.

Bud DiContino, however, saw some wrinkles in the carefully crafted plan.

"What about the unexpected?" The NSA asked. He saw Jim Coventry's head move slightly in agreement.

"In what form?" Casey responded.

"Well, take what's going on now for example," Bud said. "Say that a week before New Hampshire we find out that this Kostin fellow is actually a Russian spy sent here to supply homegrown terrorist groups with nerve gas."

"I hope that's not a suggestion of what's possible, Bud," Casey said.

"Why not?"

"Because it's ludicrous," Casey answered.

"Then pick another possibility," Bud challenged the thirty-eight-year-old political wunderkind. "Iraq. Iran. Mexico. The IRA. Hezbollah. South Africa. Israel. Which one? You know, it doesn't matter, which is my point. The unexpected, the thing that you would not have predicted with all the best intelligence, will rear up and slap you across the face just like this incident has."

"And like now it will be controlled by the proper part of the government," Casey said.

Bud would have loved to let Casey know what was still facing the country, but he had no need to be privy to that information. "The voice of the president is sometimes the only sound some people hear when things get dicey. If the Iranians 'accidentally' loose a missile at one of our ships in the Gulf, Drew Meyerson is not going to be the one the American people will want to hear from, and he is not the one the Iranians will *need* to hear from. That's nothing against the secretary of defense, it is simply a statement of fact that it is somewhat disingenuous to believe you can cast the president as a domestic manager who can delegate responsibility for the crises of tomorrow to his advisers simply because an election is looming. It's disingenuous, and it's dangerous."

"I tend to agree with Bud, sir," Coventry said. "Thinking in purely political terms, I believe the strategy Earl's laid out could backfire."

"How so?" the president inquired.

"For the same reasons Bud just presented," Coventry answered. "If you are set up as focused entirely on the domestic agenda and reality rears its head and draws your attention away, you become a target for your opponents."

The president considered the statements of his national security adviser and secretary of state while sipping his coffee. "Ellis?"

The chief of staff, his white shirt only three hours in use and already wrinkled, looked to the leader of his country, the man he had grown up with in the Golden State. "If you want pragmatism, Mr. President, then I agree wholeheartedly with Bud and Jim. But a campaign is not about pragmatism, like that or not. It's about ideology and image. A segment of the electorate buys ideology, another buys image. And it's the image factor that is going to be the challenge for you."

"Ellis, things are getting better," Coventry said. He

wasn't an economist, but he understood enough to be able to intelligently analyze the numbers coming from various agencies.

"Tell that to the guy in California whose job was just sold to China along with the steel plant he worked in for twenty years," the chief of staff countered. "Because *that* is the guy the media will have endless interviews with, along with every naysayer the opposition can drum up. You can't ignore image by throwing numbers out that are supposed to convince people who see hurt on the tube every night that things are really okay. That is also disingenuous."

Casey saw that the chief of staff's argument had scored some points with the two critics of his strategy. "And, Mr. President, the economy is only part of the domestic agenda that people are crying for action on."

The president nodded and bent forward, setting the cup and saucer on the coffee table. "I know. Crime."

"Exactly," Casey agreed. "You've made only minor dents in the overall crime rate, and coupled with big incidents that grab the headlines the image is one of stagnation on this front."

"Nothing happens overnight, Earl," the president said.

"The election of a new chief executive does," Casey reminded the president, and the rest of those gathered. "Look, we not only have to deal with what you have done, are doing, and will do on crime, we have to be able to respond to the big failures. Take the case of that Barrish asshole this week. What happened there?"

"The legal system worked in its most flawed way," Bud said.

"Wrong," Casey said. "For my purposes, which include keeping your boss in this job, it means an animal walked. That is what the voters see, and they also see it as a failure by the Justice Department to do its job, and they know who hires, supervises, and fires the attorney general." Casey unashamedly pointed a finger at the president. "This man, Bud. Ultimately, when the voter goes into the booth to pull the lever, he remembers things like his next-door neighbor being out of work, he remembers four little girls lying dead in a church, and he remembers very clearly the image of John Barrish leaving court a free man. Those are the things he remembers."

The chief of staff leaned in to take the floor. "You know, relating to what Earl just said, I had a meeting with Rabbi Levin—"

"How is he?" the president asked, interrupting. "I didn't have a chance to see him." Aside from the donations the rabbi could deliver, the president genuinely liked the man.

"He's fine," Ellis said. "He was just here for a few hours yesterday. Anyway, he had an interesting story. His synagogue was sponsoring some sort of seminars on racial tolerance. The attendance was entirely white until a couple of nights ago, when the father of one of those little girls showed up."

"Oh my God," the president said.

"He told Levin he came because he said he was starting to hate as much as the people who killed his daughter." Ellis paused for a moment, out of necessity. The emotion was real, as real as it had been when Levin shared the story with him. "The man was destroyed. So was his family. And he was there, begging for help without saying a word."

"Did someone get him some help?" Bud asked.

Ellis nodded. "The person giving the seminar, a psychiatrist from UCLA, I think, is going to do whatever she can . . . free of charge."

"Thank God there is still some altruism out there," Coventry commented.

"Mr. President," Casey began, "this is the kind of thing that will make or break you in the eyes of the voters. This man and how others perceive the future.''

Bud felt that his point had just been completely superseded by emotion, and he had a hard time arguing with that reality. One couldn't help but be moved by that story and the people involved.

But there were other stories yet to be revealed that could have a greater impact on a larger number of people. It wasn't a thought meant to minimize the tragedy of a horrid event, just a statement of fact.

"Mr. President, a great many things external to this nation can have an impact on events internal," Bud posited. "We are living with that now. A former Russian scientist was involved in the manufacture of chemical weapons on our soil. The event itself may be a domestic issue, but at least part of it began an ocean and half a continent away."

He was the leader of the most powerful nation on earth. Millions, arguably billions of people depended on his steady hand to keep them free, and he was sitting among his advisers discussing how best to keep his job. On the hierarchy of things vital to the nation it seemed very mundane to the president, but he had jumped willingly into the political arena many years before. From this vantage, though, with nowhere left to go but down, the hoop jumping and spin doctoring, farcical as it sometimes seemed, was life. It was reality.

"Earl, you said the State of the Union speech is going to be the jumping-off point," the president recalled, letting the debate of the previous moments take a backseat. "Why?"

"It's your strong point," Casey answered. "You convey ideas and feeling through words better than any president since FDR. We have to seize on that strength to get a running start. Remember, you'll have an audience of a hundred million that will be watching you in a setting that is very presidential. That's something Paul Collins and Moe Stone don't even have as a campaign tool." Collins, the Republican senator from Florida, was practically preanointed as his party's nominee some eight months before their convention. Moe Stone, on the other hand, had only to anoint himself. The former Republican congressman, seizing on a populist groundswell, was almost certainly going to run as an independent, and polls indicated there was enough support for his message of traditionalism and values to put him on the ballot from Hawaii to Maine. "Between next week when you formally announce and the State of the Union in January we'll be running a slow court press, building anticipation of the speech."

"The pressure is appreciated," the president said half-jokingly.

Casey saw no humor in the plan. "Mr. President, with all due respect, this plan may be the only way to get you reelected. You are in office at a very anxious time in our nation's history. When people are anxious they get nervous about the future, and when they are nervous they start to consider change a very attractive alternative to an unknown path they are already on. And, believe it or not, the easiest change to make is in the man at the top. NFL coaches get fired all the time because the players aren't performing. That can happen to you, too."

"I get your point," the president said, pausing for a moment and looking to Bud. "But I will not portray myself as a god of domestic policy at the expense of other important matters." The president saw his NSA smile slightly, then turned back to Casey. "I will do what is needed to get reelected, Earl, as long as it is also right. And right is not convincing the American people that, for the purpose of one day in November, we are an island. I want you to broaden your plans for this campaign. This is not a one-issue world, and I am not a one-issue president."

Let's just hope you're not a one-term president, Casey thought, drawing a long breath in. "Okay. I'll work on it. But the speech remains as the starting point. Say what you want in it, but make it good. Make it the best one you've ever given.''

"Or it may be my last?" the president asked as an addition to the statement.

Casey didn't answer the president directly. "Just make it good."

There would be no body to bury, just an empty plot of earth next to his mother and a drab marker bearing the name of Luis Hidalgo, Jr. That hollow ceremony would be played out come Monday, privately, for the family of the dead firefighter. This day, first of two usually reserved for rest, was for the extended families of Hidalgo and his fallen comrades.

"And I thought cops did it up nice," Art commented as he exited St. John's Catholic Church and saw the endless line of fire engines jamming the street in the foothills above Pasadena. Red, yellow, white, green . . . all colors of rigs had come from across three states to honor the memories of their brethren killed at 1212 Riverside.

"They will," Frankie said. That memorial service, in remembrance of the sheriff's deputies killed, would be on Monday, about the same time Luis Hidalgo, Jr., would be laid to rest . . . at least in spirit. "I can't imagine having a funeral with nothing to put in the ground."

Art pressed his way through the side of the moving crowd and stopped on the church's front lawn. "I know that's bothering Lou. It can't be helped, though."

"I know." Frankie and her partner waited as the stream of firefighters filed past. At the end of the procession exiting St. John's were the families of the men, being led out by the priest who had officiated at the service. "There's Lou."

Art watched as Hidalgo thanked the pastor and moved down the walkway with his children toward a waiting car. The A-SAC ushered his children into the vehicle with one of their aunts, then came over to speak with his agents.

"How are you, Lou?" Art asked, no verbal answer needed. The dark glasses and the puffy cheeks said all that was required.

Hidalgo nodded a bit. "Hanging in there."

"Is there anything you need?" Frankie offered.

I need you to find the bastards that made this happen. "Thanks, no. How is it coming along?"

"Slow," Art answered honestly.

"Royce?"

"Pretty much a wash on the surface," Frankie said.

"We've got three teams working him and his company exclusively," Art informed his grieving friend. "Looking for any link other than the job. Anything that smells bad."

Again Hidalgo nodded. "What's on the schedule for today?"

"Everything," Art answered. "Everybody is in. Frankie and I are going back straight from here."

"Good. You call me if you get anything," Hidalgo directed. "Anything. All right?"

"We will, Lou," Art promised. "Go home now."

The A-SAC went to the waiting car and climbed in. It pulled away behind an escort of fire department battalion chiefs.

"What are we going to do, Art?" Frankie wondered. "Three days and this thing is going nowhere. No one knows Allen, or where he's been, or who he's been with, or anything. King is Kostin. Royce hasn't done anything other than 'try to help the country.' We're at a wall, partner."

"You want to go around, over, or through?" Art asked, lightening the moment as much as possible. " 'Cause we're getting to the other side one way or another."

Art was a bull, Frankie knew. Through the wall it would be. "Back to work, partner?"

"That's the only way."

"I'm not doing it, Dad," Moises Griggs yelled defiantly, wisely standing across the living room from his father. "I'm not going to some shrink just to make you feel better."

"Lower your voice," Darren insisted, looking toward the closed bedroom door. "Your mother is asleep."

"She's always asleep, Dad. Don't you see that? There's nothing left of her."

"Shut up," Darren said, his eyes going as wide as his son had ever seen them.

"She never comes out of that room, and you just tip-toe around her like she's dead. You know why? Because she is. And so are you."

"I said shut up!"

"You both are dead because some damn crackers killed Tanya," Moises yelled, his face contorted as he challenged his father, the man he had once revered but now felt only contempt for. "And you're afraid to do anything about it."

Darren advanced toward Moises, backing him up. "You shut that foolish mouth before I—"

The right hook took Darren completely by surprise, knocking him back and sending him tumbling against the couch and end table, knocking a ceramic lamp to the floor in pieces.

"You sorry little fuck!"

"Come on, Dad," Moises said, motioning like a bully for his father to rise up again. "I'm not afraid to fight. Not afraid of no one!"

Darren eased himself to a crouch, testing his jaw with one hand as the other struck like a coiled snake at his son's midsection.

"Oooh!" Moises doubled over and gasped for air. His father had hit him!

Darren followed his strike with an open-hand slap across the face that spun Moises into the buffet. Pictures and the other family treasures cascaded off the heavy wood object.

"Mother fuck—"

This time the fist was closed, catching Moises from above and slightly behind. It hit him on the cheek like a sledge and drove him to the floor.

"You never talk like that in this house," Darren screamed, his fist coming back again. "Do you hear—"

"STOP IT!"

Darren's head swung left, toward the scream, his son's coming up from a cower.

"Stop it! Stop it! Stop it!" Felicia Griggs stood in the opening to the hallway, a worn nightgown hanging from her wasting form like a burial shroud.

"Felicia . . ."

Darren's wife looked at him with eyes that asked *why*?, and to her son with the same . . . *The pictures!*

"Mom . . ."

Felicia ran to the spot where her son was doubled over and pushed him away, her hands frantically searching the pile of broken glass and mangled photos for . . . "Tanya."

Darren watched his wife pull the picture of their little girl to her chest as she rocked back and forth on her knees. "My baby. Tanya, my baby."

Moises slid backward away from his mother, blood trickling from his lip and leaving a trail of red splotches on the hardwood floor.

"Honey," Darren said softly as he knelt down next to his wife. He placed a hand on her shoulder, which she recoiled from instantly.

"How dare you two do this!" Felicia practically spat out the words. "How dare you!"

Moises continued sliding away, the venom in his mother's stare hastening his withdrawal toward the door.

"Sweetheart, please, I'm sorry," Darren begged.

"This family is half dead already, and you two are trying to kill the rest." She looked to her son, his eyes fearful yet unflinching. He rose up from the floor and opened the front door without looking, disappearing into the night with only the sound of running feet across the porch as an explanation.

Darren, his eyes now brimming, felt weak and small as his wife's stare focused entirely on him. "I'm so sorry. Please . . ."

"I've lost just about everything, Darren," Felicia said with a sorrow so profound it seemed almost too much for one person to bear. It almost had been. "I don't want to lose you and Moises. That just can't happen. It can't."

Darren pulled his wife gently into his arms, the picture of their little girl between them. "I won't let it, sweetheart," he promised, knowing that would be easier said than done. But it had to be said, for Felicia's sake. "I won't let it."

Mile four. A month before this was the point when that steely fist would start socking him in the gut, but Art Jefferson now felt that reminder of his distance ability around mile six.

But he was able to run, to make it this far, which was a miracle to some considering his physical and emotional state just two years earlier. His daily eight-mile jogs had strengthened him in both respects. Muscles were leaner and more powerful. The heart was as good as it had ever been. And his mind, free to wander during the hour-long workout, was crisp, recharged by the solitude and the accomplishment of simply being alive.

He moved through the nearly deserted residential streets near his town house, the occasional face peering at him from behind the large bay windows common to homes in the upscale neighborhood. *A black man running at night? Here?* Art didn't let the ignorance bother him as much as it had the first time he'd been stopped by a police car after a "concerned" citizen had reported "suspicious activity." The cops were apologetic. They were only responding to a call, after all, and they had quite forcefully informed that concerned citizen that the man running past her half-million-dollar home was an FBI agent. End of the problem with her. But there would be others. There would always be others.

Still, he cherished his runs, which he sometimes took early in the morning. The present situation, though, dictated longer days, and he and Frankie had worked out a semisplit schedule so that one of them would be on duty during most of every day. She took late mornings mostly, which gave her the time to see her little girl and drop her at kindergarten before hitting the office at ten. Her mother would then pick Cassie up and sit with her until Frankie got home between midnight and one. Art usually took the six A.M. to eight P.M. part of the day, leaving time for his runs in the evening, and some for Anne.

But, being honest with himself, it was the running he was thinking of at the moment. Not Anne. Not the investigation. Just running. He was even thinking of entering a charity ten-mile run in a couple of months. The competition interested him somewhat, but it was the thought of *finishing* a ten-mile run that was his motivation. Crossing that line as everyone watched, whether he was in first place or last.

Mile seven. Still feeling strong. Not winded yet. The sound of the Eagles' "Peaceful Easy Feeling" soothing him through the headphones. A little more than five thousand feet to—*Shit!*

Art did the runner's equivalent of slamming on the brakes as the familiar Chevy pulled around from his left and cut him off using felony stop procedures.

"Dammit, Frankie!" Art cursed his partner as she stepped from the driver's side of the car. "You scared the shit out of me!"

"There was no answer at your place, so I figured you'd be doing some roadwork," Frankie explained. "This couldn't wait."

Art bent over to catch his breath, robbed by the instant excitement and not the exertion. "What is it?"

"Jacobs got something on the gun Allen had."

Art stood straight now. "What?"

"The test bullets he fired and sampled came from one of the three guns used in the Saint Anthony's shooting."

"What?" Art wondered, the word spoken slowly.

"It was one of the guns," Frankie said. "Jacobs says he's one hundred percent positive on the match."

"Allen? Working with the AVO in that shooting?"

"That was my first reaction," Frankie said. "If that's true then the prosecutors were missing some big pieces of that case."

"So was Thom," Art added. Danbrook hadn't reported any connection between the AVO and the Aryan Brotherhood.

"Maybe Barrish and his group were more careful than we thought," Frankie suggested.

"The Brotherhood and Barrish?" Art asked, looking skyward as he caught his breath. "Hart never even hinted that Allen knew Barrish." Chester Hart, an Aryan Brotherhood member serving time in Folsom State Prison, had been feeding the Bureau information on Freddy Allen in hopes of favorable consideration on outstanding charges. Little had been of use, and none of what he'd offered had even hinted at this development.

"Maybe it wasn't an AB thing," Frankie said. Behind

her partner the porchlights of several houses were going on.

Freelancing. It was a possibility, but he would not have attached this new development to that theory in a million years. "Allen offering himself up to Barrish?"

"Or maybe he was recruited," Frankie offered alternately.

"If Allen was in on Saint Anthony's then that means he was hooked up with Barrish somehow," Art observed. Both he and Frankie knew that, despite what the court said, John Barrish was as responsible for the Saint Anthony's massacre as the never-identified triggermen. With the gun Allen had on him now, though, at least one identification, for what it was worth, seemed possible. As did one other thing. "Barrish could be mixed up in this."

"But he was in detention until just a few days ago," Frankie reminded her partner.

"That hasn't stopped bigger creeps from doing bad things," Art said. He leaned on the Chevy's roof as the impromptu session of hashing the possibilities played out in the middle of the street. "But this won't be easy to dig into."

"Why not?"

"Barrish is fresh from having federal charges dropped against him," Art explained. "All we have with this is a possible link between Allen and a crime that John Barrish was technically found innocent of."

"In a pig's eye," Frankie said.

"Look, partner, you and I both know the man is guilty." Danbrook's recounting of the conversations with Barrish was enough to convince Art of that. If only his damn gun hadn't jammed, Art thought, Thom might be alive and John Barrish would definitely be behind bars for good. "But without some legal connection to Saint Anthony's this Allen link is phantom incrimination."

"You're being awful pessimistic," Frankie commented.

"No, just realistic," Art countered.

"So, what? We take this nowhere?"

Art's face twisted in a grimace. "No, we take it. But we have to approach this as if Barrish is just a possible source of information—not a suspect. Otherwise Horner will be down on our asses for harassing Barrish quicker than either of us can spit."

Malcolm Horner, the judge who had reluctantly dismissed charges against the leader of the AVO, would probably like to see him staked out on a hot day in the desert and left for the buzzards. But that was a desire, not the law, and Frankie knew from experience in the judge's court that it didn't matter if you were a racist or if you wore a badge—if you violated someone's constitutional rights you were likely to feel his wrath. Barrish was cleared of a crime Frankie knew he was guilty of, and even insinuating that he was still being investigated for such would violate the constitutional guarantee against double jeopardy.

"Are we going to talk to him?" Frankie asked.

Art tapped the top of the car and climbed in, his partner following his lead. "As soon as I get out of these sweats and into something decent." He motioned to the road, signaling his partner to head for his place. "And as soon as we can find him."

"I heard he lost his house and just about everything else," Frankie said.

"He has to be somewhere."

"And how do we find him?"

"The same way we find every self-respecting criminal," Art said. "Through his lawyer."

SEVEN

Oil and Water

Chimps were not peaceful, cuddly little creatures, Toby thought as he watched the simians battle and fornicate in the Los Angeles Zoo enclosure they knew as home.

"You know what these little guys remind me of, Stan?"

"Don't," Stanley said, avoiding looking at his brother. "Dad doesn't like that kind of talk."

"I know, but he's not here. Lighten up." Toby ribbed his brother with an elbow. "Hey, maybe these little suckers are the guys we're supposed to meet. Huh?"

Stanley turned away from the exhibit and leaned his back against the railing, watching the families and groups of friends stroll lazily by. A typical Sunday, the kind he had never known. "Toby. I think they're here."

Toby held his position, still watching the animals with amusement. "Turn around, Stan. Be cool."

"There's three of them," Stanley said after turning back to the chimps. "One is hanging back."

"Be cool," Toby said, sensing with little difficulty the shake in his brother's voice. "Don't talk unless I tell you to."

"All right." *Gladly.*

Darian Brown walked without fear toward the two men who could only be there to see him.

"The banker," Mustafa Ali observed as he walked with his leader. Thirty feet behind, standing near a popcorn vendor, Brother Roger was watching closely, noting the same thing. All three men had guns, but it was Roger's job to be aware of any attempt by police or anyone else to accost them. *Bullets are better than bowing.*

"I'll handle this," Darian said. His .357 was within easy reach under his loose coat.

Toby leaned easily on the railing, his hands clasped as they drooped over the metal bar. Stanley was to his left, and in an instant there were two Africans assuming the same position as he to his right. "Nice day."

Darian looked left at the one who spoke. He wore a baseball cap and dark glasses, as did the second one farther down. Simple measures to conceal their identity, but effective. All he could tell was that they were white, and that was enough. "You look different than when you dropped by our place."

"It's called shaving," Toby said, looking right.

"And the little boy?" Darian asked.

"He's with me," Toby answered, still meeting the African's unseen stare. "We're here to do business."

"Well, I'm here deciding whether I should trust you or kill you," Darian said, seeing the second white boy finally look his way.

"And what's your decision?" Toby asked without hesitation.

"We're not cops," Stanley said, earning himself a brief, slow look from Toby.

"Cops?" Darian chuckled, showing some teeth now. "Yeah. You two."

"Look, you said you guys would be interested in something big," Toby said with measured impatience. "As long as it was worth your while."

"Big is good," Darian quasi-agreed. "But why don't you just do it yourself?"

"Let's just say that one of our group draws attention real easily," Toby answered. "We can supply the weapons and the plans, but we need the muscle."

Darian let the smile soften to barely a grin. "Muscle, huh? Like these well-developed calf muscles of mine?"

Toby smiled fully. "Hey, why fight nature?"

The prick at least didn't waver, Darian thought. "So why should we do this for you?"

"Not *for* . . . *with*," Toby corrected. "Hey, we have one very big thing in common: we both reject the rule of our so-called government."

"Without a doubt," Darian agreed.

"We want to start hitting them hard," Toby explained. "Doing big things."

"Things?" Darian asked. "I didn't know this was more than a one-shot deal."

"Are you saying you won't go for doing more?"

"That depends on what more is," Darian answered. " 'Cause I don't even know what you want us to do in the first place."

Toby held back for a moment, knowing he couldn't give the Africans everything at once. "Does killing a shitload of folks, mostly white ones, sound like anything you'd be interested in?"

This motherfucker was for real, Darian was beginning to think. "Define a shitload."

"A couple thousand," Toby clarified. "All at once."

Darian considered the white boy's proposal. He hardly knew anything about him or the group he supposedly belonged to. Probably one of those freedom-fighting, tax-protesting bunches. But what he was saying definitely had possibilities. Big ones. It might be just the way to get his group's militant actions off to a thunderous start . . . if this all wasn't just hot air.

"Maybe more than that," Toby added as further incentive. "What'll it be?"

Mustafa leaned in and whispered something to Darian,

pulling back after a brief exchange. "If we do this *thing* for you, we want the credit."

"That's no problem with us," Toby said. That would only move their plan along all the faster. "We're interested in the end, not applause."

"I need applause," Darian said. "I like applause."

"This'll get 'em for you," Toby assured quite truthfully. "And after this first job?"

"After the first one we'll talk," Darian said.

"Fair enough."

"When is this going to happen?" Darian asked.

"The day before Thanksgiving."

Darian nodded. "I like it. And the details? Like the money?"

"Both on Friday," Toby answered. "How do I reach you to set up a place and time?"

Darian hesitated just a moment, feeling Mustafa shift behind him. "Cannon's Liquor on South Vermont. Call there and tell them you're leaving a message for Brother D. Leave a number and I'll call you back."

Smart and safe, though it would mean waiting by a phone booth for a callback from the African. "Okay."

"Okay," Darian said. "I think we'll be heading out now. Chains and cages get my blood pressure up. You can understand."

"Oh, sure," Toby answered the barb patronizingly. "But I kinda like watching the little monkeys, you know. Entertaining little fellas. Don't you think?"

"Later," Darian said with a smile, moving away from the exhibit and back toward the third member of their group.

"A couple thousand?" Mustafa said with disbelief. "Are they talking about some fucking bomb or something?"

"Dead is dead," Darian said, Roger joining the group as they passed the popcorn vendor. "It doesn't matter how whitey ends up that way."

"He said most would be white," Mustafa reminded his leader. "I don't like killing brothers."

"Some things are necessary," Darian said.

"What about the money?" Roger asked. "Did you ask about the money?"

"Friday, Brother Roger," Darian answered. "We discuss details then."

"A couple fucking thousand," Mustafa repeated, both enamored with and doubtful of the idea. "If this is for real, and we step up to this, we're going to have to drop out of sight."

"Some things are necessary," Darian repeated. He would do just about anything to see thousands of dead white bodies piled high, and even more to have such an accomplishment associated with the NALF.

"Underground, man," Roger said. "There's only three of us."

Darian understood Brother Roger's concern. They had all studied various underground movements, the most successful of which had divided themselves into several self-contained "cells" of at least four people each. It was the concept of backwatching to prevent backstabbing. Two people together at all times. A minimum of two teams of two, each person responsible for working with and watching over his comrade. With such an arrangement suspicion became an ally. Your brother had to be your brother or he would end up dead.

"What about that Griggs kid?" Darian wondered and suggested simultaneously. "Did you check him out?"

"He's for real," Mustafa reported. "His sister was one of the kids killed at Saint Anthony's."

"No shit?"

"Not a whiff of it, Brother Darian," Mustafa assured him.

"Well, Brother Moises might just be willing enough to join us for this ride," Darian said.

"He's pretty damn raw for what those folks are suggesting," Mustafa observed.

"Have you ever killed a thousand white folks?" Darian asked.

"In my dreams," Mustafa answered proudly.

"I thought not," Darian commented. None of them had, but all were willing to. Griggs, too, he believed. Something in the boy's eyes and on his face convinced him of that. The same thing Darian saw each and every morning in the mirror. "I have a good feeling about him. And about this."

"Power, Brother Darian," Mustafa said.

"Power," Roger added.

"John, Mr. Mankowitz is here," Louise Barrish told her husband as she poked her head into the bedroom.

The head of the Barrish family was resting on the bed, his head propped high against pillows and the book he had just purchased open before him. He looked over the book to his wife. "What?"

"He's here," she repeated. "In the living room, and he has some people with him."

What was he doing here? John closed the book and placed it facedown on the nightstand. "Who's with him?"

Louise looked sheepishly at the ground, then back to her husband. "A man and a woman."

There was more to it than that. John could sense it in his wife's hesitation. "What are they?"

"John . . ."

"What are they?" he asked again with gritted teeth.

"An African and a Mexican," Louise answered. "I think the woman is a Mexican."

Damn you, Mankowitz! "All right," John said with obvious irritation. "Get in the kitchen and stay there."

Louise walked from the bedroom down the hall, passing the visitors without a look as she went into the kitchen and kept herself out of view. John was a few seconds behind her.

"John," Seymour Mankowitz said, beckoning his client over.

Barrish went past the arched entryway to the living room, eyeing the visitors as he joined his lawyer nearer the front door. "What is this?"

"John, just listen to me and play this smart," Mankowitz said. "They're FBI agents—"

"FBI!?" Barrish whisper-yelled. "Are you out of your mind?"

"Listen," Mankowitz insisted. "Just listen. You just dodged a bullet with one federal case. More suspicion is not what you need right now."

"They can't screw with me about that anymore, Seymour," Barrish said. "I know my rights."

"And I conveyed those rights clearly to them. There will be no discussion of the Saint Anthony's shooting. Zero. But if you refuse to talk to them about this you can expect further scrutiny, more investigation, more visits, more phone taps." Mankowitz, despite his distaste for all that John Barrish was, held a two-hundred-plus-year-old piece of paper higher than any motivation alive in his irrational self. There was right, there was wrong. Then there was the Constitution. "You don't want that, I don't want that. So . . . you listen to their questions, and, if you can, you answer them. I'll stop any improper inquiries. Understood?"

You idiot. You worthless, legal eagle idiot. "Fine." Barrish turned and walked straight into the living room where the agents stood from the place they had staked out on the couch. He took a seat in a well-worn recliner that faced the entire room from the corner, his lawyer standing a few feet away beneath the arched opening to the front hallway. "Sit down. Please."

"Mr. Barrish, I'm Special Agent Jefferson and this is Special Agent Aguirre. We're from the Los Angeles FBI office.'' Art removed his notebook. ''We want to ask you a couple questions about someone named Frederick Allen. Do you know him?''

''I know of him,'' Barrish answered, betraying no emotion outwardly.

''How?''

Barrish shifted his gaze between the two federal pigs. The man, an African, looked to be of pure stock. No long-ago mixing of his female ancestors with the master apparent. The woman, though, was obviously the product of racial melding. The Spanish conquistadors' taking of native Central American Indians so long before was the start of her bastardized bloodline. Probably an Aryan influence somewhere along the many generations, too, he guessed. Her figure, trim and attractive, was not reminiscent of the stockier Indian ancestry that probably provided the female half of her lineage. One mongrel. One purebred. Both equally worthless, and both equally dangerous to him at the moment. His lawyer, having obviously shown the pigs to his home—and without warning—was at least right that he should just answer the questions and be done with them.

''From his actions,'' John answered. ''He killed one of your *brother* federal officers, didn't he?''

''Yes,'' Art confirmed, recognizing the tonal shift as Barrish spoke the word *brother*. ''Is there anywhere else you know him from?''

''The papers. He died in that chemical thing not too far away.''

''Twenty miles,'' Frankie said.

''Fairly close,'' Art commented. ''He was of a like mind to you in certain respects. Isn't that so?''

Barrish sniffed a laugh. ''The uneducated as to my beliefs might say that.''

''So you differed with Mr. Allen?'' Art asked, hoping to lead Barrish into at least hinting of additional knowledge of Allen.

But the AVO leader was going to have no part of that, and chose his words carefully. "Not with Allen in particular. As I said—I did not know the man. But I understand some of his views from his past and from the news that he was part of the Aryan Brotherhood. Now, just because they and my organization share a word in our names, well, that does not mean we share a mirror-image philosophy."

"But similar?" Art pressed.

"Look, I believe in separation of the races," Barrish explained. "You people always call me a 'white supremacist.' I'm a white *separatist*. I believe that Aryans, or white people of sufficiently pure blood, should have America as a homeland. I believe that you and your fellow Africans should be repatriated to the continent my ancestors so foolishly stole you from. I believe your assistant here—"

"Partner, Mr. Barrish," Frankie interjected. "I'm his partner."

"Partner." *Whatever you want to call yourself, half-breed.* "Your partner here should go back south of the border to the place where her kind abounds. It is all very simple. Now, the Aryan Brotherhood espouses the views of separation by destruction, meaning they want to separate anyone who is not Aryan from the group of the living. Some other similar groups have the same basic philosophy. But those groups, like the Aryan Brotherhood, all advocate violence as a means to achieve their end. I simply believe that the end is a foregone conclusion, and it is up to organizations such as mine, and individuals like me, to prepare my race for their destiny."

"I see," Art said.

"No you don't," Barrish countered. "But you will."

He was cool, not cocky, Art thought. He spoke his words of hate as if he knew them to be the truth. He believed he was right. What more was needed to make this man dangerous?

"Did you know of Allen before your arrest?" Frankie asked.

"Excuse me," Mankowitz interrupted. "That time period is—"

"Hold it, Seymour," John said. "I don't mind. The answer is no. Only after his actions hit the papers."

"What about Twelve-Twelve Riverside?" Art asked, following Barrish's previous answer quickly. "Have you ever been there?"

"No, but I've spent a great deal of time around Temple and Main for the last year," Barrish said, referring to the Metropolitan Detention Center in which he had been held preceding and during his abbreviated trial.

"Monte Royce?" Art said, tossing the name out.

"Who?"

"Nick King or Nikolai Kostin?"

Barrish shook his head at the African's questions. "Sorry."

"I'm sure you are," Art observed.

Barrish caught sight of the Mexican agent looking around the room. "Not what you expected?"

"Excuse me," Frankie said.

"My home," Barrish clarified. "The walls. You expected swastikas and pictures of Hitler to be my choice in decor. Me wearing a pointy white hood, spouting off about 'Nigger this, nigger that.' " He shook his head, maintaining eye contact with the agent. "You just don't get it. I'm Joe American, Miss FBI Agent. I'm your next-door neighbor." I'm your worst nightmare, John added silently, knowing what the bounds of his soliloquy had to be. "And the government you work for doesn't get it either."

"Well, Mr. Barrish, we do our best," Art said, "and *my* government does its best."

"Best." John snickered. "*Of the people, by the peo-*

ple . . . You know, the people might just decide to scrap the whole thing and start over someday. A clean slate. And make it right this time.''

''And who'll know what 'right' is supposed to be?'' Art asked needlessly. ''Let me guess.''

John simply smiled. ''Someone will know.''

''Agent Jefferson, this is going nowhere,'' Mankowitz said. ''My client obviously can't help you with this.''

Or won't. ''Well, it looks like we've wasted your time, Mr. Barrish,'' Art said, standing. ''And ours.''

''I'm sure you'll find more time to *question* me again,'' Barrish said, his meaning clearly *harass*. He remained seated as both agents moved toward the door. The African stopped short of being out of sight.

''Enjoy your freedom, Mr. Barrish,'' Art said, smiling at the man, and adding a wink that only they were aware of. It was returned with a smirk by the leader of the AVO. ''Good day.''

''We'll drop you back at your car,'' Frankie told Mankowitz as she and Art headed out the front door.

''I'll be right out,'' the lawyer said, going back to his client after the door had closed. ''John, that little speech at the end could have backfired. When are you going—''

''Get out,'' Barrish interrupted, looking up, whatever ingenuous smile there might have been on his face now gone. ''Get out of my house.''

''John . . .''

''Get out,'' Barrish said, each syllable defined by rage. A rage in the words, and in the eyes.

Mankowitz said no more. His client had always been volatile. Very challenging. But never before had he felt fear when in the man's presence. He did now.

Art saw the lawyer emerge visibly disturbed. ''Nice guy.'' Mankowitz didn't respond, instead climbing silently into the back of the car for the ride back to the city. Frankie swung the Bureau Chevy around and headed down the narrow dirt driveway, pulling far to the right as a blue minivan came at her. As they passed she noted the faces of the two male occupants, both young, their eyes wide as they peered into the front of the car heading off the property.

"He's got sons, doesn't he?" Art asked, looking to the backseat.

"Two," Mankowitz answered.

"Another generation of hate," Frankie commented. She turned the car onto the paved highway and headed east toward the freeway, putting some much-desired distance between them and the likes of John Barrish.

Toby stopped the minivan fast, sending a cloud of dust billowing forward of the vehicle. He and Stanley jumped out and bolted into the house.

"Pop?" Toby shouted before seeing his father quietly sitting in the living room. Stanley, out of breath like his brother, was right behind.

"Dad, those were feds," Stanley said, clued in by the *G* license plate.

"FBI," John said.

"Pop, I thought they took you," Toby said with a mix of worry and relief. "They had someone in the back, but I couldn't tell who."

"We thought it was you," Stanley said.

"It was that stupid Jew lawyer of mine."

"Mankowitz? What the hell was he doing here?" Toby walked over and practically fell into the couch.

"He brought the pigs. They were asking about Freddy," John said, a clenched fist rhythmically pounding the arm of the recliner. "And about the place on Riverside."

"Oh, shit!" Toby swore.

"Dad, they know," Stanley said.

"They can't know," Toby objected. "There's no way."

"Well, they know something," John pointed out. "They were also asking about Royce."

"He talked!" Stanley said.

"He didn't talk," John disagreed.

"But the papers said the feds talked to him."

"Stan," Toby said, glaring. "If Pop says he didn't talk then he didn't! Okay?!"

"But someone did!"

"Both of you! Shut up!" John sprang from the chair and began a stalklike pacing in the confines of the front room. "I don't know what they know or how they know it, but this is not good."

"Let's call it off," Stanley suggested.

"No," John responded, giving that possibility a short life. "We're not stopping." He froze at the far end of the room, looking away from his sons. "But we're going to have to take some precautions."

"Like what?" Toby asked.

"Toby, you make arrangements for a safe place for all of us to stay," John directed. "Once this thing starts we're going to have to disappear. I thought we'd just be able to ride it out, but with this . . . You know where the best place will be."

"I know, Pop," Toby acknowledged.

John continued staring at the wall and its horribly dingy wallpaper pattern. The afternoon light could do little to brighten this room with such drab decor. It would be good to get out of there in short measure. "How did the meeting go?"

"Perfect," Toby answered, pleased to be able to give his father some good news. "Friday we finalize the details and give them the stuff."

"They asked about the money, didn't they?" John inquired.

"Yeah." Toby looked to his brother.

So much for pure ideology, John thought. But their reasons were their reasons. As long as the end was the same, he didn't care about the motivation of those just along for the ride. "So they're in."

"Yeah," Toby confirmed.

John turned around, considering for a moment what transpired before his sons' return. "Friday, when you meet with them, you tell them there's another part to the job."

"Okay," Toby said, waiting for an explanation. But the wait stretched on, and all his father did was smile. "Pop?"

"I want to leave here with no strings," John said. "Do you think they'll mind?"

It was Toby's turn to smile. "If we dangle some cash in front of them and say 'kill that whitey' . . . Pop, these guys are ours. We can do what we want with them."

John looked to his youngest boy, offering him a chance to speak.

"Toby's right, Dad."

"Good," John Barrish said, thinking of the "strings" to be severed. Some things just had to be done, especially to advance the cause. What was the saying? *By any means necessary.* How ironically appropriate, John thought, considering the source . . . and the cause.

EIGHT

Transition

Darren Griggs took the tissue offered by Anne Preston and wiped his eyes, then let his head fall back against the liberally cushioned chair.

"Those tears were different from the ones you cried the night we met," Anne observed. She sat a few feet from her patient, in an identical chair. Almost sixty minutes had passed since the grieving husband and father had come into the safety of her office. A few minutes at the beginning were spent in small talk, he admiring the view through the large window behind her desk, and she showing off pictures of her daughter. That had been a good lead-in to the session, she opening with how proud she was of her daughter, Darren beginning to tell what it was like to have lost his.

But somewhere in the conversation she began to realize that this man, though in great pain, had begun the process of healing himself. How she did not know, and it really did not matter. Constructive healing, from whatever source, was welcome whether elicited or delivered.

"Do you know what my wife did yesterday, Dr. Preston?"

"What?" Anne asked, watching the man stare at the ceiling, his head back as tears of relief rolled slowly down his cheeks. These he did not bother to wipe away.

"She got up and made Sunday breakfast," Darren

revealed, as though proclaiming a momentous event. "The last time she did that was more than a year ago, the morning Tanya was killed."

"Do you think the fight you and Moises had the night before had anything to do with that?"

Darren looked to Anne and nodded, biting his lower lip. "I think so."

"Why do you think that affected her?" The best therapists have no answers . . . only questions. That bit of sage advice from an old professor had etched in Anne's consciousness by sheer repetition, and later by recognition of its value.

Darren sniffled and dried his cheeks. "I think when she saw Moises and I . . . going at each other, I think she felt she was losing the rest of her family. I think maybe her mind told her that one child lost was enough. I don't know what to call it. The survival instinct. Protectiveness."

He had the gist of it, so a slight bending of her rule was in order. "It's called mothering."

"You're right."

"I know I am," Anne said with a smile. "I'm one of them."

"I tell you, Doctor, I thought I had already lost her, and here she comes and saves me from . . . ." Darren looked away.

"Would you really have hurt your son?"

"I wanted to."

"I asked if you would have."

Darren looked through the big window to the grayish glass of the skyscraper across the street. "No. I would have hit him again, but then I would have wrapped my arms around him so tight."

"I think he would have run whatever you did, Darren."

"I know he would have. He's just so far from me, Doctor. I mean, we could be nose to nose and I still can't understand the boy. I don't know what to do for him anymore.''

"Do you think he might agree to come with you some day?''

Darren looked at the intricate rug pattern at his feet, his head shaking.

"I want you to try.''

"I haven't even seen him in two days, Doctor.''

"You don't know where he's been?''

"I have no idea,'' Darren said. "I wish he'd just come home for his mother's sake.''

Anne could do nothing to bring young Moises Griggs home. Though his father talked of him as if he were a child, as any parent would, Moises was a young man, of legal age and wanting to make his own decisions. She sincerely hoped that he was making the right ones.

"I want to meet Felicia,'' Anne said, moving the session away from what she called an impassable minefield.

Darren smiled, something he had done infrequently of late when thinking of his wife. It was a good feeling. A very good feeling. "Not just yet, doctor. She's not ready to come here.''

"That's all right. But let her know that I'm looking forward to meeting her.''

"I will.''

Anne gave her watch a glance. They were a few minutes over the hour session length she liked to stick to. She reached to her desk and brought her personal schedule book over and scanned the following week. Abbreviated by the Thanksgiving holiday, her appointments were back to back. Flipping back a page she found a slot. "Things are really hairy next week, so is this Friday good for you?''

"Anytime. Sure.''

"Okay, four o'clock.'' Anne penciled the appointment in. Later she would transfer it to her secretary's book.

Darren found it difficult to get up. Part of this arrangement was still bothering him. "I really wish I could pay you, Dr. Preston."

Anne closed her book one-handed with a slap. "Darren, you need to concentrate on you, and on your family. And we already agreed on my fee."

"I know, but you making my family dinner hardly seems like a fair exchange. You're doing all the giving."

Anne smiled. " 'Tis the season of giving."

Darren laughed softly. "Thank you, Doctor."

Anne stood and walked her patient all the way through the outer office of her secretary, waiting until he was on the elevator to turn away. "Lena, put Mr. Griggs down for this Friday at four."

"Okay. Twice in four days?"

"Next week is out," Anne said, looking over her secretary's shoulder to the following day's schedule. "Wow."

"And don't forget you've got a class tomorrow night," she reminded her boss.

"It's going to be a long one, isn't it?" Long, satisfying, tiring, and of her own doing, Anne knew, though now she was beginning to wonder if taking on two classes to teach was too much, especially with the full schedule of patients she maintained. But UCLA paid generously, and she really loved teaching. Adored it, actually. Still, time was so short, something she had begun to recognize since Art Jefferson came into her life. Though the pangs of schoolgirl crushes were well in her past, she found herself noticing when he was *not* with her. That did wonders for her concentration during those increasingly frequent occurrences. Love wasn't a bitch, she thought. It was an eye opener.

"Anne?"

"Huh?" She smiled, popping out of her silent contemplation. "I was just thinking that I might want to ease up next quarter."

Her secretary recognized the expression. "Can't get enough of him, can you?"

"No," Anne answered. "But that's nice in a way."

"Yeah, it is."

Moises Griggs walked slowly along Vermont Avenue, hands shoved deep in the pockets of his jeans and his head swiveling streetward as each set of headlights passed. This was the part of town he had never hung out in. The part of town where wearing the wrong color could get you shot. Or having the wrong look on your face. It was not a pleasant place to be, but it was the place he had to be.

He slowed near the NALF storefront, the faded neon sign of the adjacent liquor store catching his attention. His fingers fumbled through the change in his pocket. Less than a buck left. The motel room, cheap as it was, had used nearly all his money for the four nights he'd been gone from his home. Food had eaten up the rest. Now, with only a few coins left to his name, Moises was craving a Coke. Just a Coke. Something that simple, that small, and it was denied him. He sniffled against the chilly wind as he wondered if this was what his life was going to be. Want. Anger. Hate. Frustration.

The storefront to his left drew his attention back. Not with them, he thought. In there was hope. Direction. A place to be, a way to fight. A car of young men, black like him, slowed as it passed, the front passenger giving him a "mad dog" stare before driving on. "Idiots," Moises said softly. *You're killing your own people.* There were better targets for one's rage, he now realized. And the way to them was but a few steps away, a few steps that Moises took willingly.

"Brother Moises," Roger Sanders said upon turning toward the jingling bells attached to the front door. "Welcome back."

"Hi." Moises immediately noticed that it wasn't much warmer inside than out.

Darian heard the voices from the back room and came to the front. "Brother Moises. You're back. Good. Good."

Moises nodded nervously. "Brother Darian."

The NALF leader held his hand out at chest height and gave a power shake to the young man. "We know about you, Brother Moises."

The grip tightened around his hand, Moises felt clearly. "*About* me?"

"Your little sister," Roger said, stepping next to Darian. "We know what happened."

Moises looked to the floor, but a hand roughly lifted his chin up. Darian had released his grip on the youngster's hand and was now preventing his head from dipping.

"You keep your head high, Brother Moises," Darian told him. "Always high. Always proud. You don't bow because of nothing. Not because you're sad. Not because you're in chains. Because folks don't know the difference, and no one is ever going to think you're bowing to them." He pulled his hand away and tapped the boy's cheek lightly. "You understand?"

"Yeah."

Darian nodded. "Good. Now, you said you wanted to fight the last time you were here."

"That's right."

"Right," Darian said, noticing the rougher appearance of the youth. He was unshaven by a couple of days. The clothes were not clean, though they weren't soiled. He was different. "Are you ready to stand up for your people?"

"Yeah," Moises said, his trepidation of a few moments before gone completely now. *Yeah, I'll stand up. I'll stand on some cracker's head if you want me to.* "I'm ready."

"Are you afraid of dying?" Darian inquired.

Dying? I'm halfway there already. "No."

"What about other folks dying?"

Moises shook his head slowly. "I won't cry as long as they're the right color."

A smile now came with Darian's nod. "You've got a family, right?"

"I had one."

"You've got a new one," Roger said, putting a hand on the boy's shoulder.

"And this family is going to do something big real soon," Darian said. "Then we're gonna split. You got any problem with taking off?"

"I've got nothing to keep me here," Moises answered. *Just a mother and father who might as well be dead.* He hurt as he thought that.

"All right, Brother Moises." Darian looked into the boy's eyes. *Yes, the eyes.* He was right the first time he had seen them. *You're a fighter.* And soon, he knew, Brother Moises Griggs would be a killer. "Be here Monday night, ready to go."

"I'll be here," Moises said, sensing that the life he had known was over, and another was about to begin.

"His finances check out clean," Hal Lightman reported.

Art scanned the summary sheet that covered a stack of bank and business records relating to Monte Royce and his company. "Of course they do. Why should anything even remotely related to this make any sense? Nothing happened. Nothing at all. Everyone's innocent."

"What about Kostin?" Frankie asked, moving beyond her partner's frustration. "The cashier's checks?"

"The bank that issued them says he came in with cash and had the checks made out."

"Just for the rent?" she probed.

"Rent and for those chemicals and the equipment," Lightman answered.

"Nikolai Kostin was not born with that money," Art observed with some agitation. Things were moving much too slowly, even for the new and improved Art Jefferson. "He did not come here with that money. And he sure as hell didn't make all of it in his time at Royce Pharmaceuticals."

"We're trying, Art," Lightman said.

The senior agent leaned back in his chair and let out a purposeful breath. "I know."

Frankie looked up to the bearer of bad news, hoping to lighten the moment. "Don't mind him, Hal. He's still trying to decide if he likes cold weather."

"Freezing weather," Art corrected her.

"It don't get cold in Chicago," Lightman joked, his voice lowering to a whisper. "*It gets fucking cold.*"

"Thanks for the weather report, Hal," Art said.

"I'll see you kids tomorrow," Lightman said, leaving the agents to pore over the information some more.

Art looked down upon the pages, his head shaking. "Mr. Clean, huh?"

"We missed a smudge or something. I can feel it, Art." Frankie rarely called her partner by name, and then only when she was dead serious and certain of something. "He's dirty."

"I know he is." It was easy to spot someone soiled by their own actions, Art knew, and it was often a chore to keep from getting dirtied by that person. The last thought reminded him of one avenue they hadn't taken yet. "Vorhees was mixed up with Royce, even if innocently."

Innocent. Frankie rarely used that word when referring to politicians of Vorhees's type. The consummate player. Mr. Backroom Dealer who would still get in your face if it was required. Guiltless, maybe. Innocent . . . Her head shook. "We need to talk to him."

"Senator Crippen, too," Art said. "Royce said he knows them both well. Let's see how well."

"It could shed some light," Frankie agreed.

Art stood, his mind made up. It could shed some light, as Frankie said, but it would also certainly ruffle some feathers. The director was sure to get some calls about this one. "Pack a bag, partner."

"D.C." Frankie scowled. "Wonderful."

NINE
Connections

The town of Sandberg, located at the northern end of the Old Ridge Route, had seen better days. Really, it was now only a gathering of crumbling walls and amputated chimneys that had once marked a bustling way-station along the former south–north route over the mountains from Los Angeles to the agriculturally rich San Joaquin Valley. But the two-lane, winding road had been made virtually obsolete by the completion of the Grapevine portion of the Golden State Freeway many years before. Unmaintained now, the ribbon of rough asphalt was frequented only by off-roaders and the adventurous, and the town of Sandberg, nestled among a grove of oaks at the base of an antennae-topped peak, was similarly deserted. Except for this morning.

"You see them?" Stanley asked, his head almost jerking left and right in search of the Africans.

"No." Toby slowed the Aerostar past a line of buildings marked only by ankle-high bricks that outlined what remained of their foundations. "They've gotta be up the road."

"Toby, I don't like this. What if they're cops?"

Toby gave his brother a brief, disdainful look. "Do you think I'm an idiot?"

"I just—"

"Stan, Freddy's friends checked these guys out, all

right? *Brother D* is some guy named Darian Brown. You know that. I told you. That nigger's done time, enough that Freddy's Brotherhood friends knew of him. One of the other guys was a basketball player before he did time. Do those sound like cops to you?''

Stanley looked back out the windshield, avoiding the challenge. ''There they are.''

Off by the side of a muddy dirt track that circled behind a group of fallen structures a faded green Buick Electra 225 sat. Resting against its hood were the same three who had met them at the zoo.

''No rear guard this time,'' Toby observed. ''I guess *they* trust us.'' But if not, the .38 in his waistband would help settle matters.

The Aerostar turned off the ''main'' road through Sandberg, nosing right up to the big Buick. Toby took the duffel from between the seats and stepped out with his brother.

''You picked a cold enough place for this little get-together,'' Roger, his hands tucked beneath opposite arms, commented to the white boys.

''Wait'll it starts to snow later,'' Toby responded, adding a snicker.

Darian stood straight from his leaning place against the car. ''First, the money.''

Toby nodded. His father really was right about these guys. They could be bought cold. ''Stan.''

''Here.'' The younger Barrish boy handed over a soft, simulated-leather briefcase, an inexpensive model he'd picked up at Wal-Mart.

Mustafa, the only one of the men wearing dark glasses, took the case and laid it on the warm hood of the Buick, popping the twin latches. What stared up at him from the case's interior made him smile.

''A hundred grand,'' Toby said. ''It's all there.''

''It's cool,'' Mustafa said from behind Darian.

''Well, then, I guess we can talk business.'' Darian

looked down at the bag in the head white boy's hand.

Toby lifted and unzipped the duffel, removing the cylinder with one hand. "Here it is."

Darian frowned at the small object, so small that the boy's hand covered almost half its length. "What the hell is that?"

"That's no bomb," Roger said, scowling.

"A bomb?" Toby reacted, laughing. "You're right. It's no bomb." He told them what it was, taking a few minutes to cover the operation of the timing and release controls. When he was done the Africans were silent. Maybe too silent. "Is there a problem?"

Darian looked briefly back to Mustafa. "You were in the Army."

"That's what'll happen," Mustafa confirmed, remembering the training he'd received on gas attacks.

"And what do we do with it?" Darian inquired.

This took longer to explain, with Stanley producing a map and several sheets of blueprints from inside the Aerostar. "You'll have one hour from the time you activate the timer," Toby said. "You've got to be clear by then."

Darian leaned over the plans, as did his two comrades. His finger traced a path from the elevator to their target. "We just show up with a camera and tell the engineer we're there to take pictures?"

"For Mr. Stearns," Stanley said. "It's all arranged."

"But there's one other job we need done that day," Toby said. He removed a three-by-five card from his pocket, along with a folded newspaper clipping. He unfolded the latter to reveal an unflattering AP photo of the man. Really, he thought, there were no flattering shots of him.

"Who is he?" Darian asked.

"A problem," Toby answered. There was no need to share any more information than that. "Eight A.M. Here's the address."

Darian looked at the card. It was in the north valley, far from the downtown area they'd need to be in at the same time. Doing both would be impossible. *Unless* . . . Yes. It would be the perfect way to break in the Griggs kid. Roger and Mustafa could handle the big job. Yes. The first use of the cell, and the teams within that had just been established. "And I'm sure you'll compensate us fairly for this little extra."

"Fifty grand more when we meet up for the next job," Toby said.

"Which is?"

Toby smiled. "Let's just say we're going to reshape the government."

Darian's chin came up as he looked down upon the shorter white boy. His right eye was whacked out, the NALF leader saw, vibrating as the cracker grinned. "You have big ideas."

"Why go small?" Toby wondered rhetorically. "It's the government that's the problem, remember?"

"When and where?" Darian asked.

"Not so fast," Toby said. "We have to do this right. People are going to be looking after the first job is done." It took them ten minutes to decide upon a plan of action that was acceptable to both. "Once we get together again we'll go over the next job."

"Our price goes up for that one," Darian said.

"Up how much?"

Why not shoot for the sky? Darian thought. "One million."

The amount drew looks even from the African's comrades. But there was no reason not to agree to it, Toby thought. No reason at all. "A hundred up front, plus the fifty for this little extra, and the rest once the job is done."

Darian considered the payment split briefly. If these guys had that much money to throw around, he didn't want to piss them off by dickering over up-front money.

Plus, a hundred grand, what they were getting for the entire first job, was nothing to look cross at. Yes, he could do business with these white boys. Lots of business. "I guess we'll see you when we get there."

"I guess so," Toby said, giving possession of the cylinder to the African. "Enjoy."

"Oh, we will," Darian assured him. *A couple thousand dead white folks. Enjoy* wasn't the word. *Savor* was.

"The fucking bastard!" Art said, storming down the steps of the Rayburn Building to Independence Avenue. He halted at street level and turned, waiting for his partner to catch up. "I can't believe he did this."

Frankie folded the six-page typed statement provided by Vorhees's office in half, then half again before tucking it away in her blazer.

"He let us fly out here and he knew he wasn't going to be here!"

"His office says the trip was unexpected," Frankie reminded her worked-up partner.

"Unexpected my ass," Art shot back. "I should chase his butt up to Boston and nail him on his home turf."

"That wouldn't do any good, partner. Neither is this."

It wasn't what Art wanted to hear, which, considering that it came from a person he trusted his life with, probably meant he needed to hear it. That bit of self-realization allowed him to switch from a boil to a simmer. "I hate this political bullshit. You know that."

"I do, too."

Art looked around, oblivious to the glances he and his partner were rating from pedestrians as they passed. The Capitol was directly across Independence, and a turn of his head to the left set his eyes upon the alabaster obelisk a mile away. The Washington Monument. A tribute to the man who could not tell a lie. Well, that virtue had obviously gotten lost in the D.C. shuffle, especially where the Honorable Richard Vorhees was concerned.

"Do you think he's trying to hide something?" Frankie asked, the afternoon traffic sweeping by to her rear.

"Hide?" Art looked slightly away. "Avoid, partner. He's putting us off, leaving that statement for us. Generous, isn't he? Yet he couldn't have one of his flunkies give us a call. It's a game of importance. He's important in this town, we're not, therefore the rules of courtesy and forthrightness don't apply to him like they would to anyone else. Like they would to us."

"At least Crippen was cooperative," Frankie said.

"Royce should have used him instead of Limp Dick," Art commented.

"It would have made more sense," Frankie said. "Crippen's the one on the Senate Foreign Relations Committee. That's closer to what Royce needed done than House Armed Services."

"Senator Crippen is a lifer, partner," Art observed. "He knows when *not* to get involved in something."

"The funny thing about Vorhees is," Frankie began, "his statement answers just about all the questions we had for him."

"Of course it does. It's probably the God's honest truth, too. Vorhees is smart, partner. He's not going to let us say he was being evasive. Plus, what was he doing here? Doing a favor—questionable, maybe—for a contributor?"

"Don't forget keeping the country safe," Frankie added.

"*Right*," Art agreed sarcastically. He blew out a long breath. "Back to work, partner." That simple statement had a five-hour commute attached to it, he knew. The good thing was that they'd be out of this town.

"Amazing," Frankie said, looking across Independence to the Capitol. "I've been here before, seen that before, but it looks bigger every time.''

"Remember the egos it has to hold,'' Art commented, recognizing the mean streak rearing its head once again. Something had to be done about that.

"You're getting as cynical as me,'' Frankie observed with a devious grin. "I'd better get you back to Anne for some attitude adjustment.''

Art lowered his head, smiling broadly. "My plans exactly.''

"How'm I doing?'' Darren Griggs asked, no tears at all having come this session.

"Darren, I'm not the one to judge that,'' Anne answered. It was never the response a patient wanted. Things would have been easier, they invariably believed, if the doctor could just listen to them, bless them as well, and send them on their way. But it didn't work like that.

"Yeah. I know.'' Darren smiled meekly, mildly ashamed of himself for the attempt at praise seeking. "I am feeling better.''

"Good. That's what counts.''

"Felicia is doing better, too,'' Darren said proudly.

"Have you convinced her to come with you?''

"Well, actually, we were talking about that last night. I don't think she's ready to, you know, come out yet.''

"I'm sorry to hear that.''

"But, Felicia thought it would be good to have you over for dinner.''

"I'm supposed to be making dinner for you,'' Anne reminded him with a chuckle.

"I know, but it would be good for her. And . . .''

Anne knew what Darren wanted to say. "Moises.''

"I'm hoping he'll come home soon. It would be good for him to see you, too.''

"Maybe,'' Anne said. "But if he's being as rebellious as you say, he may be doing more you don't know about.''

"I've thought the same thing. I'm worried. He's a good boy, Dr. Preston, but he's hurt by this."

"I understand that. But he may need a dose of authority other than yours to prevent him from getting involved in behavior that's self-destructive. I'm not an authority figure, Darren. But I know someone who is."

The man in her life, Darren recalled. An FBI agent. "He's welcome to come."

"Good. When?"

"Is Monday all right?"

"For me, sure. I'll have to check with Art," she added. "But, I have a way with him."

Darren knew what she meant, having been on the receiving end of a woman's persuasive abilities for twenty years. "We'll see you both Monday."

TEN

Comings and Goings

"You remember him, then?" Hal Lightman said hopefully as the bank teller nodded at the picture of Nikolai Kostin.

"Yes, vaguely." The young lady, her manager standing next to her for support, looked away from the enlarged driver's license photo. "I can't remember much else about him."

"The register shows that you handled the last cashier's check that this gentleman came in for," Omar Espinosa said, trying to jog her memory. "A little more than three weeks ago. Try and think."

"It was in the morning, Sherry," the manager said, putting a reassuring hand on her teller's shoulder.

The teller's head began to shake slowly as she looked apologetically to the agents. "I'm sorry. All I can remember is the face."

"Anything about the money?" Lightman asked. "He brought in twelve hundred in cash. Did he say anything about where he got it? A job, maybe? Anything?"

"I'm sorry," she responded.

Lightman let out a breath. "That's all right. You did your best."

"We may need to talk to some of your people at a later time," Espinosa told the bank manager.

"Anytime."

The two agents left the Palmdale branch of Suncoast Security Bank, stopping just outside the glass front of the financial institution.

"It was a long shot anyway," Espinosa said. "What's she going to remember after three weeks? She sees hundreds of people a day."

"I know," Lightman agreed, leaning on the side of the Chevy and scanning the area around the bank. It was a typical strip mall, probably built in the early eighties by the looks of it. Earlier than the big building boom. That was apparent from the absence of any southwestern styling and earth tone stucco on the facade. Just a grouping of stores stretching from both sides of the bank, all the way to the side streets.

Espinosa, too, was surveying the area, which was suffering a mild case of blight. Things weren't very new compared to other areas of the high desert city. "Why did Kostin come all the way over here to get his checks? There are closer banks to his place."

"I was thinking the same thing," Lightman answered, the *why* hitting him with more force as he considered it again. "Maybe he came to this bank as an afterthought."

Espinosa saw his fellow agent looking to the row of stores more closely now. "He may have been coming here for something else."

"Right," Lightman said. "This bank may have just been in a convenient place."

"Let's check it out. You start at that end," Espinosa suggested, pointing to the east end of the strip mall. "I'll take this side."

Hal Lightman studied the numerous storefronts as he walked toward his end of the strip mall. A dentist. A doughnut shop. A sandwich place. Some offices. It was quite a hodgepodge, he thought. Of course there were also the all-too-common FOR LEASE signs, the product of so many strikes that the Golden State had against it.

Defense cutbacks. Earthquakes. It had all hit California. Except for locusts, Lightman thought, hoping he hadn't somehow suggested the plague to some higher power with his errant musing. Enough of the negative, he told himself as he entered a pool supply company at the end of the row.

Strike one, he knew, leaving the business after just a few minutes. No one had recognized the picture of Kostin. The same result from the next two businesses, a dentist's office and a doughnut shop. The next in line was a small office, obviously closed for the day. Lightman moved on, the smell of something wonderful hitting his nose before entering the restaurant.

"Good morning," a pleasant-looking older man said, greeting the agent. "We are serving lunch. Just one?"

"No, thank you." Lightman showed the somewhat startled restaurateur his shield. "We're checking with merchants in the area. Have you ever seen this man?"

The restaurateur bent forward, bringing his eyes close to the picture. His head came back up, nodding, a concerned look on his face. "Yes. Nick."

Yes! "He's been in here before?"

"Many times," the man answered, seeming surprised at the question. "His office is next door."

"His *office?*"

"Yes." The man gestured in the direction from which Lightman had come. "Is he in trouble?"

"Right next door?" Lightman asked, trying not to seem excited.

"Yes. But he has not been there in a while. Is he all right?"

"I'll be back, sir. We're going to need to get a statement from you." Lightman walked back the way he had come, stopping at the darkened office of Birch and Associates, or so the gold stencil on the glass front door said. He cupped both hands around his eyes and pressed close to the glass, examining the interior of the small office. There wasn't much to see. A desk, with no phone on it or anywhere in sight. A chair. *One* chair, actually. Some in/out boxes, all empty. Pictures on the wall, though they looked like they could have come with the place.

A front. It wasn't hard to come to that conclusion, and Lightman had already solidified the conjecture as he raced back to the Chevy, motioning to Espinosa. He had the cellular in hand, the desired speed-dial button already pressed, as his fellow agent came up. But the first words about the discovery were spoken to a very pleased senior agent quite a distance to the south.

"Seymour," John Barrish said, his time on hold longer than anytime he could recall. The relationship had changed, apparently. Was the Jew still his defender? It didn't really matter. He needed only one final thing from the legal zealot.

"John."

"I need to see you. It's important."

There was a pause, paper shuffling, the springs of an old chair creaking. "About what?"

There was no need altering the John Barrish Seymour Mankowitz had come to know. No need for sweet-talking. "Dammit, Seymour! You know I can't talk over the phone."

More hesitation. "All right. Let me check my—"

"No. I pick the time. This could be a problem, Seymour. A big one. And I'm not going to talk to any of your cohorts about this. You hear it first."

"All right. All right. When?"

"Wednesday morning. Eight o'clock, at your office."

A pencil scratched out the notation in an appointment book before the leather cover closed with a *slap*. "I'll be here." Mankowitz wanted to hang up, wanted to be done with John Barrish once and for all. He had already requested that he be removed from the case. Let some other eager young attorney have his turn with the man. But, this unexpected call did make him wonder . . . "John, are you in trouble?"

Perfect. Give the crusader a crusade and he'd be on board. It was going to be a short ride, though. "I can't tell you until Wednesday. Eight, okay?"

"I'll be here."

John Barrish hung up and smiled. "I won't," he said to the empty living room. "But someone will."

The door to Birch and Associates was already open when Art and Frankie arrived.

"Who issued the warrant?" Art asked.

"Guess who?" Lightman answered with his own knowing inquiry. "Judge Horner. He works at home Mondays, just up the road toward the mountains in Pearblossom. One of the marshals clued us in."

"Good work." Art walked into the remarkably small office. Frankie was already further in, probing the back of the small space.

"We've got two more confirmations on Kostin," Lightman reported. "Omar is getting their statements right now. A lady across the street at a tailor, and a mechanic from the Mobil station on the corner."

Art walked around the desk, which faced the glass walls at the building's front. "Did you check this out yet?"

"Bottom file drawer on the right," Lightman answered.

The drawer slid out with a screech. "Well, well, well."

"I did a quick count, with gloves on," Lightman said. "Twelve thousand dollars in fifties. Another five thousand in hundreds. They're bundled in groups."

"Make sure they stay that way," Art directed. Separate, distinct bundles could be tied to withdrawals or known amounts of cash. But then they had to know who and where it came from first. This might make that easier, especially if Royce or his company made any withdrawals or transfers that corresponded to the cash bundles.

"Nothing in back," Frankie said. "I wonder what 'Birch and Associates' means."

"It was the name of the business in here before Kostin moved in, according to the neighbors," Lightman explained. "Birch was an accountant."

Frankie noticed the drawer full of green. "I doubt he left that when he vacated."

"Hal, get the keys Kostin had at his place," Art said. "I think Jacobs has them. Do a match on this door. I want more than eyeball witnesses to place him here."

"Okay."

"You know," Frankie began, "Freddy had some keys on him when he bit it."

"That's right," Art said.

"A transfer point," Lightman suggested. "Someone brings the money here, then Kostin and Freddy could pick up whatever was needed."

Frankie looked around the unimpressive room. "This isn't a real secure place to use as a storage site for money."

"An acceptable risk," Art responded, pointing to the drawer. "There's obviously more where that came from." But one risk might not have been acceptable to one man. "You know, if this was a transfer point for our two dead guys to pick up cash, that would mean Royce would have had to do the delivering."

"No way," Frankie said, her head shaking. "If he was giving over the money there's no way he would put himself close to anything linked to Kostin. Remember, he was the conscientious employer who fired the guy . . . supposedly."

"Allen, then?" Art wondered. "The money went from Royce to him, then here for pickup. Possible?"

Frankie sneered mildly at the suggestion. "That would still put Royce with a known felon . . . unless there was a no-contact pass in between. A locker somewhere. Someplace else, maybe. I just don't think Royce would have allowed himself to be put in the same place with someone who might later turn up dirty. Not Mr. Clean."

"It got here," Art said. "Just like it got to Kostin's house." He looked directly to Lightman. "Fit this into things, Hal. Run down the place. Show Allen's and Royce's pictures to the neighbors."

"Right."

"This adds a little more sophistication to things, partner," Frankie observed as Hal left the office. Outside a line of yellow tape and two sheriffs' black-and-whites kept the lookie-loos at bay.

Art looked at the barren desktop, tapping it with a stiff finger. "Allen couldn't have thought this up. Kostin neither. And Royce?" His head shook.

"Barrish," Frankie said.

"There is a link," Art insisted. "There has to be. Something we can use to get around the constitutional booby traps."

"Give Hal and Omar a while to piece this place into things," Frankie suggested.

"A day here and a day there, partner. Time's our enemy."

It was a true analysis, Frankie knew, one that bothered her the entire drive back over the mountains into the City of Angels.

"That was the best meal I have had in years!" Art said, leaning back in his chair. The eyes of Felicia Griggs said "thank you," while those of his significant other expressed a quite different sentiment. "The best healthy meal, hon. I mean . . ."

"Stop before that hole gets any deeper," Anne suggested with a stern, motherly look. She turned to Felicia. "I'm from the meat and potatoes school of cooking. You know. Fat and cholesterol."

Felicia laughed softly as she removed the plates from the dining room table. "Well, Darren said you had mentioned that Art was partial to . . . this kind of food. I have to admit I'm a pot roast chef at heart, but I figured I could come up with something fairly healthy."

"Why do I feel like an alien?" Art asked, laughing fully after a second. "It's not like I eat dirt."

"Close enough," Anne responded. "But this was delicious, Felicia. The snow peas were wonderful. How do you get them crisp without burning them?"

"A secret from a Chinese restaurant we . . . that we've gone to." She picked up a few more dishes. "Come on in the kitchen and I'll share the secret."

Anne gathered the remaining plates and followed Felicia through a set of swinging saloon doors, leaving the menfolk at the table.

"I could eat like that every night," Art commented.

"Yeah," Darren agreed softly. He was feeling emotion. Not overpowering, just enough to remind him how wonderful *normal* really was. "Trust me, though, you can put on the weight real easy with her regular meals. Me, I could weigh twice as much if I let myself. Sometimes I slap a burger on the grill just to eat light."

Art chuckled. "Twice a year I get my treats. A bacon chili cheese dog from—"

"Pinks."

Art beamed. "A kindred spirit!"

"Have you ever had that thing they wrap up in two big tortillas? Two hot dogs, I think, and chili."

"And everything else. Yeah." Art glanced toward the kitchen and lowered his voice. "Treat time is coming up in a few weeks. I've got my partner hooked on the cuisine now. You're welcome to join us."

"You're on," Darren said with his own mischievous

look toward the kitchen. A sound from the front room, though, drew his attention away.

Moises Griggs stopped a few feet inside the house, his eyes going left toward the dining room. *Who the hell are you?*

"Moises," Darren said, loud enough that Felicia was passing him in a split second.

"Moises!" Felicia stopped a foot from her son and reached gingerly for him, laying a hand on his dirty jacket.

Darren swallowed hard, wanting to both cry and scream. But he could do neither. There was only one thing he could do. "It's good to have you home, son."

Moises looked away from his father, and avoided his mother's stare altogether. He did, however, give the two strangers in the dining room a curious look. But there was no time for introductions, and no need for them. "I'm not staying long. I just came to get some clothes."

"No!" Felicia shrieked. "Moises!" Her hands grabbed at the soiled collar of his jacket. "You can't!"

Anne pressed past the two men and came up on Felicia easily from behind, easing two hands on her shoulders. The stare of the young man fell on her as he peeled his mother's hands from his clothing.

Darren glared at his son. *You little bastard. If I . . .*

"Felicia, come on," Anne said as the woman's head dropped, tears already dropping to the floor.

Darren started to step forward, but a hand pressed firmly on his chest. He looked left into the eyes of Art Jefferson. They were pained. Filled with a sort of rage, even, but in control. *Control.* That was what was needed now.

Moises left the front room and headed for his bedroom down the hall. Art was a few steps behind.

"Are you an actor?"

Moises jerked his head back from where he knelt next to his dresser. "What?"

"Nice performance out there," Art commented, step-ping into the boy's room. "It takes a good actor to put on a tough-guy show like that. Especially for your mother."

Moises looked away and stuffed assorted pieces of clothing into a large gym bag.

"Are you a tough guy?"

"Fuck yourself."

Anatomically impossible, Art thought, and so com-mon as an insult that it no longer held even the slightest sting. "Tough guys are an interesting bunch, you know? They can talk up anything. Make themselves sound tougher than stone. But that's all words, son."

"Excuse me?" Moises said caustically. "Were you talking?" *And I'm not your son. I'm no one's son.*

Art reached under his jacket and unclipped his shield from his belt, tossing it on the bed close at the boy's side. "I know tough."

Moises paused and looked at the badge, shifting only his eyes to do so. *FBI?*

"You wanna know tough? I can tell you tough." Art walked forward and picked up his shield.

"Look, I'm getting outta here. Okay? I just gotta go." Moises continued his packing. "I just gotta . . ."

"Those people out there care about you, and I barely know them. I can see it."

They're weak.

"They've been through a lot."

Tanya went through more.

"They just want to help."

They just want to forget. I can't. Moises took a little cash that he had stashed in a drawer and shoved it in his pocket before zipping up the gym bag. He stood and turned to leave, but Art Jefferson was blocking his path. "You can't make me stay."

"This isn't the way, son," Art said, recognizing the

look in the boy's eyes. He knew what came from that kind of look.

Moises pushed his way past the much taller man and headed back toward the front room, a loud cry from his mother preceding the slamming of the front door by just a second.

"Dammit," Art said to himself. If there was one thing the world didn't need it was another black kid gone over the edge to waste his life. But he was witness to just that occurrence. He knew it. And he was powerless to stop it. "Goddammit."

ELEVEN

Creatures Not Stirring

Thirty .45-caliber rounds spat from the fat, suppressed barrel of the Ingram M-11 in less than two seconds, chewing up the squat trunk of the felled juniper.

"Whoa," Moises exclaimed calmly, though clearly enamored of the power projected by the compact submachine gun.

Darian ejected the spent magazine as smoke wafted from the business end of the Ingram and inserted a full one. He held it out to Moises. "Here. Try it."

Moises took hold of the weapon by its pistol grip, which ran perpendicular to the box-shaped body indicative of the Ingram and that doubled as the magazine housing. His off hand held the cylindrical suppressor, which was covered by a pad intended to dissipate the thermal energy radiated during firing. "I pull this back, right?"

"Right," Darian said, pointing to the rounded cocking lever atop the weapon. "That'll load a round."

Moises chambered the first .45 ACP round and tightened his grip on the weapon, both hands squeezing tight. Too tight.

"Ease up, Brother Moises. Control is what you want. You don't have to hold it as tight as a baseball bat."

"Okay." Moises looked around the desolate clearing, hidden from the hilly road north of the city by a row of thick vegetation, searching for a target. The headlights of the Buick illuminated another juniper stump a few yards beyond the one just mutilated. He shifted his feet like a batter digging in for leverage and guess-aimed from a low hold, then squeezed the trigger.

BRRRRRRRRRRRRRRRRRRR.

"Man!" Moises said loudly as the empty weapon stopped bucking. "Whoa. That is awesome." He looked closely at the target, which was not quite as torn up as the one Darian had taken under fire.

"Not bad," Darian commented, taking the Ingram back. "Pretty good shooting."

"That thing has a kick."

"A big-ass kick," Darian expanded. "But it hits harder on the receiving end."

"No kidding."

Darian inserted a fresh magazine and handed the weapon back again. "You should hear the sound without the suppressor on."

Moises' fingers scratched at the padded cylinder. "The silencer, you mean?"

"Incorrect term, Brother Moises. But unimportant right now. You'll learn plenty about weapons and how to use them right, and with the most effect. Right now you've just got to get used to it."

"Is this what we're going to use tomorrow?" Moises asked.

Darian nodded. "You'll have one, and I'll have one." He paused for a moment, studying the boy's face carefully. "You're ready for this?"

"I'm ready." Moises pulled the cocking lever back and quickly chose a new target, laying thirty rounds on and around it in a flash. A cloud of dust billowed from the ground and drifted through the blazing beams emanating from the front of the Buick. He ejected the empty and held it out for his leader. For the man he was beginning to think of as a father. "Gimme another, Brother Darian."

"Right on, Brother Moises," Darian said, smiling. A soldier was coming of age right before his eyes, and there could be no more beautiful sight than that. Other than the one they were going to create in the morning.

John Barrish had his own personal instrument of power in hand at the same moment, though his preparations were of a quieter variety. He had cleaned the silenced Beretta thoroughly over the last hour, checking for dirt and rust, aligning the sound and flash suppressor at its front end, working the action. He loaded three magazines, each with thirteen rounds of .380-caliber hollow-point, also known as 9mm short. In reality, though, he would need only two rounds. Hopefully. But if more were needed, he would use them without hesitation.

The front door opened and closed, Toby coming into the dimly lit front room a second later. "The suitcases are in the car, Pop."

John nodded. "Where'd you get it?"

"From a dealer in Lancaster. It's new, so we won't have to worry about plates."

"You paid cash?"

"Check from the bank," Toby answered. "I just told them it was from a purchase order. None of that paper-work for a ten-grand transaction. Hell, they were just glad to sell a car."

"And a place to stay?"

Toby stiffened his body and pretended to haughtily pull at a nonexistent lapel. "Arrangements for Mr. Benjamin Howell to lease a house have been made through the relocation services of Jefferson Properties of Harrisonburg, Virginia."

John smiled at the short performance. "Your doing?"

"Are you kidding? I told you Stan does this stuff good."

Toby saw the gun lying on his father's lap, resting on a towel. "Pop, I . . . I mean . . ." Toby could never remember saying the words he now wanted to utter to his father. Maybe that was best. "I'm glad it's starting."

John Barrish looked up at his son, understanding what he was saying without actually doing so. He remembered the awkwardness well from his own youth. "Your mother and Stan are already in bed, son. You'd better get some sleep. We have a big day tomorrow."

"G'night, Pop."

John smiled as his oldest boy left him alone with his thoughts for the last night in this place. In the morning they would be gone, on their way to bigger and better things. Things no one could even imagine.

TWELVE

King's Opening

Valley Oaks Memorial Park was just visible through the light drizzle, and just beyond its piano-shaped property line the Ventura Freeway was as it usually was at this early hour. Toby could see a steady stream of cars moving from right to left, heading toward Los Angeles from the bedroom communities of Thousand Oaks and beyond. Fewer crossed left to right. The city was almost everyone's destination, a thought that made him smile.

"You ready, son?" John asked, closing the back door of the Aerostar.

"I'm ready." Toby walked around the minivan, which they had parked on the dirt shoulder of Thousand Oaks Boulevard, and joined his father. They slide-stepped down the damp bank of the shoulder to a runoff ditch, then scrambled up the opposite side and over a barbed-wire cattle fence before moving up the slope. The grade was slight, and in ten minutes, their movements shrouded by the increasing misty drizzle, they had covered a quarter-mile, nearing a development of homes situated across Lindero Canyon Road from the Lake Lindero Country Club. Large homes that sat on large lots, Toby could tell through the falling haze. One house in particular drew his attention as he and his father stopped beneath an aged oak to scan their approach route.

"See the gully?" John asked, getting a nod in response. "That runs right up to that back wall. On the far side there's a high spot you can use to get over the wall."

"I see it."

"You know what to do from there."

"Yeah." Toby checked the time. "It's almost seven."

"The nurse doesn't come until nine on Wednesdays," John said, reassuring his son that there would be no surprises.

"Okay. Let's go."

The father-and-son team moved off, angling down the reverse slope of the hill, reducing the distance to the homes as they moved. There was sufficient cover, mostly in the form of oak trees and some sage, and they traversed the open spaces as quickly as the footing allowed. In eight minutes they were at the back wall.

"Three-three-four-one," John reminded his son.

"Got it." Toby continued on along the seven-foot block wall that encircled the back portion of the house at the end of Catarina Drive, while his father went in the opposite direction, toward the side of the property. The eldest Barrish boy trotted up the mound of earth at the northwest corner of the lot and peered over the wall. All was clear, with no apparent obstructions between the wall and the two-story house. A fifty-foot space to cover, Toby estimated, but then who would be watching?

He swung a leg onto the wall and rolled over, landing on his feet, and immediately trotted toward the side entrance his father had described to him. Located on the north wall of the four-car garage, the door had a single deadbolt lock. But that was to be no problem. Toby took a key from his pocket and unlocked the door, closing it and feeling for the light switch that was supposed to be there, all the while beginning the thirty-second countdown. The fluorescent fixtures over the Jaguar and the

Ford Explorer hummed, then flashed on. Beyond them Toby saw the flashing green light marking the location of the alarm box. He reached it as the count came to twelve, and punched in the four numbers on the keypad. The flashing stopped, they went solid green. He had ten more seconds to enter the next command, which was utterly simple. *System off.* He pressed the skinny black button, which made the panel go dark.

Done. Almost. He pulled the Beretta from his waistband and affixed the silencer, and waited by the door that led into the house.

The front doorbell surprised Monte Royce, causing him to jerk his cup of tea as he sat in the breakfast room. "Who could that be at this hour?" He set the dripping cup on its saucer and walked through the kitchen to the foyer, looking through the peephole before opening the—"What?"

The latch clicked and the door swung tentatively inward, the form of Monte Royce appearing in the widening gap. "Good morning, Monte."

"John . . . What are you doing here?"

"Monte." The voice, feeble but obviously female, came from upstairs. "Who is it?"

"Uh . . . No one, mother," Royce lied. "I'll be up in a minute."

"She has good ears," John observed. *What a shame.* She was the only part of this that caused him pause. But what had to be done had to be done.

"What—"

"Inside, Monte," John suggested forcefully. "Somewhere she won't hear us. We need to talk."

Royce looked past his unexpected and unwelcome visitor. The liberally landscaped front yard and its high walls blocked any view of the street, and hopefully was preventing any of his few neighbors from seeing this. "All right. Come in. Into the study."

John entered and made an immediate left, walking below an impressive open arch that led into the combination study/library. His host closed the front door and followed him in.

"What is it, John?" Royce asked again, watching as John continued walking toward the fireplace at the far end of the study. His hands were doing something to his front, but what . . . *No!*

"I wouldn't, Monte," John said as he turned, causing the elderly executive to end his retreat from the room. He closed on Royce, keeping the silenced Beretta pointing at the man's chest. "To the garage. Now."

Royce followed the instructions after a hesitation caused more by surprise than defiance. At the door that connected the garage to the kitchen he was shoved away, toward the sink. A second later another familiar face was in the room. And another gun.

"What is this?" Royce asked quietly, not wanting to disturb his mother.

"Down," John said, motioning to the exquisitely tiled floor. "On your stomach."

"John . . ."

"Now."

Royce still had no idea what was happening. Was this some sort of warning to him? Some attempt to frighten him? Did they think he was going to talk? Lowering himself from a pushup position to the floor he tried to figure it all out. But all his deductions were wrong.

"Son," John said.

Toby drew a bead on the back of Monte Royce's head from a distance of seven feet and fired one round, which drilled into his skull with the sound of a dropped egg cracking upon the floor. The old man's body jerked once, the arms actually coming in to attempt a rise, but that motion ceased in a few seconds. As blood poured from the entry wound the body went completely limp, then still.

"He's done," John said, looking to his son. "You stay here. I'll be down in a minute."

He went to the carpeted stairs and walked quickly to the second floor. The room he was interested in was at the near end of the hall, its location affording a gorgeous view of the hills to the west. John eased the cracked door fully open and stepped into the bedroom. A pair of old, yet very bright eyes immediately met his.

"John! Is it you?"

"It's me, Canadia," John answered, taking a few more steps that put him right at the old woman's bedside.

Canadia Conyers Royce looked up at the man she revered. The man she saw as the hope for her people. "You look so good, John."

"Thank you." He sat on the edge of the mattress, facing the sweet lady, the gun resting on his lap. Its presence did not go unnoticed by her.

"It's time, John, isn't it?"

He nodded, looking at her tenderly. "Things have to be done, Canadia."

Now she nodded, though very weakly. "And Monte?"

"He's gone."

She actually smiled. "He tried, John. But he was not you. He wasn't like you at all."

"I owe you a great deal, Canadia. Our people owe you a great deal."

"I've done this for the same reasons my grandfather carried the Stars and Bars," she said proudly, her eyes tearing.

"Shhh." He put his right hand on the gun and slid it toward her, resting the silencer on the pillow next to her left ear. "It's time for me to go."

"Yes." She looked straight at the ceiling, a full smile stretched across her face. "I must go, too. Good luck, John."

He said nothing more, then squeezed the trigger once. The impact of the bullet snapped her head right as a fountain of red arched onto the white bedding. John headed back downstairs without even looking at the sight, and joined his son in the kitchen.

"Done?" Toby asked, though he knew the answer already.

"Our work is done," John said. "For now. Let's get out of here."

Twenty minutes later they were back at the Aerostar, and a few minutes after that they were just one of the thousands of cars creeping along the Ventura Freeway, none of their fellow commuters wise to the fact that two murderers were in their midst.

He drove a Mercedes, which he would retire as his get-to-work car once the newest-model Corvette he'd ordered came in. His wife tagged it just a symptom of a mid-life crisis long in coming, but Seymour Mankowitz knew the real reason. He was tired of the staid, lawyerly image forced upon him by the profession he'd chosen, and wanted at least some zest in his life. Cruising from his Pacific Palisades home to his office on Reseda Boulevard each day in a jet black *rocket* would provide just that.

But, for now, it was the respectable Mercedes, which he guided into the alley behind his office in the north of the San Fernando Valley. Halfway to the narrow path's end he turned right, into the private parking lot reserved for himself and his two partners. Neither of their cars was there, which he expected. Both were already gone, on their way to Telluride for a Thanksgiving on the slopes. Him? He was here to meet with . . .

Mankowitz shook the feeling away. John Barrish was his *client* right now, and he had to treat him as such. Not as an aberration. Once the ties were severed, which he hoped would be soon, then he could allow himself to express what he truly felt. Until then . . .

His professionalism restored, Mankowitz took his briefcase in hand and stepped from the Mercedes, clicking on the alarm that sounded with a chirp. He walked toward the back of the car, the entrance to his building just beyond, but slowed as a long, old car glided to a stop in the alley, blocking entrance to the lot.

Darian put the car in park and stepped out, looking at the man from across the hood of the Buick. Moises got out from the passenger side. He was just a few yards from the clearly frightened white man. At almost the same instant both men produced their Ingrams, leveling them at their target.

"Wait! No!" Mankowitz dropped his briefcase and took an unsteady step backward. But it would change nothing.

Moises fired first, grabbing the front end of his Ingram and raising it just a bit from the center-mass point of aim he'd been instructed to use. The thirty rounds began impacting just below the lawyer's pronounced Adam's apple and stitched up the length of his face. Only a third of the .45-caliber slugs actually found their target, but that was more than enough to turn Seymour Mankowitz's head to a grotesque bloody rose of flesh and bone. Darian's shots were placed well, all but five devastating the lawyer's midsection. What remained of the body flopped backward a few feet, tumbling to the ground at the side of the Mercedes.

"Get in!" Darian yelled, checking their surroundings quickly for any witnesses. There were none.

"Did you see that?!"

"Here." Darian handed his weapon across the seat to Moises and dropped the Buick into gear, resisting the urge to stomp on the gas. Instead he pulled away from the scene quickly, but without screeching the tires. "Put 'em in the bag."

"Oh man!" Moises reached over the front seat and buried the still smoking Ingrams in a large duffel, his heart pounding. "Did you see that fucker go down?!"

"Easy, Brother Moises," Darian cautioned, though his own adrenaline level was still high. "Get yourself together."

"Right," Moises said, nodding sharply. He took several deep breaths as Darian put distance between them and their victim. *I did it. I offed him. I can do it!*

"Are you okay?"

"You bet, Brother Darian. A-OK."

Darian reached over and gave the young fighter a gentle punch in the arm. "I knew you would be. I knew it."

So did I. That thought struck Moises as somehow strange, but he was beyond harboring any concern as to why that was. It was just the way it was now. His new reality.

Priority One in the morning was always getting the Braun coffeemaker running. Wisely, Frankie used prepacked filters, and was religious about keeping the small plastic pitcher beside the machine filled with water. No running to get this or mess with measurements. Just drop in the filter, pour, and switch it on. And there was just enough time to refill the pitcher before the line of black liquid would pass the one-cup mark on the glass pot. She stepped from the cubicle on her way to the water cooler, a trip that was cut short by the sight of Hal Lightman approaching. "What are you doing here? You were on late last night."

"I was *here* last night," Lightman corrected her. In one hand was a stack of green-and-white computer printout. "When's Art getting in?"

"In a bit. I'm doing the early shift this morning. Why?"

"I think I found something."

Frankie put the pitcher down and motioned for Hal to lay the stack on Art's empty desk. "What is it?"

"I was running down Birch and Associates, looking for permits and business licenses, et cetera, and this came back from the county." He pointed to a copy of the fire department safety inspection done just three months earlier.

"It passed. So?"

"Look at who owns the space Kostin was leasing."

Frankie's eyes shifted to the pertinent information. "Green Hills Trust? This is the same place that owned his house."

"I don't care if he did pay a big chunk of his rent on that house up front—this is too much to consider just a coincidence."

Way too much, Frankie thought. "Do you have the info on the trust?"

"On my desk."

"Bring it over," Frankie said with some excitement, knowing that coincidences were often found to be conspiracies when illegality was involved. It was time to move on this, and fast. "Let's get digging."

And there was another person who'd want to join in the dig, Frankie knew. She picked up the phone and dialed with one hand. Art answered on the second ring.

Ray Harback led the two men through the airlocklike pair of doors and into the noise of the physical plant one level above 73. "This is the stuff your boss was interested in."

Roger shifted the weight of the "camera" bag on his shoulder and leaned close to their guide. "He said he wanted good shots of the flow monitor setup."

Harback nodded, one hand holding his hearing protectors. "Over here." He walked a short distance and pointed to the large outflow conduit. "This is it."

Mustafa brought up the rear as his comrade engaged

the white man in a distracting conversation. He had his own bag, but there was nothing approximating a camera in it. Not even close.

Harback felt a jab in his back and turned, freezing at the sight of the boxy-looking gun pointing at his gut. The man he had been talking to removed a similar weapon from his bag and shoved it in his ribs. "What . . . What is this?"

Mustafa gestured with the gun for Harback to back up, directing him around a corner where the ductwork disappeared into the floor. Roger laid his weapon on the ground and removed the cylinder from his bag, seeing in his peripheral vision the suppressed Ingram in his comrade's hand buck twice. He had it on single shot. A smart move, Roger thought, considering all the concrete in this space. It could have been ricochet city had any rounds missed.

"Dead," Mustafa yelled, his mouth close to Roger's covered ears. "I'll watch the door."

Roger nodded and stepped over the duct to the opposite side, seeing the access panel immediately. He twisted the twin latches and swung it up on its hinges. Next he took the cylinder. The switch he was supposed to throw was on the top, covered by a piece of tape that had held it in the unmarked *safe* position. Without realizing it he took a shallow breath and held it, then removed the tape and pressed the switch in one motion. A red LED came on, which he took to mean that the thing was now live. *Live.* That was an odd way to put it, Roger thought, considering . . .

But that it was, leaving just sixty minutes. He looked at his watch and made a mental note of the time, then closed the access panel and hopped back over the ductwork. "It's set."

Mustafa nodded and slid the still warm Ingram into the long camera bag, as did his comrade. "All right, Brother Roger. This is it."

"Let's scoot," Roger said, knowing he did not want to be anywhere close when the shit went off. Mustafa's willing acceptance of his suggestion convinced him that he had company in that desire.

The Green Hills Trust had been established in early 1992 by a smattering of well-to-do senior citizens concerned that their idle savings were not being served well by the declining bank interest rates. Real estate, they had decided, was an attractive option, particularly when the low property prices brought on by a weakening economy spurred a buyer's market. And prices would certainly go up again. Until then, when a tidy profit could be realized by selling high, a decent cash flow could be had through renting. That was the plan.

But something else had come of that venture, something Frankie and Hal were endeavoring to discover.

"These old folks own over a hundred units," Hal said, reading from his half of the printout. "It's about a fifty-fifty split between residential and commercial."

Frankie looked up from the stack before her. "You checked out the people that manage the properties, right?"

"They're as clean as clean can be," Hal answered. "They just show the properties when someone asks and collect the rent. Besides, they're just working people. No connections to anything other than the obvious."

Lightman was a healthy cynic, with a suspicious nature thrown in for good measure. If he was branding someone as clean, Frankie knew, they were. "All right, what about the members of the trust?"

"A gathering of geezers," Hal said, little hope in his voice. He passed the list of those who had bought into the trust to Frankie. It ran eight pages. "I looked at the first page and moved on. The average age has to be something like eighty."

Not the sorts to be behind this thing, Frankie thought

as she verified Lightman's analysis of the members' ages. She flipped through the list and saw no reason to lower the threshold he had set. "A mortician's dream. Some of these people are past ninety. A couple even—" *Wait. Back up.* "Hal. Look."

Lightman looked to the spot that Frankie's finger indicated. "C. C. Royce." His eyes came up, peering over the bifocals he used for reading. "Royce."

Frankie opened the appropriate drawer and removed a file that held the breadth of the information they had gathered on Monte Royce. *The bastard*, she thought, one of his statements made during their interview of him coming to mind. *"You can imagine she is quite old. . . ."* It didn't take her long to find confirmation of her supposition. "Here. Canadia Conyers Royce." She handed the pertinent page from the CEO's biography in his company's annual report. "Mother of Monte."

"Son of a bitch," Lightman commented, removing his glasses. "It looks like Mommy Dearest was doing a little recruiting of tenants for her little boy."

"It looks that way," Frankie agreed without enthusiasm. There was still the nagging question as to why Monte Royce would be involved in this. This new information only solidified a link between Royce and Kostin. It provided no connection to the man they believed was actually running the show: John Barrish. He was safe—"Hold on."

Lightman saw his fellow agent sit bolt upright. "What is it?"

"Barrish," Frankie said. "He was cleaned out in that suit a couple of years back, wasn't he?"

"Yeah. Why?"

Frankie set the Royce file aside and paged back through the list of properties owned by the Green Hills Trust, finding what they had all been looking for on the last page. "Yes!" she exclaimed, bringing her fist joyously down on the folded printout. "We have them."

"Who?"

"Look here," Frankie said. "Green Hills not only owns Kostin's house and the office he leased, they also own the house John Barrish is living in. Art and I were up there last week."

"Shit. You were right."

"This is it," Frankie proclaimed with satisfaction. But there was no time for celebration. They had to move now. "Hal, get Omar in here and get to Barrish's attorney. We're going to do this right. No legal snafus. Tell his attorney—Mankowitz is his name—that we're bringing his client in for questioning. That's all. Also tell Lou to get a tactical team ready to move on Barrish's house. Make sure he alerts Captain Orwell."

"Do you think the stuff is up there?"

"If it is we'll be ready. I'll go pick up Royce for questioning. Once we have everybody in our hands we'll get Horner to bless an arrest warrant for Barrish and Royce."

"Royce may crack now," Lightman surmised.

"What? Use his mother as leverage?" Frankie stood and grabbed her jacket. "What makes you think I'd use such an underhanded method?"

"Just guessing," Lightman said, his face plastered with a knowing smile.

Frankie reached the elevator just as Art was stepping off. He saw the look immediately. "What?"

"Come on," she said, herding him back into the elevator. "We've got Barrish. Direct link to Royce."

Art thumped the elevator door as it closed. "Dammit, yes!"

"I'll give you all the details in the car," Frankie promised.

"Where are we going?"

She smiled. "To nail one Monte Royce's ass."

Art nodded, joining the smile. It was good to start the morning on a high note. Taking Royce down was only slightly below the highest. But he could wait to nail John Barrish . . . for a while.

THIRTEEN

Body Count

"Your nine o'clock canceled," Lena told Anne Preston as she walked through the door of her outer office. A devilish grin accompanied the revelation.

"Hmmm." Anne shook her head, and headed for the door to her office. "I've got work to catch up on."

"Go see him," Lena said, stopping her boss in her tracks. "You know you want to. It's only an hour."

Anne looked to her secretary and smiled. "I knew I hired you for some reason."

"Go."

One billable hour down the drain, but the standard cancellation fee and the chance to see Art was the flip side. It was a fair exchange. "I'll see you in an hour."

"Say hi for me, too," Lena told her.

"I will," Anne assured her, then headed back the same way she had come. Five minutes later she was driving west on Wilshire on her way to surprise her man.

The drive north on the 405 took Art and Frankie a little longer than they'd anticipated, thanks to a fender bender that was clearing on the right shoulder, but the north-bound 101—actually heading in a westerly direction for that stretch—was free and clear, allowing them to reach Monte Royce's Westlake Village place of residence in less than thirty minutes. But arrival only presented a fresh problem.

"Excuse me," Frankie said as she pulled the Bureau Chevy up on the wrong side of the street, blocking the gated driveway to the Royce home. The uniformed woman looking inward through the wrought-iron bars turned toward her voice. "Do you live here?"

The woman eyed the stranger suspiciously, a reaction Frankie noticed and alleviated by showing her shield. "No, I'm the nurse for Mrs. Conyers Royce. But no one is answering the gate phone."

Frankie put the car in park and got out. Art did also and walked over to the woman. "How often do you come here?"

"Every day about this time," the nurse explained nervously. "Mr. Royce leaves once I'm here. He never leaves until I'm here."

Art looked toward the house. It was barely visible from the street, the abundance of well-tended foliage acting as a natural privacy shield. He switched his attention to the gate, particularly its locking mechanism, which operated on a simple hook-and-post principle. Press a button, the post drops, and the hook is released, letting the gate open with the aid of a hydraulic pusher. Of course one could ram the gate, but there were less dramatic ways of gaining entry. "Do you have a key to the house?"

"Yes." The nurse held out a ring with four keys on it, which Art took. "This one here is for the doors."

"Let the police know, partner," Art directed. As Frankie went to the car, he turned his attention back to the anxious nurse. "Are you concerned about the Royces?"

"Very much so. I've been trying to get Mr. Royce on the phone for twenty minutes." She glanced through the gate. "I hope nothing is wrong."

I hope the bastard hasn't skipped out on us, Art

thought alternately. "We're going to go in and check. The police will be here in a few minutes."

"I hope everything is all right."

"So do we," Art agreed, though his definition of "all right" was vastly different from that of the nurse. He looked at the wall on either side of the gate, deciding quickly that an eight-footer was a little too much. But at the north corner of the property there was the shorter fence belonging to the neighbors. Frankie came back up as Art gestured to the barrier. "Let's do some climbing."

They went to that wall—a six-footer—and used it as a step to clear the adjoining barrier. Once over they crossed the lawn and walked up the driveway, following its sweep to the front entrance. They pounded on the front door and yelled the familiar "FBI!", but there was no response. A check of several windows along the front yielded nothing, as the shades were fully drawn, so they skirted the perimeter to the north, passing the closed garage doors, and headed toward the back of the . . .

"Hold it," Art said, a hand coming up. A single finger pointed down.

The muddy footprints on the cement walkway were fresh. A second later their weapons were out. Art drew closer, noticing more details now. The prints, a single set, came from the direction of the backyard and ended at a side door. Fainter prints belonging to the same shoe—a boot of some kind—appeared to follow the same path on a reciprocal, and a different set of prints tracked over the first. *One went in, two came out.* They approached the spot carefully and listened. Art gently pushed on the door with his elbow. It didn't budge, and he decided not to try the lock. There might be better access around back. They continued on, avoiding stepping on the tracked prints, and eased cautiously around the corner. Art checked what lay before them. A damp cement path led along the back wall of the garage, then opened to a lattice-covered patio that large box windows looked out upon. They crept toward those, ears peeled for sounds of danger, weapons held firmly and pointed at the ground. Once at the windows Art rose up on the balls of his feet and looked in. It was the kitchen, and was empty . . . except for—

Blood. A pool of it covering a good portion of the tiled floor, part of its area blocked by a cooktop island. Art moved further along the window until—

Shit! "Body," Art said quietly. It was about the right size and dressed professionally. *Monte Royce.* The blood about the head and the distance prevented a positive identification, but that would change quickly. Art led the way back around to the front of the house to the main entrance. "We've got to kick it."

Frankie holstered her weapon and surveyed the door. It was solid, and would obviously take more force than she could muster alone to breach. But to either side were cement planters, about a foot and a half in height. She picked one up, dumping its contents, and grasped it in an approximation of a battering ram, swinging it back and forward in one smooth motion. Its flat, round base connected with the door near the lock, and elicited a sharp snap from the member. A second swing pushed the door in completely.

Art went through first. Frankie dropped the planter and redrew her weapon, joining him. "FBI! FBI!" they yelled together, Art covering the staircase to the front, Frankie the opening to the kitchen to the right. On the stairs' carpeted surface they noticed very faint prints similar to those outside. But to the right was where their attention was mainly focused. Listening for any signs of movement, they moved through the house, entering the kitchen after just a moment. They now saw the body from the opposite direction as before. It was almost certainly Royce. There was absolutely no doubt, however, that whoever it was was very dead.

"Dammit," Frankie said softly.

Art pointed to the same muddy footprints in the tiled floor. "Upstairs," he said.

They left the kitchen and went to the stairs. Each step was taken slowly to avoid the obvious tread marks. The agents stopped on the upper-floor landing. There were several doors along the corridor that stretched to either side. Only one of them, the second to the right, was open. The prints led to and from it. Art paralleled the tracks to the door as his partner hung back, but did not enter, using his eyes to examine the room—a bedroom—from the hall.

No. Even from fifteen feet it was clear that the scene in the kitchen had been repeated upstairs, though the stark contrast between what remained of the frilly white bedding and the explosion of crimson near the headboard took this to a higher level of grotesque.

This was not random, Art knew. It was not a run-of-the-mill burglary gone wrong. Nothing was missing that could be seen. No obvious disturbance. This was a hit. Plain and simple. And he had a good idea who was responsible for it.

"Another one," Art said. "Looks like the mother." He looked back to Frankie. "Come on."

They moved quickly back down the stairs and outside, holstering their weapons as they ran to the front of the property and grabbed on to a decorative tree to help rescale the wall. A black-and-white was rolling up just as the agents hit the sidewalk.

"Is everything all right?" the nurse inquired worriedly.

"I'm afraid not," Frankie answered.

Art trotted to the police car, making his shield obvious to the two officers. "There's two dead inside." The passenger immediately took the mike in hand. "It looks fresh."

"What are you doing here?" the driver inquired.

"We were hoping to question one of the victims."
Someone had seen to it that that was not going to happen, Art thought. "Look, I've got to make a call." Art
went to their car and heard the cellular ringing before
he could open the door. "Jefferson here."

"Art, it's Hal. We've got a mess here."

A mess? He felt his eyes widen. *Oh no.* "Mankowitz?"

"He's dead. Someone did him good. Blew the hell
out of him with automatics."

"Royce is dead, too. And his mother."

"What?!"

"Hal, get up to Barrish's house now. Fast!"

"All right."

Art knew that no more explaining was needed. What
was supposed was quite obvious. Someone was cutting
his ties to a place, and to a time. And if that *someone*
wasn't stopped fast he might just disappear . . . if he
hadn't already.

Darian set the bag with the guns in it on the floor of the
backseat. "Where'd you get it?"

Roger smiled. "From some guy's ad in the paper.
Two grand. It runs perfect."

Perfect it didn't have to be, Darian knew. Just good
enough to get them across country. "Then let's get out
of here."

Roger got behind the wheel of the Olds Cutlass, Mustafa taking the seat next to him. Darian and Moises
climbed in the back.

"Brother Moises here do good?" Mustafa asked,
looking back over the front bench seat.

Darian looked to the newest of their number and
smiled. "He did good."

Moises looked to the floor, a combination of embarrassment and a sudden nervous stomach hitting him. The
adrenaline had worn off now, allowing the reality of the

situation he'd walked willingly into to flash crystal clear in his mind. The reality, and a discovery he'd never considered. "It was easy," he said, the revelation coming not from the soul but from the heart. He wasn't sure he had the former any longer.

"Righteous things are," Mustafa said, sharing some wisdom with the boy.

Roger started the car and got them moving. He headed immediately for the Santa Monica Freeway, entering eastbound at La Cienega.

"No turning back now, Brothers," Darian said.

Mustafa agreed with a rare smile. "Power, brother."

Darian started to answer, but was cut off.

"Power, brother," Moises said, his hand extending forward.

It was a good beginning, Darian saw. And there was so much still to come.

"Ray!" Assistant Building Engineer Carl Tomei yelled as he entered the roar that filled 74. He let the door close behind and looked left, then right. Where the hell was he? "Ray!"

Nothing. Even in the steady, constant drone Ray should hear the call, Tomei knew. The hearing protectors required on this level were "tuned" to muffle the machinery noise while allowing sharper, more defined sounds, such as voices, to be heard.

But he had to be here. That camera crew he'd brought up to snoop around had already left, unless the receptionist was mistaken. Not likely, he thought. Then where was he? Tomei walked along the main feed duct, looking over its top on the off chance that Ray was checking something in an out-of-the-way place. He leaned on the duct every few yards, then continued on, giving up once there was no more area to check. "Dammit, Ray, where the hell—Oh, shit!"

Tomei saw the legs first, then his supervisor's entire

body, lying face-up on the floor. A circle of red the size of a salad plate covered his chest. "Ray!" He dropped down to the man's side and touched his face, which was whiter than he'd ever seen. "My God!" Tomei stood tentatively, then ran through both doors and down the stairs to 73, stopping at the nearest phone. Once there his actions were automatic.

"Nine-one-one, what is your emergency?"

"Seventy-fourth floor! First Interstate World Center! My boss! My boss!"

"Calm down, sir."

"He's bleeding and he's unconscious! I think he's dead!"

"Calm down. You have to—"

"Just get here! I've got to get back to him!"

Tomei tossed the handset back toward its cradle, missing badly, but not giving a damn either. He raced back up to 74 and to Ray's side, checking for a pulse this time.

"No, Ray. No." *CPR*. He had to try. Tomei scooted toward his boss's head and put a hand under his neck, lifting gently as the other hand pinched the man's nose. "Let me do this right, God," he begged, then brought his mouth down to cover Ray's.

A few feet away, however, a small microchip timer counted through the last digit of value and set in motion an action that would make Carl Tomei's lifesaving efforts fruitless; but then he would not live to know the folly of his actions.

FOURTEEN

Witch's Brew

Zero.

A small cam rotated toward a magnet suddenly energized, freeing a piston that had held the deadly contents of the cylinder in check for several weeks. Instantly, pushed by the several atmospheres of inert gas with which Nikolai Kostin had pressurized the cylinder, the VZ began to spray freely into the ventilation system. This misty liquid was instantly picked up by the forceful flow of air from the SunSnow blowers and pushed through the diving turn of the ductwork and into the treelike divider network that snaked through the bowels of the building.

The fine droplets of VZ did their first damage on 71.

The secretary looked to the A/C vent, her nose twitching at the unpleasant smell now invading her office. The noxious sulfur odor, a product of the binary method of combination, caused her to recoil, her face a grimace.

"What is *that*?" Annoyed and wanting to give Building Services a piece of her mind, she took the phone in hand and reached to the keypad, but her hand tensed before any numbers could be pressed. The appendage clenched, then shook as she looked at it, then both hands began vibrating.

What?

She looked upward, not at anything, as her neck muscles spasmed. Her head shook now, and suddenly both legs flexed like bent twigs and released, propelling her backward off the chair. On the floor her mouth went wide, as did her eyes.

No! Air! Please, God!

Her mind, beginning to feel the effects of the nerve agent, tried to comprehend what was happening, tried to give what was afflicting her a name. Heart attack? Stroke? Seizure? It was part of those things, and much more. In her muscle cells, the chlorinesterase enzyme, whose function was to act as a transmission conduit for "release," or "off" signals, was being shortcircuited. Normally, when the muscles received electrical impulse signals from the brain to contract—an "on" signal—whether involuntarily, as in the heart, or voluntarily, as in the legs when walking, the chlorinesterase enzyme acted as the messenger that told the muscle cells to relax again. But the VZ, being carried to those muscle cells by the circulatory system, was interrupting that process, preventing the muscles from relaxing after contracting. The brain, excited by the terror of the moment, was firing off signals that were being interpreted only as "on," causing virtually every muscle to spasm uncontrollably.

The woman's legs and arms were pulled into a near fetal position as her body—she no longer had control of it—jerked violently, portions slamming into furniture to add superficial physical injury to the invisible trauma going on inside her person. There was pain, but it seemed to come from everywhere at once as a blanket of ache, broken every few seconds by sharp barbs of fire, mostly from her mouth. And there was sound, a sharp cracking that seemed to come from within her head. Both estimations were correct. Her teeth, literally, were breaking as uppers and lowers slammed against each other with tremendous force, the jagged shards that remained digging into the pulpy, bleeding flesh that used to be her gums.

But the damage of consequence was to the body's most vital muscle: the heart, a muscle that contracts and relaxes, drawing blood in and pumping it out. Without the delicate rhythm in place, without being able to relax and draw more blood in, the heart spasmed uselessly. It quivered, moving no blood, a state that it, like the rest of its host, could not survive for any extended period.

Mercifully, the woman lost consciousness after two minutes, but the death that was slowly taking hold would take several more to reach its clinical state of definition. Until then, life, or some form of it virtually impossible to imagine, would continue, then surrender to the inevitable.

The same scene was repeating itself in the large offices on 71, and in the more numerous spaces on 70. And 69. And 68. It was almost without change. First the sulfur smell, then a sense of wonder, then the first twitch. Down farther, to 67, where the occupants of an entire suite of offices, crammed while wishing a colleague a happy and healthy retirement, were overcome and struck down. A fellow reveler, returning from the rest room, opened the office door to see her co-workers writhing on the floor, and splayed across desks, their mouths frothing, trying to draw in air like landed fish. Her mind went into overdrive as the sulfur smell reached her, and instinct took over. Gas leak! she thought, and bolted down the hall, unaware that she was being chased by the airborne droplets traveling through the ductwork hidden in the ceiling above her, and those being pulled along in the wake turbulence her body made as it scrambled to get away. She stopped at the elevator and stabbed madly at the down arrow, her finger breaking on the third attempt. Looking to the ceiling, and knowing not why her head was rearing back, she flopped backward and became the last victim on 67.

Then it was 66. 65. 64. 63. A full ten floors the VZ mist had been spread, and now it was having difficulty traveling through every duct, as its volume was being absorbed by its victims and by inanimate objects, such as furniture, ceiling tiles, and even, in small amounts, by the interior of the ductwork. On 62 a young lawyer, working on the day the more senior people in the firm had off, caught a faint whiff of the sulfur odor, and opened his office door. Seeing two others from his office on the hallway floor, their bodies twitching and rolling, he slammed the door and ran to the phone.

"Nine-one-one, what is—"

"First Interstate Tower, the offices of Lothrop, Bowman, and Finch. Something's wrong! Some sort of gas leak or something! I can smell it, and . . . and . . ."

"Sir? . . . Sir? . . ."

The downward journey continued, the big and powerful SunSnow blowers living up to every claim their designers had made. To 60, then 50, then 40. By the time it reached 32, a minute and a half after release, it was sufficiently dissipated that dozens of frightened workers were able to reach the phone and complete calls to 911, as well as to Building Services. On 12, Lena Carerra collapsed against the door to Anne Preston's outer office, one hand on the knob. On 74, the pagers worn by Ray Harback and Carl Tomei were vibrating on their belts, but no response was to come. A frightened junior engineer, seeing the first throngs of people pouring from the stairwells and racing toward the front doors, some dragging grotesquely convulsing friends, ran to the main security desk.

"What in God's name is going on?!" the security director screamed at the junior engineer, the sight on the monitors before him having already sent one of his officers scurrying out of the building.

"I don't know!"

"There's bodies everywhere! Look!" The security director pointed to the monitors, which received video images from the cameras mounted in every main hallway.

"They're running for the elevators and dropping. My God, what is this?"

The junior engineer, three years out of Texas A & M, stared at the piles of bodies against what seemed to be every elevator door. "Hit the alarm."

"What?"

"Shut the elevators down and hit the alarm. Now!"

The security director took care of both directions in only a few seconds. "Done."

"Are all the emergency systems up?"

"Of course they are."

"Throw the breakers."

"What?!"

"Dammit, there's something spreading around up there, and it's coming this way. Gas or something."

The calls were saying something about a strange smell, the security director remembered. *In the vents.*

"We've got to cut the environmentals," the engineer said. "The only way to do that is to simulate a power failure. The emergency lights will keep the halls and stairwells lit." *If anyone is still alive to need them.* "Now. Do it!"

The security director grabbed his keys and followed the engineer to the main breaker panel a few yards away. His key was in the safety lock when the first hint of sulfur snapped his head toward the vent.

"Hurry!" the engineer shouted, taking the keys from his petrified colleague. He pulled the panel open, ignoring the groan and *slap* of the man falling to the floor, and grabbed the main breaker switch, yanking it away from the wall as his head, inexplicably, snapped backward.

FIFTEEN

Reunion

The first Bureau forensic team arrived at the Royces' Westlake Village house just as the cellular in Art and Frankie's car began ringing.

"Jefferson."

"Art, Hal. Barrish is gone. His family, too."

Art said nothing immediately, but made a flapping action as Frankie looked to him. He had flown the coop. "Have you gotten inside yet?"

"I've got no warrant."

"Get one. Fast." Art hung up with the push of a button and started to replace the handset when it rang again. "Jefferson."

"Get downtown now." It was Lou Hidalgo.

"What? Why?"

"They may have hit with the nerve gas."

"No. Where?"

There was a pause. "The World Center, Art."

Frankie saw her partner's jaw drop, his chest heave once.

"Wha—what?"

"I don't know anything more than that, Art. Just get there."

Art clicked the phone off and tossed it across the front seat, jumping in right behind it. Frankie didn't need to be told they were leaving.

"What is it?" she asked as he accelerated away from the house, swinging a tight U-turn that made the tires scream.

She's all right, Arthur. She has to be.

"Art, what is it?"

Art told her through bared teeth as they entered the southbound 101. The rest of the drive was made in worried silence.

"Take the Fifteen," John Barrish told his youngest son from the backseat.

Stanley silently questioned the reasoning behind that routing, but expressed none of it. He simply obeyed his father's instruction and slid to the right on Interstate 10, merging onto the long, sweeping transition to Interstate 15.

"Hey, Pop," Toby said with feigned excitement as they passed under the sign marking the 15 as the choice route to Las Vegas. "We could do some gambling."

John gave a mild smile in response to his son's kidding. "I don't want to take the obvious route."

Toby's head bobbed up and down as he looked back from the front seat. Interstate 10 would have been the quicker route across country, but quicker wasn't always better. "Pop?" Toby offered, holding a bag of chocolate chip cookies over the seat. He got a head shake in response, and shifted his attention to the left. "Mom?"

Louise Barrish, hands resting one atop the other on her lap, mouthed a polite "No" and looked back out the window, watching as the mountains became clearer through the haze. Seeing the first wisps of snow, the lush green hills, the animals meandering through pastures. All the beautiful things. All the good things. All the . . .

"What are you crying about?" John asked his wife, seeing the tears roll down her face.

Louise looked toward the floor and shook her head. "Nothing."

Stanley rose up in his seat a bit and leaned toward the driver's door to get a look at his mother in the rearview mirror. "Mom? You okay?"

"I'm fine, Stanley."

"She cries over anything," Toby commented. Especially lately, he thought to himself next. *No offense, Pop, but no wife of mine will ever snivel like that.*

"I am fine," Louise repeated, wanting to deflect attention from herself. She knew what unwanted attention elicited from her husband, and the bruise he'd given her that first night back had just gone away. She had avoided any more by simply fading further and further into the background. No challenges, at least none that she could identify as such before letting them slip out. No. It was best to just stay in the shadows. To cook his meals. To keep wherever they were living clean. And to say nothing. Nothing. She felt the tears want to come again, and looked out the window to the beautiful scenery to force the desire from her mind.

"Listen," Toby said loudly as he turned the volume up on the car radio.

". . . the casualties are numerous, and area hospitals are inundated. Initial reports, still unconfirmed, indicate the cause of what can only be called a disaster that began to unfold this morning in the First Interstate World Center in downtown Los Angeles may be nerve gas. We'll have more on this breaking story next . . ."

"YEEEEEESSSSS!" Toby screamed. "Pop! Pop! Did you hear that?"

John drew in a deep breath and let his head fall back. "I heard."

"It worked! They did it!" *The niggers were good for something after all!* The thought of it made Toby roll with laughter in the front seat.

"We really did it," Stanley said, though his words

were drowned out by his brother's raucous laughter.

Toby regained his composure and looked to the backseat. His mother was staring out the window, more tears streaming down her cheeks, and his father's head was still resting on the rear deck. He looked so peaceful. So content. So . . . "Pop?"

Stanley looked in the rearview. "What?"

"Shh," Toby said. "He's asleep."

Stanley looked back to the road ahead. His father was made of steel, though some would say stone, and others ice. But there was no denying the man was made of something that others were wise to respect . . . even to fear. Stanley saved a little of both for the man who had given him life.

"Just drive, Stan," Toby said. "He deserves the rest. It's been a rough couple weeks."

"I know it's been rough." He glanced again to the mirror and the sight of his quietly weeping mother. "For all of us."

"Dammit, Frankie," Art said painfully. "She's in there."

Frankie put a hand on her partner's shoulder and rubbed firmly. She could understand the feeling of helplessness completely. Standing a full two blocks from the tower, a position enforced by the fire department's hazardous materials unit and a phalanx of no-nonsense blue suits, there was little anyone could do but stand in the steady downpour and wait. Even the members of the haz-mat team were holding back, waiting for instructions from the Army personnel on-scene.

"This can't be happening."

"Art, go easy."

"They're not doing anything."

"Orwell is in there now." Frankie dug deeper with her fingers. "He'll know what to do. And they'll listen to him."

Art nodded curtly, his eyes locked on the scene just outside the tower's Fifth Street entrance. Body upon body, some collapsed on top of others, littered the sidewalk and the empty street. *Anne could be there. She could be one of . . .*

"Damn you, Barrish. If she . . ."

"Art." Frankie gave her partner a gentle shake and gestured down the street. Emerging from the building were three men in oversized white coveralls topped by bubble helmets. "Orwell's out."

They watched together as the trio of men moved to a decontamination area they had set up a hundred feet from the building. A shower assembly, with several heads arrayed around a frame somewhat larger than the standard-size door, stood inside what looked like a large wading pool surrounded by a clear plastic tent. Several hoses snaked from the base of the containment pool to a small pump, and from there to a tank truck. The three walked one at a time through the high-pressure shower, which sprayed a mixture of water and a chemical neutralizer over every exposed portion of their protective outer suits. Once all three were through, one man used a hand-held gas probe to check for any residual contamination left on his comrades, and was then checked himself. Once satisfied, they passed through the shower once more, then through blowers in a similar tent enclosure a few yards away. Emerging from that they removed the white outer suits and disposed of them in seriously marked red drums. Beneath the outer suit was the basic camouflage "gas suit" issued to all Army personnel, though to this a nonstandard respirator and rebreathing apparatus had been added. It took just a minute for the men to step out of these restrictive garments, which two members of the team went about drying of perspiration. Captain Orwell, wearing just an olive-drab jumpsuit now, headed directly for the agents a block and a half from him.

"Is it?" Art asked as the officer drew near.

"VZ," Orwell answered, nodding, the welcome cool rain cascading over his body. "But I was ninety-nine-point-nine sure of that when I heard the first fire reports. A lot of people were saying they smelled sulfur, or the scent fireworks give off when they're set off. That's a product of the VZ binary."

"I thought these things were supposed to be odorless," Frankie said. "You know. No warning until it's too late."

"It was too late for most of the people that did smell it," Orwell reported reluctantly. The sight of bodies everywhere inside the skyscraper was burned into his psyche. He feared he'd be having nightmares about this for weeks to come. "But you're right about the common concept of how the agents can be detected. VZ is no different in a complete state. If Kostin had manufactured it as a singular product it would have been odorless. But when VZ is made as a binary there's a reaction between the two reagents that produce not only the desired agent, but also several by-products. It was the by-products that people were smelling."

"And that clued you in," Frankie said.

Orwell nodded. "We also verified it with a chemical analysis. There's no doubt."

"Is there anyone alive in there?" Art asked.

"We were only able to make a cursory inspection, but, no. I didn't see anybody." Orwell knew the agent's reason for concern. "I wish I could tell you more."

"What now, Captain?" Frankie inquired.

"I've got more personnel coming in, and we're going to get the haz-mat guys from fire up-to-speed on procedures so we can use them. Let me tell you, those guys saved a lot of lives. The first fire and police units on-scene rushed in just like up on Riverside. They look like official rag dolls now strewn all over the lobby and stairwells. The haz-mat crew held everybody back once they got on-scene.''

Frankie's head shook slowly. Dead cops. Dead fire-fighters. Dead civilians. ''Are you going back in?''

''As soon as I have more people. We need to find out how the stuff got in there. I know it was spread through the ventilation system. That's the only way it could get from the top of the building to the bottom. We only got up to ten, and there were bodies up to there.'' Orwell looked skyward briefly. ''Thank God for the rain. We didn't have to make our own here. On a dry, windy day . . . We were lucky.''

''Lucky?'' Art snapped out of his narrowly focused state of worry. ''*Lucky?* Captain, the woman I love works in that building. Tell me how lucky I am.''

Orwell looked to Frankie, who gave a very slight shake of the head. ''I didn't mean—''

Art turned away and paced several yards before stopping. This just couldn't be happening. Not Anne. Not her. Next came the selfish streak, and the pain that any thought of living without her brought on. *Not now. Not when I'm starting to live again . . .*

''Art!''

His head jerked up at the faint call, which came from somewhere in the distance. He looked right, through Pershing Square, then left, then every which way in search of the face to match the familiar voice. Or was it just a dream, a wish already dead? Something he wanted to hear but never would again.

''Art!''

It wasn't his imagination. ''Anne!''

''Art! Here!''

A hand swung back and forth in the air behind the police barricade two blocks distant. Below it was a face that he would have recognized had their separation been twice what it was. ''Anne!''

''Art! Art!'' Anne yelled, tears mixing with the rain

on her face as she jumped high to be seen above the crowd of onlookers.

Art covered the distance almost before his partner knew he was gone, and she was now racing to catch up with him. But his attention was focused forward, on one set of eyes, on one face, on the one woman he loved.

"Anne!" He reached the barricade line as she pushed forward and threw his arms around her, pulling her as close to his body as possible. But not close enough. Never could he bring her close enough to wipe away the pain, the fear that had enveloped him at the thought of her being . . .

"Art. You're okay." Anne had an equally tight grip on him, and let herself be pulled over the barricade. Neither noticed the protestations of the nearest police officer, which were ended as Frankie came up and set matters straight.

"Anne. God, I thought you were in there."

"Art, what happened?" Anne asked, her voice trembling. "Lena was in there, Art. She's got three kids. Three kids!"

Art held on tight as Anne began to sob. "Anne, it'll be all right."

"Art. The radio said someone did this. It wasn't an accident. Who? Who would do something like this?"

Art opened his eyes, releasing a river of tears, and looked to the sky. He wanted to tell her that a vile animal had made this all happen, but he knew that was a lie. This was the work of a man, a member of the only species to harbor hate as a way of life.

"Who, Art? Who could do this?"

Again he didn't answer. He simply held her close, giving her what sense of safety he could offer at the moment. There was nothing more he could do.

At least not yet.

SIXTEEN
Casualties

The president looked to his two advisers from the most powerful chair on the planet as the casualty figure numbed him into a feeling of absolute weakness. "One to two thousand? My dear God."

Bud saw the president go pale, almost the shade of the drapes to either side of his Oval Office desk. The Man was hearing an official number for the first time since the attack eight hours earlier, and had not had the luxury of a few minutes to let the enormity of the carnage sink in. Bud had, and it still made his knees weak. He surmised that the chief of staff, who stood next to him before the president's desk, was in a similar state.

"That's preliminary," Gonzales added. "The Bureau says it's probably closer to two."

The president leaned back in his chair and brought a shaky hand to his mouth. Some would be given pause at the sight, but there was a vast difference between crisis management and the reality of the deliberate murder of this many Americans. "Is everything being done to get help there?"

Bud nodded assuredly. "The Army has their chemical people on-scene, and the governor declared a state of emergency for Los Angeles County." It was a formality, the NSA knew, and really it would have little impact on such a focused event. But appearances did count, and often such measures put the public a little more at ease. The "do something" theory of response.

"Any suspects?"

"The Bureau is shifting into high gear," Gonzales reported. "Director Jones should be landing there any minute to get an update. They've been following a situation that probably led up to this. A few minutes ago we got word that they want to talk to someone very familiar: John Barrish."

The president seethed at that. They had had the man behind bars, and let him get away. But even a white supremacist murdering bastard had the right to due process, the lawyer in the chief executive reminded the rest of the man. *But how many times* . . .

"Mr. President," Gonzales began, "the press office also got wind that the *Post* is going to report tomorrow that several members of the Judiciary Committee are going to call for Jones's resignation."

"For Christ's sake!" the president swore. "They haven't even been briefed and already . . ."

"Where there are bodies . . ." the chief of staff mused soberly.

"The goddamn vultures should show a little decorum," the president suggested angrily. But he knew the reason why that would never be more than a hope. A reason less than a year away. Yes, there were vultures out there, and they were circling 1600 Pennsylvania Avenue with a vengeance. "Bud, regardless of what the Bureau thinks, what are the chances of this being an outside job?"

"Possible, but not likely. From what I know of the Bureau investigation to this point, all the indicators lend credence to this being a homegrown operation."

"If it is that bastard . . ." the president began, avoiding finishing his statement.

"The Bureau will find whoever it is, sir," Gonzales said assuredly.

The president accepted his chief of staff's analysis with a sharp nod. "I want something detailed in the morning. From all ends."

"Yes, Mr. President," Bud acknowledged, reading the request as a signal that their briefing session had ended. He led the way out of the Oval Office, making a left turn outside the office of the president's personal secretary. The chief of staff was right behind and followed the NSA to his office.

"This really hurt him," Gonzales commented. Having grown up with the president he knew better than most when he was truly affected by events.

"In 'eighty-six we lost seven astronauts and they postponed the State of the Union," Bud said. "We lose two thousand the day before Thanksgiving. What do we do with that day, now?"

"We get through it," Gonzales answered. "And we press on."

"That wouldn't sound good in print," Bud reminded the chief of staff.

"Reality usually doesn't."

Darren Griggs pressed the doorbell, the third in an hour, and said a silent prayer.

"Hello?" a young voice answered from inside, the light shining through the peephole fading as someone surveyed the visitor.

"This is Mr. Griggs. I'm Moises' father. I'm looking for him."

There was a pause as several locks clicked, then the door slowly opened. A young man looking eerily like his son peered through the still-closed screen at Darren.

"Are you Vincent?"

"Yeah."

"You're a friend of Moises'?"

"Well, yeah," the youngster answered hesitantly, the way most teenagers would to a strange adult.

"Have you seen him? Is he here?"

"Here? No, man—I mean Mr. Griggs. I haven't seen him for a couple weeks."

Another disappointment. Another negative response. Was it the truth, or just a friend protecting a friend? Darren had to know for sure. "Tomorrow is Thanksgiving, and his mother and I want him to come home. That's all. No trouble or anything. We just want him home, with us."

"He split?" the young man asked, surprised.

Darren nodded. "Please, we just want him to come back home."

"Really, I don't know where he is. I'm being straight with you, Mr. Griggs."

"I see." Darren pulled a small envelope preaddressed to his son and passed it through the screen's mail slot. "If you do see him, please give him this."

"Yeah. Okay."

"Thank you, Vincent." Darren stood motionless as the door swung shut, and as the locks clicked again, then walked away from the porch of the well-kept home in south Los Angeles. It was dark out, just three hours shy of a new day, a time when "bad things happened to good people." A time when there were few reasons to venture out.

Darren Griggs had only one, and that singular reason was enough.

"Shit!" Roger swore, his head angling forward to get a full view of the flashing lights in his sideview mirror.

"What?" Darian asked as he came out of a light sleep, an answer becoming unnecessary as a bright white light pierced the interior of the Olds from the rear.

"What's going on?" Moises asked as his own slumber was interrupted. He started to turn to look through the back window, but that action was cut off by Darian's strong left arm, which swung across his chest like a roller-coaster restraint bar.

Mustafa rose up from his curl in the front seat and carefully eyed the right-side mirror. "Just one car."

"Where the hell are we?" Darian asked, rolling the stiffness from his neck, and easing the zipper of the gym bag between him and Moises open.

"Utah, somewhere around Provo." A quick blast of siren made Roger jump. "Man, we either gotta run or pull over."

"Provo!" Darian said just below a yell. "I told you to take the Seventy!"

"I thought you said *don't* take the Seventy."

"Are you a fool! You're taking us right up to Salt Lake, Ogden, and all the other big cities." Darian's hands felt for his weapon, but it was empty. There was no time to fish for a magazine. He felt for the one Mustafa had added to the bag. It was still loaded at that time. He found his comrade's Ingram and deftly removed its suppressor without looking and blindly made certain a round was chambered. "There aren't more than a handful of brothers in the whole state and you're taking us straight into whiteville." He lowered the zipper on his jacket and slid the Ingram in the left side, safety off. "Pull over. Shit." He looked slightly toward Moises. "Whatever you do, don't lean forward, Brother."

Moises took a deep breath and put his foot over the gym bag that Darian had let slide to the floor of the Olds. "Okay."

Trooper Michael Fitzroy eased his Utah Highway Patrol cruiser to the emergency shoulder of the interstate and made sure his spotlight was focused fully on the Cutlass's interior before taking the mike in hand. "Trooper Six David, Provo, traffic stop at Seventy-five connector to I-Fifteen." Fitzroy, an eight-year veteran of the UHP, waited for acknowledgment from his dispatcher before taking his hand-held radio from its charger and stepping from the cruiser, stopping after only a half-step when the one new procedure—some called it a bother—that had slipped his mind flashed in his thoughts. A quick lean back into the car took care of it, and then he approached the older-model Cutlass on the driver's side, right hand on his holstered weapon and left hand holding the heavy flashlight high to get a good angle into the vehicle.

"How y'all doing tonight?" Fitzroy asked the driver through the open front window as his eyes scanned the inside of the vehicle. Four male blacks, no obvious open containers, no smell of alcohol or marijuana. Just the glassy stares of men who'd been on the road a long time. The driver especially, and that was his concern.

"Fine," Roger answered, looking up past the bright spot of light shining down at him. "Did I do something wrong?"

"How long have you been driving?"

"Quite a while."

"Well, you were weaving a bit back there." Again Trooper Fitzroy sniffed the air. Still nothing, but there was a bit of an edge to this guy's voice. "You crossed into the adjacent lanes at least four times."

Shithead! Darian leaned forward a bit, crossing his arms on his knees, one finger touching the cold grip of the Ingram. *I told you to wake one of us if you got tired!*

"I'm sorry," Roger said, averting his eyes to look straight ahead. "I guess I'm a little tired."

Mmm hmm. "Okay, I want to make sure of that for myself. Do you have your license and registration with you?"

"Yes, sir." Roger patted his jacket, feeling for the wallet.

"Just leave it in there," Fitzroy said. "I'm gonna give you a field sobriety test to . . ."

Damn! Once he was out of the car the pig would ask him where he was heading. Then he'd bring in reinforcements and do the same with each of them separately. *Dammit!* Darian was cursing himself now for not planning for this contingency. They should have had a singular story all fleshed out to use in just such an instance. As it was there was only one thing to do.

"... check for any impairment. Would you—" Fitzroy's words froze in his throat as the movement came quick and unexpected from the backseat. He swiveled the flashlight to the rear of the car to illuminate whatever was going on as his right thumb released the topstrap on his holster. The beam of white went not to the faces—faces might frighten, but they are not dangerous—but to the hands, which were on the occupant's lap. The far occupant was reaching across and toward the window with—*NO!*

Darian didn't know what effect the glass would have on his shots, so he swung the Ingram back and forth as he sprayed the rounds at the pig, destroying the window and sending his target falling from view.

"SHIT!" Roger screamed, ducking, then looking in the sideview mirror. "He's still out there! He's on the ground! He's moving!"

Darian ejected the empty magazine and noisily dug another out of the gym bag and inserted it. He crawled over Moises and peeked through the permanently open side window just in time to see the pig disappear behind the car, crawling on his belly. A wide trail of blood marked his path. "Stay down."

The NALF leader popped the door handle and stepped out after cautioning his comrades. Down the interstate he could see only a speck of white approaching, some distance off. But this wouldn't take long. He edged along the car toward the rear, the stubby Ingram held forward one-handed. A raspy scraping rose from the asphalt behind the Olds, which Darian could tell was the sound of hard soles pushing off the pavement. And there was breathing, or wheezing, which came and went in short bursts. As he reached the rear quarter panel the source of both sounds became visible to Darian.

"Hold it, pig."

Trooper Fitzroy, his face abraded and bleeding from being pushed along the roadway as his legs attempted to drive his damaged body to safety, paused at the sound, then rolled onto his back near the right front of his cruiser. He winced in pain as his shattered arms flopped with the motion of his torso. Both limbs from shoulder to elbow were red, pulpy strands that seemed strangely long. They, along with Fitzroy's Kevlar vest, had absorbed the brunt of the submachine gun's punishment. The trooper's gun and radio were still in their place on his Sam Browne, useless to him.

Darian stepped closer, trying unsuccessfully to skirt the swath of blood. His thumb moved the selector switch to single shot as he leveled the weapon at the pig. "How long did you think we'd just sit back and take it, pig?"

Fitzroy's expression became one of mixed pain and puzzlement, but no fear. He knew what was coming, whether the guy shot him or not. Too much blood was pouring from his open wounds. Too much for anything to matter anymore. "They'll get you," Fitzroy said confidently, his voice breathy. "Don't worry."

The short barrel centered on the pig's face. "We got you first." Darian smiled, then pulled the trigger twice, both rounds hitting true and literally exploding the top of the pig's head, which spilled toward the lowest point on the road's shoulder.

"Shit!" Roger yelled from the car. "There's cars coming!"

Darian looked south, squinting past the bright spotlight that shone almost in his face. The single dots had become multiple pairs of distant headlights, and they were coming fast. He gave the patrol car a quick look from where he stood. There was no one else in it. No other pig, and no one locked in the rear seat cage. It was a clean kill. As clean as it could get.

"Come on!"

Darian heeded that call and climbed back in the Olds through the open rear door, pushing Moises over as he did. Roger dropped the car into gear even before the door shut completely and pulled into the traffic lanes with a screech of rubber worthy of Hollywood.

Trooper Fitzroy lay in front of his idling UHP cruiser for another thirty minutes before a passing fellow officer made the grisly discovery. Within twenty minutes there were over fifty state and local law enforcement personnel on-scene. The first thing they did was call for the coroner. The second was to switch off the small Sony video camera mounted in tandem with the cruiser's rearview mirror and remove the standard VHS cassette from the recorder secured in the trunk. It arrived at the Utah Highway Patrol's Salt Lake City headquarters by helicopter twenty-two minutes after that.

SEVENTEEN
Remembrance

A hundred and twenty hours after the first person fell in the attack on the First Interstate World Center, the core of the FBI investigative team was moving beyond the "who" to focus on the "how," a question they believed was explained in the voluminous handwritten diaries of Canadia Conyers Royce.

"I'll read to you," Frankie said. Art, Hal, Omar, and Lou gave their attention as she found the first section she had marked. "Here:

DECEMBER 1985,

The 'Defender,' last month's issue, arrived today, and a very, very powerful piece was on page seventeen. By a man named John Barrish. I have never heard of him before, but he referred to Father's good friend Dr. Trent in the piece. Powerful, I do say. So clearly does he describe the negro problem that I could almost overlook that annoying habit—the same one Dr. Trent had—of calling the negroes Africans. Words, words, words. This is about more than that. I must look into this John Barrish. I definitely must."

Frankie skipped to the next passage marked by a sticky note. "And this:

MARCH 1986,

John is a charming man. He reminds me so much
of father. Intelligent. No . . . wise. That is the
word. And what power there is to his vision!''

"She sounds infatuated with him," Hal commented.

"What's that *Defender* reference?" Lou asked.

"It's some quarterly white power rag put out by an
old minister who acts as a sort of clearinghouse for all
the groups' writings," Frankie explained. "And Burlingame found an interesting ad in one from three years
back. Placed by some Afrikaner mercenary type who
said there were, quote, 'former East Bloc *specialists* eager to work for the right price,' unquote. An interesting
spin on Royce's trip, wouldn't you say?"

"I would say. You read all these?" Art asked, gesturing at the stacks of diaries.

"Every page." Three solid days it had taken, holed
up in a vacant office one floor up. Frankie, a diary writer
herself, felt she knew Canadia Conyers Royce now, a
state of familiarity that had pity and anger as tagalong
emotions.

"So she read something by Barrish and . . . what?"
Art wondered.

"This goes back further than Barrish's piece in the
Defender," Frankie explained, recalling the passages
laid upon the yellowed pages eighty-odd years earlier.
"It goes all the way back to the Civil War. Mrs. Royce's
family was originally from Charleston. Big shipping
people. Her grandfather squirreled away his money in
gold, and when the war started he fought for the Con-
federacy. He lived through it all and moved north with
his booty when it was all over. But he didn't forget his
suthun ways. He was one of the original organizers of
the Klan in Massachusetts, and his son—Mrs. Royce's
father—followed in his footsteps. The business Gramps

had set up did well and they never hesitated to support their fellow hood-heads.''

''So Mrs. Royce had a background that lent itself to John Barrish's way of thinking,'' Art proposed.

''Step one: like ideology. Step two: contact. After she read the *Defender* she started corresponding with Barrish. Eventually they met, and she liked him a lot.''

''A May-December thing,'' Hal suggested facetiously.

''In a way it was,'' Frankie responded. ''For her, at least. Women think differently, fellas. Older women like Mrs. Royce in particular. There's a romantic sort of thing about being 'connected' to a younger, powerful man. And she saw John Barrish as very powerful.

''So, step three: assistance. She started giving him money for the AVO, just like her father and grandfather had done for the Klan.''

''How much altogether?'' Lou inquired.

''She never said in the diaries, but she was loaded.''

''The money was hers, not Monte's,'' Omar reported. ''He had the business, but she had the family fortune tucked away. We ran down her accounts and found withdrawal after withdrawal, all cash. And remember those cash bundles in the desk drawer? Those match exactly in amount with several withdrawals.''

''And who—need I ask—did the actual withdrawing?'' Lou wondered needlessly.

''Mrs. Royce's signature on the papers, Monte Royce's hands on the cash. She'd okay it, he'd go pick it up.'' Omar shrugged. ''From him it somehow got to Barrish and Kostin and whoever else she was supporting. But we do know it totaled over fifteen million from the time she met Barrish.''

''Fifteen million?'' The A-SAC slid back in his seat at the head of the table. ''That's a lot of mad money.''

''Hate money,'' Art corrected the emotion.

Lou Hidalgo nodded. ''So Mrs. Royce bankrolled

Barrish because she liked him." His face screwed into a frown.

"That, and some of the nostalgic connections," Frankie expanded. "Remember what she said about Trent? That's Felix Trent."

"The guy Barrish put on a pedestal?" Hidalgo said, leafing through the thick mental file devoted to the AVO leader.

"The same one," Frankie confirmed. "Mrs. Royce's father was a friend of Trent's. In a way she thought of her connection with Barrish as a sort of divine signal." She paused, feeling a connection herself to Mrs. Royce. But it was only gender, and that was grossly insufficient to allow understanding of her actions. "The stupid old woman."

"What else do we know?" Hidalgo asked.

"The minivan the Barrishes used was found at a shopping center in Palmdale," Art reported. "Their house was deserted."

"What about the Mankowitz and Royce hits?" That was something Hidalgo was puzzled about.

"Royce and his mother were hit sometime between five and eight," Art answered.

"That was the coroner's finding," Frankie added. "But some things at the house point to a more concrete time. Royce was up, dressed, and in the kitchen. The nurse said he usually got up at six. Give him half an hour to dress and make his tea, and that puts it back to six-thirty. And the alarm was manually turned off at seven-fifteen. The security company that monitors their system records the times the systems are active for liability purposes."

"So whether Royce or someone else turned off the alarm, we have them getting hit at the earliest at seven-fifteen," Art said. "Mankowitz we know was hit at one minute after eight from the nine-one-one calls reporting glass breaking and strange sounds. They used silencers, we're certain, otherwise it would have been a 'shots fired' call. All the callers were hearing was the sound of the rounds hitting Mankowitz's Mercedes.''

"Forty-five minutes apart and different calibers," Hidalgo observed.

"Three-eighty on the Royces, and forty-fives on Mankowitz," Lightman said. "And two forty-fives on World Center's plant manager. All the spent casings were clean. Wiped before they were loaded. Smooth prints. Pro-like."

"The only people we know of that Barrish had to work with him are his family," Art said. "A wife and two sons. No record on any of them."

"This is a lot of work for four people," Hidalgo commented. "The Royces, Mankowitz, the World Center. All within an hour and fifteen minutes."

Art had no answer for that obvious and very correct observation. But there had to be one, and he would find it.

A single tap on the conference room door preceded Special Agent Dan Burlingame. His expression told those gathered to drop what they were doing. "KMOC just got a call from some group claiming the World Center as their work."

"We have a hundred claims, Dan," Art reminded him.

"Did any of those others know that the cylinder of nerve gas was in the A/C ducts on Seventy-four?"

The silence after Dan's revelation of the message's most important part was brief, just long enough for looks to be exchanged.

"I have a team going over for a copy of it," Burlingame said.

"Who made the claim?" Art asked.

"Some group called the New Africa Liberation Front."

Art's eyes narrowed. *New Africa?* What in the hell was going on?

"I made a quick check on this group," Burlingame reported. "We have them listed only as a matter of record, but LAPD has a file on them."

"They're an actual group?" Art asked skeptically.

Burlingame nodded. "I've got the address LAPD has on them."

"Liberation Front?" Espinosa said. "Sounds like a revolutionary bunch."

"That's what LAPD said," Burlingame confirmed.

"Are you saying this is a *black* group?"

Burlingame nodded to Art. He knew it wasn't the answer desired. But it was a fact. "Black revolutionaries. That's what LAPD called them."

Damn. Art looked to the A-SAC and stood. "We'll check it out."

Hidalgo stood, too. "Fast."

Art gave a crisp nod and turned to Burlingame. "The address?"

"On my desk."

"Let's do it."

Cars were like fingerprints, but infinitely more simple to dispose of. Activities and people could be traced to, or through, a car, and the Oldsmobile Cutlass involved in the shooting of Utah Highway Patrol Trooper Fitzroy made it only as far as Orem, Utah. There it was left burning in an empty parking space of a large apartment complex in favor of a Volkswagen van with a rickety box trailer attached whose owner would be needing it no more. That lasted the rest of their journey to Baltimore, then it, too, had to be done away with in favor of "clean" transportation. And more transportation.

Darian eased the just-purchased '84 Volvo sedan into the space to the right of the later-model Ford van. Its door slid open as he stopped.

"Brother Darian," Roger said, sitting in the van's first bench seat and running a hand over his newly shaved head. "Like my new doo?"

Mustafa leaned forward and looked from the front window. "We all need to look different."

Darian nodded agreement, though they'd have to retain some individuality. "As long as we're not four bald black guys running around together. And lose the hat, Brother."

Mustafa reached up and slid the brimless NALF cap off.

"Where'd you ditch the Volkswagen?" Darian asked.

"In the river back off Ninety-five," Mustafa answered, turning back to Roger. "What was the name of the place?"

"Laurel, wasn't it?" the smooth-headed revolutionary responded without surety.

Mustafa shrugged. "Anyway, it's nowhere near here."

Roger bent down and looked past Darian to the passenger seat. "Brother Moises. How goes it?"

"It goes, Brother Roger." Moises ran a hand over his still intact buzz cut. "But I'll keep my doo, if you don't mind."

"Better put some whiskers on that baby face, then," Roger ribbed. "Make that boy look full-grown, Brother Darian."

The NALF leader ignored the joking and looked to his number two. "I made the call."

"Good." Let them know that the black man knows how to strike back, Mustafa thought.

"Did you find a place?" Darian asked.

"A little apartment over by Mercy Hospital. You and Brother Moises?"

"We're going to look now."

Mustafa removed a piece of paper and handed it to

Darian. "This is the phone booth across the street from our place."

"Okay. Settle in and lay low. We'll call you a week from today."

Mustafa nodded. "Next Monday."

"Two in the afternoon," Darian said, putting the cream-colored Volvo in reverse. "Don't be late."

"Never," Mustafa promised.

Art exited the "headquarters" of the New Africa Liberation Front on South Vermont to the sound of thunder in the distance and the sight of Director Gordon Jones approaching from his car. The director's accompanying entourage was hanging back.

"Sir," Art said as Jones stopped just short of him.

The director acknowledged the greeting with a nod and looked past the agent to the nondescript front of the NALF's apparent home. "They're the ones?"

"It appears so," Art said without conviction. He saw the director notice his hedging straight away. "They have to be. No one outside the team or the Army captain in charge of the building search knew where that cylinder was found."

"Are we sure it was these guys who made the call?" Jones inquired.

"A note left inside says the same thing their call did," Art informed him. "I can't see any reason not to believe their claim."

Jones looked to his agent now. "Then why don't you sound as sure as your words?" An answer didn't come, and that didn't surprise the director. "Not the perps you expected."

"No, sir."

The drizzle that was almost nonexistent suddenly gained form. Drops tapped Art's head, while Jones opened a collapsible umbrella for them both. "I read the reports your A-SAC was sending. You were leaning toward John Barrish as a suspect.''

''Yes, sir.''

The New *Africa* Liberation Front. Jones looked again to the storefront, then back to Art. ''And now? What explains this? It doesn't exactly fit into that theory.''

From any other person, in any other tone, Art would have seen this as a mocking attack on the work he'd done so far. But it was not. The director was simply searching for answers. For *the* answer.

''Barrish was still involved with Allen, Kostin, and Royce,'' Art began. ''I'm sure of that. These guys . . . I don't know.''

''Customers?'' Jones suggested.

''Kostin the salesman.'' Art considered that.

''Selling his wares to whoever on the side,'' Jones added. ''The 'whoever' in this case was the NALF.''

Art nodded, but it was only a series of muscle contractions. He couldn't add complete agreement to that scenario. But he couldn't dispute it with any credible evidence to the contrary, either.

''You didn't screw up, Jefferson,'' Jones said. ''You had a target. A good target. No one knew there was more than one.''

Screw up? Did I?

''A-SAC Los Angeles says you're still on this. Find these bastards.''

Again Art nodded, but little was behind this gesture either. Too little, too late . . . at least for those in the World Center. ''Will do, sir.''

Jones lingered for a moment, then walked back to his car as the sky opened to a full downpour. Art Jefferson stood in the rain and watched him drive away.

EIGHTEEN
Direction

Frankie grabbed the phone on the second ring as Art paged through what information the LAPD had provided on the New Africa Liberation Front. "Aguirre."

The prolonged silence after that brought Art's eyes up. His partner's head was bobbing gently at what was being said over the phone, her pen jerking like a seismograph's stylus back and forth across a legal pad.

"Spell it," Frankie said. "O-R-E-M." She listened for a few seconds more before hanging up.

"What is it?"

"Utah Highway Patrol had an officer killed the night of the World Center attack," Frankie explained. "The officer had a camera setup running and it recorded the thing on tape. There was some bad glare from his spotlight on the back window of the car, so they sent it to our lab in Washington for enhancement. It came back this morning, with—guess who—Darian Brown shown gunning down the officer. There were three other male blacks in the car."

"It was at *our* lab and *our* people didn't recognize him?" Art shook his head.

"Well, they found the car torched right after the shooting and traced it back here," Frankie continued. "The RO sold it just before the attack to some guy. It was a cash-under-the-table deal, so no paperwork. They had no way of knowing the two were related until they got the tape back and matched it with our bulletins on the NALF.''

The drip of Art's decaf filling the pot marked the silent seconds as he thought. "Three other males plus Brown, huh? We only know of Brown and two others. They picked up someone new."

"Or someone we didn't know about."

"Hmmm," Art grunted. "They found the car in Orem?"

"Yeah."

"I assume they're running down all stolens there."

"Six the night of the murder," Frankie reported.

"Quiet city," Art commented. "Get a copy of that tape directly from our lab in D.C. Have Hal and Omar run the pictures of the known NALF members past the guy who sold them the car."

"Got it," Frankie said.

Art turned off his coffeemaker and poured himself a cup of unleaded. "Four black guys in Utah? Not the best place to hide out."

"A common place to travel through, though," Frankie observed.

"Yep." Art sipped from his mug. The small stack of plastic hot cups next to the coffeemaker was for visitors. "You know what this means."

Frankie nodded. "They've got somewhere to go."

Earl Casey surprised the president's chief of staff in his West Wing office just before lunch.

"Earl, I was just heading to Duke's for a bite. You want to join me?"

"No, thanks." Casey walked to Gonzales's desk and stood at its side. "I want you to do something."

"What?"

Casey explained his idea in less than the predicted

sixty seconds. When he finished the chief of staff was smiling thoughtfully.

"I ran it by the Man a few minutes ago, and he liked it. He even thought there might be an opening to the speech in the whole thing."

"I think he may be right," Gonzales agreed blindly, though not without some sense of what the president might be thinking. "Interesting."

"I want to do it," Casey said. "It smells right."

"Agreed."

"Will you take care of the invitation?"

Gonzales nodded and made a note to take care of it right away. "With pleasure."

Toby entered the spacious living room from the kitchen scratching his dyed and shorn hair. "How do I look?"

"Like a bad Elvis impersonator," Stanley commented from his seat by the roaring fire.

"Funny. Mom's ready for *you* now." Toby pulled a short punch at his little brother and took the seat vacated by the crackling fireplace. His father sat quietly in an overstuffed chair. Behind him out the huge window the purples and oranges of the setting sun draped the skies above the George Washington National Forest. "I like this place, Pop. The view's a lot nicer than back home."

"It's temporary, Toby," John Barrish reminded his son.

"I know. But it's nice. I think Mom likes it a lot."

John looked over his shoulder to the expanse of meadow behind the house. Five grand a month it was costing them, plus a twenty grand deposit, and for that he had a fireplace, three thousand square feet, solitude at the end of a country road near Fulks Run, Virginia, and a view of a doe browsing near the tree line. An expensive and comfortable way station, but a way station nonetheless.

"What color contacts are you getting?"

"Brown," Toby answered.

John surveyed his eldest boy's new appearance. It wasn't right. It needed something. The lines of his face were still too familiar. "Grow a mustache, and make sure your mother dyes it."

"Okay."

A log, consumed to the point of being a single roll of orange embers, collapsed in the fireplace, sending a plume of sparks upward into the dark recesses of the riverstone chimney. A burst of heat accompanied the disintegration, causing John to slide his chair back from the hearth.

"What about you, Pop?"

John touched his growing gray locks, which he'd maintained at a militarylike one inch since high school. "Shaggy red hair and a goatee."

"That'll do it," Toby commented, smiling at the thought of his father as a carrot-top.

"What about the Africans?" John inquired.

"I'll put an ad in the *Baltimore Sun* in a couple of weeks. They'll be expecting it then."

"And Vorhees?"

The sound of scissors clicking rapidly drew Toby's eyes toward the kitchen briefly. "Stan's going to start on that soon. We'll be ready. What about the tools and stuff?"

In his earlier life, before exposition of his views generated the kind of money that could finance an organization *and* support a family, John Barrish had made a modest living as a machinist. Nothing so complicated would be needed in this instance. Mostly hand tools, an arc-welding rig, and several types of metal. Light metal. Strong metal. Yes, expensive metal, but the money had to be spent on something. "I'll take care of those."

Toby nodded and let his body press into the soft cushions of the couch. They had been on the move, always busy, for so long that relaxation felt alien. But it also felt good. "Hey, Pop. You wanna go find a lake tomorrow? There's got to be one around here somewhere. We ain't got anything else to do. Maybe have a picnic, or go fishing?"

"It's winter, Toby," John said. "The fish don't bite well this time of year." The father-to-son instructions on life's important matters flashed in John's mind. His father had said something about fishing then. *Don't fish in the winter,* or something like that. He hadn't passed things such as that to his boys. He wondered if he should have.

"I didn't say we had to catch anything," Toby said. "C'mon. You, me, Stan. We'll just sit, and throw some lines in the water, and shoot the shit."

His eldest boy had a way of conversing with innocent vulgarities, John knew. He'd never gotten that out of him. But the suggestion behind the four-letter word did hold some appeal. Some day, when all that was to come had run its course, there would be much time to relax, to recreate. It might be a good time to practice for that day.

"What do you say?"

John nodded, realizing he should accept the calm before the storm. "All right, son."

NINETEEN

Arrangements

Frankie held the three-year-old police mug shot up to the freeze-frame image on the conference room's thirty-inch television monitor. "That's him."

"Roland Kirk," Art said, referring to the enhanced image of the Oldsmobile's right front passenger. "AKA Ronald Christopher. AKA Mustafa Ali." He flipped back to the man's arrest and conviction record. "Hmmm."

"What?"

"The two most recent hits—B and E, and a simple assault—go under the Ali name. He must have changed it legally."

"Converted to Islam," Frankie observed.

"This is a hell of a way to exemplify the religion." Art set the three suspect profiles side by side on the dark brown table. "Darian Brown, Roger Sanders, Mustafa Ali, and a mystery rider."

"I remember Sanders from his playing days," Frankie said. "He blew his knee out, I think."

"He also liked punching folks out," Art told his partner. "Two counts of aggravated assault, served a year at Chino."

Frankie spun Brown's profile around to face the seat she took across from Art. "Fearless leader here has one aggravated, two petty thefts, one GTA, one burglary. He beat a murder one. He's spent a total of three years inside, a combination of county and state time.''

''And for every time they were caught . . .'' Art, like all law enforcement officers, knew that an arrest or conviction on a person's record represented just a fraction of the crimes actually committed. The sad fact was that men like Brown, Ali, and Sanders put their hands in the cookie jar without getting caught more than anyone would ever know.

Art looked to the screen and rewound it to a point before the enlargements of each individual. ''Sanders driving.'' They knew now that he had purchased the Oldsmobile in a plainly illegal transaction in Los Angeles before the attack. A glance at Sanders's picture and a threat to bother the man with ''accessory'' charges had refreshed his memory quite fast. ''Ali in right front. Brown, right rear.'' His eyes locked on the small head in a darkened profile. ''The lab wasn't able to do much with him, were they?''

''The light was coming in at the back of his head,'' Frankie said.

''Looks young,'' Art observed, though there was little else he could discern. The profile as the head turned showed sharp lines, tight skin, smooth even. Short, neat hair. Familiar, almost, but then a kid in silhouette was likely to look like any other.

The tape raced back, then slid forward from the time that the left rear window exploded. Trooper Fitzroy rocking side to side as the bullets stitched across his torso, sound on the tape ending as a round cut the trooper's body mike, falling, crawling with only his legs driving him, Brown coming out, following—no, stalking Fitzroy, his mouth moving as something was said, and two shots.

Art froze the tape there. ''The bullets that killed the trooper and the World Center's plant manager, Harback, came from the same gun. That ties the two events.''

"And the prints," Frankie added. Dan Jacobs's team had pulled fingerprints from both Brown and Sanders from the cylinder found in the ventilation system. Doing so had been a trick in itself, as decontaminating the small tank with high-pressure steam and chemical neutralizers would have destroyed any prints. The solution was to take a video feed of the prints as illuminated by a helium laser and analyze those after the feed was digitized and stored as computer data. Jacobs seemed more magician than special agent at times.

Art stayed focused on the screen, rewinding then moving slowly forward as the boxy weapon in Brown's hand bucked twice. "Harback and Fitzroy with forty-fives. Mankowitz with a forty-five. Mankowitz was hit with automatic fire." Art froze the image again. "Not too many automatic forty-fives out there other than a MAC-11."

"All firing hundred-and-eighty-five-grain jacketed hollow-points," Frankie added. "But the lab couldn't batch all three." Expended bullets could be matched to a particular weapon based on the rifling characteristics of the barrel, and could also be closely matched to each other based upon their lead composition. This information was accurate enough to place bullets to specific production runs at ammunition manufacturers. But distribution and inventory anomalies at retailers made the system less than consistent in the real world. A weapon like the Ingram could spit out more than a box of .45 rounds in a second, meaning it could chew through a shelf full of boxes in no time. And that shelf could hold boxes from production runs completed six months earlier, or from the week before.

"The guns," Art said, adding no more for a moment. "Forty-fives across the board here, and three-eighties for Royce and Kostin. Freddy had a three-eighty on him."

Frankie sensed her partner's line of thought. "You think Barrish was behind all these guns?"

"He's proven proficient at it before," Art responded. The two Uzis that had been used in the Saint Anthony's massacre and found dumped at a construction site *were* purchased by John Barrish while at a festival of hate in Idaho. The law said differently, but they were dealing with reality right now. "Plus Allen had the three-eighty that was used with the other guns at Saint Anthony's. Danbrook said that Barrish told him, specifically, that he could get guns whenever he wanted."

"They're different guns, partner," Frankie said.

"But they're guns. Full-auto Uzis and Ingrams. Those have to come from somewhere."

"Just because Barrish said he could get guns, that still doesn't say he got those Ingrams that the NALF used." Frankie's rebuttal ended on a thought of absurdity, and her head shook at it. "Why would Barrish have given guns to the New *Africa* Liberation Front?"

"Why would the NALF have the VZ?" Art fired back.

The door to the conference room swung inward, ending the agents' discussion. Lou Hidalgo was behind it. "Get copies of all the information you have on the World Center, Kostin, and the NALF to Washington . . . pronto."

Art turned to face the A-SAC. "What's up?"

"The police in Maryland pulled a floater from a river. Several weeks old, they figure. A male. Right upstream was a van with a wooden trailer attached; one of those boxy jobs for moving stuff. It looks like the body was in the trailer, which came apart after a while in the river. The Maryland cops ran the plate and got a hit back to a young kid from out here. He left L.A. for Colorado the morning of the World Center attack. He had family there, apparently. He never showed. The last trace he left anywhere was a call on his phone card to his parents' answering machine. He said he was in Orem. The phone company computers put the call at a phone booth a mile from where the NALF torched their car. The kid made it just ten minutes after Brown shot Fitzroy.''

"Checking stolens was a waste, then,'' Art commented. "They just took the owner with them.''

"Denver PD just had an overdue and missing traveler,'' Hidalgo said. "So get the info to Washington. They're taking over the search for our black militant friends. We'll keep filling in background on them—anything that helps. Got it?''

"Sure.''

"Do it fast, Art. The van in the river was ten miles from D.C. as the crow flies. The 'nervous factor' just went through the roof.''

Art nodded. "On the double.''

An afternoon Conrail freight train rumbled in the background as Mustafa and Roger entered their comrades' apartment just north of Greenmount Cemetery. "Got it.''

Darian took the paper from Roger and pulled the thin classified section free.

"Gimme sports,'' Moises said from his place on the worn carpet. His hair was longer than it had ever been. Unkempt, he thought when looking in the mirror, something he did less frequently with each passing day. And he had a scraggly wannabe beard that tried to sprout fully, but itched more than concealed. Still, he had changed enough that few would recognize him. And more than mere physical alteration. He was Moises Griggs a little less each day, and Brother Moises a little more. Soon there would be only one.

Mustafa sat on the bed as his leader scanned the classifieds, and as their newest member reclined on the floor with the sports section. His perpetually flat expression changed at the second scene. "You know what you're doing, Brother Moises?''

"Huh?" Moises looked up from the football scores of the day before.

"With that," Mustafa said. In a chair by the door Roger sat, a pouting smile on his face.

"The paper?"

"The s-s-s-ports section." Mustafa spit lightly into the wastebasket next to the bed.

"What are you talking about?" Moises lowered the paper completely and propped up on his elbows.

"Hey, who's the best players, Brother?" Mustafa inquired.

"Players?"

"Brothers or crackers?"

That was easy enough, Moises knew. "Brothers."

"Which sport?"

"All of them," Moises answered. "Except maybe hockey. But who watches that, anyway?"

"Football, baseball, basketball." Mustafa made a free-throw motion toward Moises. "Brothers be good at those *games*. Oh, yeah. They be good at them. What happens next?"

"Next?"

"After they ain't so good no more?"

Moises didn't have an answer.

"Do them commercials?" Mustafa approximated a laugh. "Yeah, how many *spotes* brothers you ever see on TV when they ain't runnin', or jumpin', or throwin' a little ball? Hmm? Maybe a couple. Oooh, boy, but you can see cracker after cracker sellin' any kinda shit they can think of on the tube, or on them ugly-ass billboards, or anywhere else old cracker folks are gonna see 'em." He was letting his speech degenerate further into the old South nigger talk his father had beat out of him long before. It was for a point. "Oooh, yeah. Cracker get old, or bust a leg, or throw out a arm, well, then cracker can show his pretty white face on TV doin' somethin' else. Brother?" Lips pouted far out, head shaking. "No, brother be too dumb and ugly to do shit like that. Brother can run, an' jump, an' throw, an' put on a good show. That's what brother's good fo'. Brother puts on a good show. Good show. But brother ain't good fo' mo' than that. No, sir, massa sir. No, sir.''

The paper felt heavy in Moises' hands. His face burned with understanding. And with embarrassment.

"He doesn't lie, Brother Moises," Roger said, slapping the knee that would not stand up to the rigors of college basketball. "When this went out they didn't say 'hang around and we'll give you an education.' Unh unh. It was good-bye, Roger."

Darian folded the classifieds open to the third page and looked down at Moises from the bed. "That's propaganda, Brother. White man's propaganda. The front page are whatever lies they can think of. Lies. They call it news."

Moises closed the sports section and let it slide to the floor. There was so much to learn. So many habits from his old life that needed to be exorcised. It would take time, but he would do it.

Mustafa looked to his leader. "Did you find it?"

"Right where they said it would be," Darian answered, tapping the small five-line ad. "A week from tomorrow is the meet."

"This is a lot of waiting," Roger commented.

"Good things are worth it," Darian said. It had been damn good so far, and if their cracker partners were true to their intentions it was only going to get better.

Darren Griggs jumped whenever the doorbell rang. It was no different this Monday evening.

"Darren, hello," Anne Preston said through the barred screen as the front door opened.

"Dr. Preston." Darren's expression added a question mark to his words. Not necessarily because of his therapist's presence, but because of the vaguely familiar man at her side.

"I hope we're not intruding. You remember Rabbi Levin? He was the sponsor of the seminar where we met."

"Right." Darren smiled and unlocked the screen. "Come in."

Felicia came through the dining area, dishtowel in her hand, as the front door closed. "Honey, who was th— Dr. Preston!"

Anne saw that the surprised smile was genuine, and warm. She liked Felicia Griggs. "*Anne,* Felicia."

"Anne." The smile was now tinged with mild embarrassment.

Darren gestured to their other visitor. "Honey, this is Rabbi Levin."

"Seymour Levin."

Felicia took the large hand offered her. "I'm going to have to call you Rabbi. I hope you understand. It's my mother's doing."

"Of course," Levin said, understanding perfectly. There was a formality to his position, one shared by all men of the cloth.

"This is my wife Felicia, Rabbi," Darren said, completing the introductions. What followed was the inevitable awkward silence. "Would you like something to drink? Some coffee?"

"I have a pot on," Felicia added.

Both Anne and Rabbi Levin politely shook off the offer, exchanged a glance, and smiled at Darren.

Darren returned the expression, adding a nervous chuckle. "What?"

"Darren, Felicia . . ." Anne paused, trying to find the best words. Hell, she was still having a hard time fathoming the news Rabbi Levin had brought to her less than an hour earlier. "We've been invited somewhere."

"We?" Darren looked to Levin.

"Not me," Levin said. "I haven't the honor."

"The honor?" Darren parroted. "What's going on?"

"Darren," Anne began, "you, and Felicia, and I have been invited to come to Washington." She stopped, letting that sink in for a moment. What came next would take longer to absorb. "By the president, to be his guests at the State of the Union address next month."

Darren felt Felicia clutch his elbow, and knew without looking that her jaw was closer to the floor than it had been a second before. His was.

"I have dealings with the president's party," Levin explained, filling the shock-inspired silence. "He is very much saddened by what you have been through. By the reasons it happened. This would be good for all to see. That . . . hate does not prevail."

"Darren?" Anne saw that he hadn't moved. Neither had Felicia. "Are you in there?"

"Yeah. Yeah, I'm here." *The President!?*

"Honey." Felicia looked to her husband. "Do we . . . Should . . ."

"Well?" Anne prodded.

Darren let a deep breath drain from his lungs. "Well, I guess you don't say no to an invitation like that."

"Wonderful!" Levin exclaimed, joyously clapping his large hands once.

"It looks like we're going to Washington," Anne said, hugging Felicia.

"I guess it'll be an adventure," Darren observed.

"An adventure," Levin agreed. "That it will."

TWENTY

Consultation

Mark Reister looked to the flashing arrow next to line one and wondered when the slowdown of the congressional recess would apply to chief aides as well as their bosses. Well, someone had to oil the machinery that kept the Hill running when the big boys were away. *Away.* That didn't do justice to the slopes of Vail. But then *his* big boy didn't either. Old Limp Dick did as good on skis as one could with only one real hoof. Perpetually on the beginner's slope. It was a waste of snow, Reister thought.

Buzz.

The flashing arrow wasn't going away. Neither was the caller on the other end. *Six days 'til Christmas,* he reminded himself, and picked up line one. "Congressman Vorhees's office."

"Yes. This is Jeff Krishak from CRI in Boston. Is the congressman in?"

"Uh, no. CRI? I'm not familiar with that."

"Children's Rescue International. We arrange relief for refugee children, mostly in sub-Saharan countries."

"I see," Reister said. "I'm the congressman's chief aide. Is there something I can help you with?"

"Possibly. We're undertaking a pretty ambitious project. Something new for us. Our usual thing is to send aid, but early next year we're going to bring several children to the States to receive medical treatment. All have lost limbs because of mines and unexploded shells. And, like I said, it's a new thing for us, and we're a relatively small operation. We have the donations to handle any treatment, but we need some expertise. Someone to tell us who the doctors are we should be contacting.

"That's where we hope the congressman can help. Or, rather, his doctor. One of our board members said the congressman's doctor has to have expertise in this area, considering, and since he represents our district . . .''

Reister sniffed and smiled at the phone. Someone *wasn't* asking for a favor from his boss. *Mark this date down,* he thought. "So you just want to talk to Dr. Conrad?''

"To get his recommendations on who would be the appropriate professionals to contact.''

Hell, Reister thought, altruism! What was D.C. coming to? "I'm sure Dr. Conrad would be happy to give you some guidance.'' He cycled through the cards on his flip-file—important ones were white, virtually meaningless were blue (Dr. John Conrad was somewhere in-between)—and found the correct address and phone number. He passed the information on, accepted the caller's obviously genuine thanks, and laid the phone back in its cradle.

Seventy-five miles away, Stanley Barrish hung up at the same time.

It wasn't a long drive from their apartment, but, as Darian maneuvered through the shoppers' traffic on Fayette Street, Moises Griggs was suddenly aware just how far he'd come in a very short time. And from where.

"There's a lot of decorations,'' Moises observed, his gaze jumping from lamppost to lamppost as they passed, at the plastic Santas, red-and-white candy canes, green doughnuts of simulated pine fifteen feet above the street.

Christmas was almost here. "We used to have a big tree."

"Huh?"

Moises looked left to Darian. "My mom liked Christmas trees. More than presents, even. She used to say it was because of where she grew up. North Carolina. She said there were lots of trees there. She liked the smell." Pine. Moises drew in a breath through his nose, looking forward again and trying to remember the scent of Christmas in the Griggs household. It seemed so long ago. And it seemed like yesterday.

Darian turned off Fayette at the appropriate street, parking in a small lot behind a brightly lit supermarket. He turned off the car and checked his watch. "Whiteboy should be here." His neck twisted to look out the back window of the Volvo. "Probably is already. Checking us out, still, I'd bet."

And the ham. Moises remembered the smell of that on Christmas day. They ate about two in the afternoon, but called it dinner. He never could figure that out. But who cared about the time? That ham was always the best, and it tasted all the sweeter because they had it only once a year. His mom said it was her mother's special recipe for a smoked and barbecued ham, and it had been her mother's before that. Something like five generations old, he recalled his mother telling him. All the way back to the slave days. The same Christmas dinner his chained ancestors had shared.

Damn. Why was he thinking about this now? Why? There would be no more Christmases, at least not like the ones he'd had with his family. *What family?* That was right. It was easier to think of it that way. They were gone. Killed by the same bullets that ended his little sister's life. She'd have no more Christmases. *Practicing for a Christmas concert when she got it.*

December twenty-fifth. It conjured memories of warmth, and memories of darkness. Would it always?

Moises wondered. For him, he thought so, but what about his mother, and his father? Despite his attempts to mentally end their existence, he knew they lived on. Lived with the pain he did. Would they have a Christmas this year? *Not without you.* Would his mother make that ham? *You won't know.*

Shut up!

Presents? Hell, who cared about presents? *They'd just want you back at home.* Too late for that. Moises knew he'd cast his future already. The path was set. *They're probably worried about you.*

I can't do anything about that.

He was his mother's big strong boy. Too old to be called that now. Too old for a long time. The corner of his mouth twitched as he thought that, but the emotion was quickly squashed. *She's worried about you. You know that. She doesn't even know if you're dead or alive.*

I can't do anything . . . Moises looked straight through the windshield, to the blazing interior of the supermarket. There wasn't only food in there; there were other things. *Maybe I can* . . .

"He's here," Darian said, seeing the white boy step from a car two rows back in the lot.

"Brother Darian, I'm gonna get a Coke or something. You want something?"

"No." Darian opened the door, stepping out as his young companion did. "Come right back to the car after you get it."

"All right."

Darian saw his contact wait by the front of his own vehicle and walked to him. "You white folks like cold climates."

Toby smiled, no shades concealing his eyes this time. Dark glasses at night, aside from looking stupid, might draw attention. That was not what he wanted. "You go where the action is."

Darian looked past the white boy to the empty car. "Where's your sidekick?"

"Busy. Yours?"

"Getting himself a drink. So, you have something for me."

So true to form, Toby thought. He reached through the open front window of the car and removed a shopping bag. The weight of its contents strained the twin paper handles. "A hundred and fifty grand." He handed it to the African. "You did good on that little extra."

"Turkey shoot," Darian said, smiling. "White men can't jump, or run." He set the bag on the asphalt at his feet. "So, time for *the big one*."

"Almost."

Darian leaned against the fender and folded his arms, looking as casual and comfortable as possible. Just two guys, one white, one black, having a chat in a parking lot. "So, how do you plan to reshape the government? That's what you said at our last get-together, wasn't it?"

"I said that," Toby confirmed. "I guess 'starting with a clean slate' is a better description. You know, kinda throw everything into the shitter and start again."

"Un-huh," Darian said with a slow, cautious nod. "Details, man. We did you right back in L.A. I want the whole story now, before we go on."

Exactly one month, Toby knew. That was a long time to let the Africans keep a secret. But they would have to. It wasn't trust; it was acceptance. "The president's gonna give a little speech next month."

State of the Union. Darian knew that much, and also that it could be summed up briefly—fucked up. "Yeah."

Toby smiled before he went on. "We're gonna make it interesting."

Moises looked through the market's window to the parking lot. The cracker was jawing to Brother Darian about something. Good. That would keep him busy. He took a bottle of soda from a refrigerated case and walked down several aisles, passing magazines, a pitiful selection of wrapping paper, and a display of greeting cards before finding what he wanted. He picked through a rotating rack of postcards, choosing one with a winter scene—his mother always said she missed the snow—and flipping it over. A pen hanging by a string scrawled out the brief message, and then he went to a checkout stand, verifying first that Brother Darian was still occupied.

The checker ran the cold bottle over the scanner, which beeped once. "A dollar nine."

"Do you have stamps?" Moises asked.

"Yeah. How many?"

He handed the postcard to her, his eyes darting right as the conversation outside seemed to be slowing. "Could you put one on this and mail it?"

And mail it . . . 'Twas the season of giving, the checker reminded herself. "Sure." A few touches to her keypad brought up the new total. The customer paid her in exact change and left before she could wish him a Merry Christmas.

Darian saw in his peripheral vision his young comrade exit the market and wait by their car. In the grip of his stare the white boy was still smiling.

"Is that enough detail for you?" Toby asked.

"Who thought this fucking thing up?"

Toby shook his head slowly. "It's enough that someone did. The question is, Are you going to be able to make it happen?"

Make it happen? Someone had dreamed up a nightmare, all right. A nightmare that could be made real. "Oh, yeah. We can do that." Holy shit. This was bigger than big, Darian knew. Bigger than what he'd imagined, even after wiping out the people in the World Center.

Off the scale. And, he had to admit, brilliant, even coming from the whities. "The streets are gonna fill with blood, man."

"That'll be mission accomplished," Toby commented. *The right color blood, though.* "The name's on a card in the bag, and the address of his office. That's job one."

Darian picked the shopping bag up. "Consider it done. And don't forget you still owe us."

"Nine hundred grand." *You'd sell your mother's cunt, nigger.*

Darian gave a single nod and walked back to the Volvo. He heard the white boy pull out of the lot as he got behind the wheel.

"How'd it go?" Moises asked. He took a sip from the bottle and twisted the plastic cap back on.

Darian looked to his newest recruit. *But not the last. 'Cause after this we're gonna have an army of brothers wanting their piece of the pie.* "Good." *Anarchy. God, it was going to be paradise.* "Real good."

Senator Curtis Parsons and Congressman Jack Murphy had been to the White House many a time, sometimes to consult with the president, other times to counsel him, as leader of their party, on policy matters destined for a fight on the Hill. This crisp Wednesday morning, though, the Senate majority leader and the speaker of the House of Representatives were conveying something else: a request. That was the polite term, because they were certain it would be received for what it actually was: a demand.

The majority leader and the speaker arrived at the White House together in the back of a Secret Service Lincoln that had picked them up at Washington National an hour earlier. It was waved through the gate on West Executive Avenue and pulled to a stop between Old Executive and the West Wing. Five minutes later the na-

CAPITOL PUNISHMENT   259

tion's top legislators walked into the office of the president's assistant for national security affairs.

"Senator. Mr. Speaker." Bud DiContino had two chairs arranged facing the small couch in his office. Parsons and Murphy shed their overcoats, hanging them on the brass tree near the door, and took the seats. The president's chief of staff and national security adviser lowered themselves to the couch. "Can we order anything from the cafeteria for you? Croissants? I have coffee in the pot."

"No. No." Senator Parsons undid his tie and made a sour face at the offer. "My damn stomach's boiling. Goddamn red-eyes."

Speaker Murphy chuckled at his colleague. He had fifteen years on the man, and twenty pounds, yet the good Curtis Parsons of the fine state of Louisiana had the ailments of an older man. He also had a liking for Kentucky bourbon.

"Mr. Speaker?" Bud asked.

Murphy shook his head. "Sorry for the hurry-up on this."

Whatever *this* was, Bud thought. "Sorry we had to make it this early, but you wanted no press around."

"They're off with the boss," Gonzales explained.

"Where the hell is he this early?" Parsons asked, popping a chewable antacid into his mouth.

"Norfolk for a prayer breakfast," Gonzales answered. "For a veterans' group."

"Praying on a Friday." Parsons sniffed. "We Catholics save that for Sunday."

"The pope here protests," Murphy joked. "But, seriously, Bud, we appreciate you and Ellis seeing that this was quiet."

Bud sat forward, almost to the couch's edge. "I have to admit I'm guessing as to the reason."

Jack Murphy scooted forward also, his imposing Montana frame a hard figure to ignore. Few on the Hill had done so and walked away with their political careers intact. "Succession, Bud. The odd man out."

The NSA's face curled a bit at that. The "odd man out" was nothing more than a colloquial term for the lone member in the line of presidential succession who was normally kept away from events where all the other members were present, such as the approaching State of the Union message. It was a matter of security, a safety measure that, should some catastrophe strike when all the other members were together, ensured there would be a constitutionally recognized successor to the presidency available to assume the powers of state. For the State of the Union the choice had already been made: Energy Secretary Raleigh McCaw would do the honors, watching the constitutionally required report to Congress from the safety of his home—guarded by the Secret Service for that one evening. All very simple. All very proper.

So why were the most powerful men on the Hill sneaking into the White House to discuss the matter? *Why indeed?* Bud wondered. "The odd man out? It's Secretary McCaw. What's to discuss?"

"Whether he's the right choice," Parsons responded flatly. He didn't like McCaw, but then he didn't like the president, either. Neither, though, was behind the reasoning of his questioning.

"Right choice?" Bud snickered a bit. "You lost me, gentlemen."

"Me, too," Gonzales joined. "Raleigh did the duty last year. Energy isn't exactly tops on the agenda for the speech. He doesn't need to be there."

"He's second to the bottom, Bud, for Christ's sake!" Parsons challenged.

Murphy raised a hand to quiet his excitable colleague, then focused his attention on the president's advisers. "Listen. Curt and I don't make a habit of flying back to D.C. during recess for just nothing. We've had calls, my good men. From our friends across the aisle. They have a bug in their bonnet about McCaw. You know that. After that MicroGen bullshit he had to prove himself innocent of, and then laying it on one of *their* boys. Well, they don't like him. And they don't trust him."

"Wait," Bud said. "This isn't 1963. Soviet bombs are not going to drop during the State of the Union."

"No, but those black revolutionaries—"

"Terrorists!" Parsons interjected.

"Whatever," Murphy said. "Those fellows have the ability to do some major damage, Bud. Kill a lot of people. And that vehicle they found in the river not fifteen minutes from here is making folks on both sides of the aisle nervous. Real nervous."

"Mr. Speaker, there is no way they're going to be able to do anything during the State of the Union." Bud turned to the chief of staff. "The Service already went heads-up on that, right, Ellis?"

Gonzales nodded emphatically. "They're working close with the FBI, and from what I understand there will be an airtight lock on anything near the Capitol that night. It'll actually start a few days before, I recall. Ted O'Neil gave me a brief rundown. Plus every African-American group and organization from the NAACP to the most radical fringe has offered to help. The odds are on our side, gentlemen."

"Promises," Parsons commented. "Those did our president's predecessor a hell of a lot of good in L.A. a few years back."

"There's a damn big difference between shooting rockets at the president's motorcade, *while* it's sitting still, and sneaking a tank of nerve gas into the most heavily guarded building in D.C." Bud took a breath, realizing he was letting Parsons get the best of him.

"Tank," Parsons observed. "I saw the Bureau report on the damn thing. It's smaller than a football."

"And made of metal," Bud pointed out.

"Even you gentlemen are going to have to go through metal detectors on January nineteenth," Gonzales said. "Unless the president himself carries it in, it's not getting in."

"They could release it outside," Parsons suggested. "Upwind."

Gonzales shrugged. "There'll be gas alarms galore. Plenty of warning, and plenty of—" It was the chief of staff's turn to look to Bud. "What does the Army call them?"

"MOPP suits," Bud answered.

"Plenty of MOPP suits," Gonzales continued, "for everyone."

"An attack outside would be stupid," Bud observed. "That doesn't mean they wouldn't try it, but it would fail. Period."

"Hold on, hold on, hold on," Murphy said, repeating the mantralike admonishment familiar to all in the House chamber. "The plain truth is that enough people are uncomfortable with the idea of McCaw possibly ending up as president—God forbid—that it just won't fly. Whether you two want to admit it or not, there is a risk here. A real one where there usually isn't, and that requires careful consideration."

"Are you saying you want someone else to be odd man out?" Gonzales asked.

"Exactly," Parsons answered.

"Someone more suited to the potential," Murphy explained. "McCaw was, what, some sort of computer executive before taking over Energy? That's not what the country needs . . . if . . ."

Bud slid back on the couch. "This is really concerning you?"

"Bud," Murphy began, tapping his own chest with a thick thumb, "I'm number three on the list of succession. I was elected. People voted for me. But I'm gonna be sitting right up there behind your boss next month.

The vice president is gonna be right next to me. Pardon what comes next, but just about everyone else who can take over according to the Constitution are appointed schmucks. Normally, sure, McCaw wouldn't raise an eyebrow. But this isn't a normal time. People on the Hill want to fry Gordon Jones for what happened in L.A. last month, and they aren't sure they trust promises of security."

"It will be secure," Gonzales said forcefully.

"Fine," Murphy responded. "Then we'll all walk away happy. But McCaw has got to go. Choose someone better suited to the 'maybes,' not the promises."

"If someone doesn't take care of this before too long there're going to be public calls from some of our Republican friends for a change." Parsons's stomach rumbled loudly as the antacid began its fight with the remnants of the previous night's revelry. "Some on our side, too. That can be damn embarrassing." He pointed a long, tan finger at Gonzales. "You more than anyone should be tuned in to that. Earl Casey is going to have your ass if this blows up."

"It doesn't need to blow up," Murphy countered. There was conciliation in his voice, but also direction.

Embarrassment. Ellis knew all too well the ramifications of that. In a way he was the president's point man, walking ahead of the chief executive through the election-year minefield. It was important the rest of the term, also, but now was the time when it most counted. People wouldn't vote for a man whose own party fired a shot across his bow. No way. This wasn't worth risking that.

"All right," Ellis said. "I'll talk to the president."

"Soon," Murphy prodded.

"This week," Ellis promised.

"Make it someone everyone can accept," Parsons directed.

Gonzales nodded.

Bud stood. "That does it, then. Crisis averted."

Murphy and Parsons also rose to their feet and gathered their coats.

"Thanks for the hurry-up, Bud," the speaker said, putting a hand on the NSA's shoulder.

"Thanks for dropping in," Bud said with a slight chuckle attached, then closed the door behind their visitors. He turned back to the chief of staff. His face was blank. "Parsons can be an ass."

Gonzales quietly nodded. "Do you think there's a reason to worry?"

"Worry?" Bud sat in the chair vacated by the speaker. It was still warm. "No. Concern, yes."

"It's a hell of a thought, you know," Gonzales observed. "You know what kind of mayhem there'd be."

"That's why there's an odd man out," Bud reminded him.

"Still . . ." The chief of staff was quiet for a moment. "Do you think that's what these NALF guys are thinking about?"

Bud half-shrugged before answering. "The Bureau thinks they have more nerve gas. And that car they found in the river puts them in the vicinity. They're here for a reason. And I guess this is a good place to be if you want to do damage."

Damage. That was a mild way of putting it. How many were dead in Los Angeles? Gonzales thought. The final body count was one thousand eight hundred and twenty-two. That was damage, all right. But killing just a fourth of that number—the right fourth—in this city could mean more than death. It could mean chaos. Or worse. "You know, they may have been right to bring this to us."

Bud saw Gonzales's eyes come up to meet his. "It's not going to happen, Ellis."

"Neither was Pearl Harbor," Gonzales said in response.

TWENTY ONE

Give and Take

Montrose Road skirts the southern limits of Rockville, Maryland, running west–east between Interstate 270 and the Rockville Pike. Dr. John Conrad turned his Chevy Suburban east onto Montrose from the interstate in a driving rain, heading for home. That was a brand-new, five thousand-square-foot trilevel done in western red cedar. It wasn't cheap, but his practice was good. As good as any orthopedic surgeon's inside the beltway, the perfect place to do his kind of business. Bad backs and bum knees abounded, as did referrals. Tons of those. Enough that he had two associates working *for* him. Work weeks were four days long now, with Wednesday as a play day in the middle, and weekends sometimes ate up a Friday or a Monday. Usually a Monday. Sundays were just too short.

Life was good, the family was good. About the only thing not good was the damn road that the county never seemed to fix right. As usual the potholes, hidden under a glaze of rainwater, were assaulting his suspension and wearing the tires long before their time. Two letters already, and golf with a honcho from the roads department obviously hadn't had the desired result. *Well, now they're going to—*

The motion his Suburban made this time wasn't from a pothole. It lurched forward, pressing Conrad against

his seat. He looked to the rearview to see a pair of headlights easing back, and a flashing turn signal as the car
pulled to the shoulder.

"Son of a bitch!" Conrad swore, hitting his own signal. "The idiot doesn't know his following distance!"
A rear-ender. A *moving* rear-ender! At least the insurance company couldn't lay any of this on him . . . if the
fool had insurance. He stopped on the hard shoulder of
the road, the idiot doing the same right behind, as a line
of cars zipped by. Conrad popped his door and opened
the umbrella through the crack, then walked to the rear
of his Suburban to go through the rigmarole.

"Hey man, sorry," Darian said, gesturing embarrassment as rain cascaded off the brim of his baseball cap.

Conrad gave the guy a look, and one for his buddy
still in the car, and checked the bumper. "Oh, wonderful."

Darian bent a bit to survey the damage, pointing with
one hand and keeping the other in his coat pocket. To
his rear the passenger door of the Volvo opened. That
was the signal—no traffic from behind. "Oh, shit, down
on the fender, too."

"Where?" Conrad asked, following the outstretched
finger. "I don't see—"

The leather sap came down hard at the base of Conrad's skull, but not too hard. Just enough to stun, as
Darian had been taught by the brothers in Soledad. The
doctor grunted loud and fell to all fours. By then Moises
was up with his leader.

"Down!" Darian commanded, stomping on Conrad's
back with his boot and pushing his chest to the ground.
"Get his hands."

Moises put a knee in the small of the doctor's back
and pulled both arms behind. He wrapped a looped cord
around the wrists and drew it tight, then wound the remaining length between the arms and tied it off. Next
came the feet, and then the mouth, which was gagged

by filling it with a wadded-up sock. "Ready."

Darian looked back. No cars. To the front the large Suburban blocked the view and shrouded their actions. "Let's go."

They dragged the doctor to the rear of the Volvo, lifted him into the trunk, and slammed the lid shut. Darian then went back to the Suburban, to its interior, and took the doctor's briefcase from the passenger seat, making sure to leave no prints for the cops to find. He was back behind the wheel of the Volvo a few seconds later.

"He's moving around already," Moises said.

"Don't matter none." Darian started the car and backed away from the Suburban, then pulled out onto Montrose and traveled a quarter-mile before there was space to hang a U-turn. They passed the doctor's car going the other way and were back on the interstate, heading south, a minute after that.

"Knock knock," Lou Hidalgo said as he rapped on the metal top of the cubicle walls that enclosed Art's and Frankie's work area. Art was the only occupant at the moment.

"Morning, Lou." Art turned his chair and faced the A-SAC.

Hidalgo scratched at one ear. "I just thought I'd let you know that LAPD is scaling back their look for Barrish. There's no sign of him or his family."

"I wasn't even sure they were that interested," Art commented with mock wonder.

"Well, his lawyer and the guy paying his rent did get offed the day he and his family disappeared. I guess that makes one wonder."

"It's more than that, Lou." Art was feeling left out, amputated from the investigation that had moved to the East Coast with the NALF.

Hidalgo nodded. "I just thought I'd update you before you leave."

"Leave? Leave where?"

"You and Frankie are going to Washington to help find the NALF guys," Hidalgo explained. "To provide a hometown outlook in case it's needed."

"When?"

"Christmas day," Hidalgo answered with apology in his tone. "Sorry about the timing."

"No problem," Art lied. Anne was going to love this . . . No, she would understand. He knew better than to think otherwise.

"I'm sorry to pull you away from this end, but—"

"Don't be," Art interjected. "Gotta go with the smart money, and that's on the NALF."

"That it is," Hidalgo concurred.

Art smiled to himself as the A-SAC walked away. *Smart money, eh?* Despite having said it, Art knew he wouldn't take the bet.

Darian shoved the sock back in the doctor's mouth and closed the trunk of the Volvo, surveying the empty parking lot and the street beyond. He handed the keys from Conrad's pants pocket to Moises. "You got it all?"

"Got it," Moises confirmed. "The key with the blue tab opens the back door. The alarm box is inside the door. I press four-four-four-seven, then 'off' to disarm it."

"And rearm it when you leave," Darian reminded him.

"Right. The patient files are in the billing office. Red tab key opens that. I pull the file, flip on the copy machine, and copy the page listing orthopedic implements."

"Check it first against what he said," Darian said, hitting the trunk lid with a balled fist and saying loudly, "'CAUSE IF HE WAS LYIN' WE'RE GONNA FUCK UP HIS FAMILY."

"Got it. Match it first. Then copy it, turn off the machine, put back the file, lock up, and head out . . . and rearm the alarm.''

"And wear the gloves," Darian cautioned. "No prints."

Moises held up the surgical-type gloves. "Got it."

"Go."

Darian watched his young fighter run at a brisk clip to the wall that separated the parking lot from the back of Dr. John Conrad's suite of medical offices. He checked his watch as the Griggs kid rolled over the fence. Nine minutes later Moises reappeared over the wall with the information they needed.

"He told the truth," Moises said, handing the paper to Darian.

The NALF leader pocketed the photocopy and opened the trunk. "You did good." He reached in and pulled Conrad up by the hair, then slammed a fist into the side of his head to stun him. As he fell back Darian swung the edge of his hand hard across the doctor's throat, crushing his windpipe. He grabbed the neck with a strong hand and pressed as the man struggled in vain for air. In two minutes he had passed out. Two minutes later Darian Brown released his grip.

They drove the body twenty miles west of the city and dumped it in a thicket by the road, then drove straight back to Baltimore. There was still much work ahead and it had been a long day. Sleep was the next order of business.

"Jim," the president began, hesitating as the secretary of state waited patiently. "Jim, how would you like to be president?"

Secretary of State Jim Coventry smiled at the offer. "When do I start?"

"There's one little catch, Jim," Chief of Staff Ellis Gonzales said as his boss took a seat in one of the Oval

Office's wingbacks. "Everybody at the State of the Union has to end up dead."

Coventry lost interest in the humorous beginning of the conversation. "Wait. Are you . . . I thought Raleigh McCaw was doing the deed again."

"We have to make a change," Gonzales said. "With all the weak knees over these New Africa nuts there's some concern about Secretary McCaw's suitability should something happen."

"You were elected once, Jim," the president observed. "You'll put a lot of people at ease come the State of the Union."

"Of course I'll do it," Coventry said. Like there would be any doubt! "But it's going to raise some questions itself. The press will probably have me resigning by Monday after the address."

"Let them talk," the president said. "Besides, you'll have the best seat in the house."

"Lay in a bowl of popcorn and make a night of it at home," Gonzales suggested with a wink.

"Popcorn and a speech," Coventry commented. "Marie is going to love it."

"All you have to do is stay alive and run the country, Jim," the president said. "No big deal."

The secretary of state nodded and smiled. "This is a good deal easier than campaigning for the job."

The president snickered. "Tell me about it."

TWENTY TWO

The Rat Equation

He had come a long, long way, Anne thought, and in a relatively short time. Darren Griggs was strong, and he wanted to be a survivor. But this afternoon, on a day and at a time when 90 percent of the city was lifting glasses of eggnog and similar spirits the Friday before Christmas, the survival instinct in her patient seemed dulled. Sitting in the temporary office some twelve blocks from her normal practice, Anne couldn't deny that she harbored some melancholy herself.

"A couple minutes left," Anne said, closing her notebook. "Do you want to tell me?"

Darren smiled weakly. "I'm not trying to hide anything, Doctor. I'm just not sure it's important."

"Whatever it is it's affecting you. I sense a touch of melancholy? Hmm?"

Darren pulled a postcard from his pocket and handed it to Anne. "It's from Moises. Addressed to his mother, you can see." A touch of anger, but that faded quickly. He was coming to understand not only his own emotions and motivations but also those of his absent son.

Anne flipped it over. The front was a picture of the Washington Monument in winter. The back held a simple message: *Mom, I'm all right. Don't worry. Merry Christmas . . . Moises*

"At least we know he's alive," Darren said. "The

postmark says it was mailed in Baltimore. All the way across the damn country." *Damn.* That was the anger talking again—the anger *cursing,* Darren corrected himself.

"How did Felicia react?" Anne asked, handing the card back.

"She cried, then wondered why he's all the way across country. I guess she was also relieved that he's okay. Or that he says he's okay."

"He's making his own decisions now, Darren," Anne told her patient.

Bad decisions, Darren thought. "I know."

There was a place for therapy, and there was a place for humanity, Anne knew. And for hope. "He wrote; maybe he'll call."

"Maybe," Darren allowed. "His mother would like that."

"Anyone else?"

Darren didn't nod, didn't deny it. He didn't know if he was ready to talk to his son yet. There was one thing he was ready to do, though. He could easily throw his arms around his son and never let him go.

A stylized eagle done in dirty blue ink stretched across Chester Hart's abdomen. Above the snarling bird two words stood out in red: *White Power.* There were other tattoos on the convict's body. A cobra twisted around his arm, its bared fangs threatening from his bicep. Two impish demons held a buxom woman over a rock as a larger devillike creature impaled her from behind. Tricolor flames rose from both shoulder blades, each point of fire ending in a silvery dagger. These were all visible, worn like badges of honor and allegiance by a shirtless Hart as he pressed the two hundred pounds off his chest in the exercise yard of California's Folsom State Prison.

"You're a fucking fool, Chet," a barrel-chested white inmate commented. There were only whites around the weight set at this time of the morning. It was their time. The blacks had it after lunch. The Mexicans and any others just before dinner. It was the way of the yard. The law of the jungle.

"Whaaaaaaaat?" Hart asked as the bar shot up.

"You're gonna freeze your tits off," the inmate said, laughing. Two other inmates quietly walked away from the weight set. "It's hardly forty out here."

"Soooooo!"

Two more slinked back, leaving just Hart pressing and the inmate jawing. Someone had to keep his attention . . . for a moment.

"Sehhhhhhh-vun!"

Now a new inmate approached, sliding through the wall of white inmates that had formed a loose circle around the scene. A large paper cup was in his right hand. A glowing cigarette was in his left.

"Eighhhhhht!"

The cup holder stopped two paces short of Hart, on the blind side of tower two. Tower three was temporarily empty because of rats. There were ways to know such things, and inmates often did.

"Hart."

Chester let the bar rest on his well-developed chest and looked to the right. He saw for the first time that no one stood near him. *Shit!*

The inmate heaved the contents of the cup on Hart, aiming for the face. His aim was off. Most of the strong-smelling liquid splashed on his target's chest and ran down to the padded weight bench.

"Rats in the tower," the inmate said. "Rats in the yard." He smiled and flicked the burning cigarette at Hart. It tumbled through the air and skidded across his chest, igniting the paint thinner.

"AHHHHHHHHHHHHHH!" Hart screamed as a red hot flash washed over his upper body. It was loud, like a train rolling over him, but not loud enough to drown out the laughter. "HELLLLLLLLLP!"

All he got from his AB brethren was more laughter. As guards rushed to him, Chester Hart knew what was happening. He had been marked for death. A contract was out on him, and not just any. He could have been easily shanked with little fuss and he'd be deader than dead. No, this was a contract with a condition: kill with style. It was a message hit, and Hart knew the message all were supposed to receive—informants die a horrible death. It was his new reality now. He'd tried to live on the fence, and this was where it had gotten him . . . flesh burning, pinned on his back by a weight bar he could not lift. Yes, he had walked in both worlds, one of which had just told him to get lost.

But Chester Hart, ninth-grade education and all, was not about to surrender to the reality the Brotherhood had chosen for him. He knew this attack would not kill him. There would be a tomorrow. Not a pleasant one, but a tomorrow still. And there was always the other world, a world he knew he had a ticket to enter.

"Did you like my gift?" Art asked as Anne's head rose and fell with his breathing.

'Which one?" she asked.

"You know which one," Art said. He could feel the bracelet skim the hair on his chest as Anne ran a finger back and forth through what she called his "fur."

"It's beautiful." And it was. The other presents had been nice, and opening them on Christmas Eve with the man she loved had only made it nicer. No: sweeter. "You spoil me, G-Man. This was expensive."

"And those skis weren't?" he responded, ending her uninspired protest. It had been a perfect Christmas Eve, and he was determined to make the most of the following morning before he had to jump back into his work mode and hop an American Airlines flight to Washington National Airport. "We should have saved at least one gift for the morning."

"We're both bad," Anne said.

Art ran a hand up her bare back and massaged her shoulder, listening to her breathe. Listening to the silence. The doctor had something on her mind. Art knew what it was. "I haven't said anything, but thank you for not asking about Chicago." Art felt her breathing change, becoming more relaxed.

"I know it's been on your mind," Anne admitted. "Have you made any decisions?"

"No. I didn't really think I'd consider it seriously, but . . . I've been thinking about it."

"Your old stomping grounds," Anne observed.

"It gets cold," Art remembered. *Weather isn't everything, Arthur.* "And it's a long way from here."

Anne shifted position a bit, bringing her face closer to Art's cheek. "Chas Ohlmeyer runs the human relations department at the University of Chicago."

"Your old classmate," Art said. He was surprised at her lack of subtlety. She was saying so much in a very few words, and he loved her more for it.

"Mm-hmm," Anne confirmed. "What time is your flight?"

"Three."

"You need a ride to LAX?"

"Someone from the office is dropping Frankie and me."

"When will you be back?"

"I'm not sure. Soon, I hope. As soon as we find . . . them." What did one call the NALF? Revolutionaries. Scum. Militants. Murderers. What, indeed? And to Art there was still the question of John Barrish. Labeling him was easier: aberration. "Who knows, you may get to D.C. before I get out. When are you three going, by the way?"

"The fifteenth of next month," Anne answered. "But

that's hush-hush. I even had a visit from the Secret Service last Thursday.''

"Nerves,'' Art said. And well founded, he thought. But she didn't need to know that. ''I'm gonna miss you.''

Anne slid her arms around his neck and held on, tighter than she realized. ''You, too.''

Art knew the reason behind the gesture. It had nothing to do with his being three thousand miles from her for a relatively short period of time; it had everything to do with what would happen once they were together again. And he suspected the emotion behind her trepidation was not fear, but anticipation. It was for him.

TWENTY THREE

Points of Reference

Congressman Richard Vorhees kept the pace brisk as the cool night air washed over him. Speedwalking, some called it, that awkward-looking process of exercise or competition that made its practitioners look as though their legs were about to swivel loose of their hips. Vorhees didn't care about appearances in this endeavor, though. This was his dose of aerobic exertion for the day. At one time in his life his work had kept him in shape—jumping from perfectly airworthy aircraft into the forest to hump a ruck for days on end usually did that to one. Now this was it.

But he couldn't complain . . . too much. The job had stature, and he was coming through probably the darkest period of his political life relatively unscathed. All by being honest. As his feet—one real, one not—pushed his trim frame back toward home from his nightly five-miler along Leesburg Pike and its periphery streets, the congressman marveled briefly that he'd survived it all at the hand of the truth. Amazing. It wasn't a trend he planned to continue, though. Not that one was "less than forthright" intentionally; it was simply a matter of necessity in government. The truth often was less important than being right. There was a difference, Vorhees knew.

So he walked at night to keep his heart strong, went

home and massaged the soreness from the stump of flesh
below his left knee, showered, slept, and got up the next
day. Then off to battle, albeit a quieter kind of conflict
than that which he'd seen as an officer in the 82nd. A
quiet fight, a good fight. At the end of each day that was
what counted. Not your wounds, but that you would
fight again. That was the—

"Congressman!"

Vorhees slowed his pace at the call, putting on the
brakes fully and turning to see two people, a man and a
woman, trotting along the sidewalk to catch up with him.
Leaves from the residential lawns blew across their path,
and the motion of the man's body twisted his jacket to
the side to reveal a badge on his belt. *Shit! Not you
again. I thought I dodged your asses a month and a half
ago.*

"Congressman," Art said, stopping after their short
jog. Frankie was at his side. "I'm Special Agent Art
Jefferson, FBI. This is Special Agent Frankie Aguirre.
We were hoping you'd give us a minute of your time."

Vorhees feigned breathlessness and bent forward,
hands on knees. "I'm right at the end of my walk, Agent
Jefferson."

"It'll just take a minute," Art insisted diplomatically.

"We just have a few questions, sir," Frankie added.

Vorhees straightened, shifting his bad leg a bit for
better balance, and nodded. "All right."

"We got your statement last month when we were in
town, but there are a couple things we need to know
beyond that." Art let that hang for just a second. He
wanted more than anything to gauge Vorhees's reaction
to their just being there. It wasn't that he thought Vorhees was dirty, it was simply that he didn't want the
man to hold anything back that, though it might be embarrassing to him, would help them get their job done.
"Nikolai Kostin—did you ever meet him? Face to
face?"

Vorhees shook his head and breathed the Virginia night air deeply. "Never."

"How much did Monte Royce tell you about him?" Art asked.

"The particulars," Vorhees answered. "His position in the Russian and Soviet militaries. His expertise."

"No red flags in any of that?" Frankie inquired. A hint of skepticism flavored the question.

"At the time I thought it would be better to have his kind of expertise in our country than in, say, Iran. Or Libya. Or Vietnam."

"And Royce was vouching for him," Frankie observed. "That was enough?"

"I thought so." A little defiant, but also apologetic. It was the first lesson of excelling in D.C.: Craft your response perfectly.

"Did Monte Royce ever ask for any other favors?"

Vorhees eyed the black agent. "I don't do favors."

Of course not, Saint Richard. Let's change the wording to something more palatable, Art thought. "Assistance, then?"

"I don't recall at the moment," Vorhees said, bringing both hands to his hips to signal impatience.

"How long did you know Monte Royce?" Royce was Vorhees's link to this, Art knew. It was the place to apply pressure.

"A number of years." The response was short. *Get the message, Jefferson. You don't grill a United States congressman like this. You don't grill* me *like this.*

"Did you attend his funeral?"

Vorhees sneered at the question. *Funeral? There's your exit.* "I was busy. Agent Jefferson, if you don't mind, I have things to do. This is not a good night for me. I have to attend a good friend's funeral tomorrow." *Poor John. Victim of a bump and rob. But why did they leave his new Suburban?* The police were probably trying to figure that out, too. But at least the body hadn't lain for weeks rotting in some wooded ditch somewhere. His killers were *decent* enough to leave him by a road. It had still taken more than two days to locate it. And now the congressman had to find a new orthopedic. "If you are so interested in Monte Royce, which you seem to be from your questions, then why don't you talk to Senator Crippen."

"We have," Frankie said.

"Well, then you know more than I can give you already. He was closer to Monte Royce than I was."

But you were the one to help Royce. Art thought on that for a brief second. Maybe Royce thought Crippen would balk at the request. Maybe not. It was just the luck of the draw. Vorhees had come up short.

"If you'll excuse me?" Vorhees said, politely waiting for a nod, or some signal that his inquisition was finished.

Darian eased the Volvo through the intersection after pausing at the four-way stop, looking right past Moises at their next target. "Those are pigs. I can smell 'em."

Jesus! Moises slid a bit lower in his seat. *That's him. The FBI guy.*

The Volvo passed through the intersection and continued down Monroe. Vorhees's residence was eight houses down. Darian slowed as they passed. "Did you get the route down?"

"Yeah," Moises said, coming back up in his seat.

"What's the matter with you?"

"Nothing." *You can't tell him that pig was in your house. Who'd believe that and not think you were a snitch?* "When you said there were pigs there I got nervous."

"Pigs are pigs are pigs," Darian said. "They bleed, they die, just like anyone. Funner to kill than ordinary people, though." He'd only killed one pig up close— several had died in the World Center attack—but he was certain that would change before too long. "So you got it?"

Moises tapped the marked-up map book on his lap. Three times now they'd followed the gimp on his nightly walk, and each time he'd taken the same route. He was either cocky or stupid, Moises thought. An easy target. An opportune target.

"Let's get home," Darian said, accelerating down the street as the sight of the waddling congressman became visible in the rearview. The pigs were done with him. But they weren't.

Toby opened the long brown box and lifted the contents out with one hand. It wasn't light, but it wasn't heavy either. He knew that weight would be the key to making this work. "Looks fake as hell, huh?"

John took the prosthetic limb, cradling it with both hands. It was roughly flesh colored, though one could tell by appearance that its surface did not approach the softness of real flesh. To touch it one would know that its exterior was a hard plastic material. The top, where the stump of the limb amputated below the knee fit into a form-fitting cup, was heavier in balance, as was the bottom. At that end a crude foot was attached. It rotated on a metallic ball joint through only a front-back motion to allow the wearer to walk, though not naturally or comfortably. This was a clunker, John knew. Not a new model at all.

"Are you sure it's the right one?" John asked.

"It was in the file, and the Africans said the doc confirmed it." Toby touched the artificial limb. "And it's a good thing I was able to find this used. They don't even make this model anymore."

"Used is better," John said. "It'll look natural." But looks were only part of the equation. Function was another. That they would start with immediately. "We've got work to do."

"In the garage, Pop?"

John headed that way. "That's where the tools are."

While his father and brother toiled with the work of the hand, Stanley Barrish availed himself of a more cerebral activity a hundred and fifty miles to the east. Namely, reading the paper.

The Wednesday *Washington Post* carried the information he'd been waiting for on page five, in a little blurb that barely used two column inches to explain. *The Secretary of State. Well . . .* Stanley had read enough about the ways of appearance-conscious Washington— far more than his older brother—to know that having the secretary of state *not* attend the State of the Union address deserved more exposition in the capital's paper. Maybe that would come in the days ahead. It was only two days after Christmas, and this little tidbit had obviously been released by the White House to be buried while most of official Washington was away enjoying a long winter break. That might be so, but Stanley had all he needed to get started.

The first question to be answered was *where?* Where would the secretary of state be the evening in question? Would he watch the speech from the State Department? Probably not. It was too close to the actual event. From a secret location somewhere? If that was the case, there would be little he could do to find it. Stanley knew he had a talent for subterfuge, but he wasn't a magician. So he had to focus on what he could do, on what he could glean from sources available to him. It might take time. It might not. But he wasn't going to find the answer in the Virginia capital.

He left Richmond, where he'd stayed the night before, experimenting with the pleasures of a pretty young girl, and drove north to Washington after reading the morning *Post.* The trip on Interstate 95 took two hours to the beltway, then another forty minutes before Stanley crossed the Roosevelt Bridge to reach the District of Columbia proper. His first destination was a somewhat random choice. Almost anywhere with a public building would do, but there was one place not far that at least held some interest. A short jaunt up the Rock Creek and Potomac Parkway, past the Kennedy Center, brought him to that place: the Watergate. It was home to a dark chapter in American political history.

It was also the home of banks of public phones.

Stanley Barrish parked and entered the Watergate with the *Post* folded under his arm and chose a phone at the end of a line of three. The two to his right were empty. He opened the *Post* to its listing of phone numbers and editors and circled the number for the city desk, dialing after checking that no one was in earshot.

"Editorial, city desk."

"Yeah, this is Paulie Schwartz. Litton advanced optics. One of your photo crews needed a low-light lens, and I'm supposed to deliver it to the shoot site. But I don't know where that is. Do you have the photo assignment desk number?"

"I'll transfer you."

Simple enough, Stanley thought. But that was the easy lie. The next one would require more guile.

"Assignment desk."

Stanley looked to the photo credit under the largest photo on page five, reading the name into memory before speaking. "Yes, is . . . uh . . . Mr. Heidell in?"

"Chuck Heidell? Hold on."

It was a chancy shot, to be sure, but Stanley was banking on the supposition that most photographers for a big city paper probably spent little time in the office. They didn't take pictures of colleagues at their desks, after all. Out and about was their business. Or so he hoped.

"Chuck's out. You want to leave a message?"

"Uh, this is Billy in research. Mr. Heidell wanted me to pull any stories on a specific address for him. He wanted to see any accompanying photos, I guess. But I don't know where the house is.''

"Billy . . . are you new here?"

"Yes . . ."

"I thought so, because if Chuck ever heard you calling him *mister* he'd eat you for lunch."

"Oh. Okay. I didn't—"

"Yeah, all right. So you need, what, an address?"

"Yes. He said it's the secretary of state's house."

"Hang on."

It was *that* simple? Stanley wondered if he could bluff his way into the White House. His dad would *love* that. Probably.

"You got a pen."

"Yeah," said "Billy." Stanley copied the address onto the margin of the *Post* and thanked the photo desk. He was back in his car and heading across the Roosevelt Bridge ten minutes later, this time going north on the GW Parkway to the Lee Highway. Falls Church, Virginia, was eight miles distant.

Hillsborough Drive curved off of Lee Highway just past the Leesburg Pike. Stanley slowed the cream-colored Toyota as he entered the residential street, both because of the speed limit and to admire the beautiful homes. *Fashionable,* they were called, but the younger Barrish boy had no point of reference for comparison. He'd never lived in, or near, houses like those he was passing. They were huge, many with red brick facades that seemed calming somehow. At least he thought so.

He was not there to admire, though, and such idle thoughts would only remove focus from his task. He was there to look for one house. Just one.

But he almost missed it, the address placard blocked by a phone company truck parked facing the wrong way. Stanley passed the address, noticed he'd skipped a number, then backed up, stopping just feet from a phone company worker at the back of the open van. *Phone*

Company? He looked up at the fine Tudor-style house beyond the natural carpet of green. Number 695. *Mr. Secretary's house. And some phone trouble to boot . . . Or, maybe . . .*

"Hey, buddy."

The phone worker looked left to Stanley. "Yeah."

"My folks live down the street," Stanley lied. At least this one didn't require that a false name be used. "Is there phone trouble?"

"Nah. Just adding some lines here."

Stanley nodded, and as he did a second workman emerged from number 695 Hillsborough Drive, coming down the meandering walk to the truck. A smile joined the nod. "Great. Thanks a lot."

Adding lines? I wonder why they're doing that? Stanley asked himself as he steered the Toyota back toward Lee Highway. He didn't have to think long to convince himself of the answer.

TWENTY FOUR
Function

Almost two weeks it had taken. Now, though, they were ready for final assembly.

"Give me the cylinder," John said.

Toby handed the small tank of destruction to his father with one hand. John accepted it with two and slid it into the padded skeletal frame he'd carefully constructed from the lightest, strongest metal he could get his hands on: titanium.

Weight. That had been the determining factor in how to do it. The plan was simple enough; get the cylinder of VZ into Vorhees's leg and he'd unknowingly get it into the State of the Union for them. A timer would do the rest after that. Predicting when a speech would start and end was not that difficult in the era of network television. The president would start at a certain time, or reasonably close to it, and word had already leaked out that the chief executive, a debater from his college days, was going to break the one-hour mark with this speech. It was backwards determination. Pick a time somewhere in the window of opportunity and subtract a hundred hours—the maximum length of the digital timer they'd chosen—and the "package" would go off at the appointed minute. There were other considerations, such as how to get the good congressman to switch limbs, but that had been taken care of . . . or would be very soon. All would work as planned.

Getting to this point with the package, though, had been a test of skill and ingenuity. The prosthetic limb Toby had acquired weighed in at six pounds even, the majority of which was the inch-diameter steel support column running from the metal ball joint—or ankle—to the cup in which the stump rested. This steel column was concealed in a hollow plastic form that approximated the shape of the human calf. That was cut away carefully for later replacement, giving access to the column. The first problem was this steel rod. It was in the way, making it impossible to fit the cylinder of VZ in the limb. The other consideration was weight. Even if there were room, the added mass of the cylinder would surely convince the congressman that something was amiss.

The only solution then was to replace one with the other. The rod, as severed just below the cup connector and above the ball joint—leaving three quarters of an inch on each as a base for connection—weighed in at three pounds and four ounces. The cylinder of VZ and its associated timing and release equipment tipped the scales at two pounds and twelve ounces. An eight-ounce difference. John figured they could afford an extra half-pound without changing the feel of the limb too much. Vorhees, after all, had probably not worn it since getting his newer, lighter limb thirteen months earlier. It would be somewhat unfamiliar even to him.

Sixteen ounces. One pound. That was what John had to work with to replace the structural service of the support column, while providing room for the cylinder of VZ. He first considered actually using the cylinder as part of the new support column, but discarded that thought after being unable to convince himself that it would not damage the workings of the release and timing mechanisms. He knew all this should have been thought of before Kostin chose the cylinders and filled them, but that was the past. He now had to make the best of what he had. And he finally came up with a solution. It came to him while staring at, not out, a window.

As any carpenter worth his salt knows, when one wishes to place a window in a previously untouched wall, there is the consideration of *load* that must be addressed. Walls in general home construction are made of a series of studs that run vertically, parallel to each other about sixteen inches apart. These studs form part of the support system of the structure, transferring the load of the roof or stories above to the foundation below. When cutting a window into a wall, several of these studs have to be removed to make an opening of the desired size. This leaves the top portions of the studs hanging, unable to transfer their share of the load to the foundation, and the bottom portions jutting up uselessly. It is the top portions that are critical, though, and the solution to the problem is something called a header. Simply, it is a horizontal piece of lumber, running between the complete outer studs and connecting to the dangling studs, allowing the weight *they* carry to be transferred to the foundation through the full studs supporting the header. The header allows the load to be transferred *around* the empty space.

Why not in his mini-construction project? John had thought. *No reason at all* was the answer.

To achieve the transfer of load from the cup to the ankle he chose to create a metallic header of titanium that would curve over the top of the cylinder, looking much like the skeletal framework of a dome. This ''dome'' header then would mate with a skeletal tube, also of titanium, that had a slightly larger interior dimension than the outer dimension of the cylinder. The tube's bottom was a slightly less curved ''foundation'' of titanium that was mated to the ankle joint. The design simply took the load around the cylinder as a header and studs carry it around a window opening.

Building the system was the next step, and John went about it using all the skills he'd retained from his early days as a machinist. He had no CNC (computerized numerically controlled) machines to make the precision he desired very easy. And his knowledge, he learned, was not complete, requiring several visits to the library in Richmond and to a welding shop nearby for tutelage. But it did come together, though an ounce over the limit he'd decided upon, requiring that some plastic be shaved from the interior of the cosmetic cover.

And now it was assembly day.

"It fits perfect," John said, allowing himself a bit of self-congratulation. He deserved it at this point. *The work of a man can be judged only by its purpose.* Trent's words were true, but this piece of garage engineering was going to advance a purpose.

"All right, Pop," Toby said, patting his father's back. "You did it."

"*We* did it." John twisted the cylinder against the padding tape lining the inside of the skeleton, making certain the timing control would be accessible through the titanium "bones." He placed the dome header, now attached to the cup, over the top of the cylinder and turned it into twist-notches he'd precut into the top edge of the titanium tube. "Look away." He held a welder's mask in front of his own eyes and touched the business end of the arc welder to a single spot where the dome and tube met. A blue light flashed in the confines of the garage, then subsided. John lowered the mask and checked the bond. "Perfect."

"When do we set it?"

John did a quick calculation. "You're handing it over next Monday, right?"

"Eight at night."

"Set it at five forty-five that afternoon," John instructed. One hundred hours exactly to 9:45 on the following Friday. Forty-five minutes into the speech. John smiled.

"Got it."

"You can finish the shell after you set the timer," John said, entrusting that last step to his eldest boy. He would check it, of course. "And don't forget the charge on the inside of the shell." The small blasting cap charge, of negligible weight, would be wired to the timer to blow a hole in the shell as the VZ was released.

"Okay, Pop."

John laid the arc welder on the power unit and switched it off as he looked at the now complete innards of the device. All the rest was cosmetic. What lay before him was the power soon to be unleashed. The power to start anew.

"Would these guys try and mix with any local groups?" Special Agent David Rogers asked from his position at the head of the table. He was from the Bureau's Washington headquarters, and was supervising the search for the NALF. His question was directed to Art Jefferson.

"I don't think so. Our office pieced together a picture of a bunch of bitter loners." Art considered the question on a deeper level briefly. "I think they'd only hook up with someone if it was necessary to complete whatever they're up to."

"Well, we know what assumption we're working on," Rogers said.

"David, I'd suggest not going too narrow on their target," Art said. To his right Frankie nodded. "Not that it's probably not correct, but these guys have hit like a scattergun. L.A. Utah. Lord knows what they've done here."

"If anything," another agent suggested. "They could just be laying low."

"All right, if—"

A knock preceded an agent popping into the conference room. "Agent Jefferson, A-SAC in Los Angeles is on the phone for you."

Art looked to Rogers.

"Take it in my office," the lead agent said. "Mike, show him where."

Art left his partner in the conference and followed his escort to the office one floor down. He closed the door and picked up the indicated line. "Jefferson."

"Art, Lou. Chester Hart's AB friends tried to shut him up. And in a nasty way."

Art knew he had no reason to feel pity for the man. He'd made his own bed, and he'd given them questionable information concerning Freddy Allen in the past in the hope of trading it for whatever he fancied at the moment. But being marked for elimination by the Brotherhood was not a pleasant course for one's life to take. They were capable of some very heinous acts.

"How bad is he?" Art asked.

"They torched him in the prison yard. Quite a message. He's in the jail ward at Sacramento General now. Just came out of a coma. Art, he wants to talk."

Art's eyes rolled. "He's talked a lot before, Lou. That's his game. Talk just enough to curry some favors from us, then apologize when the stuff turns out to be less than stellar information."

"He says he's willing to spill everything he knows in trade for movement to PC at a federal prison."

Protective custody. Hart was not the one to waste a PC cell on. "Lou, he's blowing smoke."

"Art, he says it's about John Barrish."

Art hadn't expected that. "*Hart* said Barrish?"

"I thought you'd be interested in that," Hidalgo said.

"Lou, I've gotta tell you: you're on the unpopular side of a theory here. D.C. is not inclined to believe that Barrish would link up with the NALF, or vice versa. They were the ones with the VZ, remember?"

''That still wouldn't mean that Barrish doesn't have any.''

''But the NALF are the ones who've used it,'' Art said.

''Giving in, Art?''

''Like hell.''

''Good. Check out Hart. He may actually have something of substance for us this time. Hightail it back to D.C. when you're done. But keep me informed.''

''Will do.''

TWENTY FIVE

The Gleiwitz Echo

The jail ward at Sacramento General Hospital is on the ninth floor and consists of fifty beds in three separate sections. Two thirds of the beds are usually filled, mostly with arrestees or convicts recovering from wounds suffered in the jailhouse. These injuries are treated in the general nursing section. More serious injuries are treated in the surgical recovery section. The most serious casualties are housed in the ICU, or intensive care unit, where medical staff and deputies of the Sacramento County Sheriff's Department tend to their well-being and security.

Chester Hart lay in bed number four, the only resident of the ICU at the moment. His hands and arms were swathed in antibiotic-impregnated gauze, as were his abdomen, chest, and portions of his face. An IV line in his upper leg fed fluids and medicine into his system to prevent dehydration and fight off infection. A sturdy steel shackle connected him to the ICU bed by his ankle.

Art Jefferson entered the jail ward after checking his weapon at the guard station, and the ICU after donning a surgical gown, mask, and gloves. He found his would-be informant awake and staring at the ceiling.

"Chester."

Hart moved his head as far as it would go to the right, which wasn't much. His eyes traveled the remainder of the distance until he could see his visitor. He smiled at the black face behind the blue mask. "Black like you, Agent Jefferson."

"You picked a hard way to change colors," Art commented, stepping closer so the man did not have to strain.

"Chosen for me," Hart said. A wet, gurgling laugh followed.

"You got mixed up with some bad boys, Chester."

"Ah, they're just protecting their interests," Hart said. He truly believed that. He understood it perfectly, in fact. It was a credo he now had to live by.

"I hear you want to talk about something," Art said.

"In trade, Agent Jefferson." His voice was raspy. From the fire, the doctor had said. It had been sucked in when Hart breathed in its midst. The real concern was to the lung tissue, though. If that was burned in excess the long-term prognosis would not be promising. "More hospitable surroundings."

"What do you have, Chester?"

"Is it a deal?"

"Tell me what you have and we'll consider it. I have to hear it first."

Hart knew he was in no position to bargain. This pig was his lifeline. His only hope to live a long, horribly disfigured life was in barter, and it was apparent he would have to show his goods first.

"Saint Anthony's," Hart said, licking his blistered lips. "Freddy was in on it."

"We figured that."

Hart looked genuinely surprised. "How . . ."

"You've got to do better than that, Chester," Art said with raised eyebrows. Pity or not, he wasn't going to play games with this snitch for very long.

"He did it for Barrish," Hart said.

Art stopped breathing for a moment. *For* Barrish? "How so?"

"He was trying to prove a point, man, you know," Hart explained.

"Barrish? What point?"

"No, man, Freddy. Some big theory he had."

"Killing four little black girls was a theory?" Art asked doubtfully.

Hart hesitated, then chuckled. "Man, making it look like the monkeys did it. To lay the blame on them."

Art's eyes narrowed as he tried to find some reason in the statement. He recalled that the initial reports from the scene of the murder had said that two black men in masks, wearing all black except for colored rags in their back pockets, had run out of the church and disappeared over a back wall. That description lasted only until two of the guns used, Uzis, were found ditched at a construction site nearby. Those were soon linked to John Barrish, blowing away any thought of black men doing the . . .

Black men, black people, doing things for Barrish. *Interesting.* Art saw a potential symmetry. But was it really there?

"Are you saying Freddy dressed up to look black?"

Hart coughed and laughed together. "Yeah, that was his idea. Darkened his skin and everything, he said. Kind of a test, you know. He thought . . . that you could do a really violent hit on someone and blame it on the monkeys. I don't know who the other guy was."

"Wait. Blame the murder of blacks on other blacks?" What good would that do?

"Man, think, Agent Jefferson. I said it was a test. That one was against the monkeys. The ones after that would be against white folks and be blamed on the monkeys."

Art took the revelation in, pieces beginning to come together. A bigger picture was forming. "Barrish wanted to attack white people and make it look like the blacks did it?"

"It was Freddy's idea first, but John . . . liked it. He always thought about things in a historical way, you know, and he said Hitler did something like it to start the war against Poland. Something like he faked an attack by the Poles to kinda make the invasion okay.'' Hart paused, his chest rising greatly, then went on. ''But after the Saint Anthony's thing went sour he got cool on the idea. He said pretending wasn't good enough; you'd have to get the monkeys—he calls them . . . uh, you . . . Africans—to do it. Trick them or something.'' Another weak laugh. ''Yeah. Good luck.''

Get the Africans to do it . . . Trick them . . .

''He said it would set the Aryans off if you could do it,'' Hart added.

''Barrish wanted to do big things against white people by using blacks?''

''Against whites or the government,'' Hart expanded. ''He didn't really talk about it anymore. He just kind of dropped it.''

Maybe because he thought you had a big mouth. Art's head was almost spinning. Was this the explanation that would bring Barrish into the World Center attack? Barrish *had* thought of *big* attacks, and of using the *monkeys.* Of tricking them. Was this the link? It had to be, Art believed. What had seemed ludicrous to suggest now seemed within the realm of the possible.

''So? Does this get me a transfer?''

Art knew there would be at least local interest in this. The linking of Barrish to Saint Anthony's would be of interest to the LAPD, and to the DA. The state had never brought charges against Barrish because of a lack of evidence. With Hart's cooperation they would now have the evidence. Beyond that, it was still just a theory . . . not the proof Art Jefferson needed to tie Barrish to what was going on back east. But, for him, it was explanation enough.

''Well, Agent Jefferson? How about it?''

''You'll cooperate and testify?''

''Yes.''

"I'll need a stenographer to take an affidavit from you."

"I'm not going anywhere," Hart said. His mouth formed into something close to a smile. "Protection?"

"If you're not lying," Art warned.

"I'm not."

Art looked down upon the blackened form of Chester Hart, the man who'd just given him more than one piece of the puzzle. Freddy had dreamed it up. Monte supplied the nightmare. And John Barrish would make it all come true. That was only his take on it but he felt he had a good grasp on the *why* now. Only the *when*, *where*, and *what* remained.

TWENTY SIX

Indications

Darian and Moises returned to their apartment from meeting the head white boy. Mustafa and Roger were waiting for them as planned.

"Is that it?" Roger asked, eyeing the long, towel-wrapped object under Moises' arm.

"Yep." Moises went to the bed, laid the package down, and unwrapped it.

"It don't look real," Roger commented.

"It's not supposed to," Darian said. He went to the small refrigerator and took a Pepsi.

Roger picked the leg up, testing its weight. "Not too heavy." He held it out to Mustafa, who shook his head at the offer.

"Leave it on the bed," Darian instructed. "The timer's already going."

"Shiiiit," Roger swore softly, laying the limb back on the bed.

Darian pulled one of the cheap kitchen chairs into the living room/bedroom and sat. "Forget that for a minute and listen up. We've gotta talk about the schedule." He looked to Mustafa. "Did you get a new place for Wednesday?"

"We can move in that morning," Mustafa answered.

"Where?"

"Arlington. Just a few miles from Vorhees's house. You checked it out?"

Darian nodded. "You'll have no trouble."

"We're gonna do it tomorrow, right?" Mustafa asked.

"Right," Darian confirmed. "He'll be at a state dinner until at least midnight."

"Is that from the cracker?" Mustafa inquired.

"Cracker ain't been wrong so far," Darian reminded his comrade. It prevented any further question as to the information's validity. "You'll be in the clear. Cheap alarm, no dog. In, out, no fuss, no muss. Brother Moises and I will do the rest Thursday."

"What about Friday?" Roger asked.

"Friday is the big night," Darian said, showing teeth without truly smiling. "We do it together that night."

"Where?" Mustafa inquired.

"Get this—about a half-mile from Vorhees's place," Darian answered. It could have been in Tucson, for all he cared. Location was not his concern. But the lay of the land was. "We're going to need maps to figure the approach."

"There's gonna be feds there," Roger said with wide eyes.

Darian stared down at his comrade, who sat cross-legged on the floor. "Brother Mustafa has something to deal with them." The NALF leader saw his number two give a slight nod. "And if there's a fight, we fight. But we will take out the target."

The target was the secretary of state. The man who would take the reins of power when everyone in the House chamber bit the dust. After that . . . pure anarchy. It didn't take a rocket scientist to imagine what would happen next, Darian knew. Just like in the tribal conflicts that plagued African and certain European nations, factions would develop. With no legally recognized head of state, and with the black man taking the opportunity to rise up, there'd be governors, and mayors, and all kinds of folks trying to seize power. Lines would be drawn. Us against them, them against us. Him against her. State against state. City against city. The military would have no commander in chief. What would they do? Try and seize power, too? It didn't matter. Darian had to give credit to the white boys who had put this scheme into play. It was near perfect. Take away the people who wielded the power, and the people would grab what of it they could. Beautiful. It was absolutely beautiful.

"You want us to get the maps?" Mustafa asked.

"No. Brother Moises and I will take care of it. You two have a job to do."

Mustafa nodded, then looked to the quiet young fighter seated on the bed. "You ain't said much, Brother Moises."

"I'll do my talking Friday," Moises said. After that he didn't give a damn what happened. If he was alive he'd fight for the sake of fighting. Tanya wasn't even the reason anymore. Moises had thought his family was as good as dead because of her murder, but now he realized that he was the one who'd stopped living. Reason didn't matter now at all. He was on autopilot, and the only instruction his psyche recognized was *kill. Kill every white face you see.*

After Friday, that would be enough.

The sixth floor rooms, connected by a door, were comfortable, but far from lavish. Darren entered first, with suitcases in each hand. He laid these on the queen-size bed and walked to the window as Felicia and Anne followed him in. He was stiff, but not tired. His body was still convinced it was seven, not ten.

"This is nice," Anne commented. She checked the connecting door. It was unlocked, and for a moment she disappeared through it to her room to unload the two pieces of luggage she had brought.

Felicia walked up behind her husband and slid her arms around his waist. She felt the rumble of his stomach on her palms. "You should have eaten something on the plane."

"I wasn't hungry."

She knew it wasn't a case of appetite. Her chin rested on Darren's shoulder as she looked out the window with him. Across the street the D.C. Courthouse was lit against the wintry night. Snow flurries had dusted the city all day, but nothing had stuck.

Darren was looking beyond the courthouse, though. Far beyond. "He's out there, sweetheart."

Felicia hugged her husband tighter. "I know."

"Maybe he's old enough to think for himself, but . . ." Darren's breath clouded the window as he spoke. It cleared as he was momentarily silent. "I hate being this close and not being able to do anything."

"What would you do if you could?"

"Find him," Darren said, his hands coming up to caress Felicia's on his stomach. "Just find him."

Felicia would do the same . . . if she could. But she couldn't. Their son had taken a road neither of them was familiar with. They could only hope that, at some point, it would lead him home.

Darren looked away from the nighttime D.C. skyline and kissed the side of his wife's face. "I need to walk or something, sweetheart." He felt Felicia's chin move on his shoulder as she nodded. "Five hours on the plane . . ."

"I understand. There's a restaurant downstairs. Why don't you get a piece of pie." She pinched his waist and giggled. "You've got a half-inch to spare."

Darren turned, facing the only woman he'd ever loved. High school sweethearts they had been. Married right after graduation against everyone's advice. He went to work for the post office, she for a bank. Then two children, a house that was never big enough but was always *theirs*. They'd had a lot of sun in their lives, and some rain. Some real rain of late. But they had come through that together . . . "I love you. You know that."

"Really?" Felicia smiled and kissed him. "I love you, too." He smiled back, but it wasn't a whole expression. She knew what was missing. "Go get a bite and relax."

"Okay." Darren kissed her on the forehead and left the room, the hotel door clicking loudly as its twin latches closed.

Anne popped back in at the sound. "Where's Darren?"

"He needed a minute to . . ." Felicia bit her lower lip to stop the tears from coming. It worked. "It's Moises. Being here is hard for Darren because he knows Moises is just up the road a ways."

"That was weeks ago, Felicia," Anne reminded her.

"I know. Convince Superdad of that."

You couldn't talk the worry out of a parent. Not in therapy, and definitely not three thousand miles from the couch.

But maybe you could ease the parent's fears. *Maybe . . .*

"I have an idea, Felicia. Maybe there's some peace of mind for Darren." Anne got the mischievous look on her face that only one person knew. "Did Darren bring that postcard from Moises?"

"I have it," Felicia said. She retrieved it from her bag and gave it to Anne. Then she got *that* look, too. "You're seeing him tonight?"

"For a late dinner." She looked at her watch and added the three hours she'd forgotten to on the plane. "A late, *late* dinner."

"Do you think he can find something? From that?"

"We'll see."

* * *

So it hadn't been the most romantic of reunions. The restaurant, on the ground floor of the hotel Art had called home for several weeks, was hardly five-star, but it did have a very important redeeming quality: it was open. The late hour and the holiday had combined to limit their dining choices, but they were making the best of it, he with an almost decent eggplant parmesan, she with an average scampi. But together they were. That was what counted.

Anne rolled the last pinkish-orange shrimp in its buttery sauce and bit it off up to the tail. Across the small round table she watched Art lay his fork on the half-finished plate. "Not hungry?"

He leaned a bit closer, over the plate, and spoke softly, his eyes glancing at the food: "Not for this."

Anne smiled and pushed her plate aside. The shrimp were gone, but the vegetable medley had only warranted a taste. She slid a hand across the table and laid it on his. "Tired?"

He nodded.

"I miss you," Anne said as she rubbed the back of his hand. His eyes danced between hers and countless other things in sight. Something was on his mind. Something she was pretty certain of. "I wish we could have gotten together when you were back in California last week."

"It was just a quick stop," Art said, focusing on her now. He had to say it at some point, and there was no need to fear her reaction. The only thing he had to fear was what came after. Maybe fear wasn't the right word. Wary. That was better. It was a road he'd taken before, a road he thought he'd never choose to travel down again. Until now.

"You want some dessert?" Anne asked and suggested. "What could they possibly do to ice cream?"

"Anne," Art said, moving his hand atop hers, looking

at her across the remnants of highly average Italian cuisine, "I'm going to take the Chicago job." At another time in his life he might have waited for a reaction from her. Some validation before making his next declaration. Not anymore. "I want you to come with me."

Well if that wasn't direct . . . Leaving L.A. Leaving her practice. Leaving the teaching job at UCLA. She had already considered all those possibilities. Los Angeles was a place, a conglomeration of buildings and roads, a smattering of friends, but good friendships would survive some distance. Her practice was a bit harder to envision leaving, but the reality was that she had found it harder to think of healing others after so many of those she had known had lost their lives in the World Center. It was irrational, but that was the way of the human animal. Logic went only so far before emotion kicked in, and she was professional enough to know that she would need to heal before a full load of patients could count on her for the help they needed. Already she had trimmed her list by more than half. As for teaching . . . that was not an issue. The mention she'd made to Art about Chas Ohlmeyer had been a hint of sorts, but there was more to it than that—a job offer of her own, to be exact. A full professorship at the University of Chicago. Teaching *all* the time. She easily saw herself doing that. She easily saw herself doing that with Art as a part of her life.

But she saw something else, too. She needed something else. "You know I will . . . on one condition."

He knew what that was, and, to be honest, he wouldn't want it any other way. "I know. Don't think about that right now, though. I want to do it right. Proper, Miss Preston."

Anne felt the squeeze on her hand, and the funny feeling low in her stomach. "Whew. Well, I guess this meal will be memorable for more than the food."

"Thankfully," Art joked mildly. He tried to look

strong, sure of himself, stoic. But he knew the stupid grin on his face was shooting those attempts to hell. Time to set this subject aside until its proper disposition. "So, how are the Griggses?"

"Nervous, excited, sad," Anne answered. "Darren especially, because of Moises."

"The stupid kid," Art said.

"Confused, G-Man," Anne countered. She reached into her purse and pulled out the postcard. "And for that cynical transgression you owe me a favor."

Art took the card and read it. *At least he wrote home.* "How so?"

"Look at the postmark—Baltimore. Being this close and not knowing exactly where he is is eating Darren up. I know you're busy, but is there any way you could look into it? Or ask someone to?" Anne noticed a change in Art's expression. "What?"

No. It can't be him. "Suspect number four is a young black male, age seventeen to twenty-five, small frame, close-cropped hair." *He fits the description.* "Suspect number four was seen in the vicinity of the NALF headquarters on separate occasions." *He fits the profile.* "Subjects show evidence of racially tinged hatred, possibly brought on by injustices they have suffered at the hands of a different race, whether perceived or real." *And he's in the area.* Art quickly flashed on the tape of Trooper Fitzroy's murder, on the unidentified face of suspect number four. Left rear. A kid. He compared it to the face of the young man he'd confronted that Monday before Thanksgiving. The young, angry man taking off. Dropping out. Just like the NALF did two days later, after doing the damage.

"Art, what is it?"

He couldn't tell her this. It was only a suspicion. A "wild" suspicion, he tried to convince himself. "Nothing," Art said, shaking his head and forcing a smile. "I just remember that night at dinner."

"Right. That was a hard night."

You stupid, stupid kid. "He was a snot."

"So, will you?"

Art fiddled with the card for a second. He knew they could find out some things from it: the postal processing center it was handled at, what stores carried the type of card. That was about it. General information. Beyond that it would take some ground pounding. But first came the question of confirmation—or an attempt at it. "Can I hang on to this?"

"Sure," Anne said. She sensed something in his tone, almost a reluctance to ask the question. *But why would . . . Let him do his job, Anne.* "Do you think you can use it?"

Art slid the card into a pocket and toiled over the truthful answer, wishing more than anything that it could be a lie. "I'll do what I can."

TWENTY SEVEN
Staging

Art sat next to the ID technician as the woman manipulated the controls on her powerful computer workstation, trying to make the already enhanced image of suspect number four even clearer. Behind them Special Agent Rogers stood patiently.

"It's the glare," the technician said with resignation and apology, leaning closer to the twenty-one-inch monitor. On it the face in semiprofile was a far cry from identifiable. The lines that should be there to define the boundaries of the cheek and forehead were blended into the shadow deeper in the car's exterior. This was further exacerbated by the reflection of Trooper Fitzroy's spotlight off the back window. "I can't make it any clearer. Even this wouldn't hold up in court."

"What do you think?" Rogers asked. "Could it be the Griggs kid?"

Art refreshed his memory by glancing at the police mug shot of Moises Griggs that LAPD had transmitted to FBI headquarters an hour earlier. That had been taken after the boy's first and only arrest, for vandalizing the cars parked at a Beverly Hills church. Mild payback, Art thought. The Griggs kid was just getting his feet wet. Had he decided to dive in now? "It could be, David. I can't definitely say it is, and I can't definitely say it's not."

Rogers stared at the face for a moment, then shifted his attention to the postcard in his hand. "I can't disrupt what we've got running and shift a good deal of our resources to look for this kid based on a less-than-absolute ID." The agent looked again to the screen, but this time saw another face: the reflection of Art's. "Unless you're certain, I can't."

Art continued looking at the fuzzy image of what could be a young life thrown away. *Could be.* "I can't be sure."

"Sorry," Rogers said. "Thanks for the rush, Sue." He put a hand on the technician's shoulder.

"I appreciate you looking at this, David," Art said.

"That's what I'm here for." Rogers patted Art on the back, the action jogging his memory. "By the way, I've got some good news for you."

"How so?"

"The secretary of state is going to be away from the State of the Union address and Director Jones is going to be with him," Rogers explained. "Boys' night out, I guess. Anyway, the director wants you to join them."

"Me?"

Rogers nodded. "Somewhere, Art, you made an impression on the man. He heard you were in town and, well, when the director asks the likes of me if I can spare you for one night, I don't see myself saying no."

"David, that's—"

"And if I were an agent about to move up in the world, I wouldn't say no to the invitation." Rogers punctuated the suggestion with a cautionary glare.

"I don't like it," Art said.

"Go," Frankie prompted.

"Aguirre will be at the Capitol," Rogers said. "Part of our supplement to Service security."

"I'll send you a postcard," Frankie joked.

"Amusing, partner."

Rogers suppressed a grin at the exchange. "So I'll convey your acceptance?"

"Convey away," Art said. He'd had to give in to worse things in his life. One boring night with D.C. types wouldn't kill him.

Number 4387 Monroe was an extremely comfortable two-story colonial done in red brick on the outside and tasteful shades of white on the inside. Mustafa Ali was admiring the latter as he let Roger in the back door.

"Man, I hate this," Roger said as the door closed behind him. "This breaking-in shit."

Mustafa walked back to the kitchen countertop he'd crawled carefully over after having broken one pane of glass in the window to the left of the sink to gain access to the latch. He made sure the latch had been reset, then brushed some of the shattered glass onto the tiled floor, making a pattern that stretched to the refrigerator across the room. He reached into his pocket and removed a baseball, laying it on the floor near the large appliance. "Stupid kids should be more careful," he said, then headed off through the house. Roger followed with a longish gym bag under his arm.

The bedrooms were obviously upstairs, so that was where they went first. There turned out to be three on the second floor, one of which was set up as a music room of sorts, with stereo equipment and a collection of old vinyl LPs and CDs that covered the breadth of the big band era. The next room they checked had to be the one Vorhees used. Its centerpiece was a surprisingly small bed with sheets and covers tossed haphazardly up over the pillows. The congressman wasn't a neat freak at home, it appeared.

"Check it out," Mustafa directed, pointing to the adjoining bathroom. He went to the dresser and, with gloved hands, slid each drawer out carefully. Nothing. Next was the closet. It was to his right and was closed off by twin doors. He parted them and, holding the mini-flashlight in his teeth, lit up the space. What he was searching for was there, leaning in the corner like an old umbrella. "Brother Roger. I got it."

Roger hurried to the closet and lifted the artificial limb, examining it in the light. "It's close. It looks close." The obvious difference between it and the one they had in the bag was the series of straps that wrapped the upper portion, connecting it to a semirigid knee brace that itself was topped by more straps to affix the limb securely to the thigh. It was a clunker, all right. Roger had seen better on some of the brothers back in L.A. But the added gear was not a problem. They had expected it, and simply transferred it to the prosthesis they had brought with them.

"There's some marks by the ankle," Mustafa pointed out. He held the leg now while Roger opened the small makeup kit they'd brought along. A few strokes of a nonoily foundation prepared the area of their leg, and a dab of an eyebrow pencil did the rest. This they repeated for every blemish that they could find, until the difference between the two limbs was almost nil. "How does it feel?"

Roger hefted it up and down a few times, comparing the weight and balance to the real one now tucked in the bag. "About the same."

"Good," Mustafa said. "He'll never know the difference." *Until it's too late.* "Okay, put it back. Right where it was."

Roger leaned the limb back in the corner, made sure nothing was disturbed, then closed the closet door. "We did it."

"We did *this*," Mustafa said. He let the light fall from his mouth to his hand. "*It* comes Friday."

Roger agreed with a nod. "Whatever. Let's get out of here now."

"Nervous, Brother Roger?"

"Cautious, Brother Mustafa," Roger countered. He saw that it didn't convince his comrade. "Come on."

Mustafa followed Roger down the stairs. They waited ten minutes at the front door, until it was just fifteen minutes shy of midnight. They then let themselves out, making sure the latch was set to lock when closed. Only the deadbolt remained unlocked, but that was of no concern. An oversight on the congressman's part when leaving that evening. A state dinner, a dead friend. He had a lot on his mind. Such a minor slip was to be expected. A simple mistake. It wouldn't have been his first.

TWENTY EIGHT
The Switch

It wasn't a bad little place, Darian thought, but then they'd only be there a short time. Still, it did feel good to have everyone together. And the extra room this larger apartment in Arlington provided made it all the more comfortable.

But comfort was only incidental. They were there for a reason. There to prepare for the big night. There to take the last steps that would set things in motion.

"Whiteboy ain't got his head screwed on straight if he thinks there won't be cops there," Mustafa said, his powerful fingers pressing the .45-caliber shells into the stack of magazines they'd acquired for the Ingrams. He wore no gloves this time. It didn't matter if there were prints on the casings. Who would know, who would care? But if there was going to be a fight, they were going to breathe plenty of fire. No ammo worries on Friday.

"It's supposed to be low-key," Darian said. He was busying his hands with cleaning the Ingrams, as well as the half-dozen pistols and revolvers that lay on the bed between him and Moises. On the floor the "toy" Mustafa had brought with them from L.A., something he'd "acquired" from an associate in the Army some years before, lay on an open towel. It looked like a break-open shotgun on steroids. "And we'll be shooting first."

Mustafa stopped what he was doing and looked up. "There's gonna be a fight."

"Then a fight there'll be," Moises interjected confidently.

"Yeah," Mustafa said with little faith. "Virgin boy here who ain't done hardly more than pop some unarmed ratbeard is gonna take out Secret Service pigs."

"Brother Moises will do fine," Darian said with confidence.

Mustafa eyed their youngest comrade, then looked back to his leader. "Right."

"Trust me, Brothers. We're gonna do this." He laid the Ingram he'd been cleaning on the bed and took the two .357 revolvers in hand. "Brother Moises, load these. We've got work to do tonight."

The door from the living room opened. Roger took half a step into the room, his eyes on his leader. "Brother Darian."

"What?" The NALF leader didn't bother looking up.

"I need to talk to you."

Now his eyes came up. "Talk."

"In here."

Both Moises and Mustafa sensed the strangeness in that request as they looked to their comrade.

"It's important," Roger said. He backstepped into the living room, beckoning his leader.

Darian stood and went to Roger, the door closing behind. "What is it? This isn't good, talking like this. What's with you? What are they supposed to think, Brother Roger? Huh?"

Roger backed farther away from the door to the couch. "I saw something."

"Saw? Saw what?" Darian demanded impatiently. An Ingram, its suppressor affixed, lay on a piece of furniture. "You are supposed to have that weapon in your hands, watching that door, making sure that no one gets the drop on us. Is that what you were doing coming in there and saying you had something *important* to say?''

Roger bent down and reached between the cushions near the Ingram. A folded newspaper came out in his hand.

''What is that?''

Roger held it out to Darian. ''The paper. The one you got the classifieds from. Remember?''

An old paper? What . . . ''What are you doing with it?''

''I looked at the front page that day,'' Roger admitted. ''There was a story about what we did in L.A. I just wanted to take a look at it, to see what—''

''Propaganda,'' Darian said. ''You know better than to read that shit.''

''Not this, Brother Darian,'' Roger countered. ''This was talking about something different. Look at it.''

Darian unfolded the paper and immediately saw the small headline that had to have captured his comrade's attention: WHITE SUPREMACIST WAS SUSPECT IN WORLD CENTER ATTACK. Below that was a picture of John Barrish . . . and of his wife and two sons. One of those looked amazingly like the white boy with the funky eye that they'd been meeting with.

''That's him,'' Roger said.

Darian looked up from the story.

''That Barrish guy is the one who got off for killing those girls at the church on Crenshaw!'' Roger said in a suppressed shout. ''Brother Moises' little sister was one of them!''

''You had this all the time?''

Roger nodded. ''I didn't want to, you know . . . That thing sounds like we were working for him.''

Darian read some more, then crumpled the paper into a ball. ''It says he wasn't a suspect anymore.''

''Brother, his kid was the cracker we were meeting with!''

Roger always had been the most timid of the NALF's

small number. Now he was more than that. "Have you shown this to the others?"

"No. I didn't want to believe it myself. But . . ." Roger looked to the carpet, then to his leader again. "I can't do this no more. It's been eating at me. These guys aren't no tax protesters. They're killers, man, and they've killed our people. Do you think Brother Moises would be doing this if he knew who the crackers we've been dealing with are?"

Darian squeezed the ball of newsprint smaller, and pressed it into his pocket. *You shouldn't have read that, Brother Roger. It's too late to stop now. We've come too far. And now you can't come any farther.* He stepped closer to his comrade. "Go get the others."

Darian stepped aside, toward the couch, to let Roger pass. When he did, Darian reached quickly to the couch and took the Ingram in hand. He spun and raised the weapon in one smooth motion, taking the selector switch from safe to single shot with his thumb. As Roger's hand was reaching for the bedroom door, the NALF leader shot him once in the back of his head.

A second later the door to the bedroom opened inward, Roger's limp body collapsing completely to the floor at Mustafa's feet. "What . . ."

Darian lowered the Ingram. The sound of the shot had hardly been louder than a phone book dropping to a solid floor, but that report, and the thud of Roger's body tumbling against the bedroom door, had been enough to alert the other NALF members.

Moises pushed past Mustafa, his eyes flaring at the bloody sight. "What happened?"

"He wanted out," Darian said matter-of-factly. "He got it."

"Out?" Mustafa asked. "What do you mean?"

Darian tossed the Ingram across his front to the couch. "Out, Brother. Out. He was going soft on us."

Mustafa looked to Roger's still body. "Brother Roger?"

"Why do you think he wanted to talk to me away from you all? He didn't have the stomach to say it in front of you." Darian kicked the body's feet. "Candy ass. He could have blown it all if I'd let him back away from this. He would've started shooting his mouth off. We could have all been burned by him."

"Damn." Mustafa stepped over the body.

"But how are we going to do it without him?" Moises asked.

"We're just going to do it. Period. Now get those guns ready, Brother. We've got a job to do." Darian looked to Mustafa. "So do you. Get this pile of shit out of here."

"Bud, how's your day?" Secretary of State James Coventry asked over the phone.

"Half up, half down," the NSA answered blandly.

"An even split? Lucky you. Listen, Gordy's going to be over at my place to watch the address tomorrow."

"Oh?"

"He's not exactly the Hill's favorite person right now," Coventry explained. "Anyway, I thought you might like to join us."

Bud smiled to himself. "Heard about the compromise, did you? I keep my mug away from the cameras and Earl won't throw a fit if the president talks about Iran." There was a bit of sarcasm in the NSA's relation of the political reality he'd been cast into.

"Just the smiling faces of HUD and Interior for the networks to see, I gather."

"You gather correctly," Bud confirmed. Earl Casey was pushing hard to craft this as a domestically centered campaign, leaving the NSA's domain somewhat in the shadows. But a campaign was just that. Reality dictated the true importance of Bud DiContino's expertise.

"Sure. Sounds like a plan. Who's bringing the beer?"

"I'll provide refreshments," Coventry answered with a chuckle. "Oh, and Gordy's inviting one of his agents who's in town. You'll remember him: Jefferson."

"Art Jefferson? Yeah. A good man. He filled in a lot of the pieces after the assassination. I met him once. What's he doing here?"

"Working with the D.C. Bureau people tracking down those militants."

"What time?" Bud asked.

"Anytime before nine."

"Sounds like a good time," Bud observed.

"We can make it so."

Congressman Richard Vorhees rounded the corner at a fast clip, splitting a pair of walkers coming at him on the sidewalk. "Evening."

"Evening."

Vorhees looked briefly over his shoulder as he moved away, his eyes admiring the women's backsides. Both were easily over forty, but it had never been proven that a woman lost her can at that age. At least not to him it hadn't. He looked forward again with an added bounce in his step and pushed himself along the final mile of his walk, realizing this was the only exercise he'd have for two days. His card was full for the following evening, as it was for anybody who was any—

"Freeze, fucker!"

Vorhees stutter-stopped, the rubber soles of his shoes actually skidding as the dark figure jumped from the shrubs on the right and blocked his path.

"Get 'em up, dickweed!"

"Easy, easy," Vorhees said, his eyes fixed on the kid's hands. Those were the most dangerous parts of a man. These held a revolver that was pointed at his crotch.

"Get 'em UP!"

Vorhees showed the kid his hands. *Male black, five-four, maybe five-five. Dark clothing.*

"Give me your money!" One hand came free of the gun and reached out. "Now!"

"I don't have any," Vorhees said, trying to commit more details about his assailant to memory before a fear-induced adrenaline rush made such an effort fruitless. *Dark bandanna drawn across his face, maybe dark blue, and—*

"Your watch! Now!"

The gun waved as Vorhees pulled his watch off. He saw that the hammer was cocked, and the punk had his finger on the trigger. It would only take a twitch. "Here."

The thief shoved the watch in a pocket and took a half-step back, slowly, without any haste at all. That seemed strange to Vorhees, but more so were the eyes. They glowed in the harsh reflection of approaching headlights, and he could see them travel down his body, past the obvious aim point of the gun, and to his leg. The gun followed the eyes the final distance.

"You ain't chasin' me, fuckhead," the thief said.

I'm going to be shot. The realization hit Vorhees before the punk even spoke. The eyes, the gun, the movement. A switch was reflexively thrown. *Combat. Unarmed versus Armed. Move quick. Disarm. Eliminate.* He was an 82nd Airborne trooper again, moving toward the enemy, hands in motion, one going for the gun, the other for the upper body for a control hold. There was an abundance of clothing to grab. Moving. Reaching. Almost . . .

BANG.

Vorhees saw the flash, sensed it even on the skin of his left hand, and felt his weight shift awkwardly. It threw the aim of his right hand off, and by now that claw of fingers set to grab had become a fist prepared to strike. It made contact with something hard, with a soft top layer, but he did not see what. He was falling left and back, one arm reaching now to break his fall. His mind searched for pain. Where was he hit? Where was . . .

There? He realized where just as his butt hit the sidewalk. *My God, how lucky could I be?*

Moises Griggs was through the shrubs and across the field of short, brown grass beyond less than thirty seconds after the shot was fired. He jumped through the open door of the waiting Volvo. The door closed on its own as Darian sped away, heading quickly for the Leesburg Pike.

"Did you get him?"

"Yeah," Moises said. He pulled the black knit cap off and wrapped it around the .357, tossing both into the backseat.

"In the leg?" Darian pressed, his eyes darting to the rearview. *No flashing lights. Whew!*

"Yeah. Yeah." Moises pulled the bandanna down to hang around his neck, then put a hand to his forehead. "Man, the motherfucker hit me."

Darian looked right. "Shit, you're bleeding."

Moises rubbed above his left eye and felt the wetness. It stung at the touch. "Shit."

Darian drove with one hand and pulled his young comrade's head over for a closer look with the other. "He gouged you."

"Huh?"

"A big ol' hunk of skin is gone, Brother Moises." Darian let his head go. "It's gonna be a scar. A good one."

Moises took the bandanna from around his neck and pressed it to the wound. It stung, but it didn't hurt. It did not hurt. "Fuck it."

That's the attitude, Darian thought. As he did the first

police cars, light bars flashing, passed left to right behind them.

"Where are you hit?" the police officer asked as he knelt down. Two civilians had already come to the victim's aid.

"The leg," Vorhees answered, laughing nervously. He saw the cop looking at him and thinking "shock."

"It's a prosthesis."

The police officer watched as the victim pulled the left leg of his sweatpants up. He held the beam of his flashlight on the sight. "Unbelievable."

Vorhees heard more sirens approaching as he stuck three fingers into the gaping hole halfway between his knee and the artificial ankle. He moved them around, making a clinking metal sound. "Blew the hell out of it."

"Better it than you," the police officer said. He ran his light over the rest of the victim. "What's that?"

Vorhees noticed the blood on his hand for the first time. "It's the punk's. I laid one on him."

The police officer examined the bloodied hand. There was a large class-type ring on the third finger, some pieces of torn skin jammed between it and the finger, and—he looked closer—yes, even some short hairs still embedded in the skin. "Don't touch anything with this. I want to get this in an evidence bag. The leg, too, I'm afraid."

"It's no good to me anymore," Vorhees said.

"But how . . ."

"Don't worry." Vorhees laughed a bit, silently likening himself to a car. "I have a spare. An old one, but it's got a few miles left in it."

TWENTY NINE

Trojan Horse

John Barrish stepped from the house near Fulks Run for the last time and gazed eastward over the trees. The morning sky glowed with a jaundiced hue that filtered through sheer fingers of clouds flowing northeast, the cold nip of winter stinging his cheeks. It was a beautiful morning. It would be a glorious day.

"John."

He turned just his head toward the voice, then looked away from his wife's face.

Louise Barrish came from the house, wearing the closest thing she had to a winter coat. It did little to stave off the sharp chill. "John, Toby is leaving soon." She said this to his back. Silence followed. "How long will he be gone?"

"A while."

Louise drew her arms tight against her chest, gripping opposite elbows. "John, does it have to happen?"

Trent wrote once that *"doubters are not followers. Instead they favor proximity to the bold, for it is with them that they find nourishment for their weakness. Doubters need visionaries to justify their existence. The lion is a visionary. The grizzly is a visionary. The slug is a doubter. Doubters are prey."* Do not feed the doubter, John recalled Trent proposing. It was better to let the behavior starve.

"So many people are dead already," Louise said, her voice having a surprising edge to it. "Do more have to die?"

"Toby will make the call tonight, then he'll be back," John said to the forest. Sparks of light flashed off the ice-covered trees as rays of sun began to crest the horizon.

"John, think about this," Louise implored. She stepped closer, even though she could see her husband's fist ball at his side. "How many more?"

"Make sure you make a big dinner. I'm sure he'll be hungry."

"John . . . Don't do this. Stop it. You can stop it."

"Don't let a doubter become a challenger. Challengers are parasites that infect he who allows them quarter."

"Please, John." He was so young, so strong, with such powerful convictions, such grand ideas, such determination. How could she not have fallen in love with him then? So long ago. Now she understood the reality of it all. Her reality. One did not love John Barrish. One either hated him or respected him. Louise knew now that she was unique among those groupings. She was a creature of two selves. She did not love him. Infatuation at one time, maybe. Starry-eyed adoration. But never love. Respect, yes. Fear, most definitely. "Don't make our sons like you. Don't."

John unclenched his fists and slid them into the pockets of his jeans. "Steak. We have some steaks left. Toby and Stanley both like steak."

"John!"

He looked over his shoulder at her. "They're my sons! They're nothing like you! They never have been, they never will be!"

Her eyes were glistening, her cheeks red. Neither were from the cold. "Please!"

Now he turned his whole body and faced her, just

looking, not lifting a hand, not making a move. It was a posture he had mastered against more worthy doubters. This one, like the others, would not become a challenger. "One other thing, Louise: if you say anything, do anything, even think anything that crosses me in front of the boys, I'll kill you."

Her body didn't move an inch, but internally she cowered, hunching down into the smallest fetal position she could imagine, hands shielding her face from the monster that stood over her like a giant. The monster looked down upon her, then walked past. It could have stepped on her if it wanted.

It might still, she knew.

"I can't believe we're here," Felicia Griggs said to her husband as they were escorted to the upper level of the House chamber.

"I'm in a suit," Darren said. "Believe it."

"I can't get him in a suit even for church," Felicia joked, looking back to Anne.

"I can't get mine *out* of his," Anne responded, realizing from the shocked look on her newest friend's face that there was too much interpretation possible in that statement. "You know what I mean."

"I know," Felicia said.

"There was a lot of security outside," Felicia commented. "There were soldiers on the roof of the Supreme Court building."

"Just a few," Darren reminded her, though he had noticed, too.

"Art promised it was safe," Anne assured them. Of course *he* was miles away watching the whole thing as the guest of some government bigwigs. Well, they were guests of the biggest bigwig, Anne knew.

The House usher stopped and motioned a left to the guests of the president. "This way. To the second row on the right. You'll be behind the first lady."

Felicia froze momentarily, as did Anne. Collectively they thought, *The First Lady!*

"Come on," Darren prodded. He led them down the steps, past the half-filled rows to the seats indicated by the usher. It was still early, and the House chamber was only sparsely populated, but more legislators were entering every minute.

"Do you think there's someone selling peanuts?" Anne asked.

Felicia giggled at the joke and looked toward the podium where the president would be speaking. They were above and to the left of that spot, one of the choicest seats for the yearly event. It was where those whom the president had chosen for special recognition of some sort sat, along with the first family.

"Do you think she'll bring the baby?" Felicia inquired.

"Not if he yells like he did at that speech the president gave last summer," Darren answered.

"The child has lungs," Anne commented.

"I think he's cute," Felicia said in defense of the little boy. She squeezed her husband's hand as thoughts of another little boy filled her head. Darren, not surprisingly, squeezed back.

He shouldn't have been surprised, but Art Jefferson was when Secretary of State James Coventry met him in the foyer with a long-neck hanging lazily in one hand.

"Jefferson. Good to see you." Coventry shook the agent's hand and took his overcoat. It was dry outside, but cold and breezy. "Did the guard dogs give you any trouble?"

Art noticed the smile attached to the inquiry, but doubted that the two Secret Service agents who'd given him the once-over out front would appreciate the secretary's characterization. "Just doing their job, sir."

"I know. Come on in." Coventry led the evening's

final arrival into the main area of the foyer. A long, sweeping staircase curved up to the left, forming an arch over the passageway to the back of the house. To the right was a parlor, and beyond it a dining room. To the left, through twin doors that were open, was the secretary's study, and the gathering.

"This is a nice house, sir," Art commented. Nice, big. It was definitely beyond his means, but soon there would be another set of means to add to his. And he would have to start looking for a new place. *Correction*, he caught himself . . . *they* would be looking.

"Thanks," Coventry answered, bringing Art into the study. Bud DiContino and Gordon Jones stood to greet him. "You know this fella."

"Mr. Director." There was no way around the formality, Art knew. Mister this, mister that. All evening.

"Glad you could make it, Jefferson," Jones said.

"And you've met Bud DiContino."

"Yes. A couple years back."

"Good to see you again," Bud said, shaking the agent's hand.

"Have a seat, Jefferson," Coventry offered. "Take your jacket off. You want a beer?"

Oh, wonderful! He was being told to get comfortable *and* have a brew in front of the director! Art could see it was a loose-tie and rolled-up sleeves night, but he had a gun on his hip—although Jones did, too, and his Smith & Wesson was there for all to see.

"Relax, Jefferson," Jones suggested with an amused smile. "Consider it a night off."

"Yes, sir."

"Beer?" Coventry asked again as Art hung his jacket with the others.

"Do you have any nonalcoholic stuff?"

"One light-light coming up."

Art took a seat next to the national security adviser on one of the room's two couches. Two chairs completed the U around the coffee table, and at the far end, built into a large display case that held some of the secretary's memorabilia, was a good-sized TV.

"I wish you were in D.C. under better circumstances," Bud commented.

"To be honest, I try not to find many circumstances to *be* in D.C."

Bud smiled and looked to a grinning Jones. "He knows the first rule of surviving this place, Gordy: stay away!"

Jones chuckled quietly. He wasn't a man given to overt laughter. "So, Jefferson, the word is you're going to Chicago."

"I called Bob Lomax yesterday and accepted."

"What's this?" Bud asked.

"Jefferson is going to be the new assistant special agent in charge of the Chicago field office," Jones explained. He looked back to the agent. "You'll like Lomax."

"I worked with him in Chicago about a dozen years back," Art said nodding.

Clinking bottles announced the secretary's return. He handed Art a bottle, and the second round to the others, then sat in one of the chairs. Jones was next to him in the other.

"Good seats, gentlemen," Coventry observed as the TV picture showed a filling House chamber. "Bud says you have someone there in the guest box?"

"Yes, my . . ." *Well, she's not really your girlfriend anymore.* ". . . fiancée."

"Congratulations, Jefferson," Coventry said.

"A new job, a new wife," Jones commented.

Bud lifted his long neck. "To a successful marriage and warm winters in Chicago."

Art lifted his bottle with a wide smile. "Hear! hear!"

* * *

The Volvo had been ditched in favor of a brand-new minivan whose owner wouldn't miss it for a few hours yet. Darian was behind the wheel, easing it carefully north of the Leesburg Pike. In the back, Moises and Mustafa were making final preparations.

"How long since you've fired that?" Darian asked.

Mustafa swung the front of the break-open M79 grenade launcher upward, closing the breech-loaded weapon and making it ready to fire. In its chamber was a 40mm fragmentation round, and affixed to the bandolier slung across his chest were eight more. "About six months. But you never forget, Brother Darian."

"Good. You know what to do." Darian looked to Moises in the rearview. He sat straight in the second bench seat, the headlights from oncoming traffic washing pale over his face. "We're almost there, Brother Moises. You ready?"

Moises looked straight ahead, his hands tight on the Ingram, and only nodded.

Fire. Darian saw it in the stare. Saw it on the face. A fighter had been born.

The metal detectors were four wide for House and Senate members, and were located just off Statuary Hall to the south of the grand rotunda. Begrudgingly, the elected representatives of the citizens of the United States had accepted this "indignity" after stern warnings by leaders of both political parties, but the lines were slowed by secondary checks after keys and various other items set off the sensitive instruments.

"Can you believe this?" Congressman Cal McCrary asked, as he and his fellow representative from the Commonwealth of Massachusetts inched closer to the portals manned by the Secret Service.

"Ridiculous," Congressman Richard Vorhees agreed, the discomfort in his knee transferring more to his face as time wore on.

"Sore tonight, Dick?"

"Tonight, today, tomorrow, next week. Until I get a new leg."

"Count your blessings, my man," McCrary said. "You were lucky." He checked the shade of his surroundings. "I think they enjoy killing middle-aged white men despite the statistics. Thank goodness yours was a lousy shot."

"He didn't want me chasing him," Vorhees explained. "It was no accident he shot me in the leg. I'm just glad he picked the one made of plastic and steel."

"Flesh and bone are expensive to replace, eh?"

"Don't I know it?"

The mass of bodies became lines nearer the metal detectors. Vorhees followed McCrary through, and, as he expected, set off the buzzers. "Down here."

A senior Secret Service agent, aware of the congressman's condition, stepped forward. "We'll just wand you, sir."

Vorhees lifted his arms, letting the agent run the metal detecting wand up and down both sides of his body. The only reaction was from the prosthetic limb.

"Okay, sir. Go on in."

Vorhees nodded and continued on, entering the House chamber just as the networks were throwing their "Presidential State of the Union Message" graphics up for a nationwide audience.

John Barrish sat with his youngest boy in front of the TV. Louise Barrish was nowhere to be seen.

"There he goes," Stanley said at the sight.

John said nothing, but wore an uncharacteristic broad smile. It was no coincidence that this formed as the somewhat less than cheerful Congressman Richard Vorhees took his seat in the fourth row. "What time is it?"

Stanley looked at his watch. He knew what his father wanted to hear. "He should be doing it now."

Sixty miles away, Toby Barrish was hanging up the pay phone at a truck stop just off Interstate 66, leaving a confused and alarmed 911 operator talking to a dial tone.

THIRTY
Setup

Article II, Section 3, of the Constitution of the United States of America charges the President with the responsibility of, from time to time, reporting to the Congress on the state of the union. That seemingly simple obligation had developed over the years into a pivotal time for many presidents, an occasion when their legislative agendas and special programs for the coming year were to be presented to both houses of Congress. With the coming of television coverage of the State of the Union message, image was thrown into the mix of factors deemed important. Combining that with the general seriousness of a constitutionally required address, there was a choreographed quality to the event.

After the vast majority of legislators had entered and located their seats—committee chairpersons and members of great seniority always had the choicest seats near the front of the chamber—the Chairman of the Joint Chiefs of Staff and the Joint Chiefs came forward up the center aisle and took their seats in the second row on the left, as one looked toward the podium. On the riser behind the podium the vice president stood on the left, acting in his capacity as president of the Senate, with Speaker of the House Jack Murphy on the right. An American flag hung vertically behind them. They had the best view up the center aisle—which is slightly off-center to the Republican side of the chamber—and were the first to see the House doorkeeper make his first trek a third of the way in.

"Mr. Speaker, the Chief Justice of the United States and the Associate Justices of the Supreme Court!"

The bellowed announcement was followed by a procession of the nine men and women who formed the judicial branch of the United States government. They walked up the aisle to unrestrained applause and turned right to take their front-row seats on the GOP side of the chamber. The applause subsided after a moment and then the doorkeeper made his second of three appearances that night.

"Mr. Speaker, the President's Cabinet!"

Again the clapping began, with some cheers this time, as the long line of Cabinet secretaries moved forward, accepting greetings and shaking hands as they did. At the front of the chamber the senior and most important Cabinet positions turned left, taking the front row on the Democratic side. The remainder of the Cabinet turned right into the row behind the justices of the Supreme Court. Smiles were the expression of choice.

But the revelry eased as the speaker tapped the gavel, drawing all attention to the center aisle for a final time. The House doorkeeper again came forward.

"Mr. Speaker, the President of the United States!"

The chamber erupted in applause and cheers as the president entered, followed by a beaming Senate Majority Leader Curtis Parsons. The president progressed slowly toward the front, taking some hands pressed toward him, ignoring others out of sheer necessity. He greeted the chief justice at the head of the aisle, then walked to the left past half of his cabinet, stopping at each. He ascended the raised platform next and stepped up to the podium, taking a quick glance at the Tele-PrompTer to confirm that his speech was scrolled to the beginning. The raucous welcome continued as was customary, one of the few times the United States Congress outdid its counterpart across the Atlantic in London in the area of enthusiasm expressed. He looked up to his left, seeking out his wife, and smiled at her, thinking how strange it was to see her without their son. But this was not the place for him, nor the time. He was, hopefully, fast asleep by now.

The barrel-chested speaker pounded his gavel repeatedly, bringing the exuberant members of Congress to a very temporary simmer. Murphy smiled over the chamber that was his domain before speaking. ''Members of Congress, I have the high privilege, and the distinct honor, of presenting to you the President of the United States.''

Once again the assembled legislators rose to their feet and demonstrated their respect with continuous, if somewhat superfluous, clapping. After a minute the gavel began to strike again, the sharp wood-on-wood crack slowly overcoming the enthusiasm. The applause began to fade, those on the right side of the aisle taking their seats first, then those of the president's party. When it was quiet the president found his place on the Tele-PrompTer, glanced upward again, though this time to the row just behind his wife, then looked out to the men and women to whom he was here to report on the State of the Union. He wondered if they would want to hear what he had to say.

''Thank you. Thank you very much. Mr. Speaker, Mr. President, members of Congress, my fellow Americans . . .'' He paused, thinking of the words he was about to speak, wanting to do that instead of simply reading them. '' . . . I stand before you tonight as leader of the greatest nation on earth, a nation that has triumphed over tyranny abroad, and tyranny at home. A nation that has seen the good, the bad, the indifferent in the rest of the world, and has seen the same at home. A nation whose future is limitless, and whose past has challenged it to do better. I stand before you to say that there is much that is good about this nation, but good is not better, and we live today in the shadow of the darkest part of our past, the remnants of a tyranny that infects us all and makes any progress we achieve on other fronts as tenuous as the proverbial straw man. I speak of that which separates us, and makes us all victims.

"But I stand before you not only as your president to tell you this. I stand before you as the great-great-grandson of slave owners to say that the divisive hate which grew from the actions of my ancestors is here, my fellow Americans, and we have seen with tragic clarity in recent months that it is alive. I stand before you to say that before anything else can truly be accomplished with an eye toward perpetuity, that hate must be confronted, and rejected."

The action outside had subsided considerably. No more legislators rushing up the steps of the Capitol's east front. No reporters scurrying about looking for the last tidbit before the show. It was quiet where Frankie Aguirre stood. Disquietingly so.

"Let's hope this is the dullest spot in town tonight."

Frankie looked left with a start. David Rogers had come out from the Rotunda and now stood next to her. "So far, so good."

Rogers glanced at his watch. "He's a windy one. How much you want to bet the next hour seems like twelve?"

Frankie surveyed the mostly deserted landscape out to the Supreme Court building across First Street. No one wanting to do harm could even get *that* close. The outer perimeter this night began a quarter-mile farther out at Fourth Street, and ringed the Capitol for a similar distance in all directions. Secret Service. FBI. Park Police. D.C. Police. DEA. ATF. They were all out there somewhere, manning the barricades that blocked streets leading to the Capitol. Marines were atop several buildings in the vicinity with shoulder-fired Stinger antiaircraft missiles at the ready just in case a threat materialized from the air. Sewers sealed. The Senate subway closed. Every precaution had been taken. Frankie knew she was standing at the most heavily guarded spot in the country at the moment. No one was getting in.

"This is too clean," Frankie said, puffs of white breath billowing with each word.

"Huh?"

She gestured to her front. "Wouldn't you think that someone wanting to hit this place tonight would know there'd be security like this?"

"Sure, but that does not mean they could find a way through it."

Frankie thought on Rogers's statement for a moment. It didn't settle her. "We missed something, David."

"Or our chain is being royally yanked."

"Maybe," Frankie said, though the rising sensation in her stomach allowed no more surety in that response. "Or maybe not."

Think, Frankie. Think through it again. From square one, and fast.

The president waited for the applause to subside before continuing once again. "But the hate I speak of has no boundary. No one person, or group, or ideology holds domain over it. But all people hold domain over the power to reject it, to look away when the opportunity to hate presents itself, or to stand up and confront it when hate challenges us." He looked up again, seizing immediately on the strong eyes that bore down on him. "Some of us have been hate's victim more than others. I want to introduce to you three very special people. Darren and Felicia, would you please stand. And Dr. Preston."

The three guests of the president stood, receiving a dose of welcoming applause from the members below.

"Members of Congress, these three wonderful people have experienced the depths of despair, and the heights of renewal. They have seen the result of hate. Darren and Felicia Griggs have experienced it more personally than most of us ever will with the loss of their daughter to an act of hatred at Saint Anthony's Church in Los Angeles along with three of her friends. And Dr. Anne Preston has worked with them to see that their lives are not also destroyed by this senseless act. The weak use hate as their ally, the strong reject it. But the sting is painful all the same. Darren, Felicia . . . our sympathy is for your loss, our admiration is for your strength." The president was the first this time to lift his hands in applause.

The front door to the secretary of state's house opened after a quick knock. One of the two Secret Service agents guarding the front entered and came straight to the study. Coventry lowered the volume and stood to meet him. "Yes?"

"Mr. Secretary, Fauquier County Emergency Communications just got a nine-eleven call saying that four black males are planning to kill you tonight."

Art and Jones both stood upon hearing that, followed quickly by Bud.

"The caller apparently overheard these guys talking," the Secret Service agent explained briefly.

Coventry looked back to Jones. "The militants?"

"It would fit," Jones said. "I think."

"But why would they let themselves be overheard?" Bud asked.

Blame the monkeys. Art recalled that statement from Chester Hart. "Is someone running down where the call came from?"

"State Police have a unit on the way to the call site."

The gathering was quiet for a moment before Coventry spoke. "Is there anything . . ."

"It could be a crank, sir," the agent theorized. "Or, who knows? But our team out back got the same word, and the State Police is sending two cruisers by just in case. Just relax, sir. We'll take care of everything."

The four men watched the agent exit to the front.

"Interesting," Coventry said as he turned. He saw Jones staring at Art. "What?"

"Jefferson?"

Art didn't hear the director's one-word inquiry. His mind was racing through the possibilities that this new piece of a very interesting puzzle might present. *Blame the monkeys . . . Have to get them to do it for you . . .* But why the call? *A setup?* "A setup."

"A setup what?" Bud asked.

Art looked left toward the rear of the house, then to the windows on his right. Whiteness swept across the curtains covering them. *Headlights.* Then a brighter flash, and a sound familiar from so long ago. Familiar and frightful. "GET DOWN!"

The front door blew in just as Art's warning was heeded.

THIRTY ONE

Strike

The side door of the minivan was already fully open when Darian slowed the vehicle a hundred feet shy of 695 Hillsborough. Mustafa took aim through the opening with the M79 as he did, drawing a bead on the front door of the secretary's house. He breathed, noted one target already near the door, another coming out through it, and squeezed the trigger. The six-ounce 40mm grenade leapt from the fat barrel with a metallic *pop* and arced gently toward its aim point, impacting low on the small stone porch a hair more than a half-second after firing.

Hundreds of shrapnel fragments flew outward from the explosion, a good deal of it tearing into the two Secret Service agents standing just feet from the point of impact. Both were killed instantly, and the remaining blast and fragmentation did the rest of its significant damage on the wooden front door of the secretary's house. The seven-foot-high slab of oak was split in the middle and pushed into the foyer by the force of the blast.

Darian accelerated to the house and stopped in front. He hopped out, weapon in hand, Moises joining him in a race to the smoking door. Mustafa had already reloaded the M79 and stayed with the car. He caught sight of a form coming up the driveway of the house and fired straight at it. It disappeared in a flash and a scream.

Jesus! Art lifted his head in time to hear a second explosion and immediately drew his weapon. He was on his knees and looking at the shattered front door as shadows fell across the opening.

"Get them back!" Art yelled to Jones, who also had his weapon out.

The director pulled the secretary up and toward the kitchen. Bud followed, looking back at Jefferson just as he began to fire toward the front door.

"SHIT!" Darian yelled, two shots hitting the doorjamb to his right. He stuck the Ingram through the opening and sprayed fire to the left. Moises saw movement toward the rear of the interior and fired half a magazine that way.

Art saw the stubby weapon just before it fired. He rolled left and retreated in the same direction as the others had. He found them in the kitchen, the director covering the arched opening to the foyer.

"Everyone all right?" Art asked.

"Yeah," Jones reported. "They've got firepower."

"Where are the Secret Service guys?" Coventry asked. There was no response. He knew what that meant.

Art lifted his head a bit and looked over the island to the far side of the kitchen. There was a door, shades on it drawn. The two Service agents guarding the rear were supposed to be out there, but Art hadn't heard any fire from them. Had the second explosion taken them out? He then looked behind, checking the abandoned study. Empty. And . . . His eyes saw the steps rising from an alcove off the kitchen. "Does that go upstairs?"

Coventry nodded.

* * *

Darian and Moises stepped back from the front door together. The NALF leader had communicated his wish to Mustafa with a clear hand signal. As they hunched behind large cement planters to either side of the porch a third grenade was fired. It penetrated to the rear of the house before exploding.

The NALF entry team went in behind it.

The detonation of the small but powerful fragmentation grenade threw all four men in the kitchen to the floor. Despite the protection of a counter, shrapnel tore through the room. One shard of metal tore a gouge across Bud DiContino's forehead.

"Damn!"

Coventry pulled the NSA farther back in the kitchen, finding more shelter back behind the island and nearer the sink.

"This is not good," Art said to the director.

"We need cavalry."

As Jones said that the kitchen was peppered by automatic fire from two weapons.

Darian reloaded, as did Moises, and advanced along the left wall of the foyer. He stopped, went to his tiptoes, and fell back to his young comrade.

"Back there," Darian whispered, pointing toward the kitchen. Moises peeked around him briefly. "I'll move there, you cover my rear. That room back there. That's where the shots came from."

"Got it." Moises backed up, taking a position at the base of the stairs, his eyes sweeping left and right as his leader inched deeper into the house.

Jones held up two fingers in a V. *Two guns.*

Art nodded, looking behind once again. In the study he saw a shadow fall from the foyer. He looked back to the director and mouthed *behind us.*

It was obvious they had to do something. They were outgunned—at least two automatics and someone lobbing grenades at them—and outmaneuvered. Art looked to the small staircase again. Or were they?

You cover here, Art mouthed to the director. He then pointed up, then down, then to the front of the house. Jones nodded and slid a bit to the left. When he looked behind Art was already heading fast up the stairs.

Mustafa glanced at his watch. A minute and a half already. It seemed more like an hour. He had already discarded the M79 in favor of his Ingram, suppressor off like the others, and was hunched down between a government sedan at curbside and their minivan. Windows all along the street had lit up, and he was beginning to hear sirens in the distance. Things were going to have to happen fast, or else it would get—

Movement to the right!

He rose up, looking over the roof of the car, catching only a glimpse of a shadow, but that was enough. The Ingram bucked as he aimed and tapped the trigger. Sparks flashed off the sidewalk as wild rounds hit the cement. Auto glass shattered. Metal was punched. Orange flashes . . .

The lone surviving Secret Service agent fired from over the rear deck of one of the Crown Victorias, taking one of the attackers by surprise. Six rounds from his Sig Sauer pistol found their mark, felling Mustafa Ali. He fell into the open side of the minivan, then to the ground. The agent, sporting some nasty but superficial shrapnel wounds to his head and shoulders, backed away to the other Service Ford and got immediately on the radio. He passed out after putting out an "agent needs help" call.

Art was up the stairs to the second floor and moving down the hallway he hoped led to the main staircase as fire from outside made him pause. When it died he continued, stopping as the upstairs landing opened before him. He peered carefully down, trying to keep his cover, and saw Moises Griggs standing at the bottom of the staircase.

Dear God, don't make me have to kill him.

Director Jones held the Smith & Wesson 1076 two-handed, wondering if the lessons he'd learned so long before as a Bureau street agent would help keep the bureaucrat he'd become alive. One thing was certain: his ears were still good. They were easily picking up a clearly identifiable sound: shoes on broken glass. And it was getting closer. Much closer. Just on the other side of the counter.

Art knew what he might have to do. And he would . . . if it came to that. But there was another avenue of approach.

He saw the Griggs kid keep shifting his gaze from the study to the rear of the house, completely ignoring the stairs and the landing. If he could get close enough, just close enough to—

Coventry had a napkin from a drawer pressed against the NSA's head wound, but that wasn't enough to staunch the flow of blood. The sticky liquid already covered Bud's face, and most of his shirt. The secretary needed to get pressure on the wound, something to hold it tight. *My tie.* He pulled the striped piece of silk loose, and looked toward the front of the kitchen, where the director was . . .

No. Above the counter, silhouetted in the light, a dark figure was advancing, pointing some sort of gun into the kitchen and right at—

"Gordy!"

* * *

Art heard the yell and saw Moises step away from the stairs. He took that opportunity and made his move. With his weapon trained on the young man, he ran onto the landing and down the stairs, reaching the third step and vaulting the banister with one hand as shots rang out from the kitchen.

Director Gordon Jones made his move, too, with fear but no hesitation, and as he did he saw the barrel of the easily recognizable Ingram submachine gun swivel from its aim at his friends farther back in the kitchen to him. His own weapon was coming to bear also, quicker, and he fired two center-mass shots at the gunman.

Darian Brown felt the shots impact like large spikes. It startled him, but he pulled the trigger of his weapon anyway and swung it right, stitching a path of bullets across the kitchen until the magazine was empty. Then two more spikes drove into his chest and he fell backward, eyes open, but only blackness before them.

Art came over the banister and onto Moises Griggs with one hand around his neck and the Smith & Wesson pressed into the soft back of his skull. They tumbled backward to the debris-littered foyer, Art spinning him facedown as they did. The Ingram was pinned to the floor under Moises Griggs, his hand still gripping it.

"Kid, show me your hands! Now!"

Moises pulled at the weapon, trying to get it free.

Art pressed the barrel hard into the back of Moises' head and put as much weight on his body as he could. Sirens blared outside, getting louder. "I WILL KILL YOU!"

"Go ahead!" Moises screamed and tugged.

"Don't do it, Moises! They set you up! They used you! Used you all!" Finger on the trigger, ready to pull.

Moises eased his struggle a bit, the claim from the

pig striking a nerve. "What do you mean?"

"Who were you doing this for, Moises?! Huh?! DO YOU EVEN KNOW?!!"

Doing for? How does he know about . . . "Why?"

Less resistance now. *Keep it up, Arthur.* "Because they tipped us off!" Art had to take another shot now. He had to reach the kid. "They were white, weren't they?"

Stillness. "How . . ."

"Moises, they were the ones that killed your sister. The same ones."

What? "Tanya? No."

"Were they young or old, Moises?" Art saw in his peripheral vision the director step into the open to cover the kid.

Tanya? "Young."

The voice was almost resigned now. Art recalled what he could of Barrish's sons. They had to be the ones dealing with the NALF. John Barrish would have been too recognizable. He had to convince Moises. "One of them, did he have a lazy eye?"

Eye? Oh, God, no! Brother Darian had talked about the white boy's weird eye, even calling him Popeye a few times. "Yes. God, no, please. It can't be!"

Art holstered his weapon and pulled at Moises' gun arm, freeing it—empty—from under his body. With no resistance from the now sobbing young man he brought both hands back and cuffed them together, then rolled him off the Ingram and pulled him to the stairs. He then looked to Jones. "Is everyone in there all right?"

"Bud is hit, but it's a head graze," Jones reported. Anything on the head had the potential to be a bleeder. "Jim has it covered."

"You got one, sir?"

Jones nodded without glee. He'd never shot his weapon in anger during his entire career. This was a hell of a way to make up for that.

All at once there were screeching tires and sirens droning to a stop in the street out front. Virginia State Police officers were in and around the house without delay. Art, however, was not finished with Moises Griggs.

"Look at me." When the young man didn't Art lifted him by his jacket and pinned him against the wall. Moises made eye contact then. "I want you to listen good, because I have no time to fuck around." Art glared through the young man's tears. "What else did you do? The nerve gas? Where is it?"

Moises hesitated, not knowing what to do, what to think, or even if he should be alive. He was lost where he stood.

"Moises, don't fuck with me. Is it at the Capitol?"

No response, just mild sobs.

Hit him with it, Arthur. "Moises, your parents are there right now. Tell me! What else did you do?!"

Mom? Dad? No. God, no . . .

"WHERE IS IT?!"

Then it came like a flood. Art, however, heard only the first three words. Once he did he let Moises Griggs fall to the ground and ran outside to his loaner. On the cellular he dialed Agent David Rogers at the Capitol.

Word was going out quickly that something had happened at the secretary of state's Falls Church home, and that a mysterious 911 call might have something to do with it. The Virginia State Police unit assigned to check out the call's point of origin, a truck stop off I-66 near Marshall, made haste in doing so. After just a minute of questioning the waitresses and a few patrons of the small café at the stop, the troopers had a brief description of the youngish man who had made a call from the public phone located at the end of the counter. One waitress remembered the man's strange eye, a descriptive point the troopers immediately seized on thanks to the broadcast from their communications center, and one trucker remembered seeing the "screwy-looking guy" get into a Honda, dark green, maybe. Another trucker recalled the car cutting in front of his rig as he entered the truck stop, zooming away up the entrance to westbound I-66.

With that the troopers had something to go on. They radioed in the information, and within minutes there were seven VSP cruisers, marked and unmarked, converging on the stretch of interstate between Marshall and I-81. A helicopter was also racing that way from an assignment near Winchester.

David Rogers flipped open his cellular and heard the excited voice of Art Jefferson. He handed the phone immediately to Frankie as requested.

"Aguirre."

"Frankie, it's inside," Art said quickly, somewhat winded.

"What? How?"

"Vorhees . . . He was picked on purpose . . . That's why Royce didn't use Crippen . . ." Breaths, heavy, fast. "Frankie, it's in his leg! Get it!"

Frankie's eyes went wide as she handed the phone back to Rogers. It was more of a toss, really, and all he heard was "Oh, my God!" from her as she bolted into the Capitol.

As she did, phones and radio circuits all over Washington suddenly came to life.

The VSP helicopter began scanning the interstate from a point five miles west of Marshall, flying at two hundred feet and a hundred miles an hour as the trooper observer surveyed the light traffic through powerful binoculars. Just past the Highway 522 connector he got a hit. A mile and a half back an unmarked cruiser was tasked with making a quiet pass of the vehicle to ID the driver. It accelerated past a hundred to make up the distance. The word now was that the suspect was not to be stopped, just followed. It was where he was going that was important.

"Get out of the way!" Frankie screamed. Secret Service agents grabbed at her, and it took Rogers running behind her with his shield held high to free her more than once. "It's in there! It's in there!"

Access to the center aisle was blocked by two large Secret Service agents who stepped to block Frankie's path, but moved aside as something came through their earpieces. She pulled the twin doors out and ran down toward the front of the chamber.

". . . with an added seven federal prisons to—" The president looked straight ahead as a commotion spilled into the chamber from the hall, but had no time to react. That was done for him. Two Secret Service agents came from either side, grabbed the chief executive by his suit jacket, and dragged him off the podium as the House and Senate members jumped to their feet.

In front of Anne and the Griggses, the first lady sprang to her feet, and was as quickly whisked off by her security detail. Anne and Felicia watched that, while Darren kept his attention on the floor below.

"It's Frankie! Art's partner! Look."

Anne jerked her head to the right and caught sight of the woman her future husband trusted his life with. She was climbing over a sea of fleeing bodies to get to one man.

Frankie got her hands on Congressman Richard Vorhees's coat and pulled him back into a chair without explanation.

"Get your hands off me!" Vorhees screamed.

"Leave him alone!" a fellow representative protested.

Frankie heard none of it, and held Vorhees back in the seat with one hand while the other ripped at his pants. "Which one is fake?! Now!"

"Are you mad?"

Rogers made his way over the crush of bodies and put a chin lock on the congressman. "It's in your god-damn leg, idiot. Now which one is it?!"

"In my leg. You mean . . ." The shot in the leg, the window broken by a ball whose owner he could not find, the awkward balance of the spare. Oh my God! "The left! The left! Get it off!" His hands ripped at his trousers now. "Get it off!"

The flow of mostly middle-aged men increased as a lightning bolt of understanding swept over the chamber. *It was in there. With them! Near them! On him!*

Frankie pulled with both hands and tore the pricey material from cuff to above the knee, exposing the limb. Vorhees undid the several straps with fingers that had completed the operation countless times before, and without hesitating Frankie took the limb, still wearing the congressman's leather shoe, and dove through the mass of bodies to get out of the chamber. This time a path seemed to open for her.

She headed straight for the exits to the west front of the Capitol, moving away from the masses heading for the east side. The doors were held open for her by agents who shielded their faces and cringed as she passed. One had managed to get a respirator on.

The cold air slapped her for some reason as she emerged, limb in hand. She stopped, took a breath, heard Rogers come out behind her, heard sirens start up some-where in the distance, saw agents clearing the way be-fore her, and asked herself just what she was going to do with it.

Think, Frankie, think! She didn't know how much time there was. Seconds. Minutes. Not long, she was certain of that. The president was three quarters of the way through his speech. There was a frighteningly small window of opportunity left to dispose of the thing. But how to do that. A breeze was blowing at a good clip, negating just laying it out on a patch of lawn to go off. She had to get it somewhere safe, somewhere it could be contained. Somewhere it would be . . .

Her eyes fell upon the small reflecting pool beyond Grant's monument. *Water.* Orwell's statement about 1212 Riverside flashed in her head. *"The best thing would be to just pick the whole house up and set it in a vat of water."* Not with a building, maybe, but with a leg . . . yes!

Frankie heard Rogers yelling something at her, but there was no time for response. She started down the steps to get to the pool. It was just under a quarter-mile away.

"State police just made a pass of a car their air unit spotted," one of Jones's Washington agents reported to the director as they stood in front of the secretary's battered Falls Church home. "It looks like Toby Barrish."

Jones looked to Art, as did Coventry and a hastily bandaged Bud DiContino. "You were right."

Art swallowed and nodded, accepting the compliment. He saw Moises Griggs lying proned out on the lawn and knew he would have rather been wrong about everything.

"They're following him to see where he goes," the agent continued. "HRT is just getting airborne."

Again Jones looked to Art. "You want in on this?"

"Badly."

"Block off a street and get a bird here for us," Jones directed.

"Gordy, any chance I can be there for the party?" Bud asked. His wound was quite superficial, and had been quickly cleaned and taped shut by VSP trooper.

"Are you up to it?"

"If it means seeing the man that did all this," Bud began, "yeah. I'm up to that."

Jones pointed a finger at his agent. "Get that bird here fast."

Frankie had visions of reliving her high school softball days and pitching the limb into the reflecting pool from twenty yards away, but her sensibilities stepped in and drove her to draw much closer before letting the hunk of metal and plastic fly. She slid to a stop and watched it tumble end over end through the air, sailing into the wind, diving for the rippling surface of the pool, and finally splashing foot-first into the water. It disappeared beneath the surface, the wake disturbance rolling over to cover it. Frankie bent forward, hands on her knees, took a deep breath of relief, and spit it out with eyes gone wide as the limb bobbed to the surface. It was floating.

Lee Highway was completely blocked in both directions by VSP cruisers and FBI vehicles, allowing the Park Service Jet Ranger room to land.

"Park Service?" Bud asked as he instinctively bent forward and trotted toward the blue-and-white helicopter.

"It was the closest thing," Jones reported. He climbed in, followed by Bud, then Art.

"Everybody ready?" the pilot asked from his seat on the right of the helicopter's cockpit.

Everyone nodded and slid into headsets. As the bird lifted off and headed west, Art Jefferson did one more thing to ensure that he was ready: he inserted a full magazine into his Smith & Wesson.

If her mind had been racing before, it was on afterburner now. *The goddamn thing is buoyant!* Frankie looked around for something to weight the limb down with, but could see nothing. She'd just shoot it and hope to sink it that way, but that might just as easily set it off. Her gun would do no good here . . .

Or would it? *Yes!* Frankie ran to the pool's edge, to where the limb had been pushed by the steady breeze, and pulled it out. She laid it on the ground and knelt next to it, removing her belt and the holstered weapon attached to it. She wound the combination around the limb tightly and secured the buckle as tight as possible. It wasn't the use intended for her Smith & Wesson model 1076, but if its forty-plus ounces would do the trick it would count as straight shooting in her book. Standing once again she underhanded it fifteen feet into the pool and watched it settle into the water, sinking, falling, sinking, and staying underwater.

"Jesus," Frankie said, watching and waiting, then jumping as a dim flash pierced the surface, which boiled briefly. She became very conscious of the wind in her face, the wind coming at her from the direction of the pool. She held her breath, knowing that would do no real good if any of the VZ had breached the surface, then pulled a lungful in and took stock of herself.

She was alive. She let out the breath and took in another. Then another. The night air tasted sweet to Frankie Aguirre. Sweet with success.

"It's heading south on I-eighty-one," the pilot of the Park Service heli reported over the intercom after receiving the radio report from the Virginia State Police heli fifty miles distant. "And the Hostage Rescue Team bird is on-station with them."

"Good," Jones said into the boom mike touching his lips. "If I say 'floor it,' does that have any meaning to a heli jock?"

The nose of the Park Service Jet Ranger dipped, the pilot smiling as he did the aerial equivalent of putting the pedal to the metal.

Jones looked left to Art. His gaze was fixed forward. "We got it in time," the director said. That report from the Capitol had come minutes ago. "She's okay, Jefferson."

Art nodded.

"HRT is the best," Jones reminded him over the intercom. "No hostages here, but they're the best SWAT team in the world. We'll get them."

Another nod. Art knew they would "get" John Barrish, but somehow that seemed inadequate. They should have had him a long time ago.

THIRTY TWO
Takedown

Toby stopped the Honda fast in the driveway and ran into the house. His father and brother were in front of the TV in the living room.

"What happened?" Toby demanded. "The radio said someone broke into the place and ripped his leg off!"

John Barrish sat hunched forward on the edge of his chair, muscles tensed, nostrils flaring with each hot breath.

"That's what happened," Stanley confirmed. The TV now was cutting between news crews trying to get information on the happening. They would not be the only ones. "Dad, we've got to get out of here."

"He's right, Pop," Toby agreed. He pulled the .38 from his waistband. "They could find us."

Who? Who had blown it? Who screwed up? WHO RUINED MY PLAN?

"Pop," Toby pleaded. "Come on. We've gotta get out of here."

John looked to his sons. They were right. They would have to leave, would have to run to fight again. He picked up the Beretta resting on the end table and stood. "Stanley, get your mother. She's in the bedroom. Toby, throw some food and ammo in the car. Now!"

* * *

The FBI and Park Service helicopters landed on State Route 259 near Chimney Rock, two miles from the house to which the blacked-out VSP air unit, flying high and using its FLIR (forward looking infrared), had carefully followed the Honda. A trooper familiar with the area briefed the team on the lay of the land, then all involved piled into vehicles, some commandeered, and headed toward Fulks Run.

"Get the food, Louise," John commanded. His wife looked at him with dead eyes and dropped canned vegetables into a paper sack.

"Pop, Stan's grabbing some clothes for us," Toby said as he popped his head into the kitchen. "I'm putting the guns and stuff in the car now."

"I want to be on the road in five minutes," John said.

"You got it," Toby assured him, then headed out the front. The lights of the Honda were still on. Not good for the battery, but it had only been a few minutes. Toby walked toward the rear of the car, arms full of ammo boxes and extra weapons, his pace slowing as light glinted in several spots from the dark forest. He looked behind. The car's high beams were reflecting off the large front window and into the trees, illuminating . . . what?

"FREEZE! FBI!"

Toby dropped the load in his arms and drew the revolver from his waist. He was just bringing it up when a volley of fire came at him. He felt a fire in his belly, fell backward, and crawled toward the open front door, gun in hand. Ten feet was all he could manage before he passed out and died.

"What?" John's eyes flared. He spun toward the front room. His youngest son ran by the opening toward the front door, Louise following. The leader of the Aryan Victory Organization knew those to be foolish acts. He looked left. A second later he was through the back door and running into the woods lining Fawley Hollow.

"What's going on?" Jones asked the HRT leader as gunfire erupted up the road that was the only access to the house.

The black-clad agent listened to the radio chatter in his earpiece briefly. "They spotted us coming in. We had to drop one."

"Is a perimeter up?" Jones asked. Art was listening intently to this question.

"Not yet."

"Dammit!" Jones swore. "Get the helicopter overhead. Now. Jeferso—" He looked past the HRT leader. Art was moving up the road, gun drawn, at a dead run. "Jefferson!"

"Toby!" Stanley yelled at the sight of his brother lying facedown on the cement driveway. A circle of darkness was expanding from beneath his stomach.

"Toby!" Louise screamed as she tried to push past her youngest boy. He saw beyond his brother, small flashes of intense red light—*laser aiming devices!*— coming from the trees. His left hand shoved his mother to the ground inside the house as he stepped out, aiming at the lights with his weapon, and squeezing off shots. More came back to him.

"STANLEY!" Louise screamed as her baby boy fell back into the house, bullets tearing into the walls. She reached for him and pulled his limp body out of the doorway. "Stanley?" She brushed his hair, and laid a caring hand on his chest. It was damp, warm, and still. "Stanley? STANLEY! NOOOOOOO!!!"

John Barrish is weak. Art thought this as he trotted off the road and into the trees, making a wide sweep to the right of the advancing HRT line. *John Barrish is a small*

*man. A coward who uses others to do what he is afraid
to do. John Barrish will not stand and fight. John Barrish will run. No. John Barrish will slink away.*

Art had dealt with bigger men, but not with bigger
dangers. For John Barrish was the keeper of a virus.

Trees flashed by as Art moved through them toward
the woods to the rear of the house. The ground to his
right sloped downward, and he heard the sound of water
gently running. He heard something else to his front.

The virus.

Art slowed and crouched. He realized his white shirt,
even though soiled, was standing out in the darkness of
the forest. He pulled it and the T-shirt beneath it off,
barely noticing the chill. Twenty yards ahead he saw
movement crossing his path left to right. The form was
lighter than the darkness.

*You almost killed the woman I love. You could have
destroyed my country.* Art stepped easily right, finding
footing on the slope as the form ahead slowed and took
cover behind a tree. Sounds off to the left announced
the arrival of the HRT at the rear of the house. Art eased
forward, using the trees as a screen, inching closer, foot
by foot, yard by yard, until he could see the virus from
behind. It was lying on the ground twenty feet away
staring back upon the route it had taken.

Covering your rear? Art thought. *Wrong rear.* He leveled his weapon at the prone form of John Barrish. There
was a twig at his feet. He could step on it, make a sound,
force John Barrish to move threateningly at him. Then
he could kill John Barrish. Then he could kill the virus.
He could do that, and no one would ever know. No one
would ever know. He wouldn't even care.

But someone would. And Art Jefferson knew he could
not hide a darkness such as that from her.

"Barrish!"

John twitched at the sound from behind.

"FREEZE!"

The gun was in his hand. He would just have to roll, aim, fire.

"DROP IT! NOW!"

That voice. John knew it. But from . . . He looked behind, moving only his head. Light from the rear of the house illuminated the bare-chested African's face, and his stainless-steel gun.

"SHOW ME YOUR HANDS!"

John heard the command, but the tones said *Don't. I want to kill you. Make me kill you.*

Art maintained his partial cover behind a tree and watched John Barrish roll slowly on his side, hands empty, compliant.

"Show me your hands!" Art commanded.

Barrish did, as footsteps came from the direction of the house. HRT agents approached and lit up the area with their weapon-mounted lights. Red dots danced on John Barrish's body. Art lifted his weapon clear as two agents moved in and cuffed the man, then lifted him to his feet after searching him. They walked him to where Art stood.

"You want him?" an agent asked.

Art answered by grabbing Barrish by the elbow and leading him through the trees to the front of the house, HRT agents following. Director Gordon Jones and Bud DiContino were waiting in the driveway by a VSP cruiser.

"Good catch, Jefferson," Jones said. His expression said *Stupid move, Jefferson*. But it was the words that counted.

"Sir, this is John Barrish." Art gripped the elbow a bit tighter and lifted the man.

"Did you Mirandize him?"

"HRT did when they cuffed him," Art reported.

Bud studied the man for a moment. Small. So small. Size said so much in this instance.

"So it's a crime to run when men start shooting at

your house without warning?'' Barrish asked defiantly.

Art spun him so they were face to face. "No, it's a crime to murder eighteen hundred people." And how many more? Art wondered.

Barrish smiled. "You have no proof of that."

"Yes they do."

Barrish turned to the voice. It was Louise, standing just a foot or so away, hands cuffed behind, blood soaking her clothing. Her face was tear streaked, but she was no longer crying.

"Louise . . ."

"You killed my sons! *You* killed them!"

Art held Barrish steady, making him face his most damaging accuser.

"And you killed the others, John. I know that, and I will tell everyone who wants to hear exactly what you did. Everything, you goddamn bastard!"

Barrish glared at her, wishing he could get his hands free for just a moment. She was weak. The doubter had become a challenger.

"And one other thing," Louise said to her husband's face. As he stared across at her she stepped forward and brought her knee up, full force, into his groin before the HRT agents could pull her back.

"Get up," Art said, lifting the doubled-over racist to his feet. He was moaning in pain and gasping for breath. Two agents from the HRT came up and took Barrish from him, leading him to a VSP cruiser separate from his wife. Art watched as they were both driven away.

Bud DiContino reached out and offered his hand to Art Jefferson. "Thank you."

Art shook the NSA's hand with some puzzlement. "For what?"

"For stopping this."

Art shook his head. He might have smiled, but could not manage that expression at the moment. "I didn't stop anything." He looked at the bloody corpses of the two Barrish boys lying where the HRT had laid them in the driveway. "There'll always be another like John Barrish. Animals reproduce, remember?"

"Right," Bud DiContino agreed. This would never be over.

EPILOGUE
State of the Union

There was no need for them to be present, but there was reason, though neither Art Jefferson nor Frankie Aguirre could adequately put it in words. Less than a month after the night that most would like to erase from their memories, the agents stood beneath a wintry afternoon sun and watched the aircraft belonging to the United States Marshal's Service descend and land on runway two-five left at Los Angeles International Airport. The aircraft slowed, swung left, and taxied back toward them before stopping at the transient parking area on the airport's south side. A ramp truck pulled to the front door, and a minute later three U.S. marshals led a manacled and shackled John Barrish down the steps and toward a waiting van that would take him to the Los Angeles County Men's Central Jail to await trial. The eight deputies at the van to receive him were all black.

"Appropriate, wouldn't you say?" Frankie asked.

"A bit of a show," Art responded. It might have been, but now that John Barrish was in chains, maybe it wasn't altogether bad to complete the role reversal. It was for his benefit only, but Art wondered if it would make much of an impression on the man. Would anything? he asked himself.

With no delay John Barrish was placed in the rear of the black-and-white van, a deputy on either side, and within a minute the three-vehicle caravan was heading out from the airport for the forty-minute drive to his new home . . . for the time being.

"I hope he chooses gas," Frankie commented as the trio of vehicles disappeared into traffic.

"There's still a trial to come, partner." And Art knew that would be lengthy and messy. The incarceration in San Quentin. Then ten or fifteen years of appeals. Then, if John Barrish hadn't been done away with already, it would be the chamber or a gurney. Gas or lethal injection. *Gas,* Art thought. Frankie was right. It was the appropriate way for him to go.

"At least he's here and not tied up in a tug-of-war," Frankie commented. The authorities in several jurisdictions back east had gladly approved the extradition of John Barrish to California so that he might face capital murder charges—several thousand of them—in a jurisdiction itching to add another to the long line of death row inmates. Then there was the question of Moises Griggs. "The kid is going to go down with him," she said with no glee.

Life without parole. Was it better than death by gas or lethal injection? Art didn't know, but Moises had obviously decided that cooperating in the prosecution of John Barrish was worth the trade. There was also vengeance in the young man's heart, a burning desire to avenge the murder of his little sister. Then, he could consider his own future.

"It's a waste, partner, but it's of his own doing," Art observed dispassionately. That wasn't how he felt, but it was how he had to look at it.

Frankie nodded agreement, but the reasoning was deeper than that. "Think of it. The kid was drawn to the very people who killed his little sister because he became like them." She was able to laugh. "Let some psychotype loose with that one." There would be plenty of those wanting at Moises Griggs, she suspected.

"Speaking of psychotypes, has Anne settled everything yet?"

"All set," Art said, allowing a smile. "We leave Tuesday."

Frankie smiled back at him, though the lump rising from her chest was threatening a different display of emotion. "Who am I going to eat chili dogs with now?"

"Bacon chili cheese dogs, partner," Art corrected. "Your little girl. Cassie would love 'em."

"When she's eighteen, maybe." Frankie chuckled, then fell silent as the moment became awkward.

"Well," Art said for the sake of saying *something*.

"Well, partner, two days," Frankie said, cheering herself up with thoughts of the wedding to come this Saturday. "Do you remember how to be married?"

"I'm hoping to learn the right way," Art answered. "Speaking of which, what have you got planned for the afternoon?"

Frankie noticed the innocent look in his eye, and knew it meant quite the opposite. "Nothing . . ."

Art started walking for their car, his partner for the next few days following him. "Do you know any good jewelers?"

She froze midstep. "Art Jefferson! You don't have a ring yet!"

"What?"

Frankie shook her head at him. "You don't know how to be married, but you sure know how to be a man."

"There's a difference?" Art joked, then climbed in the car with the full expectation that a lecture would be his to endure. A lecture he would cherish always.

The Secret Service frowned upon it, but the president was the president, and if he wanted to take in the night sights of the Mall from the vantage point of the Truman Balcony, well, he could do so. Standing next to the man,

Bud DiContino could understand why his boss was so obstinate on that point.

"It's beautiful tonight, sir," the NSA commented. Looking due south he could see the brilliantly lit obelisk that was the Washington Monument. One sight among many that gave the capital city its charm at night.

The president, though, was looking to the southeast, at a diffused glow rising from the containment tents that had been set up around the Capitol reflecting pool. The decontamination process had begun immediately, and would continue for some time. They had been lucky, the chief executive knew. Very lucky. "Have you thought of what would have happened if Barrish's plan had worked?"

Bud saw what the president was gazing toward. "The important thing was it didn't, sir."

"It was too close."

"Yes, it was," Bud agreed. There had been too much distrust of the Bureau by the CIA, too much insulation of theories by the Bureau itself, and too little understanding of the threat posed by people like John Barrish. Already there was one casualty: Gordon Jones. His tenure at the Bureau was in doubt when the World Center attack took place. Having a similar attack almost come to be in the laps of the Congress was too much. Whether justified or not, he was gone, and a replacement was yet to be named.

So the lessons were obvious. Learning from them was a process just beginning.

"I feel like we were fighting a vapor cloud on this one, Bud. Something that you can see, that you know is there, but that you can't get a grip on. It's unnerving."

"But not unbeatable," Bud reminded the president as a chilly wind kicked up from the west.

The president leaned on the white plaster railing and stared toward the glow for a long moment as he thought. "How long is it going to take, Bud?"

The NSA recalled the report from the Army special-ists responsible for the cleanup. "About six weeks, sir."

The president looked to his NSA and smiled, seeing immediately that the man realized he had given the right answer to the wrong question. "I think it's going to take a bit longer than that, Bud."

"Me too, Mr. President."

The Following is an Excerpt From
SIMPLE SIMON
the Riveting New Thriller by
Ryne Douglas Pearson
Available in Hardcover From
William Morrow and Company

North of Tokyo . . .

Keiko Kimura stood near the foot of the bed, a sheer white peignoir hanging from wispy straps to veil her still-enticing form, thinking both that the American's fledgling erection was unimpressive and that his blood was going to be the devil to get out of fine silk.

But she could not deny the rapture of that warm red wetness rolling over her, or the heights to which a scream could take her, and looking upon the pale body that was willingly four-pointed to the bedposts, she knew that ruined lingerie was an acceptable trade.

"Do me, mama-san." The American beckoned with eyes hungry and limbs tugging joyously at the bindings he had insisted upon in pursuit of some masochistic fantasy. "Hurt me."

"You want Keiko to spank you?" She skated one foot across the wood floor, then the other, until she stood bedside, black hair draped over either shoulder and dark eyes sweeping his body. As she sat upon the mattress, her tongue slid into view and slowly wet her lips.

He smiled, teeth bared, chest heaving. His erection began to improve. "I want you to *punish* me."

Primal forces boiled within her as he spoke *that* word. *Punish*, she thought. So perfectly did he speak it, so clear and pure was his desire for it, that Keiko replayed the intonation over and over in her mind. After a very few repetitions she felt herself getting wet.

"Come on, mama-san, I'm needin' this bad, and I'm needin' it soon. . . ."

Keiko rolled her head once and then looked squarely at the American. His face was dotted with glistening beads of sweat. She imagined each tiny drop as a pearl of redness—blood tears that he was crying . . . crying for her.

Ooh, sweet one, she thought, the warmth rising within, lifting her almost to the precipice before she called retreat. *Too much. Too much so soon.* There would be time enough for pleasure, but as was necessary, business had to come at some point before her plaything was dead.

"Come on," the American demanded now, with gritted teeth.

"You gotta do something for Keiko first," she said, and slid a hand through the black curls on his chest. She found his nipple and squeezed it between thumb and forefinger.

"Unnhhh," he groaned, his face contorted in the beginnings of an ecstatic agony. Or so he believed.

On the end of each finger was a perfectly filed natural nail, and with these Keiko now pinched. Hard, very hard, so much so that the American was drawn from his burgeoning erotic state to recoil from this *real* pain.

"Hey! Easy!"

With a force less impressive than might seem necessary, Keiko dug deep into the nipple and jerked her hand away, tearing it from his body, flinging the bit of soft pink flesh aside. It hit the off-white wall, leaving a bright red starburst on the slick surface before falling to the floor.

"*You crazy fucking bitch!—*"

He pulled and bucked and twisted and fought. Blood

sprayed from his wound, flecks dotting Keiko's face and the peignoir she had briefly fretted over. Her tongue appeared again and licked spots of blood from above her lip. Its taste, its simply being *on* her, made staying focused on the business end of things very difficult. Almost impossible. "You gotta talk to me, Joe."

"Joe?" the American asked through the pain. He didn't know that all American men were Joes in his tormentor's mind.

"You not the only one paying Keiko tonight, Joe." Her mouth tingled with the salty, coppery taste of his essence. *To bathe in it*, she thought. Soon, though never soon enough. "Someone wants to know what you know."

His brow wrinkled at her words. A warm crimson trickle ran down his ribs. "You're a fucking psycho! Know what?"

Keiko's face expressed something—not a smile or a scowl. Nothing easily identified. *A beastly look upon the human form*, the American thought. Then he saw a knife come up from the side of the bed in her bloody hand.

"You know," she said, holding the knife delicately by its shank, drawing slow figure eights in the air above his face.

"Know what?" he shouted, nearly pleading now.

Now she smiled, lowering the knife to begin a hard night's work. "It don't matter, Joe. You gonna tell me everything about everything, and I'll sort it out." She pricked the tip of his nose and drew the blade slowly across her tongue, savoring the taste. His being was so fleeting, as would be her own ecstasy. In the morning, with this job behind her and with this plaything cast aside, the cravings would begin anew. With the cravings there would come a need. And for that need there would be someone, somewhere, who would provide satisfaction. Until then . . . "Just enjoy it, Joe. We got all night."

* * *

Art Jefferson had been back in Chicago less than two months when he made an enemy of United States Attorney Angelo Breem.

"What in God's name was that, Jefferson?" Breem demanded after catching up to the FBI's number two man in Chicago on the courthouse steps and grabbing him by the elbow.

Art looked seriously at Breem's spindly hand, and the U.S. attorney wisely withdrew it. "What was what?"

Breem, still exasperated by his sprint to find Art after court had adjourned, pointed a shaky finger at the man he considered a turncoat. "You know exactly what I'm talking about. What you testified to on that stand is going to let Kermit Fiorello walk!"

Art turned and took a step up so that he stood on equal footing with Breem. He towered over the zealous prosecutor by six inches. "I told the truth."

"Christ, Jefferson! You know Fiorello's guilty! Guilty as sin! He's responsible for at least six contract murders, two of which we could have nailed on him, plus the racketeering charges, if *you* hadn't gone soft!"

"Soft?" Art asked, his head cocking. A vein rose beneath his left temple. "Listen to me, Mr. U.S. Attorney, if you had had your *P*'s and *Q*'s straight, there would have been no need for me to testify at all. Your case was weak from the get-go. And so you decide to call me in to dredge up some ancient history on Fiorello? That was fifteen years ago, Breem. It had nothing to do with the paper-thin case you had until ten minutes ago. I didn't kill your case; it committed suicide."

Breem seethed, his fists balling at his side. He would have loved to swing at the cocky black agent. Mr. Big Shot coming back from his time on the Coast. "He is guilty, Jefferson."

"You think I don't know that?" Art asked, leaning to get in Breem's face. Breem's features were pale and abrupt. "I was chasing Fiorello when you were at the prom."

"Then why did you say he had nothing to do with the Carerra murder?"

"Because he didn't!" Art backed off and shook his head. "If you'd bothered to check with me before calling me to the stand, I could have set you straight on that. But no, you base your whole case on that one crime. If Fiorello had Carerra whacked, then he had to do the same ten years later to Tangini, and then to Picone, et cetera. He did Tangini and Picone, but not Louie Carerra. Any agent who was around back then could tell you that." He stabbed a solid finger at Breem's red tie. "You didn't do your homework, and because of that, Kermit Fiorello is a free man once again. Thank yourself, Breem, before you blame someone else."

With that Art showed the U.S. attorney his back and trotted easily down the steps, ignoring the visual daggers being thrown his way. He cared little for people like Breem. All high-profile talk, all grand drama in the courtroom, and no real smarts to carry the basics of a case from start to finish. Breem wanted to go places as fast as possible, and in this case he'd gone a damn sight too fast. It seemed that every damned U.S. attorney wanted to get to D.C. and a nice office in the Department of Justice as quickly as he could. Well, Angelo Breem's path to the top had just been detoured, and Art had no illusions that the pipsqueak would blame him for it until the day he died.

So what? Art asked himself as he reached the bottom of the steps and headed down Dearborn to grab a bite at Nico's. He'd made worse enemies in a long career with the bureau. What could one measly U.S. attorney do to him?

Number 6601 needed surgery.

Circling the earth at 150 nautical miles in a ninety-eight-degree sun-synchronous orbit, the two-billion-dollar piece of electronic and imaging wizardry known as the KH-14 was just a year into its planned ten-year life span when the same shuttle that had placed it into orbit, *Atlantis*, blasted off from Florida's Cape Canaveral an hour before dawn. On the fourth revolution *Atlantis* rendezvoused with the reconnaissance satellite and precisely matched its course and speed. They were man-made moons in tandem orbit of Mother Earth.

As the sun set on the East Coast, two men from the planet Earth exited *Atlantis* and moved via MMUs (manned maneuvering units) the ten yards to number 6601. One astronaut carried tools. The other carried a small case the size of a shoe box. It shone silver in the clear sunlight of space.

The astronaut with the tools opened an access panel on the huge satellite's side, below and aft of its number two solar panel. He worked carefully and removed four bolts that held a red box in place. One cable went in the red box, and another came out. He disconnected these and pulled the red box free.

It took him twenty more minutes to put the silver box in and reconnect the cables.

After finishing the surgery, the astronauts took the red box with them and reentered *Atlantis*. They were to continue with the "scientific" activities of Mission 98-A for another eight days, then land back at Cape Canaveral, weather permitting.

Number 6601 required only five minutes to recover from surgery, just long enough to recalibrate itself with controllers on the ground at several secret installations across the United States. The first thing it did was spit a stream of electronic gibberish toward the earthbound receiving stations. All of them answered back with the same gibberish. They understood each other. But no one else did.

Number 6601 had just been taught a new language.

* * *

It was very late when the father sat in the rocker in the corner of his child's room and helped his son onto his lap. The son wore white flannel pajamas highlighted with tiny blue snowflakes, and when he curled up in the strong arms, his nose pressed into the crook of his father's neck. The son detected the faint scent of motor oil, and this comforted him. He slid his thumb into his mouth and closed his lips around it.

"Wander boy, wander far, wander to the farthest star," the father began to sing softly. His pitch was off, his rhythm tortured. The son found assurance in the song sung his father's way; it was the only way he knew. *"Wander boy, wander far, dreams are what you're made of."*

Eyes closed, and the son began to suck his thumb. The father stared blankly at a bare wall and continued the melody. He had long ago stopped asking God to heal his son. He accepted him now. *"Under a tree by a house, by a field washed with rain, lies a boy all alone with his thoughts and his dreams."*

The father loved his son. He had sung to him every night of his life but one. It was their special time. *"Wander boy, wander far . . ."* At this point he continued only in a hum. *"Hmm-hm-hm-hmm-hmm-hmm-hm-hm-hmm."*

The son fell asleep in the safety of his father's arms.

Half a world away there was no safety for the son of another father. His body was already cold.

But in the quiet of this Midwest home there was only peace as the father hummed the lullaby, his son resting serenely as the night marched on. The ritual was unchanging.

For now.